ABOUT THE AUTHOR

Lloyd Shepherd is the author of several highly-acclaimed historical thrillers. A former journalist and digital producer, he also co-presents a podcast, 'The Curiously Specific Book Club'. His website is www.lloydshepherd.com

ALSO BY LLOYD SHEPHERD

The English Monster

The Poisoned Island

Savage Magic

The Detective and the Devil

AFTER LONDON

LLOYD SHEPHERD

LLLJ BOOKS - LONDON, ENGLAND

Facial recognition technology will be used for the first time at the Formula 1 British Grand Prix to try to stop criminal activity.

Northamptonshire Police said it would be used to spot those who pose a "risk of danger to the wider public".

That could include wanted criminals, those involved in serious crime, or "unlawful protest", the force said.

Det Supt Richard Tompkins said officers had "thought long and hard" about the use of the technology.

BBC NEWS ARTICLE, JULY 2023

DAY ONE

1

The stars were out. Jupiter and Saturn sat comfortably alongside each other, shepherding a half-filled moon. The sky had been cleared by a bitterly strong wind, and she cursed a half-dozen times trying to light the cigarette. The impossible lighter - which always seemed to light despite being visibly empty for weeks now - burned hot on her thumb as the flame finally took, and she took in a deep sweet drag and held it for a good long while, exhaling eventually, watching the smoke catch the cold night air somewhere up towards the heavens. The transgressive thrill of a stolen cigarette at the age of fourteen.

It had been six long hours since she'd last been up here. Six hours of walking and carrying and keeping her head down and her face neutral while the very important men and women filled their glasses and tilted their heads together and chatted about whatever it was very important men and women chatted about at parties. It was only her third time serving at one of Brother Thomas's *soirées* - *soirée* being a word she'd never heard until Thomas had come up to her after chapel one morning in the old gaol and asked her, in his smooth way, if she would like to join 'his little band of helpers' and 'officiate at one of my *soirées*.' It hadn't been a request, of course, but he'd at least made it sound like one. He was classy like that.

Six hours ago, she'd stood with the other Brothers and Sisters who were in attendance this evening, watching from the grass terrace in front of the house as the boat left the jetty on the opposite shore of the Strait. When the boat reached the jetty on the Island side, she saw there were around a dozen of them, and something about this particular intake of guests suggested that Brother Thomas was attracting a different class of guest, these days. There was an air of entitlement, of studied indifference to anyone of a lower grade, that marked these guests out as more demanding than the usual local VIP's.

And so it had proved. The men were mainly disinterested, but some of the women were actively hostile. Two of them were dressed barely decently, and became drunk quite quickly, hanging off the arms of the men they were with and studiously ignoring the help. One older man had a voice so poshly English she had to force herself not to smile. Most of the people looked different to those who had been here before. She had been a year on the Island - a year away from the Salford orphanage - but she recognised good tailoring when she saw it. The men's suits fitted them better than their own faces, the bodily lines of the two drunk women were brazenly on display, while a third woman, perhaps the most important guest of all judging by the way she held court, wore an immaculate trouser suit that was cut even better than anything on the men. She was terrible, this one, barking orders at the Brothers and Sisters who were serving, complaining about the food, and at one point staring at Jenny with such an intensity that she felt guilty without quite knowing why, as if the woman could see into Jenny's own fragmented past and draw conclusions.

The thing she noticed most of all was how well-fed they all seemed to be. Bellies bulged in a way she had not yet seen in her fourteen long years. Food on the Island was not as scarce as it had been in Salford, but it was hardly plentiful. Here in the house, though, there was bounty indeed, cascades of meat and vegetables and fruit and wine, even champagne and rich chocolates.

She had watched them, in her way, keeping her eyes firmly down most of the time but stealing the occasional glance, catching a hand touching an arm or even the small of a back, hearing a firm, harsh whisper of caution, smelling a delicious cloud of glamour coming from one of them, a woman or a man, she did not know.

And then the food had come in, richer and more amazing than any food she had ever seen, and she had caught Brother Thomas's eye, because he'd been watching her, of course, watching her like a hawk, as he watched them all. She'd felt the old familiar stir of defiance at being caught doing something that was not allowed, in this case gawping at the stupendous feast laid on for these very important people. But he'd smiled, and then made a rueful shape with his eyebrows.

I know. Amazing, isn't it?

Did she listen to what these people said? Not really. In the days to come, the detective would ask her that. *What did they say? What did they talk about? Who said what to whom?* But nothing would come back to her, because in truth she'd been too busy to eavesdrop. When the important people were chatting and drinking and eating, she'd been scurrying around, lifting and carrying and placing and wiping, and the occasional glances and sniffs and touches were all she'd been able to take in.

After a few hours, the important people moved to other parts of the house, and the Brothers and Sisters who were in attendance were left to clear up. There were bangs and crashes from those other, unseen parts of the house, and once she heard the high, hysterical giggle of a woman, but the workers paid the noises little mind.

She'd made a round of the bedrooms, sneaking away to take a look at the bits and pieces the guests brought with them. Some of the rooms were locked, but most of them were open, and she'd spent a while picking her way through their belongings. Before she'd come to the Community, she might have tried nicking something, but she wouldn't have dared now. She had too much to lose.

She'd finished her work ten minutes ago, and had crept away for this little moment of stolen solitude on the roof. One of the Brothers, called Ethan, older and, she thought, quite beautiful, had shown her the little stairway off the old office corridor at the top of the house, the first time she'd worked here. They'd shared a cigarette, huddled against the wet Welsh rain that had fallen that night, but Ethan had not been working tonight, so she'd found her own way. She would be in Trouble if Brother Thomas realised, but Jenny had been no stranger to Trouble before she'd come to the island, and although she'd developed a secretive, quiet approach to disobedience since coming here, she knew that one day she would go too far and there would be Trouble (she imagined this in the tired social worker's voice in Salford, his soft Liverpool accent mournful: *Don't get into Trouble again, Jenny. Keep your head down over there*).

Her thoughts were interrupted by the sound of the door on to the roof opening, and for a moment Trouble was very much on top of her, and in the space between the door opening and the person who opened it appearing Jenny's imagination raced towards her expulsion from the island, picturing herself walking back over the bridge to the mainland carrying the same sad little red suitcase she'd arrived with.

A woman came through the door, a cigarette already in her mouth, a lighter already flaming into life as she slipped out into the cold air. She was wearing a smart tailored coat, which hugged her thin figure, and her fine red hair was pinned tightly to her head. Jenny recognised her as one of the people at the party, but she'd not been one you took particular notice of, hanging around at the fringes of things, even helping to pour the wine and serve the canapés, perhaps the only guest who had actually spoken to the helpers. This woman walked up to the little fence that lined the parapet at the front of the house, and lit a cigarette. Jenny could see her hands shaking. She stepped a little closer. The woman was talking to herself. One word, over and over again, a bad word.

Then the woman saw her, and looked visibly startled.

'Bloody hell! You scared the life out of me!'

She had a soft Welsh accent. Jenny could see a plain white blouse beneath the coat, and a gold cross hanging from a chain, and she could smell the woman's exquisite scent. She thought the woman was very beautiful.

'What you doing up here?' the woman demanded.

Jenny raised her cigarette.

'Same as you,' she said, the instinctive defiance coming back into her voice, thoughts of Trouble receding. She imagined this woman wasn't allowed up here, either - though she obviously knew the place well enough to find her way out onto the roof. Perhaps she was a *soirée* regular.

'You lot allowed to smoke, then?'

Jenny didn't answer that. She deflected, a skill she still possessed even after a year of dutiful prayer on the Island.

'You were at the party,' Jenny said.

The woman snorted in response.

'No *party* for me, my love,' she said. 'No posh food or drinks for the little old drones. I was working, like you. Though at least I get paid.' She pulled on her cigarette, pulled her suit jacket tightly around her, looked up into the sky. 'Christ alive, it's *freezing.*' She glanced at Jenny. 'Sorry.'

'Why are you sorry?'

'Well, I shouldn't be blaspheming, should I? Not in the presence of a Sister of the Community.' She looked up into the sky again.

'I don't mind,' said Jenny.

'Well, still.'

The woman shifted her gaze down and out over the little iron railing which stood at one of the two points where the roof jutted out over the terrace below. She stood still for a moment, the bitter wind pushing her back slightly. She wore comically high heels, Jenny noticed. She looked terribly thin, not used to the riches that this evening had served. The woman continued to smoke, looking repeatedly up and down, into the sky then out across the Strait.

'Always freaks me out, you know,' she said, at last.

'What does?' said Jenny.

'That they don't watch here.'

So that's why she'd been looking at the sky. Obvious really, Jenny thought.

'Weird,' said the woman. 'Very weird. Them not watching. You almost get used to them being there, all the time.'

She looked at Jenny.

'What's your name?' she said.

'Jenny. Sister Jenny.'

'Hello, Sister Jenny. I'm Anthea. I don't suppose you're meant to be up here.'

'No. No, not really.'

'Hmm. But who's going to know, right?'

Her eyes went back to the sky.

'If they're not watching, you could get away with anything,' she whispered, as if to herself.

The woman didn't say anything further, and Jenny watched her for a moment longer, and wondered about asking her for another cigarette, but there was something sad and unsettling about the woman, so she muttered 'well, good night,' and turned away, back to the staircase down into the house. The woman didn't reply.

2

t was almost midday when Detective Inspector Ted Wood found himself at that corner of Wales where the mountains of Snowdonia tumble down into the sea, and, just like the first time he had come here, the sun was there to greet him, piercing the blue-grey cloud with such clarity that a peal of choral music seemed needed. God himself seemed to be pouring his mind onto the waters.

'Bloody hell,' said Ted, as he had probably said the first time he'd seen it, a dozen years ago or more.

He had left Manchester two hours before, and while the traffic had been thin his little Dyson had barely the puff for sixty miles an hour, so progress had been slow. Perhaps if he'd arrived half-an-hour earlier or half-an-hour later he'd have missed this light show. Wales dispensed her splendours in small enough chunks. If you were unlucky enough to miss one, well, another might be along very soon. Or it might just start raining again.

The Expressway curled round the shoulder of Penmaenmawr and then turned inland, and Ted followed it, taking the sign to the Menai Strait Bridge as he'd been instructed. Angela Leybourne's call this morning had been odd - she rarely called him other than to complain about something or other he had or hadn't done. He couldn't remember the last time the call had been about a new case. Even a suspected double homicide, like this one.

'The house is called Plas Newydd,' she'd said. 'It's on Anglesey.'

'I know it,' Ted had replied.

'You know it? How come?'

'I've been there.'

'Well, do you remember the way?'

'A55 all the way, I think.'

'I've been told to tell you - take the Menai Strait Bridge, not the other one. I didn't even know there was another one.'

'The Britannia Bridge.'

'How poetic. Well, only lorries in transit allowed on that one. So steer clear. The Brothers will meet you on the Island end of the Bridge, and they'll take you to the house.'

'The Brothers?'

'Look it up, Ted. But get moving.'

He'd taken the time to *look it up*, as Angela had suggested, before he got moving. He'd consulted the ugly police tablet with the basic internet access, and he'd got the essential details on the Brothers of the Community of St Lidwina, custodians of the Island of Anglesey, by appointment to the King.

The newish signs on the Expressway clearly echoed what Angela had told him, sternly forbidding non-freight traffic from staying on the A55 towards Holyhead. Cars were directed left on to the A487 towards Caernarfon. A right turn to the Menai Strait Bridge was available, but with additional admonitions that 'Community Traffic Only' was permitted. Ted took the right hand turn, and after a while the road dropped down to a roundabout, and doubled back on itself before coming back up on the bridge, Telford's extraordinary thing, flying out from one piece of rock to another, spanning the Strait, hanging from its two towers on an iron cobweb. He blinked slightly at the way that turn of phrase had popped into his head. They weren't his words. Something Peg had said, on that earlier trip, in the time before.

There were no cars crossing the bridge in either direction, no holidaymakers driving to rented cottages or fixed caravans as he would have seen on that previous visit. Those were only echoes from a disappeared past. Ted drove the Dyson along one of the two narrow lanes that crossed the bridge. He passed under the first tower, at the Mainland end of Telford's bridge, and started out across the span of the Strait. He glanced up in the rear view mirror, and, seeing nothing behind him, stopped the car, put it into Park, and got out.

He was above the water. The wind whistled along the Strait and the view would have been another heart-stopper if the view had been what he was looking at. But it wasn't.

The drone hadn't followed him onto the bridge. It hung in the air, visible beyond the tower Ted had passed through. It was one of the smaller ones: four rotors, each rotor about the size of a side plate, the body in the shape of a claw reaching down, holding four cameras, so that it could see all around itself, in front and behind, to the left and to the right. Ted thought he could see a microphone, too. The latest drones could pick up speech, if they got close enough, and close enough could be surprisingly far away.

An identical device had been waiting for him when he stepped out of the house in Manchester, and had tracked him as he got into the car and drove away. A drone-chain had obviously been placed on him - a sequence of machines, each identical, one handing over to the next as its power drained, dropping automatically to a charging point on a nearby pylon, the new drone tracking for the next however-many miles before its batteries, too, wound down. All of it happening without you even noticing, because by now barely anyone noticed the drones. But this kind of attention was unusual, for him. Drone-chains were usually only for certain types of Important Persons who were deemed to need their little electronic flying familiars. They were never for the likes of him. He was being watched in a different way to the usual.

They looked at each other for a while, the detective and the drone. He could imagine it signalling back to the nearest base station, waiting for instructions, whether from a human or from some independently-running piece of software, he couldn't tell. After perhaps 30 seconds, it sprang away from the tower, and away from Ted. The move was so sudden it made him jump. The drone flew back towards the roundabout he'd just driven around, and out of view.

'Well,' he said. 'Well, well, well. It's true, then.'

He watched the empty air where the drone had been for a good while, before turning and climbing back into the car. The Dyson continued across the bridge.

In front of the second tower, at the Island end of the bridge, a gate had been built that wasn't remotely in keeping with the elegance of Telford's design. It was an ugly thing, constructed from what appeared to be a random selection of scaffolding poles. A uniformed officer was standing with his arms crossed, next to three men in brown robes. All four of them watched as he drove up. He wondered what they'd made of the old detective getting out of his car halfway across and staring back into the distance.

He stopped the car, got out, said 'Detective Inspector Ted Wood,' to none of them in particular, holding out his old Met Police badge which the powers-that-be allowed him to continue using. The officer looked at the badge, smirked slightly, looked at Ted and pressed the call button on his radio, which squawked in reply. The three men in robes just stared at him, as if he were some exotic species.

'Lieutenant Lancaster,' the uniform said into his radio.

'Lancaster here,' the radio squawked in reply.

'The Manchester detective's arrived,' said the uniform.

The word *detective* had a derisory emphasis. The lad's accent was central-casting-Welsh, the kind of accent that might have been used for comic effect on an old BBC sitcom. But they didn't show old sitcoms on the BBC anymore. Nothing from before, seemed to be the rule. Don't depress people. Don't bring it back up. As if the past was something you puked.

'Let him through,' buzzed the radio. 'Show them the pass.'

The officer took his hand off the radio.

'OK, Detective Inspector,' he said. 'If you'll come with me.'

They walked over to the three men in brown robes, the uniform holding a slip of paper out like a gun. One of the robed men took it.

'Could I ask for your badge, please?' the robed man said. He was a thin young man, with a West Country accent. His brown robes were dirty, his face unshaven, his hair untidy. He looked like one of the homeless lads who used to sleep in the underground passage by Charing Cross tube station.

'Why do you need my badge?' Ted asked.

'I need to inspect your credentials,' the man in the robe said. 'I have the right.'

Ted turned to look at the uniform.

'Help me out here, son,' he said. 'Does he have the right?'

'You're not getting on the Island without his say-so,' said the uniform, in that rich Welsh accent. 'We don't like it, but that's the way it is.'

Ted handed over the badge. The man in the robe peered at it briefly but carefully.

'Detective Inspector,' he said. 'Is that your rank?'

'Aye, son,' Ted said. 'It's my rank.'

'And the Metropolitan Police? Is that a Manchester thing?'

'It's an old badge, son. It's still valid.'

'OK. And what do I call you?'

Ted glanced at the officer next to him, who was busy suppressing a smile.

'You call me Detective Inspector Wood,' Ted said. 'It's an old-fashioned term, but it's still current. Constable is another old-fashioned term. This idiot alongside me is called Police Constable Metcalfe. I'm his superior, as he's about to find out if he doesn't wipe that idiotic grin off his face.'

Ted watched the man in the robe as he looked first at Metcalfe, and then back at Ted. Now it was his turn to suppress a smile. Ted wondered if he'd made an ally. The man in the robe pulled out two pieces of dishevelled card. He handed one of them to Ted.

'Right then, son,' Ted said. 'Let's get this chicanery done with.'

The man in the robe began to speak. Ted followed along on the card he'd been given. One of the two other men in robes scribbled in a battered leather-bound notebook.

'I, Brother Enoch of the Order of Saint Lidwina, do welcome you, Detective Inspector Edward Wood, into our Community. Under the provisions of the Religious Communities Act, I do hereby give you permission to come into our Community, on condition that you do agree, in front of these witnesses, that you understand the provisions of the said Act and will comply with them during your time on the Island and after your visit.'

'I do hereby comply with the Act and all its provisions,' Ted said. He hadn't read the Act, or its provisions. But those were the words on the card.

'Your name and rank for the record, please,' said the robed man, the so-called Brother Enoch.

'Detective Inspector Edward Wood, Manchester Division, His Majesty's Police.'

'And the date, please.'

Ted gave it.

'Amen,' said all the robed men. Brother Enoch looked at Ted, and tilted his head to one side.

'Amen?' Ted said.

'Welcome to Anglesey,' said Brother Enoch.

Ted handed the card back to Enoch, who himself handed it to one of the other two brothers.

'I will accompany you in your car, if that's acceptable,' Brother Enoch said. 'I can show you the way.'

'Of course,' Ted said. He and Enoch climbed into the Dyson, as the other two men in robes opened the makeshift scaffolding gate. Ted didn't even look at Constable Metcalfe.

3

'People always find it somewhat strange,' said Brother Enoch as they drove through the gate.

'Strange?' said Ted.

'The drones stopping at the bridge. Some people find it odd. No longer being observed. That's why you got out of your car, isn't it?'

It should feel like a fog lifting, thought Ted, *but it doesn't*. It was more like being caught suddenly naked.

'I knew they weren't allowed on the Island,' he said. 'But it is a weird sensation.'

'God is our only witness here,' Enoch said.

'I hope not, son. Good old-fashioned witnesses may be all we have, in this case.' Ted couldn't help smiling. 'Like the old days, isn't it?'

Brother Enoch said nothing to that. He had no opinion on the old days. Ten years must have seemed like a lifetime to one so young. And it must have appeared odd to him, Ted showing enthusiasm for a homicide case. Death wasn't the sort of thing that was supposed to make you nostalgic.

The car made its way between the extraordinary iron girders which hung from the two towers and then plunged into the road itself, disappearing into some anchoring below. When Ted had last been here, this space had been crammed with cars. Now the empty road seemed to glide into a canopy of green.

A man was standing, alone, at the edge of the bridge, looking over the iron railings to the trees below. As they approached, he turned towards the car. He seemed to be the same age as Ted, dressed in jeans and a leather jacket, completely bald. He may have weighed as little as nine stone. Ted could see that the man's cheeks were wet. His head turned and followed their progress as the Dyson went past. Ted looked in the rear view mirror. The man continued to watch them as he receded behind.

'An inmate?' Ted said.

'We prefer they be called the Suffering,' Enoch said. Ted could almost hear the capital S.

'He has the explosion sickness?' Ted said. He hadn't seen anyone with a case that bad in maybe five years.

'We do not recognise the term,' said Enoch. 'The main thing is that he suffers. And that is why he is here.'

'He looked like he was thinking of jumping.'

'Perhaps he was.'

'You're not going to talk to him? Stop him, or something?'

'If he has decided to depart this world, we will not stop him, Detective Inspector. We will keep him comfortable while he awaits what is to come.'

'You just let them kill themselves?'

'That is between the Suffering and the Almighty.'

'Church thinking has changed a good deal.'

'Hasn't everything?'

They came to a roundabout, on the far side of which

was an old supermarket, its name still decipherable in the W I OSE letters that stood above the entrance. Then there was an abandoned petrol station, and another roundabout. Soon they were passing under the Expressway which ran across Anglesey to the port of Holyhead. *Only lorries in transit allowed on that one*, Leybourne had said. An old decrepit brown tourist sign pointed to Plas Newydd and the Sea Zoo, then they were driving past a row of white bungalows and a long, long place sign.

Llanfair Pwllgwyngll. That's what the place is really called. Some English pillock made up the longer name.

The words came creeping back down the years. Laura's words. And then Peg, in the back seat, had claimed she could say the long version of the name, and she'd tried, starting well enough but then getting tangled up in it, tripping over the strange sounds and laughing as she went, and then they were all laughing as they drove along in the massive Mercedes estate, a car as big as a county.

'Detective Inspector?'

Ted glanced to his left. Brother Enoch was looking at him.

'Is everything all right with you?' the young man said.

'Sorry. Miles away.'

'You sounded like you were trying to say something in Welsh.'

It was never nice, discovering the voices in your head were speaking out loud.

'You have memories of this place, perhaps?' said Enoch.

'Came here with my family.'

Enoch didn't say anything, and there was something to the way he moved his head that made Ted want to smash him in the face.

I am not Suffering, you sanctimonious God-bothering bastard. I am not about to jump off a bridge. Don't you think of me like that. Don't you bloody dare.

They drove a little further.

'Not far to go now,' says Enoch.

I know, Ted thought. *I bloody know, don't I?*

He told himself to calm down.

The Dyson turned off the main road, and came out into open countryside, a long, straight, possibly Roman road pegged in by a beautiful stone wall. They'd had a row here, hadn't they? Or just a small disagreement? Laura had wanted to stop at some ancient monument, and he had wanted to head on to the house, because he had been hungry.

'Isn't there an old burial mound or something down here?' Ted said.

'Bryn Celli Ddu,' said Enoch. 'It's a bit further on down the road. Have you been there?'

'No,' Ted said.

'But you've been to the Island?' Enoch said.

'Yes. Back when it was still called Anglesey.'

'We still call it Anglesey.'

'And do you visit this place? This Bryn Celli Ddu?'

'It is a sacred site, to us.'

'Let me guess,' Ted said. 'You only visit on Midsummer's Day.'

'Yes,' said Brother Enoch. 'We go there on Midsummer's Day, and we say prayers for the dead and for the Suffering, and when the light falls on the chamber, we sacrifice one of the children.'

Ted laughed, despite himself.

'We are allowed a joke, after all,' Enoch said.

Even on a homicide case?

Ted thought it, but said nothing.

Another achingly familiar brown tourist sign read *Plas Newydd* and pointed to the left. There was something about those brown signs that always made Ted's heart droop. Remembering a time when people put up helpful brown tourist signs.

He drove the Dyson into the flat, neat car park, the spaces for cars surfaced with small pieces of slate which looked remarkably well-preserved. No weeds in the slate gravel. The verges well trimmed. Almost as if the last 10 years hadn't happened.

The last time, they'd walked up past a sign showing a map of the Estate and into the ticket office and gift shop. They were greeted by a smiling young woman who'd asked them if they were Members. They were not members - Laura had always said joining the National Trust meant you were 'officially old' - and he'd handed over the entrance fee, which Laura had correctly guessed would be comfortably expensive.

He found Enoch looking at him again, waiting patiently, as if he didn't want to interrupt the inner voices. His scrawny, kind face was carefully neutral. Ted looked back at him, and looked away again.

'Do you wish to park here, and walk down to the house, or shall we drive down to the service entrance?' said Brother Enoch.

'Was the car park used last night?' Ted said. Enoch pondered the question.

'The minibus, perhaps - bringing the Brothers and Sisters from the dormitory at Beaumaris.'

'Why were they here?'

'To attend upon the guests.'

'Free waiting staff, is it?'

'That's one way of looking at it.'

'But the guests did not park here?'
'No. The guests arrive by water.'
'From the other side of the Strait?'
'Yes.'
'Well, then. We'll walk, Brother Enoch.'

4

gly bloody thing, isn't it?' Laura had said. The house was coming into view down below as he and Enoch neared the edge of a long-abandoned cricket pitch.

The ground sloped steeply towards the Strait. The house stood square and solid against the backdrop of Snowdon on the far side, the mainland side. The stone was grey. The roof was grey. The sky, now, was grey. High, Gothic windows lined the ground floor, with smaller versions of the same above them. The roof consisted of half-a-dozen pitches tiled with slate, punctuated by chimneys and small towers topped with what looked like upturned wine glasses. There was probably a technical term.

Ted sensed that Enoch was beginning to drop back. He stopped and turned to face him. Enoch's face betrayed him. He did not want to see whatever there was to see down there.

'Would you rather wait for me by the car?' he said.

'Would that be acceptable?' Enoch said.

Ted held out a hand.

'My thanks to you, Brother Enoch,' he said.

Enoch looked at Ted's hand with surprise, and then gingerly removed his own from the pocket of the robe. His grip was tentative.

'You don't need to wait,' Ted said. 'I'm sure you have other duties.'

'Yes,' said Enoch. 'That wicker man won't build itself.'

He turned away, having allowed himself another joke. Perhaps it was his way of coping. Ted watched him for a moment as he climbed back up the path towards the car park. Then Ted turned, hoisted his backpack back onto one shoulder, and started walking down the path once again. The house rose up in front of him as he descended, becoming bigger and bigger until it seemed to dwarf the figures that were standing beneath it.

Between the end of the pathway and the house was a paved area, and here was what Ted supposed to be the scene of the crime, or one of them. It was marked by a cluster of uniforms standing in random, shabby disorderliness. It was a dispiriting sight. His first possible live case in he didn't know how long, and not a single one of them looked like they knew what they were doing. This was what passed for professional policing, these days. No perimeter set. Officers wandering around. No tent to preserve evidence. Whatever had happened here, it was highly unlikely to be discovered by basic forensics. And as for DNA - well, Ted doubted it. It was shocking, in its way. Probably none of them had ever secured a crime scene. Most of them looked like children. They'd probably qualified since London, under the new dispensation. These days, uniforms were sent where they were sent by the software. Constables fetched people and they locked them up.

And detectives? Who investigated anything, these days? Weren't there better ways of detecting now?

He had to go through the whole stupid rigmarole again, just like at the Bridge. He showed them his Met Police badge when they asked for it. They peered at it, and then they peered at him like he was some exotic creature - an American film star, perhaps - who had shown up wearing something amusing, like a wetsuit or a tutu. They said the words *Detective* and *Inspector* with the same half-exposed sarcasm of Police Constable Metcalfe.

And all the time he was lying there, the dead man, the back of his head planted in the concrete, his open eyes gazing up to the sky. Like Enoch, he wore the brown robe of the Community, but this man's robe looked significantly newer and cleaner, apart from along the shoulders, where the blood from his shattered head had seeped along the concrete and stained the cloth. His arms were flung out to the side. He was wearing sandals over bare feet. Even the sandals looked strangely well-appointed. The toe nails were beautifully groomed.

There were only two non-uniformed figures in the group standing around the body. One was a woman of about Ted's age in jeans and a hooded sweatshirt who scowled at Ted as if he'd nicked her parking space. The other was a younger man in a dark blue suit.

'Detective Inspector Wood,' this young man said. He was wearing standard-issue Security Service Police civvy kit - the suit, the white shirt, the neutral tie. He carried a police radio. He looked like an FBI agent from one of those films made in the 80s but set in the 50s. Well-spoken, an unplaceable English accent that spoke of an expensive school somewhere. He sounded like a fund manager. Did they still have fund managers? Come to that, did they still have expensive schools? But most importantly, he managed to say Detective Inspector Wood without sounding like he was taking the piss. He said it carefully, as if he'd practised it.

'That's me,' Ted said. He held out his hand.

'Lieutenant Edward Lancaster, sir,' the young man said, shaking Ted's hand. 'I'm to act as your local liaison.'

'You're Security Service?' Ted said.

'Originally, sir,' said Lancaster. 'But I've had the police training. Hence the uniform.' He nodded downward at his own suit, and gave a trained smile.

'One of the new breed,' Ted said.

'I suppose so,' said Lancaster.

'Don't worry, it doesn't bother me, son,' Ted said. 'If MI5 wants its officers to become policemen, that's up to them.'

This wasn't true. It bothered Ted like crazy that the police force was now part of the Security Service. But it wasn't this lad's fault.

'Is it really so obvious that I'm not originally police?' Lancaster said.

The straight back. The crisp shirt. On second thoughts, it wasn't a fund manager Lancaster looked like. He looked like a Mormon, like the ones they saw in that musical, the one Laura said she would never, ever be bringing Peg too, even though she'd laughed like a drain.

God, Ted, can they really say that?

'Only obvious to an old lag like me, son,' Ted said. 'And call me Ted.'

The smile stayed in place.

'Perhaps when we're off the clock, sir, if you don't mind. Protocol.'

'Right. Of course, Lieutenant.'

The woman in the jeans and the hoodie didn't say anything, so Ted spoke to her.

'Just visiting, is it?' he said.

'Diane Priestley. I'm scene of crime.'

'On your own?'

'Yes.'

Ted looked up at the enormous house, and back at her. She raised an eyebrow.

'All offers of help gratefully appreciated,' she said.

'You've had a look around?'

'Well, I've been waiting three hours,' she said. 'So, yeah, I've had a look around.'

Unlike deferential Lancaster, Priestley exuded a bitter lack of respect which Ted found himself appreciating, as if she were the only other grown-up in a room full of kids.

'I can't do anything about the drive from Manchester,' Ted said.

'But why,' she said, 'did you have to come all the way from Manchester?'

Ted looked down at the dead man at their feet.

'Well, that's a bloody good question, isn't it?' he said.

There was a strained silence.

'Any indication what happened here?' Ted said, eventually. 'Apart from the fact he obviously fell from the roof.'

He looked at Priestley.

'Nothing so far, no,' she says. 'But I've barely scratched the surface in there. It'll take weeks to explore the whole place, if I'm on my own.'

'Did you take a view as to time of death?'

'That's one for the forensic pathologist,' she said.

He tried not to roll his eyes.

'I'm not asking for a court statement, love. Just your thoughts.'

'I'm not your love.'

Ted sighed, more at himself than at her. He must be more tired than he realised.

'No, you're not,' he said. 'Apologies. I'm knackered, to be honest. Cut me a bit of slack here. What does the body look like to you?'

Priestley sniffed. Ted wondered if she was smelling the body itself.

'I'd say he died today, early morning,' she says. 'No putrefaction that I could make out. Birds haven't been at him.'

It wasn't much. To be honest, it was less than half of sod all.

'OK,' he said. 'Thanks. You're not from round here?'

'No.'

'Not from the South, either.'

'No, thank God. Nottingham.'

'Ah, Nottingham. Never been.'

'Don't bother.'

'Right,' he said. He turned to Lancaster. 'What do we know about the deceased?'

There was a shift in the mood. Lancaster himself looked suddenly uncomfortable, as if Ted had just insulted a bishop.

'You don't know about Brother Thomas, sir?' he said.

'No. Should I?'

This was still true. Ted knew very little about the Community of St Lidwina, and even less about its brothers. It was one of the many reasons he found his own presence here to be baffling.

Lancaster cleared his throat, as if he was about to read an obituary from the paper.

'Brother Thomas was formerly known as Thomas Jenkins,' he says. 'He was one of the original founders of the Community here, along with the Abbot.'

Ah, well now. Ted looked at the body again, his interest piqued despite his exhaustion. The violent death of a founding brother of the Order of St Lidwina would have set messages pinging all across the north-west. Maybe there was some sense in sending someone from outside. But why him? And all the way from Manchester?

One of the uniforms was staring at them while they spoke.

'Help you, son?' Ted said.

'No,' the officer replied.

'No, sir,' said Lancaster, coldly. The uniform looked at him, and stood a little straighter.

'No, sir,' the uniform said.

'Something to be getting on with, constable?' Ted said. 'Whatever it is, fucking get on with it.'

The uniform went back to whatever pointless task he was supposed to be undertaking. Ted looked up at the house.

'And what was this place to Brother Thomas?' Ted said.

'The house, you mean, sir?' said Lancaster.

'Yes. Why was he here?'

'He lived here.'

'Is it a dormitory or chapter-house or something?'

'No, sir. Just him.'

Ted whistled.

'Doesn't seem very…. monastic,' he said.

'No, sir,' said Lancaster. 'It doesn't.'

Was that disapproval Ted could hear?

'Did he go off from the windows, or roof?' he said.

'Roof,' said Priestley. 'Some loose masonry up there and around his body. He knocked something off when he came down.'

'And no cameras. No drones. No footage.'

'No sir. Not on the Island.'

He knew this, of course. But of course he asked,

because it had become hard-wired in all coppers. There should have been footage, probably quite high-definition footage, there should have been facial recognition and activity analysis, there should have been instant algo-rithmic calculation of suspects and likely levels of red-handedness. But there wasn't.

He was actually a detective again. Not a call-centre operative.

He thought for a moment. He'd imagined this was a simple mop-up job. He thought he'd been sent here just to show willing. He still thought that, pretty much. But there were wrinkles here. And some of them were sharp enough to set his antennae twitching.

He looked down at Brother Thomas. His lean, clean-shaved face pointed up towards his God, though the look of horror on his face suggested the experience had not been all he was hoping for.

'He looks terribly surprised,' he said.

Lancaster looked decidedly uncomfortable with this observation.

My days, the lad is very green indeed.

'Not as surprised as the other one,' said Priestley, bitterly.

Ted looked up to the house.

'Right then,' he said. 'Let's go and see her.'

5

The three of them - Ted, Lancaster, Priestley - set off to go into the house, leaving the uniforms standing around the body of Brother Jenkins, aimlessly, sullenly, deliberately and pointedly useless.

'Has the other body been identified?' said Ted.

'Yes. She had ID with her. Her name was Anthea Mortimer. She works for a PR firm in Chester called Moncrieff Associates. The boss, James Moncrieff, was at the party as well. He was interviewed along with the other guests this morning.'

'You did the interviews?'

'Yes, sir. All recorded and uploaded to Witness already.'

'OK. Will I have heard of any of the other guests?'

'Yes, sir. I think so.'

The lad paused.

'Rachel Whitehouse was here.'

Ted stopped walking for a moment and looked at him.

'Rachel Whitehouse? As in the Defence Minister? That Rachel Whitehouse?'

'Yes sir.'

'Why on earth was she here?'

'It was a meeting of the Investiture organising committee.'

Oh Jesus. Of course. The Investiture.

'OK. OK.' Ted tried to keep the strain out of his voice, and started walking again. A dead man of God was one thing. A dead woman was another. A crime scene involving Rachel Whitehouse was another. A connection to the Investiture of the new Prince of Wales was one more, the cherry on the top of this anxiety-inducing cake.

What the hell has Angela sent me into?

They arrived at the front of the house. Huge French windows, all of them locked, gave out onto the lawn, which ran in a steep green slope down to the sea. This was, in fact, the front of the house. It was a place designed to be seen from the water. An old brick wall stood at the edge of the water's edge. Were those cannons down there?

'Wasn't this place owned by some Marquess or other?' he said, to neither of them in particular.

'The Marquess of Anglesey, I believe,' Lancaster said.

'So what happened to him?' Ted said.

'I don't know, sir,' said Lancaster. 'The door at the far end is open. It's where the staff come and go.'

'The brothers and sisters, you mean?'

'Yes. They left the house around midnight.'

'The guests were left to themselves?'

'Yes. That's how they normally did things. The Community staff returned at seven this morning. That's when the bodies were discovered, and we were called.'

They came to the far corner of the house, and into a small walled yard. Lancaster opened a door to the interior. An old familiar smell caught Ted's nose.

'Toilets,' Ted said. 'There used to be a cafe here.'

'You've been here before?' said Lancaster.

'Years ago.'

Lancaster seemed about to ask a question. *Did you come here with your family?* Once, it would have been a normal thing to ask. It wasn't normal anymore, because it might lead to other questions, questions that British people were uncomfortable with, questions like *Are they still alive?* Especially when the person you were asking used to work for the Metropolitan Police. Ted saw Lancaster deciding to keep his mouth shut.

'Hang on,' said Priestley. 'You're not wearing the gloves I gave you.'

Lancaster looked at his hands, then looked at the handle of the door he'd just opened, like a guilty schoolboy.

'Oh, gosh,' he said. 'Sorry.'

Priestley rolled her eyes and handed him a pair of latex gloves. She gave a pair to Ted, and they exchanged a look.

These young'uns. What can you do?

The door opened onto a big open space. There were tables and chairs arranged in front of a large screen. The room seemed bizarrely normal, like they'd stumbled off a medieval battlefield into a productivity seminar.

Lancaster walked over to a door on the far side. Priestley and Ted followed him into the main part of the house. There'd been a funny kind of museum, here. It was gone, now, but the memory came back, sharper and stronger than any of the memories that had come over him since he'd first seen the sun cresting the edge of Penmaen-mawr, barely two hours before.

'Is that a wooden leg?' Peg had said, peering into one of the glass cases.

'Apparently,' he had replied, reading the notes. 'The first Marquess lost his leg at Waterloo.'

'Seems an odd thing to do,' Peg had said.

'I don't think they mean the station, sweetheart,' Laura had said.

'Ha ha,' Peg had said. 'I mean, it seems an odd thing to do, to lose your leg.'

Ted had been laughing. They had all been laughing.

He followed Priestley and Lancaster through the empty space which had been the museum. They were now walking back along the length of the house, through beautifully-appointed living rooms and spectacular vestibules. There were paintings everywhere, countless aristocratic eyes glaring down at them from shiny canvases. In a long thin room there was an enormous mural showing a mythical harbour scene. Ted stopped to look at it, and eventually Lancaster and Priestley, noticing that he was no longer following, did too.

'It's by Rex Whistler,' Lancaster said.

'I know,' said Ted. 'He stayed here before he went off to the war. He was supposed to be in love with the Marquess's daughter. Look.'

Ted went up to one end of the painting, and pointed to a depiction of a young man.

'That's Whistler,' he said. 'He's sweeping up rose petals. It's said to be a reference to his love for the Marquess's daughter. A few years after he painted it, he was dead - killed in the War. And look here. Have you seen the wet footprints? They follow you round the room. Wherever you go, they look like they're coming towards you.'

He was talking to Peg, down the years, but she wasn't there, and when he looked back at the other two, Lancaster was frowning, while Priestley looked oddly delighted, as if the Manchester detective had suddenly burst into song. Ted brushed the surface of the mural with his fingers, and turned to follow them out of the long room.

At the far end of the house was an elegant study lined with bookcases. Again, he remembered it from that previous visit. The then-custodians had 'preserved' it as the study of the Marquess, with books and papers covering every surface, and in one corner an old CD player surrounded by boxes of discs, all of them of classical music. It had been studiously messy. Ted walked around it now. It was tidy, neat, organised, with a big screen in one corner in front of an elegant leather sofa.

'We'll need an inventory of the stuff in here,' Ted said.

Lancaster made a note.

'Right, sir.'

'No computer,' Ted said.

'They don't use them,' Lancaster said.

'They don't use computers?'

'Well, they prefer not to. Obviously they do for some things. But not the way we do.'

'Why not?'

'They believe in our right to be forgotten. So no data storage.'

'They prefer to write things down,' said Lancaster.

'So not a right to be forgotten,' Priestley said. 'A right to be remembered inefficiently.'

Ted looked at her, and then at Lancaster. The young man's face was flushed red. He looked both annoyed and embarrassed, as if he might have said something to Priestley if Ted hadn't been there. Ted wondered if the two of them had already fallen out over matters spiritual.

They went upstairs, where there were more opulent bedrooms looking out over the back of the house and the Strait. In one of these rooms, with huge windows looking out over the water, there was a desk with a laptop computer open on it, and a metal cantilevered lamp. A brown wardrobe the height of a small woman, the height of Priestley.

The dead woman was lying face-up on the bed, eyes and mouth open, an expression of anxious surprise for the still-living world. Her arms were tied, at the wrist, to the posts of the headboard. Her red hair was pinned up neatly and tightly. Her achingly thin body was clad only in underwear, ordinary, cheap-looking stuff that seemed terribly at odds with the shoes, one of which had fallen from its foot and was sitting on the grey carpet below, its heel obscenely long. It must have been appallingly uncomfortable, and her look of polite shock seemed almost apologetic. *Oh! How did I find myself here? And what on earth am I wearing?*

'Hello, Anthea,' Ted said, quietly. 'What on earth happened to you?'

6

Ted didn't stay long in the terrible little bedroom. Priestley indicated what he had already suspected, though it would have to wait for the pathologist for confirmation - that Anthea Mortimer had probably been strangled, by person unknown. The bed was unmade, and messed up in such a way that some kind of struggle was suggested, either enforced or consensual. The montage was pornographic, the shocked open eyes less so, and it was to those eyes that Ted kept returning, as they seemed to him to tell a story that was at odds with the scene - the bound hands, the vulgar heels. But you could only read so much into a pair of dead eyes.

They went out of the bedroom, and on to the end of the corridor, under Priestley's direction. A door on the landing was marked Private, but was open.

'Did you open that?' Ted said to the two of them.

'No,' said Priestley. 'It was already open.'

Ted walked through the open door, finding himself on a utilitarian staircase, the kind of thing one might find in a hospital or a council building, with fire doors punched through with frosted windows and a long, plain corridor painted in a municipal green-brown which made him feel terribly nostalgic for the old police station on Lavender Hill. This floor felt completely out of keeping with the rest of the place, like the local council had taken over Brighton Pavilion.

Ted tried some of the doors. They were all unlocked. Some had numbers on them, in a 1970s typeface that was in keeping with the anachronistic feel of the corridor.

There was another municipal-style fire door, and behind it a smaller set of stairs leading up into the roof. At the top of the stairs was a small door, perhaps five feet tall.

'Who opened this one, then?' Ted said.

'Same again. It was open when we got here,' Lancaster replied.

Outside, the wind was suddenly upon them. It was beginning to get dark - putting the time at late afternoon. Lancaster had a torch, and was shining it along a gap between two pitched roofs. They walked along the middle of the roof, following the spine of the house. Halfway along there was a small set of steps, climbing up and over one of the roof pitches and onto the far side. Ted followed Priestley through a gap between the pitches, to a small space between the slope of the roof and the stone parapet. He looked over the edge.

Brother Thomas lay below, a large dark halo surrounding his head and upper body. His dead eyes gazed up at Ted. The lights they had turned on inside the house were flooding the pathway and patio. Long shadows stretched out from the uniformed officers clustered around the body, dark fingers inching their way back up the path that led to the car park. The air was clean, salty and sharp.

Priestley pointed down to the brickwork that lined the edge of the roof. Ted could see that one of the bricks had come loose, as if knocked by something.

'So, maybe he goes over here, and kicks the brickwork as he goes over?' said Ted.

'So, either a very clumsy suicide, or he was shoved by someone,' said Priestley.

'Clumsy suicide?' said Lancaster.

'It's not a high wall,' said Priestley. 'If you were going to jump, you'd just step over it.'

Ted nodded.

'That's my take, too.'

He saw one of the uniforms say something to a colleague, down below them on the ground.

'You have something for us, officer?' he shouted. The man started and looked upwards.

'No sir,' the officer shouted back, in a thick Welsh accent.

'Then sort this crime scene out, man. If we're going to do this, we're going to do it properly. I want a perimeter set for 20 feet around, and I want a tent over that body, and I want the house fenced off as well.'

The local uniform looked around him.

'But it's getting dark, sir.'

'Yes, chum, it's getting dark. It does that, every day at this time. Now get moving, and get this scene sorted. I want two of you manning it all night.'

The old cop shows used to talk abut hunches and niggles, witchy kind of thoughts which detectives had to tell them something wasn't quite right.

Go with your gut. It's getting bigger, but you can normally rely on it.

It was Laura's voice, from somewhere down the years.

His gut had stopped getting bigger - guts were a thing of the past, these days. But it was still speaking to him, nonetheless.

And it said: *watch out, Ted.*

The car park below Caernarfon Castle was almost empty. The daylight went two hours ago, and though there were streetlights up above in the town, down by the river and the sea it was dark. There were a few yachts berthed in the little marina. It surprised Ted to see them, to find that people still had yachts.

He'd forgotten the way the Castle walls loomed over the car park and the river and even the sea. The old building was enormous - an impossibly massive statement in pale stone, Edward 1's implacable message to the defeated Welsh still echoing down the centuries. But there was no light from the Castle. It stood apparently unoccupied, but he knew that was not the case. It was indeed occupied, in new and interesting ways, but the occupants did not advertise themselves as being at home.

There was someone watching him, nevertheless. The drone had picked him up as soon as he'd left the Island, appearing from who-knew-where as he drove off the Menai Strait Bridge. It now hovered above him while he stopped to take a look up at the Castle. It was odd, the way its temporary absence on the Island made its presence more jarring now. Like he'd forgotten how to forget about them. He found himself imagining some operative somewhere looking down at him on some high-definition screen on a business park somewhere between here and Manchester. Of course it might be flying on automatic, and if there wasn't an operative now there would be one later looking at the footage picked out for them by the software. Ted imagined them thinking the same thoughts as he did. 'Big castle. Strange yachts. No light.'

He hadn't thought like that about the drones for years. Hadn't thought about thoughts, or about the operatives, or about the system behind it all as something sentient. It had been impossible *not* to think of it like that in the early days.

And if the drone could see him thinking? Could see inside his head? It wouldn't find anything surprising in there. It would see the three of them in the old Mercedes, the car as big as a county, arguing about where to park. Laura wearing that summer dress she'd bought at the last minute, for a visit to Glyndebourne, somewhere they'd never been before and hadn't known the dress code for.

Random, disconnected memories which should have been fading by now, like everything else. Ted thought of the local constables sneering at his title - *Detective Inspector*. It was a phrase already passing from memory. CID. That was another one. *Criminal Investigation Department*. He'd been a Detective Inspector in CID. The words and letters had been branded on his soul. They still were. But now they were like a reminder rather than an identity. Or, perhaps, a *memento mori*. Now there were new words. Security Service. Digital Intelligence. Witness.

But he was here. He was *still here*. Here in Caernarfon, like the three of them had been years before, but alone now, standing by this funny little Dyson, plugging it into the Service charging column with the Royal seal, entering his PIN and setting the time. Everything looked the same, but everything was different. The castle, most of all, looked to have stayed as it was, its seemingly endless walls rising over the river and the estuary, timeless but forgetful. Seemingly untouched by all that had happened, on the outside at least. Inside, he know, it was a very different story. No tourists were allowed *inside* Caernarfon Castle anymore.

Amazing how thoughts could come and go all in a rush, pictures and memories opening up in fragments of seconds, time suspended, sequences crushed, chains of happenings shoved into compressed dots, like pills, MDMA, concentrated meaning....

Stop, now.

Was that Laura speaking?

Was it always Laura speaking?

Was it *ever* Laura speaking?

No.

It never was.

'It always rained when we used to come here,' he said, out loud. 'Peg used to hate the weather.'

No reply.

Tonight, the air was cold. The grey sky had given way to purple night as the clouds cleared. Here in the dark car park, with no light pollution, he could see stars strung across the heavens. He could even see the Milky Way, its smudged magnificence making him feel queasy. You weren't supposed to see skies like this in cloudy Wales. It felt impertinent.

You up there, God? Maybe chatting to your recently-deceased priest?

He pulled on his suit jacket from the back seat of the car, closed the door and locked it, wiping his hand on his trousers as he put the key back in his pocket, the dirt from the car's surface seeming to jump onto his fingers by some weird process of attraction. He found himself looking for the pay-and-display ticket machine, before stopping himself. He couldn't shake the habit. No-one paid for parking anymore. The Dyson was filthy dirty, but so were the other cars, apart from the one on the other side of the charging column to his own, a thug-black BMW imported from Europe, sucking up power into itself. He walked away, up the side of the Castle.

At the top of the hill, he turned into the square. It was filled with neat piles of metal, which on closer inspection turned out to be stacks of temporary railings, ready to be turned into temporary barriers for an expected crowd. Old, almost decrepit advertising hoardings had been filled with colourful new portraits of the teenage prince, beaming the practised Hollywood smile over the benighted pavements of the old country. In four days time, he would be invested as the new Prince of Wales. He stopped to read a plaque set into an ugly piece of concrete right in the middle of the square, commemorating restoration work and celebrating the support of one Robert Mountjoy, Leader of the Council. Ted wondered if anybody had put a plaque like that up since London.

Ted realised he was starving. Lancaster had told him he was to meet the chief crown prosecutor for North Wales at a restaurant called The House of Constantine, on a road 'opposite the Castle', but he struggled to find the place at first, heading by force of remembered gravity towards the old shopping centre before remembering that the medieval part of Caernarfon - where the restaurant was situated - lay alongside the castle, in little streets held in by the remnants of medieval walls. He turned back, and found the little alley running down from the Castle. 'Hole In The Wall Street' it was called, and it sat directly beneath one of the old walls.

The House of Constantine was small and upsettingly well-preserved. He didn't know what the name was meant to represent - it sounded presumptuous, but was it? Light poured from its front window, even though it was now almost nine o'clock and the other places on this street had long ago shut up shop.

As he opened the door to the place, he tried to remember the last time he'd visited a restaurant.

8

There was only one man sitting inside. He was talking on his phone. He beckoned Ted over to the table. A waitress stood at the back of the room. Ted nodded at her and smiled. She sort-of smiled back, but it looked more like she was in pain.

Ted assumed the man on the phone was the man he was there to meet: Allan Davies, the chief crown prosecutor for North Wales, the local equivalent to Alison Leybourne, who held the same title in Greater Manchester. Criminal justice in Britain was still, notionally, in the hands of people like Davies and Leybourne. Prosecutors were still responsible to the King for bringing cases involving criminal activity to trial, and the police were responsible for presenting the facts of those cases. But, increasingly, the evidence used was supplied by the Witness system - the drones and the software that ran them. And that system was run jointly by the Security and the Intelligence Services - and, in the shape of men like Lieutenant Lancaster, the Security Service increasingly employed its own police. And so two systems sat alongside each other, the old and the new, both suspicious of the other, though everyone knew the old system, the prosecutors and the police, was being allowed to wither and to die, a tired anachronism. Prosecutors like Davies and Angela Leybourne were political animals, these days - players in a grander game than the one that had gone before.

Davies kept his conversation going just long enough to put Ted in his place, and he then put his phone down on the table. It was one of the latest Korean smartphones, not the bog-standard government-spec, American-built brick Ted was forced to use, for half-forgotten security reasons. Davies seemed particularly proud of his phone, almost stroking it as he put it down. His suit was slick and expensive and somehow threatening. Ted remembered the black BMW in the car park and wondered if it belonged to Davies.

'Detective Inspector Wood, I presume?' Davies said, holding out a hand but not standing, and not introducing himself.

'Yes, sir,' Ted said, dutifully enough. He shook the man's hand, and sat down at the table when invited, like a good little boy. The waitress at the back of the room seemed to think about coming over to them, and then changed her mind.

'You've had a busy day, Wood,' Davies says, dropping Ted's rank and speaking to him as if he were an employee, or perhaps a pupil in a public school Latin class. 'A long drive, and I hear from Lieutenant Lancaster that you've already visited the Island and got things ship-shape over there. He says our local flatfoots are jumping up and down already.'

Local flatfoots. Jesus. And he'd *heard from Lancaster*, had he?

'Well, sir, it's not every day I get a direct call from a crown prosecutor about a case,' Ted said.

'And what did Alison say?'

'She was very direct,' Ted said. 'She said this investigation was important to her.'

'It's important to all of us,' said Davies. 'And it's a bloody mess.'

He was clean shaven and shiny, his teeth pearly white. His accent was English and crisp. His handshake had been practised and he held himself with an easy, dominant manner. His hair was grey and immaculately cut.

'This is a delicate situation, Inspector,' said Davies. 'You've been to the crime scene, so you've seen the place. The Island, and Plas Newydd.'

'It's an impressive place,' Ted said. 'For the house of a monk.'

'Ah well, Thomas Jenkins was much more than a *monk*, Inspector,' said Davies. 'A great man. A visionary. Brother Thomas is known.... *was* known to a great many of us in North Wales. He and the Abbott - well, the *country* owes them a debt for what they have done for us. Look, before we get into this, how about a glass of something while you look at the menu?'

He clicked his fingers, imperiously. The waitress walked towards them, carrying menus. She placed them down on the table. They were expensive, leather-bound things, brazenly opulent. Davies smiled at Ted, his perfect teeth in gleaming shark-like rows. The drink question hung in the air for a yawning second or two.

'I won't, thanks,' Ted said.

The grin on Davies's face widened momentarily, and then narrowed into an expression which was probably meant to be sympathetic but wasn't.

'Oh, I'm sorry,' says Davies. 'You don't drink?'

'Not while I'm on duty, sir.'

'You consider dining with me a duty, Wood?'

'A duty if not a chore, sir. I'd still rather not have a drink.'

God, the silly little games these men played. Davies raised an eyebrow, then muttered 'give us a minute' without looking at the waitress. She left, and Ted watched her go. She never looked at him.

'They're open late?' Ted said, and then instantly regretted it. Davies smiled, smugly, and patted the opulent menu as if it were a child which had performed an impressive arithmetical trick.

'I made them stay open for us, Wood,' he said, in a simpering tone. 'There are *some* benefits to being Chief Crown Prosecutor, you know.' The initial capital letters resounded round the room.

The waitress had resumed her place at the back of the room. She caught Ted's eye for a moment, and then looked away. He assumed the kitchen staff were also waiting, somewhere hidden. Waiting for the Mighty Prosecutor and his Important Guest to make their order, eat their food, and fuck off. Ted despised Davies's petty vanity, but he also remembered that this man's boss reported directly to the King, notionally at least. He could almost hear Laura's voice: *Be careful, Ted. Keep a lid on it.*

He opened the menu. It only took a glance to show this was a place catering to the wealthy and powerful. Fresh lamb, new potatoes, enough pastry on the dessert menu to keep a small Midlands town in butter for a week. The word *organic* appeared a good deal, which was shorthand for 'not grown with American GMOs on a super-farm'. Since London, Britain had become sort-of self-sufficient in food, partly because of the incursion of US agricultural technology and practices, but mainly because people ate less. A great deal less. Food was expensive. Most of the population lived on the less expensive frankenveg and frankenfruit - it tasted like dust, and there was not enough of it. Rationing was a daily reality, but one organised by facial recognition and software, not little books like after the last war. But in places like the House of Constantine, important men and women could enjoy their grub, safe in the knowledge that no chemicals were harmed in the growing of their food, unworried by the fact it cost four times as much as the everyday stuff, unaware that their bellies were expanding while the rest of the population tightened their belts, literally and figuratively.

Ted thought about saying something - perhaps a sardonic 'they must know a good farmer' - but, following Laura's whispered (to him) advice, he kept a lid on it. But he refused to look up at Davies. He knew the game here. It was how corruption took root - *had* taken root in Britain. It disgusted him.

But there was organic lamb on the menu, and the imported wines would make it slide down very nicely. If he were to drink one of them, which he would not be doing. He needed a drink, the need curling around his gut and hissing. But he wouldn't be letting Davies see that.

He heard the waitress come back, and looked up from the menu. Her hips were narrow and her cheekbones stark. The poor thing didn't eat off this menu, then.

'I can recommend the steak,' said Davies. 'It's what I'm having. Medium rare, no potatoes, green salad.' He said all this without looking at the waitress.

'What's quick to cook?' Ted said, thinking of the kitchen staff. She looked at him like he'd belched.

'It's all cooked to order,' she said.

Well, he'd tried.

'I'd like the chicken breast, please. With chips.' He

smiled at her, because the menu said *French fries*. Of course it did. She stared back at him, as if he had spoken in another language, before reading the order back to them. She said 'French fries'. Her voice, unlike her face, was bright, practised, bubbly.

'And bring us a bottle of something Italian and red,' said Davies. 'Not too expensive. Say 70 quid.'

She glanced at Davies, despite herself, and flushed as red as the wine he'd ordered. Davies didn't notice, but Ted did. Even here, in a restaurant presumably used to such showy extravagance, someone saying 'not too expensive' and '70 quid' in the same sentence was an affront. The waitress wrote something on her pad, and went away.

Wanker, Ted thought.

'To business,' said Davies. 'Thomas Jenkins. An important man. Knew a lot of people. The Community is something in the line of a local charity. Everyone contributes. And the town benefits. People coming and going. Families dropping off patients, you know the sort of thing.'

'Don't they call them the Suffering?' Ted said.

'Well, yes, but we know what they are,' said Davies. 'They're sick and they're dying. The Community is like the religious hospital monasteries of old, Wood. Caring for the old and the sick in the name of God.'

'One could almost call it a leper colony,' Ted said.

Davies frowned.

'People with explosion sickness are not lepers,' he said, coldly.

'No, I agree,' Ted said. 'Which is why I find it odd we shove them onto an Island a long way from anywhere. Out of sight, out of mind. Literally.'

'The comparison is invidious. Not to say offensive. This is not *a long way from anywhere*.'

Davies looked angry. Laura, if she were here, would be repeating her warnings.

'My apologies,' Ted said. 'Today was my first visit to the Community. It was striking, and I am probably a little raw.'

Davies raised an eyebrow and performed a little shrug.

'I sympathise,' he said. 'The place can be a little intense. Did you talk to Lancaster?'

'I did.'

'A good man. A man on the up. We have high hopes for him.'

'He's MI5, though, right?' Ted said. Davies frowned again. *I need to stop making him do that.*

'You mean, he's not old-fashioned Police,' said Davies. Which is exactly what Ted had meant.

'It's a new world,' Ted said.

'Yes, Wood. It is. We are part of the Security Service now, hand in glove, as they say. It is how it should be, and it works. And we will continue to make it work.

'Lancaster seems like a good man,' Ted said, carefully. 'A man of faith, I think.'

Davies didn't respond to that.

'You must be wondering why I asked for you to be sent here,' he said. 'All the way from Manchester.'

'I had wondered. Alison…. Mrs Leybourne was not exactly forthcoming.'

'Well, Wood, the thing is, men like you are a rare breed, these days.'

'Men like me?'

'Policemen. Detectives. Men of the old school.' Davies grinned. 'We need someone who's capable of working a case in the old way.'

'Because of Witness.'

Davies frowned, yet again, as if he'd been building up to that flourish.

'Yes. There's no-one like you left in Gwynedd. Possibly anywhere in Wales.'

'There's hardly anyone like me in Manchester, sir,' Ted said. 'I had basically assumed those days were gone.'

'But now they're back. On the Island, at least.'

'Seemingly so,' Ted said. 'With Witness not watching the Island, you need to solve this the old way. Chain of evidence. Scene of crime.'

'Method, motive, opportunity,' said Davies. 'Isn't that the mantra?'

'It was.'

'Well, I just asked Alison to send her best man. You see, Brother Thomas occupied a rather unique position in the official hierarchy. Since the news broke, I have been under some pressure to ensure a reliable hand on the wheel. We'd like this one done by the book.'

Davies said this like he was boasting about vanquishing a boy in the school playground. Ted found the smell of ambition on him overpowering, even over the man's expensive cologne. And how much of what he was saying was pure nonsense? Most of it, perhaps. He was not, by any stretch of the imagination, *Alison's best man*. He wasn't Alison's anything. And anyway, did Davies really ask Alison for help? Whose caper was this, anyway?

The waitress came and opened a bottle of wine at the table. The smell of it flowed into his nostrils, lighting up parts of his brain that were normally pitch dark. The waitress poured Davies a glass and went to pour Ted one, but he put his hand over the glass, eventually, just in time, right at the last possible moment, but the pause before he moved his hand, ah, it had felt like a lifetime. He could take a drink, by God. He'd not smelled anything like this wine since Paris, that boring bloody conference on Europol and the British Situation three years ago. The waitress left, and he picked up the bottle from the table and read the label. It was Italian, and his mind flew back to a hotel above the Positano cliffs, a room with a balcony and a sea view, impossibly expensive on his copper's salary, a treat for two nights. Peg was with Laura's parents. They had eaten dinner down by the sea, a warm salt smell in the air, sardines and tomatoes and delirious bread - 'I can't, honey, I just can't, too full' - and now they were falling asleep with the window open while the ancient breeze lapped at the curtains. Her skin had been.....

He looked up to see Davies grinning as he held the wine bottle, a broad avaricious smile, the smile of a cat toying with a bird. Then the man's phone vibrated on the table with an incoming message. Davies picked it up, looked at the screen, and nodded, putting the phone back down. He didn't refer to the interruption. The theatre of it all was preposterous.

The waitress came back, this time with their food. Ted looked at it, and wondered how many times the kitchen staff had spat in it. There was a tasty-looking sauce smothering the chicken breast which suddenly felt less appealing. But he was starving.

Davies piled into his plate without even acknowledging the waitress. She hovered for a moment - he imagined her pondering a question. *Will you be wanting dessert, or shall I let the kitchen staff go?* Ted even considered answering the question before it was asked. *No, let them get off, love.* But he couldn't do that. Davies could have had this place closed down with one call on his sleek, top-of-the-range phone.

The waitress retreated. Ted bit into the chicken, trying to forget what might be in the sauce. It was delicious. The tastiest thing he'd eaten in months. Maybe even years.

'So, what were your impressions of the crime scene?' said Davies, his mouth half-full of food richer than almost any British mouth had tasted in a decade, speaking through it like he was eating a high street plastic burger.

'It was a mess,' Ted said. 'No formal process, no perimeter, local plod wandering up and down. I had to bark at a few of them.'

'Making yourself popular already, eh?'

'If this case is as important as you and An…Mrs Leybourne suggest, I'm afraid I'm going to have to make myself pretty unpopular, yes.'

'Quite right, quite right.'

'Did you not visit the house yourself?'

'No, no, not at this stage. Much better to leave it to you chaps.'

Ted tried to imagine Davies standing over the woman's dead body in the bedroom. The image made him feel a little sick. It was almost Hitchcockian.

'And did you draw any early conclusions?' said Davies.

'We won't know much until we look at the forensics.'

There wouldn't be any forensics, is what he was really thinking. But he was damned if was going to think out loud about this case in front of a man like this.

'But suicide is the most likely explanation?' said Davies. Ted noticed he wasn't shoving steak into his face any longer. He was watching, attentive. Worried?

'Suicide? The woman was face up on the bed, tied at the wrists.'

Davies blushed a little.

'Ah, no, I meant… well, I don't quite know what I meant.'

'The woman was definitely killed, I would say. As for Brother Thomas - we shall see. If he did kill himself - well, one explanation does present itself, doesn't it?'

'He killed her, and then killed himself.'

'Yes.'

'That would be…. an undesirable outcome.'

'Undesirable for whom?'

'For everyone.'

Davies went back to his food, chewing thoughtfully on a piece of meat.

'Did you know Thomas Jenkins?' Ted said, after a moment.

'Of course. I am a regular visitor to the Island,' the prosecutor said. 'As you will see when you check Witness.'

'No doubt,' Ted said, evenly.

'But that is not unusual. Most of the local dignitaries visit the Island regularly. We are proud of it, after all. Indeed there has been talk of the King himself paying a visit.'

'When?'

'In four days time. The Investiture, you know.'

The pressure of the situation was thrown back into his face. Four days before the Investiture of a new Prince of Wales, to be attended by his father the King, there had been a double murder at a house almost opposite Caernarfon Castle, the site of the ceremony. And one of the victims was a co-founder of the Community of St Lidwina. Which had been operating under a charter from the King himself. The chicken sat suddenly rather heavy on his stomach.

'The King was….what? Planning to stay at Plas Newydd?' Ted said.

'No, nothing like that. But it has been an important site during the planning of the Investiture.'

'Important?'

'Well… Now we come to it.'

The steak was almost gone. Davies poured himself another glass of wine.

'You see, Brother Thomas and the Abbot, Brother Nicholas, they form… or rather, they *formed* an intriguing partnership. Brother Nicholas is very much the *spiritual* lead, but Brother Thomas is…. Well, was, the *temporal* partner.'

'I don't understand.'

'Well, you have been to Plas Newydd. It is a splendid place, is it not? Not at all, well, *monastic*?'

'It seemed like a palace.'

'Just so, just so. And it was the place where the great and good who visited the Island tended to stay. I have stayed there myself.'

Davies smiled, mock-humbly. Ted pictured the house, its well-appointed and, more to the point, well-preserved rooms.

'You mean, it operated as a kind of hotel? For *the great and good*.'

'Rather more than a hotel, Wood. More of a…. convention centre.'

'Convention?'

'Away from prying eyes.'

At this, Davies raised his eyes to the ceiling. It was a common enough gesture in Britain, these days.

There was great danger here, Ted suddenly saw. Meaning danger for himself.

'Do you mean to say, Brother Thomas made his house available for off-the-grid meetings?'

'Well, I wouldn't have put it quite like that.'

'Meetings that weren't recorded by Witness.'

'Well, the *attendees* were recorded, of course. Witness can see them travelling to the Island. But yes, once on

Anglesey, Witness has no means of monitoring those sessions. But that became essential, you see?'

'Essential for what?'

'For the government! Some things need to be hidden away.'

'The government hiding things from itself?'

'Well, no. Not quite. But in some ways…. yes, possibly.'

Davies was struggling to explain, and Ted could see why. He was reluctant to hand over any information about Plas Newydd, but the man couldn't help but project himself into the heart of things, dramatising his own importance, dropping in supposed insider knowledge like a grandmother gossiping with a neighbour over the garden fence.

'How often did you visit the Island?' Ted said, not trying too hard to avoid a sharp tone.

'Me? Oh. Every month or two, I suppose.'

'For unmonitored meetings?'

'For various things. Departmental business, mostly. Alison was sometimes there, too.'

Ted hadn't thought of that possibility. He filed it away for now.

'And when was the last time you spoke to Brother Thomas, if I might ask, sir?'

'Well, if it's relevant, I suppose…. a month ago, perhaps. A group of us went to discuss arrangements for the Investiture.'

'You met at the house? At Plas Newydd?'

'Of course, yes.'

'And how did he seem?'

'Oh, his usual self. He was good at a party. The Abbot is a rather more private individual. He tends to limit himself to the needs of his flock. Brother Thomas always had more of an idea on the *political* dimension. Hence his temporal role.'

'I did not fully comprehend the political dimension prior to this conversation,' Ted said.

I am even beginning to sound like this bastard.

'Well, I hope I have been able to help with it,' says Davies, before taking another gigantic swig of wine.

'But it still doesn't change the facts, as they stand, sir.'

'The facts?'

'That this looks like it may be a murder followed by a suicide.'

'Yes, I do see that,' says Davies. 'And it may well be that this - you being here, and such - is all, well, something of a *performance*. But we do need to be seen to be making an effort.'

'Making an effort? I hope you'll allow me to do my job, sir.'

Davies took another sip of wine, slowly, pointedly, and didn't respond to that.

'I've booked you a room in the Lloyd George Hotel, on the square,' he said. 'It's yours for as long as you want it. I need this case closed, DI Wood. Quickly. I understand it may be an open-and-shut kind of thing, but please just follow whatever procedures you might have, and let's get a report together. Shall we say by the day after tomorrow?'

'For appearance's sake?' Ted said, unable to stop himself. Davies glared at him, one finger tapping on his expensive smartphone, and Ted wondered if, despite all his efforts to be a good little boy, he'd ended up making an enemy anyway.

9

The Lloyd George Hotel was as disturbingly smart as the House of Constantine - out of place, inappropriate to the times, the haunt of government and intelligence types. Ted hadn't seen places like this back in Manchester, where even the police headquarters had an exhausted air. The hotel exuded the same *look at me, son, I'm important* bollocks with which Davies had stunk up the restaurant.

The young woman on reception - the same angular, hungry sharpness as the waitress in the restaurant - smiled professionally and remotely, and it was only when he'd signed the digital register with a thumbprint and a face scan and she'd asked if there was any luggage that he realised he'd come to Caernarfon with nothing at all. How had he managed to do that? He'd left the house as soon as his conversation with Angela had ended. Now he was checking into a hotel the best part of a hundred miles away, with no change of clothes for the morning.

There was a small selection of tourist tat for sale at reception, including a range of T-shirts emblazoned with the face of the young man who would become the Prince of Wales in four days time.

'Do you have one of those in a large?' he asked the receptionist.

She looked at the display, and she looked back at Ted. There was a smile on her face now. It was the first genuine facial expression he'd seen since he parked the car down beneath the castle. People guarded their faces, these days - or they wore a theatrical mask, like Davies had. The software had become good at reading faces, and inferring what went on behind them.

'Seriously?' she said.

'I've come here without a change of clothes.'

'And you want to wear a T-shirt?'

'Well, I'm only planning to go to my room and go to bed. I was hoping I could get the shirt laundered overnight.' *And hang out my underpants over the bath*, he did not add.

The receptionist looked at her watch.

'It's pretty late,' she said, doubtfully. It was there then, suddenly - the status thing. She looked at him, a polite look on the surface, but a wary one behind it. He was able to read it pretty well. *Here is a man who wants his shirt cleaned. He could be an important man. If he's not important, what is he doing at this hotel? So I'd better do as I'm told.*

That was one of the things that had changed. It perhaps hadn't been intended, but the coming of Witness had seen the rebirth of an older form of deference, and like so much to do with Witness the change seemed to have been welcomed. A return to 'old-fashioned values' was something to be celebrated. A country where people knew their place, and were happy to stay within it.

He came close to telling her not to bother about the shirt, but then she spoke.

'Should be fine,' she said. She went and rifled through the T-shirts, pulling one of them out. She held it out to show him, and they both laughed. The T-shirt was an appalling thing, but it was not as appalling as this faked bonhomie between the master and his servant.

'Should I leave you the shirt now?' he asked, trying to be helpful now.

'What, change here in reception?'

'I don't mind if you don't,' Ted said..

'Neither do I,' a third voice said, from behind him. He turned to find a smartly-dressed woman waiting quietly for her turn at reception. 'Surprise!' she said, making pretend jazz hands.

'God, I'm sorry,' Ted said. He turned back to the receptionist. 'Look, why don't I nip into the toilet and change while you deal with this lady?'

'Seriously, my friend,' said the smartly-dressed woman. 'You can strip down in the reception for me, any day.'

She was American. Of course she was American. This was turning into a scene from an old sitcom. Ted took a closer look at her. She was elegantly made-up and coiffured and dressed, nothing gaudy, just a general sense of wellbeing, education and social poise. Guessing her age was an impossibility, but Ted thought she might be older than he was. There was an authority about her that wasn't at all aesthetic.

'In the name of preserving our renewed special relationship, I think I'll head upstairs and bring the shirt back down,' he said.

'Shame!' said the American woman.

'You should be relieved,' he said.

He thanked the receptionist, and left her and the American to their business. He climbed the stairs to the first floor, his tired feet on beautiful carpet, his hands brushing against expensively-papered walls and carefully-polished banisters. From somewhere within the hotel he heard the sound of piano music. Laura would have known what it was. It sounded pretty generic to him.

Up in the room, his eyes went straight to the minibar, if only to confirm that there was one. It was a recently-installed thing sitting in the cabinet underneath the screen. He changed, and walked back down to the reception in the ugly T-shirt, a walking advert for the monarchy. The girl on reception smiled as he walked up to her, that practised, professional smile that made him want to scream. The American woman had gone.

'Nice T-shirt,' she said. 'Fits perfectly!'

'Thanks. Here's my shirt.'

He handed it over, and she took it from him, and they looked at each other, and something passed between them. It was one of those silent spaces that people sometimes shared with each other now. It was a look that spoke silent volumes: *There's no-one here to wash your shirt. We don't do that anymore. No hotel does. So I'm going to do it. I might even have to take it home and wash it, and dry it, and iron it. But I'll pretend it was done by a 'service'. And you'll pretend as well. Because you might be important. And I don't want to attract the wrong sort of attention. I don't want you looking me up on Witness, checking my history, looking into the people I know - family, boyfriend, girlfriend, kids, whatever. Those kinds of things can be dangerous, these days, and you might be important, and this transaction, this ludicrous bit of business over a shirt, might expose me to the power that you might or might not yield. And the camera above me and the camera behind you are both recording this whole elaborate, preposterous charade. Our transaction is being recorded, and we are forever linked now, inside Witness and its impossible memory.*

A girl and a detective exchanged words at this place, on this date, at this time. Nothing suspicious logged. Keep the face neutral, pretend to smile, and for pity's sake don't do anything to attract attention.

It was, in so many long-standing ways, a typically British moment. Maybe that was why so few people complained about Witness. It enforced old modes of behaviour. Did people *like* this stilted politesse? After all, wasn't it just like the old days?

'Thank you,' he said. 'You've been most kind.'

'A pleasure, sir,' she said, but her eyes were tragic, so tragic that he found himself wondering how good Witness's facial recognition was, whether this look on her face might trip some kind of trigger. You saw this occasionally, if you looked carefully enough. Another human being, intelligent, trapped in a world without prospects of betterment, doffing the cap and tugging the forelock and silently screaming. 'Good night.'

He turned away from her, and went back upstairs, and shut the bedroom door. He looked around. There were two cameras - a wide-angle thing beneath the ceiling light, and another one above the door. He opened the minibar anyway. A square of white light, broken by shining cylinders. A kind of altar. He knelt down in front of it, as if in worship. They knew well enough that he drank too much.

All his memories of drinking were episodic, moments sharp-edged as cloudless May mornings. Singing Neil Diamond songs with a bunch of Met lads at a conference afterparty in Lake Tahoe. Looking for a cab in Paris with Laura. And that one night. That last night. Beginning the ninth pint in a corner of the pub, Laura at home with Peg, the night before London, the night before everything changed.

He was terribly drunk that night. He could remember it all, every little detail.

It's the mornings after that have slipped away. That particular morning most of all. But then it was never there.

She came to him, then, as she sometimes did, there, as he knelt before the minibar. She didn't say anything - she never said anything - but it was her, kneeling on the floor beside him, not a memory, real, now, in the moment. He could see her sharp, perfect knees against the dark carpet, and he knew every indentation and bump on them, like the dark mark on the left one where she'd knocked herself against a fountain in Rome. There was no sound as she knelt down beside him. Her knees had once cracked like gunshots.

He reached out to touch her hand, and his hand shivered and shook like that old song by the Cure she'd always loved and he'd always hated. His fingertips brushed against the sharp electric surface of the carpet.

He took his hand away, and put it inside the minibar, felt its cool air, and grasped one of the bottles. A vodka. Some nondescript brand, a fake Russian name, the spirit probably distilled in a half-empty business park on the outskirts of Gateshead or Carlisle, because who gave a shit about point of origin anymore? He opened it, and drank it down in one glorious shot. He put his hand in again, took out another bottle. Rum. A picture of a pirate on the label.

The minibar would send its data back to the hotel chain's head office, and from there it would be sent on to Witness. *Detective Inspector Ted Wood is drinking again*. He had finished the vodka he'd bought at the shop near his home last night. And the whisky he'd bought the night before. And the eight beers he'd had in the pub in Stockport the night before that. All the data - from cameras, card transactions, stock control, the RFID receiver in the minibar - added to the statistical entity that was Ted Wood, Melancholic Alcoholic.

He went over to the bed, carrying the remote control and the rum bottle. He switched on the screen. By default it was switched to the live video feed, a randomly selected camera on the public network. This one was on the square outside. A fox walked across the open space. There was no human around. He clicked the remote control. This camera was inside a pub, almost-empty, a few men inside, some at the bar, some at tables, the barman talking to one of them.

Click.

A high-level drone, looking down on Caernarfon, the shape of the Castle pixellated out, because it belonged to The Family, and from the Family Witness turned its face away.

Click.

A CCTV camera on a street corner. A woman passing, hurrying home.

Click.

A drone following a car down a road. He didn't recognise the road.

Click.

Public cameras inside a car. A taxi, perhaps. Some kind of semi-public vehicle. The driver's face - young, semi-bearded, gaunt, bored - and the shape of his passenger.

Click.

The reception, here at the hotel. The woman on reception stood silently, head bowed. She was reading a book.

Click. Click. Click.

The lives of people followed by the cameras of Witness. The live feed which anyone could watch, at any time. The thing Ted did instead of watching real television. Like so many.

He drank, one bottle after another, clicking through the feeds. Laura did not return. And so, the night rolled by.

DAY TWO

10

is head was silent apart from the sound of his heart thudding. The cotton of the pillow felt like sandpaper.

Ted slid into wakefulness like a body sliding into a swamp.

The first thing he saw when he lifted his head from the pillow was the minibar. Or, to put it more honestly, that was the first thing he looked for, like a flower opening to the sun.

The minibar's door hung open. The light inside was on. It created a rhombus across the carpet, and in that rhombus were tiny empty bottles, the detritus of a party in a doll's house.

He was here in the hotel room, but he was also back there.

He was lying in the glorious double bed in Streatham. The sun was streaming through the big old windows. The light always turned those windows into something holy, the glowing patterns badly in need of choral music. He was confused by the light at first, because the only thing his brain could recall, initially, was that *the curtains had been closed*. Who had opened them? He rose to the surface of the day on a bubble of confused questions.

Peg was sitting on the side of the bed. She was small, no more than six or seven. He realised that he felt sick and old and that his head was throbbing like an approaching elephant. Peg handed him two white pills and a glass of water.

'Mum says breakfast is ready,' she said. 'And she says you're a stupid bastard who can't take his drink.'

The half-hidden lisp was still there. She would lose it in a year or two, and they would miss it for a week or two, and then it would be forgotten among the screeching chaos of all the changes that were carried in by those incessant waves of growth. Every day different. Every day remembered, even now.

He closed his eyes. He tried sitting up. The hotel pillow slid out from under his shoulder, and his head slipped down again. He groaned. He opened his eyes again, and for a single crystal moment Laura was there, her back to him, her brown hair untidily scrunched up around the top of her head and the pillow below, and in that moment he could smell the two of them, the morning smell, the smell that had grown up with them, slowly adapting to the years as they passed, changing in detail but never in character. He reached out his hand and felt nothing but the cotton surface of the hotel duvet. Suddenly, he felt it everywhere. He was naked in the bed, a dying man on a windy hillside, a man waking up in a field having fallen from a plane, a man washed up on a tropical beach, his mouth full of saltwater.

On the wall of the hotel room was a black-and-white picture of a young woman's face on a beach somewhere, the wind artfully blowing her long hair away from her perfect eyes, which gazed at him with flagrant invitation. The picture reminded him of another picture entirely.

Hibakusha. He had read the word in a book from before London. A copper who read books. That had been his thing, his USP, the quirk he was known for in the station. This book had a black-and-white cover showing a Japanese woman sitting on the remains of a wall, her long black hair tied up but coming loose, a piece of it blown by the wind across her suffering face. Beside her, and supported by her, sat a child with close-cropped hair, dressed in a sleeveless woollen jumper. Behind them was a blurred, half-seen image of destruction, a leafless black tree in the foreground seeming to loom over the frowning child. The book's title was *Hiroshima.*

The book had described, in precise, devastating detail, the impact felt by those on the ground when the Americans dropped their bombs. The word *hibakusha* appeared in the last quarter of the book, the section dealing with the longer-term aftermath. The Japanese avoided the word 'survivors' to describe those who had lived through the twin apocalypses of Hiroshima and Nagasaki. They had instead used the word *hibakusha.* In its literal translation, the word meant 'explosion-affected persons.'

That word - *hibakusha* - had seemed like a refugee from a novel, not a work of non-fiction, as this book had been. It seemed a little on the nose. It was so perfectly *Japanese,* almost insulting in its caricature. *Explosion-affected persons.* A phrase expunged of the horror of its genesis.

Except, as he would come to see, the horror was there all the time. The man or men (or men and women, or woman, or demon) they all now called 'Guy Fawkes' had set the timer or flicked the switch or just dropped the box on the ground, and they were left with only horror. Explosion-affected persons. Yes. That was exactly what they were, all of them.

The *hibakusha* of Britain.

Him included.

He made it into a standing position, and walked to the light switch. He winced when the light came on, and then started when he saw a face staring at him from the wardrobe. A terribly familiar face. A young man, smiling charmingly. The prince. The face was on a T-shirt hanging from the wardrobe door. How did the T-shirt get there?

A fragment of the previous evening came back. The receptionist and the dirty shirt. It sounded like a short story title from another time. *The Last Detective's Last Case.* Another for a growing collection. He had bought the T-shirt to wear while that poor woman washed the shirt he had driven to Wales in.

He walked to the bathroom. His own terrible face stared back at him from the mirror above the sink. He could see the prince on the T-shirt peeking over his shoulder.

'Rule Britannia,' he muttered into the mirror in the bathroom. 'Britannia rules the waves.'

His grey, shapeless, drooping body stared back at him.

'Britons never, ever, ever shall be slaves,' his disgusting self replied.

11

He opened the bedroom door after showering, the strange T-shirt worn underneath his suit jacket, making him feel like the ancient manager of an Eighties rock band. Even the cringing hangover felt appropriate, the residue of a night spent with roadies and hangers-on in some sleazy downtown bar.

The clean shirt was dangling on the outside of the door. It smelled fresh, and had been carefully ironed. He went back into the bedroom, and changed out of the terrible T-shirt and into the clean shirt. When was the last time a woman had cleaned and ironed a shirt for him? He remembered a night after a conference somewhere, a cheerful detective sergeant from Aberystwyth, all squeezes and clasping. She'd ironed his white shirt with the cheap hotel iron the next morning. Why had she done that? He wondered about it, even now.

He walked downstairs. A different angular, sharp-cheeked young woman was standing behind reception desk, and he wondered where last night's receptionist was now. She probably had a second job. Or even a third. He felt guilty, again, about making her wash his shirt.

His head was crystal-fragile but he planned on flooding his body with carbohydrates at the hotel breakfast buffet, which he assumed would be as un-rationed as the menu at the previous night's restaurant, this being that kind of place. The dining room was full of people sitting in ones and twos, split between men and some women who looked like state bureaucrats or politicians, none of them particularly recognisable, and obvious visitors, some of them also obviously American.

It never failed to amaze him that people still came to Britain, especially Americans, even though it was ten years since London and, he supposed, any lingering fears of terrorist attack had subsided back to their pre-London levels. Or perhaps even lower than that, given Witness. Americans probably outnumbered Europeans in Britain, these days. The special relationship, measured in visits to the gift shop. There were still castles and churches to see, and after all, the fallout had not reached Stonehenge. And then there was the Community, which attracted its own diaspora of religious types and gawkers. And even then, he remembered with a little shudder, there was the Investiture. Of course. They were here to see royalty.

The American woman from the previous night was sitting by herself at a table near the buffet, finishing off a coffee and holding a tablet computer. She smiled as he walked past.

'My friend,' she said, 'I don't know who is braver. Me for braving this damned climate. Or you for braving your obvious hangover.'

He smiled weakly, unable to dredge a response from his wrung-out brain. Her face became serious. She was dressed for the day, in that committed and professional way

Americans had. Her hair alone must have taken an hour. She looked powerful, strong, decisive. Qualities one rarely saw anymore.

'You ok, fella?' she asked.

'I had a few last night,' he said, mock-ruefully. She frowned at that, and he could imagine what she was thinking. Had he already had a few when they'd spoken in reception? Or had he had a few after that, alone in his room? He hadn't gone out again, not with the curfew.

He nodded at the buffet.

'I need to get some fatty food into me,' he said.

'Well, good luck getting through the day,' she said. 'The weather's going to be a pig.' She glanced down at her coffee. 'But not as much of a pig as this coffee. This country really is on its knees.'

And she looked down at her tablet again. He felt dismissed.

He plunged into the coffee which the American had so dismissed but which tasted better to him than any he'd had in a long, long time, and juice and eggs and potatoes, which he piled into himself with grim efficiency, trying to bury the hangover. As well as the coffee being good, it was more food in one place than he'd seen in a good while - than anyone he knew had seen. Then he want back to his room because he felt like he was going to throw up. He managed not to.

He left the hotel and walked back past the Castle, heading down to his car. Men in yellow vests were beginning to put out the metal barriers he'd seen the previous night. Yesterday's mild weather had given way to a cold, damp day, rain heavy in the air but not quite breaking free from a descending sky.

The Castle's grim solidity was, if anything, even more manifest this morning. The rest of the town seemed to bow its head down towards it, a supplicant estate. Normally the Castle would be open to tourists, but now it was closed up, the insides presumably being readied for the Investiture. The King had begun a process of renewal and fortification not seen since those old days of Edward Longshanks, the man who had built this grim fortress. With its ancient law courts gone - and, some said, its ancients laws as well - and its wealth melted into originating carbon, the only things Britain had of its old self were stories and histories. *Tourism will save us*, went the argument, ignoring the rubble where Westminster Abbey had once stood. Caernarfon's enormous polygonal towers now gleamed with fresh paint, the white and yellow intended, it was claimed, to reclaim how the Castle was intended to be seen by its original builders. No money had been spared - the additions were in similar stone to the original, and the old walls had been freshly mortared. Caernarfon Castle was not the grey-brown colour of a ruin. It was the white-and-red of a magnificent royal palace. You could go inside and dream of Arthur and Guinevere. 'Heritage porn,' Laura would have said.

He looked up and behind. A drone hung in the air watching him - the same model as the one that had accompanied him from Manchester. Perhaps - who knew? - even the same actual drone.

'Good night's sleep, son?' he said to it. 'Suck up some juice, did we? Hanging upside down in a barn like a fucking vampire?'

He gave the thing - and whoever or whatever was operating it - a thumbs-up and then turned down the hill to the car park. Being rude to machines hadn't made him feel any better.

12

The North West Wales division of Witness was based at Parc Menai, a sprawling business park not far from the second of Anglesey's bridges, Stephenson's Britannia, the one which was now closed to all but cross-island freight traffic headed for the ferries at Holyhead.

The business park was the kind of place that would once have been marked by trimmed grass verges, tidy car parks, and boards advertising companies dealing in bathroom supplies, accident claims, plastics and logistics. There were still dozens of boxy office blocks, but the verges had run to weeds long ago, and the open spaces in front of the units were almost all empty.

The Witness building was the exception. The gigantic white box sat at the edge of the park, nestling right up against a grand-looking old private estate behind it. The offices oozed the same slick corporate health as the old glass-and-steel towers of Canary Wharf which, he believed, still stood, though empty now - an infestation of buildings along the river, the cranes that had tended to them either still or dismantled. He couldn't remember the last time he'd seen a crane.

Outside, there were so many drones in the air here that he could no longer make out his own personal companion amid the airborne electrical swarm. Above him, mostly invisible, were the high-level drones, which could stay airborne for days. Plas Newydd, the house which he'd haunted the evening before, was maybe a quarter of a mile from here, across the Strait. A man had fallen from a roof and died within eyeshot of this place, and Witness hadn't seen a bloody thing. It must have been driving them potty.

Good.

Inside, there was the expected security theatre - cameras, thumbnail sensors, X-ray machines, a careful burrowing through his ancient Fjällräven backpack. Lancaster was waiting for him as he made his way past these customary interruptions and into the office itself.

'Guv,' said Lancaster, holding out a hand. 'Welcome to Menai Witness.'

He said *guv* as if he were auditioning for a part in a television drama.

'I feel like I've come for a job interview,' Ted said.

Lancaster grinned. He seemed a far more relaxed individual than the uptight, nervous fellow who Ted had met on Anglesey the previous evening. But then Witness had always felt more the property of the Security and Intelligence services than the police. Lancaster was on home ground.

'We're just through here,' he said.

He followed Lancaster through what looked to be, to all intents and purposes, a call centre. People sat inside individual cubes, most of them with two screens in front of them. One screen was for video - either live, or pulled up from the archive. The other showed data relating to the video - profiles, histories, connections to other profiles. No-one looked up at Lancaster and him as they walked through. These employees had fallen into the dataset, like people used to do with their social media feeds. What was going on inside the screen was always going to be more interesting than what was going on out here in this dull office, because what was in the screen was what was in the world. The office was the artificial reality. Why gaze over the top of your cubicle, when you could gaze across entire towns?

They passed a kitchen, in which two young women were talking while cameras in the top corners of the room recorded them and tracked their time away from their desks.

He watched Lancaster as they made their way through the building. The younger man nodded a dozen times at different people as they passed. He was waved through security which, while not uncommon, did mark him as a senior officer with high levels of clearance. Again, it struck him how much the lad looked like he was back in his element. Last night, on the roof of that strange Gothic house on the other side of the Strait, he had seemed displaced and anxious. Here, he was master of his domain.

'Get much sleep, Lieutenant?' Ted said.

Lancaster smiled ruefully.

'A few hours,' he said. 'How was dinner?'

'Filling,' said Ted. 'So, what facilities have they given us, then? Palatial situation room with views of the sea, is it?'

'Just a small office, I'm afraid.'

'Shame. I was half-hoping they'd have put us in Caernarfon Castle itself.'

Lancaster laughed at that.

'There was talk of putting Witness in there, once,' he

said. 'That place is still a fortress. The walls are stupendously thick. Edward knew what he was doing when he commissioned a castle.'

'Not a popular view round here, I'd have thought,' Ted said.

'With the Welsh? No. Probably not. But Edward's my hero.'

'Where are you from, Lieutenant? Your name makes you sound like a descendant of the old fellow.'

'Well, my Dad always claimed we were descended from the earl of Lancaster, who was Edward's brother. Never bought into it myself. And we grew up in Watford.'

'Did you lose people, son?' Ted said.

'Everybody lost people, Detective,' Lancaster replied.

Not one for surrendering information about himself, Lieutenant Lancaster. Ted found himself admiring that, after the boastful pantomime Davies had subjected him to the previous evening. But he'd said *we* when talking about Witness. Lancaster was Security Service, not Police. He may have done the training, but that wasn't the same thing, whatever the manuals and department announcements tried to say. Police were police. Spooks were spooks. There had been good reasons for the old demarcation of roles. He could remember the MI5 mob, who would descend on Met investigations every now and again. The way they carried themselves always reminded him of that old song. *We were no match for their untamed wit.* Posh boys and girls, usually, cracking toilet jokes in Latin.

Things probably hadn't changed all that much. With his starched shirt and tailored suit, Lieutenant Lancaster was doing his best to blend in. But the fact was, he didn't. Coppers were crumpled. The best ones, anyway.

Glass-sided meetings rooms were arranged around the desk-cubes. All these glass-sided rooms had people in them

- perhaps a dozen meeting rooms in all. Witness practised what it preached - glass walls were the norm here. Everything was visible to anyone who cared to watch. Cameras were everywhere, too. Everything was logged - every keystroke, every kitchen conversation, every arrival and departure. If Witness could make the real world like this, it would. And in many ways, it had.

Lancaster led him into one of the glass-sided rooms. Inside sat Diane Priestley, the scene-of-crime officer from the night before, hunched over a screen. She nodded at him, he nodded back.

'Here we are, guv,' said Lancaster.

He hadn't expected much, and he hadn't got it. The room was one of the smaller ones. There were three terminals inside, each with the same dual-screen set-up that sat on all the desks outside. An interactive whiteboard that doubled as a screen had been placed at one end of the room.

'I'm only here to check in,' Priestley said. 'I need to get back out to the house. It was a waste of time, trying to inspect the place in the dark.'

She was full of resentment, but then, in the old days, this room would have been bubbling with sullen resentment. A copper brought in from outside! To interfere with *our* case! But that older kind of resentment didn't exist anymore. People were too tired, too busy, too poor, too hungry to worry about others muscling in on their turf. And besides, there weren't any other coppers in the room. There was a young recent trainee from MI5 and a scene-of-crime investigator who probably barely had a job anymore, thanks to Witness.

And him. Ancient, superannuated him.

'Right, then,' he said. 'What have we got?'

Lancaster sat down and turned to his terminal. The

whiteboard flickered into life, becoming another, bigger screen. It showed a view of the Witness database, the bit of the system that no member of the public ever got to see. Ordinary folk could watch most of the live video feeds, just as he had done in his hotel room the night before, but they didn't see the archive, and they didn't see the database - the thing that held it all together, the source of Witness's power.

At the centre of the screen was the face of Brother Thomas. He was sporting a well-trimmed beard, and his dark hair was cut short. His skin was tanned, his teeth white and exposed in a big smile. He looked like he'd be good company, or at least be happy to sell you a time share. He grinned into the camera as if he'd got great news to tell you, perhaps about God, or about the status of your investments. The eyes, though, were the real tell - no smile there. Just a piercing gaze, unafraid and appraising.

'Is that a Witness picture?' Ted asked.

'It is but it's pretty old,' said Lancaster. 'Before the new rules on smiling.'

Around this central picture was a cluster of headshots. These were all more recent Witness pictures. All the faces held the same, Witness-approved expression. You were not allowed to smile in this official photograph, the one that was on your ID. Something to do with measuring the distance between the eyes, the nose and the mouth.

'Is that the only picture of Thomas Jenkins we have?' Ted said.

'It's the most recent,' says Lancaster. 'Since the formation of the Community, people have only had to supply an updated picture on travelling to the Island.'

'OK,' I say. 'Give me the bio.'

'Thomas Jenkins,' says Lancaster. 'Aged 64 at the time of his death. Gwynedd man, born and bred. Before entering the Community, he was a pretty well-known character around here. Lots of connections to people still around. He was a property developer.'

'A *property developer?*'

'Yes.'

'Odd grounding for a man of the cloth. Any family?'

'No siblings or children. But he was married.'

'To who?'

The picture of Thomas Jenkins shrank away, and another picture appeared. A young, startlingly attractive woman, even in her formal, unsmiling Witness pose. Her dark hair was tied up - as Witness required for profile pictures - and her face had a green-eyed, clean-edged intensity. She looked at the camera - and thus, at Ted - as if daring them, any of them, to try it on.

'That's a recent picture?' Ted said.

'Yes. Less than a year old. Lucy Jenkins, born Lucy Brock. She's 34 now.'

'Thirty years younger than Jenkins?'

'Yes.'

'Dirty old bastard,' Priestley whispered.

'And where is she now?'

Lancaster pointed over Ted's shoulder and, for a moment, Ted imagined the woman was in the room with them.

'She lives just over there,' said Lancaster. 'One of the houses on the Y Neuadd estate - it's right up next to Parc Menai, you'll have seen the gatehouse when you drove in. It's Thomas Jenkins's old place. He did the development, back in the day.'

'And they remain married?'

'Yes. No formal separation or divorce. The Brothers and Sisters of the Community are required to take a vow of celibacy, and to renounce all family ties.'

'The usual God-bothering rigmarole,' said Priestley. The look Lancaster gave her could have soured milk.

'OK,' Ted said. 'Now show me the female victim.'

The face that sprang into view on the white board told him little - no smile or grimace, no twinkling eyes or down-turned lip, no nervous brow or fearless eye. Witness did that - it reduced people to these flat two-dimensional avatars, fungible into ones and zeroes. But even so it struck him, hard, how in contrast this pleasant face on the screen was to the figure on the bed back in Plas Newydd. Anthea Mortimer looked like a perfectly ordinary young woman, an innately cheerful one, despite the forced pose. Even in the bleak flat language of a Witness photograph Ted thought he could see an open and honest character. Which was, of course, ridiculous of him.

'Tell me what we know about her, please,' he said.

'She lived in Chester,' said Lancaster. 'Worked for a public relations firm.'

'And do we know in what capacity she was attending the meeting?'

'As an executive assistant, is how it's been described to me. Her boss was also there.'

'Bring up the graphs, then,' Ted said. 'For both of them.' Lancaster did so, silently.

The screen reloaded. Now, the pictures of Brother Thomas and Anthea Mortimer were at the centre of a cloud of tiny headshots, which hung around them, moving slightly, as if in orbit. Ted always wondered about that odd hanging-in-the-air movement, about what it was supposed to signify.

'Bloody hell,' Priestley said. 'Was there anyone he *didn't* know?'

It was true. Ted had never seen such a cloud of faces around one person that looked anything like the cluster around Brother Thomas. On the screen his face swam in an ocean of connections. The connections varied in transparency or opacity, indicating how close the relationship to Jenkins was, as calculated by the Witness software. The system's databases included analysis of activity on Witness itself - places visited, people met, frequency and length of such meetings - alongside third party data - financial transactions, medical investigations, insurance claims.

Had you been you to school this morning? Witness knew. Did you take a sick day? Witness knew. Did you take your grandchildren to the seaside? Witness knew. With facial recognition, it could even take a view on whether or not you enjoyed yourself.

And the thing was: it worked. Of *course* it worked. Ted had tracked down one murderer based on an old Facebook post from two years before London. From his desk. Using Witness. He never left the office. The killer was now dead. There had been a trial. It had lasted half-an-hour.

Court backlogs were something else that didn't happen anymore.

And because it worked, people were OK with it, for the most part. As long as another Guy Fawkes didn't blow up another city, it was all just fine.

Ted went up to the whiteboard, as if to scan the pictures, but really just to think. The cluster of pictures around Anthea Mortimer's serious-yet-sunny face was terribly thin in comparison with that of Brother Thomas.

'Bring up Anthea Mortimer alone,' he said. The screen reloaded, removing Jenkins and his cloud of acquaintances. Now it was just Anthea's Witness graph. A mother and father, each of them looking old and exhausted. The father's face had the word *Deceased* written across it. A young man, a brother, with the same word obscuring his features. Her boss, named James Moncrieff, a slick-looking character with smooth features and perfect hair.

The parents lived just outside Conwy. The boss was currently in Caernarfon, though his home residence, like Anthea's, was in Chester..

'Send the address details of Lucy Jenkins and the mother of Anthea Mortimer to my phone,' he said. 'I'm going to pay her a visit. And while I do, Lieutenant, I want the full info on everyone who was in that house yesterday sent to my phone.'

'Yes, sir. Of course.'

'But not a data dump, Lancaster. I don't want to have to unpick it myself. I want a report, do you understand me? Something I can read.'

An uncertain pause. Now Ted did turn round, and Lancaster, who presumably had been staring at his back, looked down.

'Do you understand me, Lieutenant?'

'I…. yes, sir. Of course.'

'Right then. Let's get to it.'

13

The young woman stood at the stupendous window, gazing at the rain, nursing what Ted imagined was expensive malt whisky. The window looked out on an equally stupendous garden. Beyond the garden was the Strait, and beyond that, Plas Newydd. Thomas Jenkins's old house looked out onto Thomas Jenkins's new house, although it looked through a veil of water.

She was casually but expensively dressed. The house itself was similar. She cried looking up and out, as if in defiance. Ted saw the whisky in her hand trembling, as if calling to him. It was barely 10 in the morning.

'Are you sure you'd not prefer to sit down?' he said.

Lucy Jenkins, the widow of Thomas and, he assumed, now the owner of this house and all that was in it, if she hadn't been already, shook her head, once to each side, defiantly and firmly, and took a gulp of whisky. He could almost feel it sliding down his own throat. His own head was throbbing again, the hotel carbohydrates and paracetamol having lasted barely two hours.

She'd given him a similarly expensive glass, but it

contained only corporation pop, as his Dad used to call tap water. She'd popped a few ice cubes in as well, and they'd clinked loudly as she'd handed him the glass.

'I don't suppose there's any chance of its being a mistake?' Lucy Jenkins asked, still looking out of the window, her voice wet with crying. Her accent was at odds with the glamorous silhouette - she looked like an Agatha Christie lady of the manor, she sounded like an Agatha Christie kitchenmaid. He recognised the flat vowel sounds of Kent, achingly familiar.

'The body hasn't been formally identified,' he said. 'I'm afraid I'll need to ask you to do that. When it comes to it.'

'If they let you have him back,' she said, bitterly.

This startled him.

'What do you mean by that?' he said.

'St Nick will have been making calls.'

'St Nick?'

'The Abbot. The saintly bastard has his pals all over.'

'This is… Nicholas Higgins? The man who founded the Community with your husband?'

'That's the one.'

'You don't care for him?'

She turned to him, putting her head on one side.

'Must be odd, being you,' she said.

'How so?'

'Well, I say something slightly nasty about someone, and you're on it like a cat on cream. *You don't care for him.* No, Sherlock. I do not care for the Abbot. I wish he was dead. He stole my husband. Well, him and his bastard side-kick upstairs.'

She turned back to the window, and raised her glass to the sky.

'Well, he's with you now, arsehole,' she said. 'You're welcome to him.'

She put the glass down on a table.

'Rain or no rain, I need some air,' she says. 'Take your chances, Detective, and come into the garden with me. Grab an umbrella.'

The Jenkins house was a modern glass-and-concrete thing inside the grounds of an old estate, called Y Neuadd, which was situated almost directly next to the Parc Menai business park. On Lancaster's advice, Ted had driven in round the back of the place, past multiple KEEP OUT and TRESPASSERS WILL BE REPORTED signs, and dozens of cameras which swivelled to watch him as he passed. There was a massive old house at the centre of the estate, which looked almost deserted as he passed it. Lucy Jenkins could be found between the old House and the Strait, in her ground-hugging, many-windowed modernist cathedral.

Outside, the garden of the house was exquisite, fenced off from the surrounding estate and, like the house itself, planted with eyes only for itself. The estate was a kind of parkland, with some terraced gardens running to weeds and a copse by the water which looked like it once was groomed but was now as unwieldy as an old man's eyebrows. But this garden was very different. Ted watched Lucy Jenkins as her eyes followed the flowers and plants, ticking them off, taking inventory. Her garden, then, not her husband's. He wondered if that had always been the case. She spoke, cogently, as her eyes flicked around the beds. The rain on their umbrellas made sharp tapping sounds, irregular and oddly soothing.

'Tommy used to like to walk around out here, when he was still living with me,' she said. 'He used to say I was an artist for what I did out here.'

'Did he help?' Ted asked.

She smiled. Her tear-wrecked face was the more awful for it.

'I do plants,' she says. 'Tommy does people.'

She breathed in, the air shuddering slightly.

'Did people,' she said, quietly.

'What can you tell me about your life with him before he left you, Mrs Jenkins?'

'Why?'

'I don't know why. I'm just assembling a picture.'

She breathed in again, and out again, leaned down and pulled out a weed, and then began shredding it with her fingers as she spoke.

'Tommy was an early riser,' she said. 'He'd be up by six, hitting the gym in the basement. He was a fit bastard. He was in his fifties when we married. Did you know that?' She looked at Ted. 'Well, of course you bloody knew that. Stupid question. Lots of people thought I married him for his money.'

'Did you?'

'Of course I did. I was 20 years old, for Christ's sake. But....'

'You loved him.'

The fingers shredded through the last bits of green matter, and the remnants of the weed fell on to the immaculate lawn.

'You from London?' she said.

'Yes.'

'Gravesend, me. Ever been to Gravesend?'

'Once or twice.'

'I was walking in Snowdonia when it happened,' Lucy Jenkins said. 'Can you imagine? On my own up a sodding mountain when some bastard blows up London. I wanted to head south, but they closed everything down. You remember? Even the sodding roads. Me Mum was in Kent. Never saw her again. She died a year later.'

'It was a bad time,' Ted said.

'Bloody right it was a bad time. And Tommy made himself scarce. So I faced it on me own.' She sniffed. 'Mum ended up in one of the hospitals. Not somewhere you wanted to end up, back then.'

'How long had you been married by then?'

'Three years.'

'Where did you meet?'

'Estate agent conference in Stoke. He was one of the speakers. He was a good speaker, too. I was training. Walked up to me in the bar that night. *Buy you a drink?* he said. *Cheeky bastard,* I said. *I know what you're after.* And he laughed. *Too right I'm after it, you're bloody gorgeous.* That was it. Not exactly *Brief Encounter,* is it?'

She was crying a little again, but spoke clearly enough.

'Anyway. We got married two weeks later. Two weeks! Me Mum didn't mind - he charmed the knickers off of her. He was already planning this place - built it in a few months, and me moving in got a few tongues wagging, I can tell you, middle-aged man moving his hot totty into a luxury house. Tommy didn't care. Said he'd planned the place for me, even if he'd not met me yet. Called it The Gilded Palace of Sin.'

'So it was all sweetness and light? Right up to the point he left?'

'Are you married, Detective?' she said.

'I was. She died. In London.'

'Oh,' said Lucy, putting a hand on his arm. 'I'm so sorry.'

She left her hand there a moment. It was a measured gesture. He told himself there was a good deal more to

Lucy Jenkins than the carefully-cultivated image. He told himself to watch it.

'I think I'd know, now,' said Lucy, taking her hand away and returning to gazing at the flower beds as she spoke. 'I can read men better now. But I was barely 23 when he started drifting away. I don't know I could ever put a finger on it. When it started, I mean. I can remember when he told me he'd found God. It was a warm, dry day. Very unWelsh. I was digging around in one of these beds - I'd got the gardening bug good and proper by then, probably because Tommy had been spending less and less time here. And he came out and started talking to me, small talk, and then he said 'Babe, I've been talking to God,' and he carried on talking, not to me but to God. Church every Sunday, prayers every morning, the whole bloody works. Then bloody St Nick. And then one day, he left. Got up, did a bit of a workout, had some breakfast, then he came upstairs. He was…. well, shall we just say he wasn't finished exercising, and needed a bit more horizontal action, and leave it at that? Then he had a shower, left the house. I imagined he'd gone straight to work. This was only a few weeks before London. But he didn't come home that night. Or ever again.'

'Where did he go?'

'To the wotsit. The Community.'

'The one led by Nicholas Briggs.'

'St Nick. Yeah. That one.'

'What did you do?'

'I went over there. Well, I tried to.'

'To the Community?'

'Yes, to the Community. It was over at St Asaph's, then. I drove over. But I didn't know where to go. I mean, where was he? Where the fuck is St Asaph's? Didn't find him. Drove home. Cried. Went to bed. Didn't hear from him for six weeks. Until after London. I sat here, in this house, on my fucking own, while those bastards did for London. And then he showed up here. With Brother Nick. They told me what they were planning. We had dinner. We all sat down one side of the long table, Brother Nick and his disciples, while some Italian twat painted us.'

Ted laughed, despite himself. He found himself liking this young woman a great deal.

'Yeah,' she said. 'You've got to laugh to stop yourself crying. St Nick saying grace at my fucking table. And then stealing my fucking husband.'

'What communication did you have with Jenkins after he left?'

'Ah,' she says. 'Well. That's where things got really interesting. You need to know about Tommy's little hobby.'

'His hobby.'

'Yeah. I told you. He cultivated people.'

'You did.'

'Well, this house turned out to be a handy tool for him, Detective. As did his trophy wife. Or trophy-sort-of-ex-wife. Not that we ever divorced or anything.'

She turned from the flower bed, and gave him me a not-unpleasant look of appraisal.

'Why you here, Inspector?'

'I'm interviewing you.'

'Nah. I mean, why are you *here*. In Wales. Tommy stepped off a roof, didn't he? That's what you said. Why the investigation? And why are you doing it?'

'It's a good question.'

'It's the only bloody question. I mean, you can, for instance, call up your little machines and find out whether I have ever been over to the Island, right?'

'I can.'

In the old days, the question would have been masked

by another, less direct, query: *Where were you on the day he died?* But Witness knew the answer to that. Lucy Jenkins hadn't been any nearer to the Island than this house and garden, apart from one visit, three years before, when she'd driven her car up to the Menai Strait Bridge. She'd stepped out and walked up to the Brothers on the Island side, had stood ten feet away, and had given them the finger with both hands.

He took the phone out of his pocket, and showed her the still of that visit that Lancaster had sent to his phone. She laughed.

'Yeah, that was a bad day,' she said. 'I'd been drinking a good deal that day. In fact, your little machines could probably have had me up for driving under the influence. But no, Detective Inspector Wood. I didn't want him dead. There's been too much dying around here this last decade.'

She handed him his phone back and placed her hands into the pockets of her jeans.

'God, on the other hand,' she says. 'I'd kill that fucker tomorrow.'

She looked at him, another appraising look.

'So, I should probably tell you what I do for money, these days.'

'Is it relevant?' he said.

'Could be. Follow me.'

She went back into the house, and Ted followed her inside. She led him up the stairs and into a small room with a massive picture window of the Straits. On the other side, he could see Plas Newydd. It struck him that she and her departed husband could almost have looked at each other from each other's bedroom. It was rather sad.

'I don't know if it's ironic or fated or what,' she said. 'But this was his study. He must have looked out on that house a thousand times.'

On the desk in front of the window, there was a screen. A standard screen, plugged into either a satellite or cable feed for the BBC and the live video feeds, like the ones he'd watched in the hotel room the night before. He remembered, now, that there'd been no screen down in the living room. She watched what she watched from up here, where she could see the pictures of the world around her, look up, and see Plas Newydd, which was not on any of those pictures. He felt suddenly very sorry for this glamorously sad woman.

She turned the screen on. It was set by default to a low-satellite view of her house from above. At the edge of the view, he could see the grey line which marked the edge of the hidden zone of the Community, masked from Witness. Lucy Jenkins hit a button on the keyboard, and the image switched to a fixed camera looking out onto the Straits. In the distance, he could see Plas Newydd. The image was like a mirror of the one from this window.

'Where is that?' he said.

'End of the garden, down some steps, and you're there.'

'Is it on Witness?'

'Of course it's on Witness. Everything's on Witness. But it's my camera. I installed it.'

'So Witness *can* see the Island.'

'Well, in a way. It can see it from cameras pointing at it from the Mainland. It's only the aerial stuff that's masked. And your clever bits of code don't get to munge people's faces.'

This made sense, of course. No-one was stopping people taking photographs or videos of the Island from their phones when they were on the Mainland. This was essentially what Lucy Jenkins was doing.

'So why am I looking at this?' he said.

'Because, Detective, I had this camera put there for a specific reason. I wanted to be able to watch the people getting on to the boat.'

He looked away from the screen, and at her.

'What boat?'

She held down a button on the keyboard, and at other end of her beautiful garden the camera panned down, causing Plas Newydd to slide off the upper edge of the view. At the bottom of the screen a large motor launch appeared.

'That boat,' she said. 'The Community paid me to welcome their special guests, give them a drink when necessary, and then get them over to Plas Newydd. And when their meetings or seminars or team-building bollocks was finished with, I welcomed them back and sent them on their way. I worked for my husband while he worked for God.'

'It's your boat?'

'No, it's not my boat. Ask Emyr Phillips about it. Britannia boatyard. I had nothing to do with the boat.'

She raised a glass to the big house on the other side of the Strait.

'So long, you bastard. Just what the hell do you expect me to do now?'

14

I t was half-an-hour's drive to Conwy, time that he might have spent in silent conversation with his dead wife and daughter. Before yesterday, that's exactly what he would have been doing. But his hungover brain had something else to grind through now - a case. After so many years, a case. Names, faces, connections - a present reality more vivid than the incessant past.

He called Lancaster. The lad's earnest young face appeared on the car dashboard as the call was put through. Clean chin, white teeth, not a hair out of place. He looked even more like a Mormon on a screen than in the flesh.

'Talk me through the guests at Plas Newydd,' he said when Lancaster answered. No greeting or chatter. 'Starting with how many of them went over in the boat.'

There was a pause. Ted briefly wondered if Lancaster was trying to work out who was calling him. Or whether he was recording this call for his own personal use. Many people did. You didn't even have to ask the other party anymore.

'There were 13 of them,' Lancaster said at last. 'I've spoken to some of them already.'

'OK. Well let's start with the most important and go from there.'

'Rachel Whitehouse,' said Lancaster.

Yes. Rachel Whitehouse. The bloody Defence Minister, who had somehow been inserted into the centre of his case. She wasn't the Secretary of State for Defence, and most people would struggle to recognise her face or recall her name, but she was one of the top twenty politicians in the country.

'She's the chair of the Investiture organising committee,' said Lancaster. 'I spoke to her PA in Caernarfon, a woman called Angharad Rees. She told me the Plas Newydd event had been arranged for months. It was designed as a final wrap-up followed by a social - drinks and dinner.'

'Why the secrecy? Why not on the Mainland?'

'She said most of their committee awaydays had been held at Plas Newydd. No particular need for secrecy, she maintained - they just liked the place.'

'And this woman, this… Angharad?'

'Yes, sir.'

'You said she was the Minister's PA in Caernarfon? She has a specific local assistant?'

'Yes, a temporary hire for the duration of the Investiture organisation process. Mrs Rees says she's coming to the end of that contract.'

'She was the only one attending with the Minister?'

'No, the Minister brought along an aide from her office. A man called Peter Holmes. I spoke to him as well. He's staying in Caernarfon with the Minister. He's normally based at the Cabinet Office in Birmingham. He's been seconded to the Minister for the Investiture.'

'Civil servant?'

'Yes, sir.'

'Full profiles available for these, I take it?'

'Yes, sir. Completely clean, as far as Witness is concerned.'

'OK. So that's the Minister, plus a PA, plus an aide. That leaves ten.'

'One of whom is the deceased, sir.'

'OK, we'll get to Anthea. Tell me about the other nine.'

'Sir Anthony Mayfield. He's a private secretary to the King. He came with one of his staff, a man called Lawrence Greenwood. I spoke to Greenwood; the two of them are staying at a private residence outside Caernarfon. They're based at the Castle during working hours. Greenwood told me they'd travelled up from Highgrove the night before the party. Neither of them had met Brother Thomas before, or had ever been to the Island. No connections on Witness between either of them and either of the deceased.'

'Did he say how he found it?'

'Found what, sir?'

'Going to Plas Newydd. Staying the night. Avoiding the prying eyes.'

'I asked him if he noticed, sir. He said it barely occurred to him.'

'OK. Keep going.'

'Robert Hughes and Eurwyn Collins. They're local bankers, they put a lot of money into the Investiture. I haven't spoken to them yet, but Greenwood told me they're basically angling for knighthoods in the next honours list. They both bought their assistants.'

'Assistants? Can I assume all these assistants were

women, on the young side, relatively impoverished backgrounds?'

'Yes. That about sums it up. Mair Collier and Diana James. I spoke to Miss Collier.'

'And what did Miss Collier have to say?'

'She said it was a lovely evening.'

'Did she explain why she was there?'

'She said she was there as a professional assistant to Mr Collins.'

'And who is she?'

'She works at one of the supermarkets in Caernarfon. They both do.'

'Seriously?'

'Seriously, yes.'

'Unique skills for an Investiture organising committee.'

'I made that point, sir.'

'And how did she respond?'

'She said she didn't appreciate the implication.'

'Did you ask her outright if she had sex with Mr Collins?'

'I did. She told me to mind my own business and what did that have to do with anything?'

'Were they paid? For their 'professional assistant' duties?'

Ted rather suspected that Lancaster would not have thought to ask that, so he was surprised by the younger man's answer.

'They were, yes. £200 each.'

'Not bad, with a party thrown in.'

'No, sir. Not bad.'

'OK. So we have the Investiture organiser with two companions, the royal secretary with one, and two bankers, each with their so-called assistants. That makes eight. Who's left?'

'Frank Daniels. He's the chief executive of the Welsh History Society. Advisor to the committee, by all accounts. He was accompanied by his daughter. She also works for the Society. She's called Beryl. I spoke to her. She said it was a nice evening, excellent food and wine, but they went to bed pretty early. Mr Daniels, it seems, is not one for staying up.'

'Which leaves?'

'The deceased, sir. And her boss.'

'OK. Anthea. Why was she there?'

'She was with a man called James Moncrieff. He's head of public relations for the Investiture. Based in Chester. Firm called Moncrieff Delaney.'

'And what does he have to say for himself?'

'I haven't been able to speak to him yet, sir. It appears he's checked out.'

'Checked out?'

'Of his hotel. He was staying at the Lloyd George.'

'He's scarpered?'

'I can't say, quite, sir.'

'It does seem a bit odd, though? The fella who's doing PR for this whole affair setting out four days before the things about to kick off?'

'Three days, sir.'

'OK, Lieutenant, three days.'

'I was just arranging for him to be picked up, sir, when you called.'

There was a pause on the other end of the line.

'Lancaster?'

'Just a moment, sir….. Something odd.'

'Odd.'

'He seems to have turned off the Expressway, sir.'

'He's not going to Chester?'

'Seems not, he's…..'

Another damn pause. And then Lancaster spoke again, urgency in his voice.

'Sir, I think he may be heading to the same place as you.'

'What, Anthea Mortimer's mother?'

'Yes, sir. That's the direction he's heading.'

Ted shoved the throttle down. The engine pitch on the Dyson began to scream. He picked up all of 10 miles per hour in speed. He didn't want Moncrieff breaking the news to Anthea's mother. And he certainly didn't want the bastard spinning any yarns which might affect what she'd say to the police.

'You're ten minutes away, sir,' said Lancaster.

'Maybe not in this stupid fucking car,' Ted replied.

'You're about to lose signal, sir. The Conwy tun....'

And then Lancaster was gone.

15

He was in the tunnel for barely two minutes, the Dyson whining its way under, he assumed, the River Conwy. As he emerged at the other end his phone and satnav burst back into life. The satnav directed him off the Expressway and onto a road that doubled back along the river and began to climb steeply. Meanwhile, he hit the number to reconnect with Lancaster.

'Where's Moncrieff?' he said when the lad answered.

'He's there, sir.'

'In the house?'

'Yes, sir.'

'Shit.'

He slammed the throttle down but the bloody battery-powered piece of crap barely went above forty on the steep hill. The satnav took him off to the right, climbing even further into a nondescript area of sixties and seventies housing, with messy verges and rusting vehicles. He saw an expensive red German machine outside the house before the satnav dinged at him that he'd arrived.

He stopped the Dyson. He ran up to the front door, his

old crippled heart racing away at a pace that shamed the Dyson, and slammed five times on the decorated glass insert.

'Police!' he shouted through the letterbox. 'Police! Open up right now!'

He saw a shape through the frosted glass.

'Hello?' a woman's voice said, sounding shaky. 'Hello, who is it?'

'It's the police, ma'am. Please open the door immediately.'

'Yes, of course.'

'DI Wood, Manchester CID!' he said to the broken-faced woman opened the front door, her cheeks wet with tears. Ted saw a tall man standing behind her, a few feet away, and pulled the woman towards him. She fell into him, already crying again.

'What the fuck do you think you're doing?' said the tall man from inside the house. 'What the actual fuck do you think you are doing?'

16

He sat with a cup of weak milky tea in a polite living room which could have featured comfortably in a TV sitcom from any of the last four or five decades. A companionable two-person red leather sofa, two personable matching red leather armchairs, a flame-effect gas fire in a ceramic surround, a television which refused to dominate the room, a rug with an odd geometric pattern.

And photographs. Dozens of them. Standing in frames on the mantelpiece. Hanging on the walls. On the side tables, three of them, looking like a nested set, now separated and placed beside the two armchairs and at one end of the sofa. Mostly, the photos showed the same three faces - a man, a girl, a boy. Many of them had backgrounds of alternately sun- and rain-drenched beaches - the same beach, by the look of it, the faces getting older but the beach staying the same. Ted, thanks to Witness, recognised the girl, even though the photograph must have been ten years old. She was always the smiling one. The father was stern-faced, balding, glaring into the father as if it had said something to him he didn't like. The boy changed as the photos progressed, the smile fading, until he took on the same face as his father. But through them all the girl remained smiling, a smile as big as a beach, as warm and welcoming as hot sand. And the woman who owned this house - well, she never appeared. Presumably she had always been holding the camera.

Ted sat on the sofa, leaning forward, elbows on knees, in Listening Policeman mode. James Moncrieff sat with his legs crossed and his face like thunder. Mrs Mortimer had sat - actually, it was truer to say she had collapsed - into the other armchair after dispensing tea. The room had been silent for several long moments.

'Mrs Mortimer, I am truly sorry for your loss,' Ted said, at last. 'And I'm very sorry I didn't get here quickly enough to break the news to you myself.' She looked at him for a moment, her eyes pleading for some form of explanation, or at least a sign that something else was possible, that this was all perhaps some hideous mistake. Seeing nothing but professional sorrow in his face, she looked down again. The words he'd spoken were meaningless and trite but also required of him. She understood that. It was what British people did in these situations. Ted turned to the other person in the room.

'Mr Moncrieff, I'm going to have to ask you to wait in the kitchen. I need to speak to Mrs Mortimer alone.'

Moncrieff breathed out through his nose. He was a thickset, tall man, his head shaved against creeping baldness, his tanned smoothed skin testament to good food, regular exercise and access to expensive cosmetic imports. He wore the kind of well-fitting blue suit which had to have been tailored just for him. You didn't see suits like that anymore, until you did.

'I'm not waiting in the kitchen, DI Wood,' he said. 'I

came here as a courtesy to Mrs Mortimer, and thank God I did, otherwise she might have been terrified out of her wits by your banging on her front door. God knows what this poor woman's neighbours must be thinking.'

You don't give a shit about this poor woman or her neighbours, Ted thought to himself. *You're just covering the angles.*

'Mr Moncrieff, I need to question you,' Ted said. 'You can wait wherever you want, but I'm still going to question you. And if you try to leave, I will have you stopped and arrested. I can do that. As you know perfectly well.'

It was nice, wasn't it? Being able to lean on people like Moncrieff in this way. Ever since London, police authority had been growing. It was a pervasive fact of British life. When Ted spoke, he spoke with the voice of a mighty organ of control. It was what people wanted. And every now and again there was a joy in using it on men like Andrew Moncrieff.

But then, a small voice from the past, an echo of a half-forgotten fragment of bitterness.

Your Dad arrests people, Peg. It's what he does.

Moncrieff stood up.

'I'll wait in the car,' he said. 'At least I can do some work in there.'

He turned to the woman in the armchair. His concerned face, when he switched it on, was professional and entirely appropriate.

'Mrs Mortimer. My very great sympathies. My loss is but a fraction of yours, but even so, it is very great. I cherished your daughter.'

Without acknowledging Ted again, he left. And then Ted was alone with the mother's grief.

'Mrs Mortimer, I know this must be very hard,' he said, again feeling like he was reading the words off a card. Moncrieff's words had been original, direct, sympathetic -

that was his job, after all. A poor old policeman could hardly be expected to compete.

She looked up at him.

'What is? What's hard?'

'Talking to me, at a time like this.'

'Talking about Anthea, you mean,' she said. 'But the thing is, Inspector, all I want to do is talk about Anthea.'

She picked up the photo of the smiling girl that stood on the table beside her, raised it to her lips, and kissed it.

'All of them gone, now. Just me left.'

'When did you last speak to your daughter, Mrs Mortimer?'

'Last night.'

That shook Ted.

'Last night? But....'

'Oh, I know, I'm only being silly. I know she was.... I know. No, you see, she left me a message. A voicemail. On my phone. And very often, you see, I don't notice that she's left me a message. We used to laugh about it. She'd phone me, and she'd say 'I left you a message, Mum,' and I'd say 'Oh, did you?', and she'd laugh and call me a silly old idiot, or something. So anyway. I listened to her message last night.'

'Do you still have it? The message?'

'I don't know. Do they stay on your phone? After you've listened to them?'

'If you don't delete them - yes. Yes they do.'

'Oh, well then, let's look.'

She got up from the armchair and went over to a sideboard. A red leather handbag - matching the chairs and the sofa, Ted noticed - sat there, and she reached in and took out a phone. She sat back down, touched the screen a few times.

'Oh, yes, here it is.'

She passed him the phone.

'You can listen to it.'

'Do you want me to put it on speaker?'

'Yes. Yes, I think that would be nice, Inspector.'

So he pressed play on the message (she was called 'Ant' in her Mum's contacts) and listened. She had a singsong Welsh accent, a sort of breathless excitement behind the words, as if everything was amazing. He didn't look at the mother while he listened to the dead daughter.

Hi Mum, it's me! Listen, Jimmy's asked me to go with him to Caernarfon tomorrow, and guess what? We're going to stay on the Island - on Anglesey! Haven't been there since we were kids! I'll be there tomorrow night, and then Jimmy's going to stay in Caernarfon and I'll get the train back. I'm thinking I'll stop at Conwy on the way back. Maybe we can meet for a coffee? Hope so! Anyway, I'll ring you when I'm on the train. Love you!'

He pressed pause carefully. The last thing he wanted to do was delete this final message.

'What did you do when you didn't hear from her?' he said, looking up at her for the first time. She was crying, silently and almost without noticing.

'What do you mean?' she said, after a moment.

'Didn't you expect her to call you yesterday?'

'No. I didn't hear the message until last night. Quite late it was. I called her phone, but it just rang and rang, which was a bit odd, because normally it goes to the answer thing. I was a bit worried. But Ant's always so busy. Sometimes I don't hear from her for days and days.'

'She lived in Chester?'

'Yes. For five years now. She moved there when she got the job with Mr Moncrieff.'

'Any boyfriends?'

'I think she meets the occasional fella, yes. Nothing serious, though. She doesn't go into details, and I don't ask.

She's always a bit too smart for the lads, you know? They prefer a stupid girl. I find.'

She looked down at the photo in her lap.

'Her brother always used to say that, you know. *You're too smart for your own good, Ant-girl.* That's what he used to call her, Ant-Girl.'

'And you lost him too?'

She nodded.

'Yes, dear. Yes.'

She looked at him suddenly.

'You're not from round here,' she says.

'No. I'm not.'

'You sound like you're from the South.'

'Yes, I am.'

A pause. A very familiar pause.

'London?'

'Yes. And then St Albans.'

'Oh. That's quite well-to-do, there, isn't it?'

'Some of it is, yes.'

She looked down again.

'Your son?' Ted said, gently. 'London?'

She nodded again, the tears returning.

'The both of them,' she said. 'Him and his Dad.'

'The photos,' Ted said, nodding around the room, at no particular point, because the photos were everywhere. 'The ones on the beach. Anthea mentioned Anglesey in her call. Were the photos taken on Anglesey?'

She smiled at him, as if she were oddly proud of him.

'Well, you're a sharp one, Detective. Yes. They're all on Anglesey. Trearddur Bay. Do you know it?'

'No, I'm afraid not.'

'Oh, it's a beautiful place. Beautiful. We had a little house up there. On Ravens Point. My Da left it to me in his will. He called it Cigfrain's Rest. His little joke.' She sighed. 'All part of that bloody Community now, of course. He saw to that.'

He saw to that. People had many different ways of saying it. Almost as if they were talking about God, and in a sense, Ted supposed, they were. Whoever had brought that device into London - the man or men now universally known as *Guy Fawkes* - had seen to a lot of things.

17

James Moncrieff was in his car talking into his phone when Ted came out of the house. A drone hung in the air above them. The local uniforms had returned to base.

Moncrieff was animated even if he couldn't be heard through the glass. He didn't notice Ted for a while, so focussed was he on the conversation. Ted wondered if he knew the call was being recorded - presumably he would be moderating his words accordingly. Witness would have automatically activated full-fat phone monitoring for all persons of interest in the Plas Newydd case. Of course Moncrieff would have known that.

He walked towards the car, and Moncrieff, noticing him, ended his call. He stepped out of his car.

'We can talk in the car if you'd prefer,' said Ted.

'I'd rather not, if it's all the same to you,' said Moncrieff, leaning back on his red German tank and crossing his arms, a study in insouciance.

'Who were you talking to?'

'None of your business.'

Ted smiled at him. It wasn't a phrase one heard very much anymore. Moncrieff saw him smile, and for a moment his executive insouciance wobbled a little. That little surge of power, again. So intoxicating. So dangerous.

'So how was it?' Ted said. 'Your little jaunt to Plas Newydd.'

Moncrieff thought for a moment before answering.

'Detective Inspector, was it?' he said, at last.

'That's it.'

'I missed your name.'

'Wood. DI Wood. And if we've quite finished trying to establish dominance, perhaps you'll answer my question.'

Moncrieff smiled, a humourless, ugly thing. Ted pictured him strangling puppies.

'DI Wood. Let's not play games. I know damn well you can stick my details into Witness, and get yourself a nice little printout of who and what and when. And it'll tell you that I've been to Plas Newydd more than a dozen times.'

'Well, save me the job. Explain why.'

'Brother Thomas and I knew each other before London. I handled public relations for his property development firm.'

'Can I take it you are not a man of God?'

'Not particularly. What kind of God blows up a little old lady and her family and thousands of other people?'

It was a gauche statement. The kind of thing people didn't say. Moncrieff was testing him.

'So you did not share Thomas Jenkins's need to set up a religious community?'

'No, I did not. But I did sense a business opportunity. I knew Plas Newydd well. I suggested to him that he set it up as a centre for corporate meetings - with a unique selling point.'

'That it would be invisible to Witness.'

'Indeed. Of course, one has to be careful. I needed to keep the government onside with the idea. Made it clear that all comings and goings to the Island would be visible to Witness. And then, of course, I suggested it might be of use to them.'

'Them? The government?'

'Indeed. Some Ministers might, for instance, value the chance to meet people out of sight of the cameras owned by other Ministers. You know how these things are.'

'No, I don't.'

'Well, if you're the Chancellor, and you've got a tricky session with the chair of the Federal Reserve about Britain's dicky trade imbalances, you might fancy a private chat away from the eyes of the Defence Secretary. Who, as you know, shares responsibility for Witness with the Home Secretary. A delicate balance.'

Moncrieff folded his arms, warming to his subject.

'You can think of Plas Newydd as a safety valve,' he said. 'A place to, literally, let off the steam of persistent surveillance. I've even suggested they replicate the model in other places. Bit like a freeport. Remember those? A place beyond jurisdiction, where the normal rules do not apply. We don't even allow phones or terminals at the dining table or in the lounge. It's designed to be off the grid.'

'And was that what Rachel Whitehouse wanted? Somewhere beyond prying eyes?'

'Hardly. She's mad for Witness. She'd push it even further than we have - compulsory cameras in people's homes, stuff like that. No, she just wanted somewhere nice and a bit different to celebrate completion of the Investiture celebrations. And she needed to keep the money and the nerds happy.'

'Money and nerds?'

'Robert Hughes and Eurwyn Collins. They're basically

paying for the damn thing. The Family being a little hard up, these days.'

'They're paying for the Investiture?'

'Well, partly. The rest has been raised from the local community.'

'And nerds?'

'Well, nerd. Frank Daniels. The Welsh bloody History Society. Bastard doesn't even sound Welsh, but to hear him speak you'd think he was descended from Owain Glendower.'

'So, this was a social affair. Plain and simple.'

'Plain and simple. That's right.'

'With special entertainment laid on for the special guests?'

Moncrieff smirked.

'Our banking friends were kept busy,' he said. 'Let's put it that way.'

'And what was Anthea doing there?'

Moncrieff closed his eyes, and sighed.

'Ah, Anthea. Bloody hell. Poor, poor woman.'

He looked at Ted.

'What do you mean?' he said. 'When you ask what she was doing there.'

'In what capacity did she travel to Plas Newydd?'

Moncrieff stepped away from the car and took a stride towards Ted. For a moment, he looked like he might throw a punch.

'If you're implying….'

'Mr Moncrieff, calm down. I'm not implying anything. Just tell me why Anthea was there.'

'As my assistant! Fucking hell, DI Wood, she was working!'

His eyes narrowed.

'But why would you think….'

He stopped.

'Bloody hell, DI Wood. What are you saying? Was there something about the way she was found?'

'I can't reveal that, Mr Moncrieff. Just answer my question, please.'

'OK. OK.'

Moncrieff seemed suddenly shaken, and it occurred to Ted that this corporate shark held genuine affection for Anthea Mortimer. Which was why he'd come here, he supposed.

'We took the boat over at 7pm,' he said, at last. 'Dinner was at 8.30. Anthea was at dinner but she was keeping an eye on the staff and the arrangements. We ate for a couple of hours, very pleasant. The Minister in particular seemed relaxed. And Thomas was his usual self.'

'Usual self?'

'Ah, DI Wood, Thomas Jenkins could have charmed a roomful of angry feminists. He is… was grace itself. You need someone like him at a dinner like that, to bring everyone in, keep the conversation oiled. He was a master at that stuff.'

'So what happened after dinner?'

'We moved to the lounge. Beautiful room, looking over the terrace and the Strait. The Minister made a little speech. She thanked the bankers, who were properly pissed by then. As were their companions. The sluts were particularly noisy.'

Feminists and sluts? Moncrieff was sounding like a Seventies comedian. You found more and more men like this. London had set back questions of identity and correctness by decades. There was little time to worry about such things when there was too little food to eat.

'And then?'

'The nerd and his daughter headed upstairs straight

after the speeches. Shame, the girl is a pretty thing. I quite fancied my chances, to be honest. The bankers and their friends disappeared around midnight. The Minister and Sir Anthony Mayfield went soon after. I remember joking to Anthea that maybe they were fucking, the joke being that he's a massive queer. We hung around for another hour or so.'

'So that's you, Anthea, Angharad Rees, Peter Holmes, and Lawrence Greenwood,' said Ted, referring to his phone.

'Correct.'

'Had you met the two men before?'

'Greenwood, yes. He's been up a few times. Holmes was new to me, seemed like an all right bloke. Angharad Rees… well.'

Moncrieff looked down at the ground, a smirk on his face.

'What about Angharad Rees?' said Ted.

'Well, DI Wood, as I said, this was a social occasion, we all liked to let our hair down.'

'You're saying you slept with her?'

'Wasn't a lot of sleeping going on, but yes.'

'Did you get up during the night? See anything? Hear anything?'

'I had my hands full. Literally. She's a bonny lass.'

'I think I get the picture, Mr Moncrieff.'

'Well, then, no. I didn't hear anything.'

'Until the next morning?'

'Right. When your lot woke us all up, and told us what had happened. Ruined the rather nice lie-in I had planned. With a handful of Welsh tit.'

'They questioned you, and then you left?'

'Yes. We left. The Minister didn't hang around. Understandably. Angharad and Holmes popped off with her, mid-morning, I would say. We hung around for another hour or so. I tried to see Anthea, but they wouldn't let me anywhere near her. But we could all see poor Tommy. Jesus.'

Moncrieff shook his head.

'Never had him down for one of those,' he said.

'One of those?'

'A killer. Tommy was a lot of things, and probably had a few skeletons in the closet. You don't succeed as a property developer without cutting a few corners. Know what I mean? But I never, ever had him down as a killer. Especially a suicidal one.'

18

Ted drove from Conwy back towards Caernarfon, but turned off the main road at Bangor. The hospital was on a hill above the town, behind a maze of residential streets. He pulled into the vast car park. There were perhaps a dozen cars in the weed-strewn expanse.

He remembered hospital car parks in the old days of the NHS - expensive, clogged-up, seemingly incapable of ever meeting demand. Just like the NHS, in fact. Not anymore. The remains of the NHS were a few A&E departments in those parts of the country which prioritised that kind of spending. Most hospitals had collapsed within a year of the Incident, the money to fund them drained away into the nuclear sump. Some volunteer doctors and nurses managed to keep parts of the system operating, but the drugs ran out within weeks. The private sector sprang into life, and there was a market for it, because there was always money, even with Westminster a smouldering wreck there was money. Meanwhile the needy, the ones who the NHS had been built for, fell back into older ways. Ted had heard cases of women selling themselves to men in return for access to drugs for their children - he had even investigated some, in that strange hazy time after the blast when he still went into work every day, though by then 'work' was an abandoned DIY store on the Kettering ring road as the London exodus of officialdom sucked everyone even out of St Albans, twenty miles north of the blast zone. He remembered one black market pharmacist who operated out of an old veterinary surgery in Leicester. He kept a bed in one of the consulting rooms so 'services' could be provided instantly. The man survived two days in prison before the husband of a dead cancer patient beat his brains out with a tray.

There was always talk of bringing the dear old NHS back, but somehow it never got past whatever arcane spending committee dealt with those things. If you wanted to get well, you paid for it. It was said that an open market in healthcare was one of the conditions of the Romney plan which partially sustained what was left of the economy in the aftermath of London. Ted supposed he'd never know the truth of that.

And to think, they used to ask questions in Parliament about NHS car parks.

What remained of the old mortuary service in Gwynedd was still based here. Traditional mortuary services collapsed as quickly as anything else in the wake of the Emergency. How could post-mortems possibly be performed on a population that was dying at such a rate? If a body was found - and bodies were found, across the country, not just in the radioactive shadow of London - the assumption was that its owner had departed at his or her own hand. The suicide rates were enormous. Everyone, it seemed, lost someone, and some lost everyone. That's when people started talking about 'explosion sickness' - a catch-all phrase for a basket of conditions, some physical, some psychological, some, perhaps, even spiritual. Clogging up the arteries of the dying health service like the sewer fatbergs the newspapers used to write about in the time before London.

He looked up as he walked through the deserted corridors of the hospital. There were cameras everywhere, their tell-tale blinking red lights the opposite of camouflage, a flagrant statement of intent. The country was watching - perhaps some old fellow in his dusty living room mourning his dead wife was watching the broken detective make his way through the hospital, a real human drama amidst the wreckage.

There had been a cursory effort to sweep the place, but the windows were filthy and, in some cases, broken. An ancient and rather sickening version of that old familiar hospital smell, a combination of disinfectant and rubber and decaying flesh, lingered like Ted's own memories.

In the mortuary he discovered a precise and beautifully-spoken South Asian man, who introduced himself as Dr Gunasekara. He was in scrubs which, though they looked like they had seen better days, were scrupulously clean.

Dr Gunasekara was not alone. Two Brothers of the Island were with him. One of them was Brother Enoch, the lad who'd driven with him to Plas Newydd. He looked as scruffy and unwashed as he had the previous day. Ted didn't recognise the other one.

'Are you in charge?' Dr Gunasekara asked after introducing himself.

'That's a philosophical question,' Ted replied, looking at the two other men in the room. 'Or perhaps a theological one. I don't know.'

'These men have no right to be here,' said the doctor.

He had a high, indignant voice, and Ted found myself admiring the man's refusal to be cowed. It was no longer easy, being an Asian doctor in Britain, even with those clipped privately-educated English tones which suggested that Gunasekara was not 'Asian' in any meaningful sense. 'They entered without permission. This is a sterile environment.'

Ted looked around at the filthy mortuary. He very much doubted its sterility. But the doctor was serious enough. Ted turned to the Brothers.

'Enoch, this is not acceptable,' he said. 'We have to be able to do our work here.'

'The Abbot sent us,' said the other Brother. He spoke with a Scottish accent, which was in itself surprising - there were few Scots left in England these days, since the independence vote soon after London. And his voice had a reassured self-importance. This was a man used to being listened to. 'He wished us to reassure him that the remains of Brother Thomas are being respected. He asked us to pray over him.'

'So no prayers for Anthea Mortimer, then?' said Ted.

The Brother smiled, a small, cruel, anachronistic thing that made Ted hate him.

'Of course, DI Wood. We will pray for the woman too.'

'And you are?'

'I am Brother Michael. I am the Abbot's adviser on external relations.'

'External, meaning me?'

'Meaning you, yes, DI Wood. But I do need to see that the formalities of our faith are observed.'

Ted looked down at the two bodies, shrouded in green sheets.

'I don't even know Anthea's faith,' he said.

'Anthea believed in our Lord,' said Michael.

'And you know this how?'

'Because I spoke to her. I was at the party.'

'You were? Then we should speak.'

'I have already arranged for you to come and speak to the Abbot and, if you wish, myself. Tomorrow morning, on the Island.'

Michael's face was impassive. Enoch looked terribly uncertain. Ted wondered if he had ever even seen a dead body before. Ted found himself hating the Abbot for sending this young man on this particular mission. Could Michael not have handled matters on his own? The man looked like he'd seen his share of cadavers. Perhaps even made a few, in the time before.

'Let them have their prayer,' Ted said to the doctor. 'And then please explain to them your procedures for storing the bodies, such that they can reassure the Abbot.'

Dr Gunasekara grumbled mildly over a briefcase in the corner, while the two Brothers knelt on either side of the trolley on which lay the body of Brother Thomas. Brother Michael spoke the first part of the prayer:

'God, omit not this man from Thy covenant,
*   And the many evils which he in the body committed,*
*   That he cannot this day enumerate.'*

Then Enoch spoke:

'Be this soul on Thine own arm, O Christ,
*   Thou King of the City of Heaven,*
*   And since Thine it was, O Christ, to buy the soul,*
*   At the time of the balancing of the beam,*

At the time of the bringing in the judgment,
   Be it now on Thine own right hand.'

Then both Brothers spoke together.

'And be the holy Michael, king of angels,
   Coming to meet the soul,
   And leading it home
   To the heaven of the Son of God.'

Without thinking about it, Ted whispered 'Amen' along with them and found himself looking at the floor. When he looked up, he saw the doctor glaring at the three of them with an expression of loathing. The Brothers stood, and then knelt on either side of the body. They repeated the prayer. This time, Ted said nothing.

'Please, speak with Dr Gunasekara now,' Ted said. 'And then return to the Island, and explain to the Abbot what you have seen.'

Michael, the king of angels, nodded and turned to speak to the doctor. Enoch had eyes only for the bodies. Ted shut his own eyes for a moment, wondering at that strange prayer, spoken in this even stranger place, and another memory came breaking over him. Laura standing alone, outside the crematorium at the point where the drive bent round from the car park. He had been looking at her through the car windscreen. Her belly swelled out beneath her black dress. Peg was inside that glorious swell, tiny and perhaps already listening, as she would come to listen, so carefully and attentively, and not always for the best. The great chimney of the crematorium rose behind them, and Laura was holding her hands in front of her round belly, looking down at the ground with her eyes closed, and he could see her lips moving, speaking a prayer only for herself and her father, whose ashes, even now, were somewhere being scooped into a container, and whose particulates were rising up through the chimney and into the sky.

Coming to meet the soul, and leading it home.

Just who was Michael, king of angels, anyway?

'They've gone,' said Gunasekara, appearing beside him, making Ted start. How long had he been daydreaming? 'What a preposterous display of superstition *that* was.'

Ted didn't say anything. He almost asked the little doctor about *his* religion, and whether it was something he still practised. He even thought about asking him what he was still doing here, in England, why he hadn't gone back to 'wherever his family originally came from,' as the current official formulation had it. So many like him had left, ejected from a country that now despised them where once it had depended on them. No-one knew who brought death to London, but it was extraordinary how many people assumed his face was brown, and that he prayed five times a day. Ted caught himself assuming things about this little doctor, and he hated it. They had all become monsters.

'Well, then,' said the doctor, as if he could hear these grubby thoughts. 'Let's get started.'

He pulled back the first sheet, all the way back. Anthea Mortimer's dead face seemed less surprised than when he had first seen it, because now her eyes were closed. Gunasekara pulled the sheet all the way down, exposing Anthea to the decaying air of the hospital. Someone had removed the cheap underwear. Ted's eyes ran down her body once, before scurrying back to her face, and then finally looking away.

'I've already had a good look at this young woman,' said Gunasekara. 'Her main injuries are bruising around the neck. See?'

Ted looked. Gunasekara was pointing a little torch at Anthea's neck, making up for the dim poorly-funded lighting in the mortuary. The light picked out the vivid bruising.

'There are no indications of fingers, just a single line of bruising. So I would estimate she was strangled with a ligature of some kind. Did you find anything?'

'No. But she was tied to the bed.'

'Ah. Well, I'm afraid this kind of injury can be associated with nighttime extremes.'

'Nighttime extremes?'

'I'm sure you can work out what I mean, Detective Inspector. This may conceivably have started out as something consensual that went too far. I have seen it before. People have become startlingly reckless in these difficult times'

The doctor pulled the sheet back over the nakedness, for which Ted was grateful. He couldn't bear to look at it anymore. He caught Gunasekara looking at him, as if he were just another interesting cadaver.

Injuries on the inside only, Doc. Accelerated wear and tear on the outside.

'Were there any indications of recent sexual intercourse?'

'None whatsoever.'

'Are you sure?'

'Perfectly sure. I'll check again, if you like.'

'So if this was related to horseplay, it preceded the main event.'

'Well, those are not words I would have chosen, but conceivably.'

The doctor turned and handed Ted a small metal bowl. In it were a set of keys, a pen, and a sheet of folder paper.

'There were hidden in the dead man's robes,' the doctor said.

'Hidden?'

'There was a pocket inside the robe, with a button to keep it closed. They were inside.'

Ted found himself growling inside. Had no one searched the body properly? He pulled on some latex gloves and lifted up the keys, the pen, and then unfolded the piece of paper.

It was a seating plan, with the names of the party guests alongside their seats. Some were annotated, dietary preferences mostly, though Ted noticed there were ages written down against the two women from Caernarfon, and a sum of money, presumably to be paid for services rendered. Next to the name of Frank Daniels was written a curt and unmonkish *Llanfaes bullshit.* Near the bottom right corner, in the same handwriting, was scrawled *19 RPT.*

Ted grabbed an evidence bag from his backpack, and dropped the pen, the note and the keys into it.

Meanwhile, Gunasekara had lifted the sheet from the second body. Brother Thomas lay naked before them, his skin grey and stiffened. His eyes were now closed. Does that mean, Ted wondered, that one of the Brothers brought the lids down before they carried the body here?

'Landed on his back?' said Gunasekara.

'Yes. Well, he was found that way. What do you read into that?'

'Nothing in particular. Some of them are face first. I always think they're the really determined ones. But I've got no evidence for that. The plural of anecdote is not data, as they say.'

Now the Brothers had gone and he was getting on with his job, he sounded almost cheerful. He put on a head-torch and began close inspection of Brother Thomas's body, moving down the torso first and then up along the arms. It seemed to be the first decent inspection he had made. Ted looked at Thomas Jenkins's face. It was hard to read anything of the pattern of the living man from his dead face. The hair was cropped and grey, the jaw sharp and strong, the nose, it seemed, broken. The shoulders and chest were well muscled - he remembered what Lucy Jenkins said about Jenkins visiting the gym before going to visit God. A fit man, beneath the robes.

'There's a lot of broken bones in here,' said Gunasekara, partly to himself as he prodded the dead flesh. 'Consistent with a fall.'

'Cause of death?'

The doctor looked up at Ted from his close investigation. His head-torch temporarily blinded him.

'Well, I'd say he died from massive head trauma,' he said, with the suspicion of smile.

'That's it?'

'What else do you want, Detective Inspector?'

Ted sighed, and tried to control his temper. The doctor was not trying to be unhelpful, but something about his precise, high-pitched voice was beginning to grate, not to mention the bizarre bonhomie he now seemed to be affecting. Ted tried to push down the bigot that apparently now lived in his head.

'What kind of head trauma?'

'The killing kind.'

Something in his face must have shown his irritation, because Gunasekara looked suddenly almost apologetic.

'It's one of those situations where the cause of death is so resoundingly obvious that it's hard to see past it,' he said. 'I'm going to take samples so we can screen for drugs and such-like.'

'He was a monk.'

'Well, it's standard procedure.'

'Is there any indication whether it was murder or suicide?'

'None whatsoever.'

'He could have been dead already?'

'Do you know anything that might lead you to suspect that?'

'No.'

'Well, then.'

'What about other injuries?' I say.

'Well, let's see.'

He looked back down at the body, felt along both legs. Then he turned the body onto its side, and looked at the head injuries which, they both assumed, ended Brother Thomas's life. He switched off his head-torch, removed it, and picked up a small handheld torch, which he used to closely inspect the ruined scalp and skull. Grey splotches of brain were mixed up with the appalling hard-edged whiteness of the skull, smashed into pieces.

'Hmm. Hello.'

'Found something?'

'Possibly. Look.'

Gunasekara shone his little torch into the deepest part of the destruction.

'Can we assume that I don't want to look? Just tell me.'

'Hang on.'

Gunasekara picked up a pair of tweezers, and began to fidget around inside the back of Brother Thomas's head.

Ted's struggle not to vomit intensified. After a few moments, the doctor held up the tweezers.

'So, what's that doing there?' he said.

'What is it?'

'Looks to me like a piece of brick.'

'And what of that?'

'Well, as I understand it, Inspector, this man landed on concrete. So how did he end up with a piece of brick embedded in his skull?'

It was a good question.

19

The office of the Crown Prosecutor for North Wales was in an ugly glass-and-brick building on the outskirts of Caernarfon, a place that seemed to have been designed by a toddler with a bucket of Lego. Ted parked his Dyson outside on zig-zag lines which had been worn away by indifference. He grabbed his backpack, and slung it over his shoulder as he got out. He noticed, in passing, another plaque, commemorating the same Robert Mountjoy who'd made his presence permanent in the Caernarfon town square. It reminded him of the signs scattered across Westminster, commemorating some deputy head of planning or other for signing pieces of paper when he was asked.

A young woman at reception scanned him in and asked him to wait. She had none of the angular desperation of the women at the hotel or the waitress in the restaurant. The money was in law enforcement. You didn't need to be polite to people to get it.

Davies made him wait a full fifteen minutes, having summoned him in the first place via a peremptory text, received just as he was walking to his car from the mortuary at the Bangor hospital. Ted supposed this is how men like Davies chose to express their authority - by being an arsehole.

Waiting time would be difficult, because it was thinking time. Ted tried to distract his busy mind, which had slowly dug itself out of the routine hangover, by watching the screen in the lobby, which flicked between cameras in central Caernarfon. The steady drizzle outside gave the images a European arthouse cinema feel - not that anyone watched European arthouse cinema anymore. Not the way that they used to anyway. Ted gazed on umbrellas carrying people along pavements, finding the images almost soothing.

'DI Wood,' said Davies, striding through the lobby with his hand held out, in a deliberate busy fashion. What was that word that younger people started to use before London? Performative. Prosecutor Davies was very performative. 'How delightful to see you,' he says. 'This way, this way. We are in the board room.'

They walked into the heart of the building, which had none of the exhausted, unkempt air of most public buildings since London. This place was well-maintained, clean, almost bustling. The court rooms were in session, and men and women sat on chairs in the corridors, waiting to be called. So many of them, Ted thought. If Witness was anything, it was efficient. The room for doubt had been bricked in.

The 'board room', as Davies had described it, was a medium-sized affair with windows out onto the street, containing an expensive-looking slab of wooden table which wouldn't have looked out of place in an old City bank. Seated at this table were two men, both in suits, sipping hot drinks. One of them had just put a biscuit into his mouth. He was a stout-looking fellow, affecting a combover of suspiciously dark hair. The other one looked fit and ascetic, his tanned skin as suspiciously coloured as his companion's dark hair.

'Gentlemen, this is Detective Inspector Wood,' said Davies, coming into the room. His attitude had changed completely - he was all deference in the face of these two men. 'DI Wood, this is Robert Hughes,' - the man with the biscuit in his mouth nodded - 'and Eurwyn Collins' - at which the slim, tanned executive switched on a smile as expensively white as the Taj Mahal and bowed his head at Ted as if he were the Rajah himself.

'DI Wood,' said Collins, standing up and walking round the board table. 'So lovely to meet you. Such a tragedy. Such a senseless, awful tragedy.' His accent was softly Welsh, every word polished like an expensive slate cheese board. A man who only said what he meant to say.

Ted shook the hand offered to him, but didn't sit down when Davies urged him to.

'This is somewhat irregular,' he said, ignoring the frown Davies sent his way. 'I would prefer if these interviews be conducted, separately, at Witness headquarters.'

'You can fuck right off, Wood,' said the stout man, Hughes, spitting a little piece of biscuit onto his lapel. 'We're only here because Allan asked us to come and speak to you. We gave our statements to whatever flunkies you sent out to Plas Newydd yesterday. If you want anything else, you can speak to our fucking lawyers.' Hughes spoke with a West Country accent, which did nothing to smooth off the violent contempt of his tone. Collins sat down again, his face reflecting none of the violence of his colleague's words. He looked beatifically calm, in fact.

'I suggest, DI Wood,' said Davies, who had now taken his own seat, 'that you take advantage of the opportunity afforded by these two gentlemen and ask them any questions you might have while they're here and willing to speak to you.'

Hughes grinned like a happy shark. Collins raised his eyebrows ruefully, and shrugged. *What are you going to do? I can't do anything with him.*

Ted told himself to keep a lid on it, and did as he was told. He sat down. Collins shoved the plate of biscuits towards him. Ted ignored it.

'Tell me about this party,' Ted said. 'How was it arranged?'

'It wasn't a fucking party,' said Hughes, furiously.

'Well, not *officially*,' said Collins, smiling sheepishly. 'We were there to work.'

'And what work would that be?' said Ted.

'We have been helping Rachel with the organisation of the Investiture,' said Collins.

'Rachel Whitehouse? The Defence Minister?'

'The very same,' said Collins. 'We had a final round of decisions to make - tweaks to seating plans, sanity check on waiting staff, confirmed security arrangements, that sort of thing.'

'And we had to listen to the sodding Castle guy droning on as well,' said Hughes.

'The Castle guy?' said Ted. 'You mean Frank Daniels?'

'Of course I mean Frank Daniels,' said Hughes. 'Whoever had the bright idea to attach him to this committee wants bloody shooting.'

'That would be James,' said Collins.

'James Moncrieff?' said Ted. 'The PR guy?'

Hughes smirked.

'Don't let that smooth bastard hear you call him that,' he said. 'Corporate communications, don't you bloody know.'

'And what was your involvement?' said Ted.

'Our involvement?' said Collins.

'With the Investiture,' said Ted.

'We're paying for the bloody thing!' said Hughes.

'Well, not quite,' said Collins, smiling indulgently. 'We have arranged for local businesses to supply the necessary funding to allow the Investiture to happen in a manner in keeping with its heritage.'

'By putting the squeeze on?' said Ted.

'Careful, Detective Inspector,' growled Allan Davies. 'Show some respect.'

Ted ignored him. Hughes glowered. Collins smiled.

'And how was Thomas Jenkins involved?' Ted said.

'Tommy helped us with the funders,' said Collins. 'Invited them to Plas Newydd. Showed them round the Island. Worked his unique charm.'

'Tommy could charm the knickers off a nun,' said Hughes.

'Tommy? He was a friend, then?'

'We've known Tommy for years,' said Hughes. 'Used to fund his property stuff back in the day. We all helped each other. I thought he'd gone off his rocker when he signed up for this God-bothering bullshit. But he's made it work.'

'Made it work?' said Ted.

'Ask Briggs,' said Hughes.

'The Abbot? Nicholas Briggs?'

'Ask Briggs what Tommy did for him. Oiled the wheels, didn't he? Kept in with the right people.'

'People like Rachel Whitehouse?' said Ted.

Hughes smirked. Collins did the same, looking down at the table.

'Something amusing?' said Ted.

'Well,' said Hughes. 'Let's just say the Minister hasn't been very comfortable with the way we do things up here.'

'And what way would that be?' said Ted.

'We're all local, aren't we?' said Hughes.

'You don't sound particularly local,' said Ted.

Hughes glowered at him.

'Cheeky fucker, aren't you?' he said.

'I'm a Detective Inspector of His Majesty's Police, Mr Hughes. If you don't like the way I do things, you can complain to my superior. Now, perhaps you could elaborate on what you mean by 'the way we do things up here'?'

Hughes stayed silent. Collins took over. Quite the double act, these two.

'What Robert means to say, DI Wood, is that it's a pretty tight-knit community up here. We all know each other, and Tommy was a big part of that community. The Minister expected things to be a little more… well, shall we say a little more formal?'

'And in what way were things informal?'

'Well. I suppose we have both been guilty, Robert and I, of leaning on a few chosen entrepreneurs, to use your words. Unlocking their potential investment, shall we say. It's important to the community that we put on a show for the new Prince of Wales.'

'And Tommy… Brother Jenkins…. he helped with all that?'

'Oh, very much so. Hosted countless evenings at Plas Newydd. It really helped us reach our targets. The Minister has found it all a little unorthodox.'

Ted looked at Robert Hughes, and held his eyes for a moment. Contempt dripped from the man's fat face. So Ted addressed the next question to him.

'I understand you had a couple of companions with you,' he said.

The fat eyes narrowed. Ted could see the real man now - a bully, and dangerous with it.

'Is that a fucking crime, DI Wood?' he said, softly.

'Depends on whether or not they were paid, doesn't it?'

'They weren't fucking paid.'

'Then why did they go?'

'Bit of fun. Decent grub. Some champagne. What girl wouldn't?'

'And who arranged this 'bit of fun'? I assume you didn't wander down the supermarket and find them for yourselves.'

'None of your fucking business.'

Ted sat back in his seat, and waited. Hughes had gone into a staring contest with him. Ted could hear Davies shifting uncomfortably in his seat. Eventually, Collins broke the silence.

'Lucy Jenkins,' he said. 'She always arranges the invitations.'

Invitations. That was one word for it.

He stood up.

'Well, gentlemen, that will be all for now.' He took a final swipe at Hughes. 'You've been intermittently helpful. Please don't fly to Dubai, or whatever it is people like you do.'

He turned to leave, then stopped, and turned back.

'200 quid, by the way,' he said.

'200 quid what?' said Hughes, looking close to an explosion.

'What the girls were paid. 200 quid each. That's procurement. And I have evidence. Just in case I need to do a little leaning of my own.'

He left the office, trying not to slam the door, and rather failing. He heard Davies speaking in the room as he walked away, and then he heard the door opening again. He sighed.

'DI Wood!'

He stopped, and waited for Davies to catch him up.

'What in God's name do you think you're doing?' said Davies, in a loud whisper. His face was red.

'I'm investigating a potential homicide, sir. What did you think I was doing?'

'Do you have any idea….'

'Any idea who those men are? Yes, sir, I do. Witness has a lot of information on them. Some of it is quite interesting. If you'd like me to share any of the details, just ask.'

A gamble - he hadn't read the Witness file on the two bankers. But he assumed that Hughes, at least, would have some juicy elements in there.

'Robert Hughes and Eurwyn Collins are *giants* in Caernarfon,' Davies said in an angry hiss. 'They are not used to being spoken to in the way you did in there.'

'Really, sir? You do surprise me.'

'You made them sound like a pair of street crawlers!'

'And what would you call it, sir? Paying young impoverished women to spend the night at a strange house in their company?'

'They told you! There was no payment involved! Not from them, at least!'

Something occurred to Ted. He probably shouldn't have said what he said next. He heard himself saying it, but by then it was too late.

'Did you ever attend any of these parties at Plas Newydd, sir?'

'For pity's sake, man! What is wrong with you?'

'Did you, sir?'

'It's preposterous to call them parties, and I do not appreciate your tone, Detective Inspector.'

Ted supposed he had come to hate Davies by now. He thought he might even want to hit him.

'The thing I don't understand, sir, is this. Why go in a

boat, when there's a perfectly operative bridge? Keeping it a secret from the Brothers, were we?'

'Oh for Christ's sake, Detective, do reel it in,' says Davies, his voice tight. 'As you already know, I went to Plas Newydd a few times. It's hardly a scandal.'

But he was already looking deflated, conscious of the ground becoming slippery beneath his feet.

'Well, forgive me for saying so, but it does seem faintly scandalous that the local chief prosecutor has been consorting with the subject of a murder investigation.'

Davies went quite pale.

'It's a suicide, detective. It's a fucking suicide! He killed that poor woman, and then he killed himself.'

Ted raised his eyebrows.

'That's your theory, is it, sir?'

'Again, Detective - watch your bloody tone with me. As I *say*, there was nothing *clandestine* about my visits to Plas Newydd, Inspector. We weren't the first to go there. We've always known about Brother Thomas's little *soirées*. They are important to the Island, in fact. Quite a few benefactors got their first taste of the place via Brother Thomas's little boat. Stay a night or two at Plas Newydd. Sample the place a bit. We spent some time there, had some nice food and wine. Networking, they used to call it. And then we went home. Brother Thomas is…. was *extraordinarily* good with people, you see.'

'And yet you didn't see fit to recuse yourself from the case. Or maybe you did - is that why Angela brought me in?'

'Detective, for the final fucking time - watch your step.'

'I think it's a fair question.'

Davies face had gone cold. He had looked, by turns, angry, anxious, and incredulous. Now, though, perhaps

Ted was seeing the man for the first time. A thug in a suit with a framed qualification hanging on the wall.

'Angela warned me you weren't always the sharpest knife in the drawer, DI Wood,' said Davies. He spoke slowly and clearly. 'When we were told you were coming, she warned me. I thought we understood each other. Do we?'

'Do we understand each other?'

'I am your superior, DI Wood. You are an ageing police officer with dubiously relevant skills. Don't mistake this… situation for a career renaissance. You are to provide the detail of what happened to Brother Thomas, and that is it. Those are the boundaries of your investigation. Is that quite clear?'

'Perfectly clear,' Ted said..

'I'm sure you'll be hearing from Angela,' Davies said.

'I'm sure I will,' Ted said. 'And I'm sure she'll be hearing from me. And while we're being clear, Prosecutor. I'm here to do a job. To find out what happened to Thomas Jenkins *and* Anthea Mortimer, and to find out why I'm here at all. There's something about all this which is out of whack, and I do not think I'm being told everything. I'll carry on digging until I'm told not to, and taken off the case. If you've got a problem with that, speak to Angela Leybourne yourself.'

'Oh, you can be sure of it,' Davies said.

They did not shake hands. Davies turned and went back into his board room.

20

'dunno where she is, do I? She's supposed to be on shift right now, and she's not here, is she?'

The harried, hassled supermarket manager looked about 13 years old, and well out of his depth. His domain was a brick building on the outskirts of Caernarfon commanding an extraordinary view of the Strait. Like a dog salivating at the sound of a bell, Ted's mind went back directly to another supermarket car park, this one on a Croatian island, Peg half-in and half-out of a car seat, crying, Laura struggling to do up the straps, and him listening and watching while he filled the boot of the rental car. That view had been amazing too - but young parents have little time for views.

Lancaster looked at his phone. He held it out to the manager.

'Is that their address?' he asked.

The manager didn't even look.

'I don't know their bloody address, do I? All I know is they live together. If you see them, let them know if they don't call me today, I'm giving their jobs to someone else. Not like there aren't people desperate for work, is it?'

They let the poor lad go. A local woman began haranguing him instantly in Welsh, gesticulating at the near-empty shelves and waving a phone in her face, presumably complaining about some failure of the notoriously-flaky government rationing app. Ted and Lancaster made their way out to the car park.

'Is it far?' said Ted.

'No, sir. Only a few minutes from here.'

'Right then. I'll follow you.'

Lancaster got into his car, a considerably newer and better-appointed machine than the Dyson. It was another little signal that this lad was not all he seemed; that he either worked at a different level of influence than he made out, or was marked out for such a role. He'd spent the day so far compiling a full Witness dossier on all the Plas Newydd attendees, which he'd sent to Ted. He'd met Ted here at the supermarket.

Ted followed him out of the car park, up the hill towards the mountains, coming to a halt on an ordinary-looking street with an unpronounceable name that looked and felt, to Ted, exactly the same as the street that Anthea Mortimer's mother had lived on. They parked up, and walked to the front door of a surprisingly large semi-detached house, with a concrete bird bath leaning to one side in the unkempt front garden. All the curtains were closed.

Lancaster rang the door bell. There was no answer. He rang it again, then leaned down and shouted through the letterbox.

'Police! Open up, please!'

There was nothing for a moment, then a shape appeared behind the frosted glass of the door. It seemed to stand for a moment, considering, and then the door opened, and a young, round-faced blonde woman peered out at them.

'Show me your ID,' she said. 'I'm not letting anyone in without ID.'

Lancaster flipped open his police badge. Ted did the same.

'What do you want?' the young woman said.

'I spoke to you or your friend earlier today, on the phone,' said Lancaster. 'We want to talk to you about the other night. On Plas Newydd.'

The woman breathed out, shakily.

'Oh, bloody hell. Do I have to let you in?'

'Why wouldn't you?' said Lancaster.

'I don't know, do I? Do I have to?'

Ted spoke.

'It's OK,' he said. 'We can talk here if you'd rather. Are you on your own in the house?'

'No.'

'Are you Mair?'

'That's right.'

'And Diana? She's inside?'

'She is. Yes.'

'OK. What are you so frightened of, Mair?'

She gazed at him, wide-eyed. The she opened the door a little wider.

'We had a phone call,' she said. 'You had better come in.'

She stood aside for them, and they went in.

The house was tidy and randomly furnished, as if assembled from cast-offs from other houses. There were posters on the wall, some of them framed, some of them peeling away, all of them showing pop stars and films from America. Ted wondered where all the British pop stars had got to. He struggled to remember any since before London.

Another woman stood at the bottom of the stairs. Where Mair Collier was blonde, Diana James was dark, but they both had the same round cheeks and stark, frightened eyes.

'Shall we go into the lounge?' said Ted. Diana turned and went through a glass-panelled door, and they followed her.

'Cup of tea?' said Mair, and Diana glared at her.

'Why would you be making them tea?' she hissed. Ted wondered if she'd had run-ins with the police in her past.

'Nothing for us, thanks, Ms Collier,' he said. 'May I sit down?'

Mair, looking embarrassed at her friend's outburst, indicated a purple sofa half-covered by a vaguely Indian-looking throw. Ted sat on it. It smelled of cigarettes and cheap perfume. Lancaster stood by the window.

'You were saying you received a phone call,' Ted said.

Mair looked at Diana, who nodded, as if giving permission.

'This morning,' she said. 'Just after you lot called.'

'Man, or woman?'

'Woman.'

'Did you recognise her voice?'

'No.'

Lancaster scribbled the details down in his new notebook. The call had come through while they were getting ready for work. Mair had answered. A woman had told them to be careful, they were being watched, and if they said the wrong thing to the wrong person, there would be repercussions.

'Repercussions? That was the word this woman used?'

'Yes.'

'What do you think she meant? About being careful?'

It was Diana's turn to speak, at last.

'We assume she meant: be careful about talking to you lot,' she said.

'Us lot? The police?'

'That's right.'

'Talk to us about what?'

Diana sighed, exasperated.

'About the other night on the Island, isn't it? That's why you're bloody here, isn't it? Or has Mair got a sodding parking ticket?'

Mair sat down then, and burst into tears. Diana rolled her eyes, and went over to her, rubbing her shoulders.

'I told you!' Mair said. 'I bloody told you this wasn't right, didn't I?'

Ted looked at Diana, who looked back at him. He felt he didn't need to ask a question, and he was right. This woman was fiercely intelligent, he saw, probably frustrated and bored by her life, trapped in a country which made her work in a supermarket and do a bit of after-hours sex work to keep the rent going on this grimy, draughty block of brick.

'It was just for a bit of extra cash,' she said, after a moment, keeping a hand on Mair's shuddering shoulders. 'She said we'd be paid a couple of hundred quid each to go to the party, dress up nice, have a few drinks and a decent meal, and keep a couple of old bastards company for the night.'

He could have interrupted her then, done the full *you mean you were prostitutes* thing, but he could see in her eyes that she knew what she was saying, and she knew what he was thinking, and she didn't give a damn.

'The *old bastards* being Robert Hughes and Eurwyn Collins?' he said.

'We didn't get any names, not officially. But yeah, that's what they were called. *Bobby and Eurwyn*, that's what His Nibs called them.'

'His Nibs?'

'Sir Wotsit. The royal fella.'

'Sir Anthony Mayfield?'

'Yes. Him.'

'He was friendly with Hughes and Collins?'

'They all were. Apart from the history fella. And his daughter. She was nice.'

A car had arrived to pick them up at 7, she said. They'd been driven down to the jetty and taken over to Plas Newydd in a boat with the other guests. There'd been a boring presentation of plans for the Investiture, given by the 'swanky twat' from Chester, James Moncrieff. Then there'd been drinks, and a dinner. By now Mair had stopped sobbing, and interjected by saying the dinner was 'bloody spectacular.' Then more drinks, lots of them, and not just drinks either, if he knew what she meant, though they didn't partake. Then they went up to their bedrooms, Diana with Robert Hughes, Mair with Eurwyn Collins. Diana's eyes flashed warning signals at this point - *don't ask me about this bit, draw your own bloody conclusions* - so Ted let it pass.

'And Anthea Mortimer? How did she seem?'

They hadn't spoken to Anthea and she'd said very little all night. Mair thought she was shy, and Diana agreed.

'She didn't pair up with anyone?'

Diana scowled.

'Pair up? It wasn't a swinger's session.'

'Did you notice her with anyone, then. Spending time.'

Neither of them had.

So Ted asked about Brother Thomas, and even Diana seemed to lighten up a bit at the mention of his name.

'Oh, he was always lovely to us,' she said.

'Always remembered our names,' said Mair. 'Not everyone's like that.'

'So you'd done this before?' said Ted. The two of them glanced at each other.

'Yeah. A few times,' said Diana eventually.

'And did Brother Thomas go to bed at the same time as everyone else?'

'No,' said Diana. 'He stayed up a while, I think. He said something about sorting a few things out before bed. A lot of clearing up had already happened, I think. There was a little army of them, kids in their brown robes, sweeping up after us. By the time we went to bed, the place was spotless.'

'So he wasn't doing the clearing up, or anything like that.'

Diana smirked.

'I don't think Brother Thomas was the kind of man who cleared up, for anyone. Perhaps metaphorically speaking.'

'So everyone else went to bed at roughly the same time?'

'I think so. Can't be entirely sure. I hand my hands full trying to keep him away from the kinky stuff. Thankfully the fat twat went to sleep as soon as he'd done the dirty the once.' She glared at him now. 'Whatever he might have said to you.'

'He hasn't said anything about such matters,' said Ted, picking his way carefully round the words *such matters*.

There were a few more questions, and then they got ready to leave.

'One more thing,' said Ted.

'All right, Columbo,' said Diana. She smiled for the first time. And Ted, genuinely, smiled right back.

'You said *she. She said we'd be paid a couple of hundred quid.* Who was the she?'

She raised an eyebrow.

'I think you probably know the answer to that, don't you?'

'Lucy Jenkins?'

'Yeah. Lucy.'

'You know who her husband is, I take it?'

Diana rolled her eyes again.

'*Everybody* knows who her husband is, don't they?'

Ted and Lancaster made their way to the door, but now Mair Collier called them back.

'Excuse me? What are you going to do about this phone call?'

Ted paused at the door. It was important, he supposed, to project a relaxed air. Because he was almost as worried about that phone call as the two women were.

'You definitely didn't recognise her voice?'

'No,' said Mair. 'I'd never heard it before.'

Ted looked at Diana.

'You didn't hear it?'

She scowled, understanding what he meant - Mair could not be relied upon as a witness, especially an aural one.

'No. I didn't hear it.'

'We'll look into it,' said Ted. 'Sergeant Lancaster here will let you know what we find.'

21

And so, he arrived at the Castle.

It was remarkable, really, the way this whole part of Wales was informed by the extraordinary masses of Edward I's fortresses. For more than seven hundred years they had defined the politics of this part of the world, and to some extent the geography too. The new King knew this, of course - he had finely tuned antennae for such matters - and he also knew that the Investiture of his son as Prince of Wales was a political moment, arguably the biggest Royal event since he had himself ascended to the throne. That event had passed with barely any pageantry in the wrecked weeks after London, when even the BBC had gone dark and the event had to be streamed over an American-owned video network from a scrambled-together patchwork of hand-held cameras.

But the BBC was back now, and the King was determined to make the most of the moment. It wasn't just Royal protocol at stake - it was the image Britain projected to the world. Broken-backed and exhausted and, yes, hungry after London, the country needed a rallying cry and a pageant, and the King wanted to provide it.

Ted didn't believe a word of it. And thinking about it too closely made him feel sick to his stomach. His investigations were projected against a national, even international, backdrop. Why weren't there more people on the team? Why just him, Lancaster and Priestley, for pity's sake? Didn't they want this mystery solved?

He had tripped up on that question a number of times now. He even wondered if the answer was obvious: no, they didn't want this mystery solved. There had been no mention of the case in the press - he assumed all the interested parties had been gagged, and in any case this kind of story would be subject to D-notices which, these days, were as common as Welsh rain. They'd suppressed it, and one way of confirming that suppression was to keep a small team on it, the smallest possible, and bring someone in from outside whose absence from Manchester would cause scarcely a ripple. Looked at like that, he could see the logic of it. And it made him even more suspicious of Lieutenant Edward Lancaster. What was his role here? Help the investigation? Or keep a lid on it?

If there were answers, he doubted they'd be here in Edward's fortress.

They'd tried to visit here with Peg, in that long ago beforetime. But the car park had been full, and Peg had been fractious and not at all interested in castles or kings, and couldn't they go to the pier at Bangor instead? So they'd gone to the pier.

Which meant he wasn't prepared for the overwhelmingly forbidding GO AWAY air of Edward's gatehouse. No expense had been spared in building a bespoke, high-security pipeline for entry into the Castle interior. It began at the bottom of the ramp into the street, where two armed

Security Service officers with dogs checked his police pass. One of them accompanied him up the ramp and into the gatehouse itself. Here, within Edward's fearsome set of six separate portcullises, the Sec people had built a full screening system inside a tunnel of clear perspex, such that the VIPs who attended the Investiture would still be able to see the Castle fabric while they were being processed by all the surveillance power Witness could command. His face was scanned, his palm and finger were scanned, his jacket had to be removed and scanned, a Sec officer with a crewcut patted him down, and he was separately scanned for any signals from electronics which might be on or even in his person. Rumour had it that some people were installing transmitting or signal blocking kit in their skin, but Ted had never seen that demonstrated.

And even when that was all over and he was ushered inside, he was accompanied by a Sec officer who did not identify himself. Ted could not avoid comparing the welcome with Brother Enoch's methods on Anglesey. He thought there were instructive similarities and differences.

The castle interior consisted of endless grey-and-cream stone and neat, manicured terraced lawns. Seating had been constructed to surround a central dais which was covered in a half-exposed clear perspex dome, on which sat a single chair. The chair was for the current Duke, and soon-to-be Prince of Wales. A lectern stood to one side of it. The last Prince of Wales to be invested here had made a speech in Welsh, they said. Ted thought it unlikely such a thing would happen this time. The lad was barely in trousers.

The Sec officer led him down the terraces to a second courtyard, smaller than the main one into which they'd entered. Another temporary construction had been added here, with generators and cabling suggesting an administrative facility of some kind. He followed the Sec officer inside, and was there met by a young man in a well-tailored suit who greeted him with a handshake and - Ted actually wondered if he was imagining this - a snap-together of the heels.

'Detective Inspector Wood,' said the man, in a cut-glass English accent. 'Welcome to Caernarfon Castle! What do you think of the place?'

'You are?' said Ted, deliberately avoiding the charm. The young man did not seem to notice.

'Lawrence Greenwood, assistant to Sir Anthony, at your service.'

'And is Sir Anthony here?'

'But of course! He is waiting for us in his office. Thank you, Mitchell, that will be all.'

Greenwood turned away and Ted caught the Sec officer scowling at him. The officer caught Ted looking at him in turn, and the two rolled their eyes in the time-honoured way, class allies again across the departmental divide. Ted followed Greenwood.

Sir Anthony Mayfield's 'office' turned out to be barely a cupboard at the side of the pop-up facility, but even so he had managed to turn it into a small slice of Aristocratic England, with what appeared to be a pair of crossed spears purloined from some far-flung corner of the Empire, as well as a photograph of a younger Sir Anthony with the old Queen and her middle son. It was at this picture that Sir Anthony was gazing when Ted was shown in by his factotum.

'Ah, DI Wood! Delighted to meet you, delighted.'

Sir Anthony shook Ted's hand delightedly. He had a refined but oddly manic energy, and would have been much taller than Ted if he stood up straight. As it was he was a little stooped, as if trying to hear what the shorter people were saying. He sat down behind his desk, and waved Ted into a seat. Greenwood stood behind Sir Anthony and to one side, hands behind his back, as if waiting for a food order.

'Now,' said Sir Anthony. 'Plas Newydd. Dreadful business. Absolutely terrible.'

'Yes,' began Ted, forcing himself not to *sir* him, feeling an old chip biting into his shoulder in the face of effortless *noblesse*. 'We have your statement, but I was wondering if you could give me some insight into the purpose of the meeting.'

'Delighted to. Anything I can do to help.'

Sir Anthony leaned back in his chair, and put his hands behind his head. It was clearly a common position for him.

'It was my idea, actually,' he said. 'Not especially happy about that now, of course, but yes - I suggested it. Wanted to keep the money boys happy, of course - one must *always* keep the money boys onside, DI Wood - and I thought our history fellow would like to see Plas Newydd as well.'

'The history fellow? Frank Daniels?'

'That's the chap. Knows his onions but a trifle dry and he didn't take to me, I'm afraid. Not like the English have covered themselves in glory in this corner of Cymru, is it? But he'd been a great help to me. We've been here for six months, you know, planning this little affair. The Defence Minister also wanted to meet the money boys, and she was also intrigued by the Community.'

'She wanted to know more about it?'

'Oh, I should say so, yes. Frightfully interested. She rather monopolised poor old Brother Thomas , I'm afraid. She had never met the fellow before, and gave him a positive *grilling*.'

'Did Brother Thomas spend any time with anyone else?'

'Oh, yes, indeed. He spoke to all of us. He is rather a fine worker of the room. Oh, bless me - I mean he *was*. Hadn't seen a finer exponent of the art since Obama visited us back in the Noughties. But I would say he spent most time with Her Nibs.'

'Her Nibs.'

'Ah! Sorry. Our little joke. It was our nickname for La Ministresse. Rather unprofessional. But she is rather vulgar, I would say. Her little entourage were all a bit below-stairs. Wouldn't you agree, Greenwood?'

The factotum nodded.

'Oh rather, yes sir.'

Sir Anthony beamed and turned back to Ted. It was a comic performance, but Ted had little doubt it was a *performance*. This man meant everything he said, and meant everything he said to be heard. And he didn't care whether you found the thing offensive or not.

'And how well did you know Anthea Mortimer?'

'Oh dear God. Poor, dear Anthea.'

Sir Anthony removed his hands from behind his head and leaned forward. He brought his hands together in front of his mouth, his lips pursed.

'Lovely young woman. So bright. So full of life. She has been an absolute force of nature on this project. It's not always been easy, you know - there are many in this part of the world who see the Investiture as a disgusting anachronism, forever tainted by its association with Edward Longshanks. But she arranged countless Q&A sessions, displays, roadshows, the works. I believe having a local woman like her front up things has proven *essential*. She is a great, great loss.'

'And her boss? Moncrieff?'

'Oh dear me, no. Awful chap. Wouldn't buy a footstool off the fellow.'

'Did you notice anyone with Anthea during the party? Did you speak to her?'

'I did not. In answer to both questions. I mean we made small talk. But I wouldn't say I had a conversation with her. What about you, Lawrence?'

Greenwood leaned forward, almost conspiratorially.

'Well, there was a little unpleasantness around the room allocations, sir.'

'Oh dear me, yes! There was! I had completely forgotten.'

'Unpleasantness?' asked Ted.

'Yes. Anthea and Brother Thomas had a bit of a set-to, I remember. She was unhappy with the room I had been allocated, as it happened. Perfect nonsense to me, of course. I could not have cared less. But when Anthea raised it with Brother Thomas, the fellow became quite intransigent. Rather told her off, in fact, which she did *not* take kindly to. Anyway, it was all cleared up.'

'Your room was moved.'

'Indeed. My room was moved. Anthea and I swapped, as I recall.'

'And then all was well.'

'Oh indeed, all was well. We only raise it for completeness.'

Ted noted *We.* He thought that little revelation might have been stage managed. Sir Anthony meant for him to take note of it.

'Did you stay up especially late?'

'No, I think not. I tend not to these days. I was in bed around midnight.'

'And you?' Ted said to Lawrence Greenwood.

'I went to my room soon after Sir Anthony retired,' said Greenwood, officiously.

'And you both stayed in your rooms? All night?'

'DI Wood, I'm not at all clear I understand your implication.'

Sir Anthony's fake bonhomie was still on show, but for a moment he allowed Ted to see beneath it. His eyes told Ted to be careful.

'No nighttime visits to the loo?'

'Ah, no. The rooms at Plas Newydd are blessed with en suites. Handy for a fellow my age, you know!'

There was little else. Like all the other guests, Sir Anthony had been woken by the noise of the police arriving outside his window, and had given his statement at the house. Lawrence Greenwood said the same.

As he was leaving, Sir Anthony came round the desk to shake his hand and show him out.

'Now. This business. I trust it will not *interfere* with things, DI Wood? The Investiture is rather important to the nation's wellbeing, you know.'

He put one hand on Ted's shoulder as they walked back out through the pop-up unit.

'I don't see why it should interrupt things, sir, no,' said Ted. He thought that, before London, he might have said something along the lines of *it will take as long as it takes, Sir Anthony - it's a double murder inquiry.* But such clear priorities were more muddied, these days. Who was he to say that a murder was more important than a crowning, these days?

'Good man, good man. And tell me, I rather expected to find Lieutenant Lancaster accompanying you. He is a fiercely clever lad, you know. Knew his uncle. We were at Cambridge together. Expect he's off beavering away on some database or other, hmm? That's what you chaps spend most of your time doing, these days. But as I always say, DI Wood, databases are only as good as the data you put into them, correct? Ah, and here's someone else I expect you need to talk to. Glendower!'

A small, bald man with round glasses looked around at the shouted name, already scowling. Sir Anthony smirked.

'He *hates* it when I call him that,' he whispered, conspiratorially. 'Zero sense of humour about such matters, these Welsh fellows. Be on your guard! Glendower, put down the trowel and the sour expression and come and meet Detective Inspector Wood. He is charged with examining the sad events at Plas Newydd.'

The small, bald man, who was not carrying a trowel, walked towards them.

'Frank Daniels,' he said, holding out a hand. 'Not Frank Glendower. Sir Anthony here finds our cultural heritage mystifyingly amusing, I must say.'

'Oh, Frank, the heritage is glorious. It is your *attitude* to it that is amusing! Anyway, I will leave you fine gentlemen to it. I have a ceremony to run. Good day to you both!'

With which Sir Anthony spun on his heels and began to march back to his office. Ted had the distinct sense of having been dismissed by a private schoolmaster.

'Men like that give you English a bloody bad name, you know,' said Daniels. 'Patronising wanker.'

He looked like he might spit on the grass, but thought better of it. He glared at Ted, as if daring him to have any kind of a problem with what he'd just said.

'He spoke rather highly of you, actually,' Ted said.

Daniels rolled his eyes.

'He's the master of empty platitudes, that one. Now. How can I help you?'

'Perhaps you can start by telling me why you were at the party?'

'Because I was on the committee,' said Daniels. 'We were all invited. Me and Beryl, my daughter, were advising the committee on the historical aspects of the Investiture. Its role in Anglo-Welsh relations. That sort of thing.'

Ted asked him the same questions he'd been asking everyone. No, Daniels had not seen anything suspicious. He had found Brother Thomas to be an odious fellow, 'cut from the same bloody cloth as Sir Anthony,' had spoken as little as possible to the two bankers - 'crooks' - their escorts - 'dolly birds' - or the politician and her entourage. He softened only when speaking of Anthea Mortimer.

'Bloody tragedy. Bloody awful tragedy. She was a lovely, lovely young woman. Don't know how she could stand working with that idiot boss of hers. You know she hired me?'

'She did?'

'She'd read my books, you see. I had a particular interest in the original investiture. He was still building this place when they crowned him - little Edward the Second. He stole everything we had, and then he made his son Prince of Wales just to rub salt into the wounds. Even went to the lengths of turning Arthur into a bloody Englishman. Knew what he was about, old Edward did. When it came to building castles or building myths. Got to admire him, really. But I wish the bastard had never lived.'

They were walking back into the big courtyard while Frank Daniels gave his little speech. A young woman in dungarees with filthy hands and face walked over to them. She looked concerned.

'My daughter, Beryl,' said Daniels. 'Beryl, come and meet the police fellow who's looking into what happened to poor Anthea.' Ted noted he made no mention of Brother Thomas.

'It's a bloody tragedy, it is,' said Beryl Daniels. She held out her hand and then noticed how dirty it was. 'Oh, sorry, sir. I've been helping some of the fellows put cameras in the towers. Filthy job, it is, but we want to make sure they don't a mess of the stonework. You know how these TV types can be.'

Ted had no idea how these TV types could be, but nodded anyway.

'How well did you know Anthea, Ms Daniels?'

'Oh, call me Beryl, love. Haven't been called Ms Daniels since I was at school. Yes, Anthea and I were mates, I would say. Had a few drinks and a bit of a laugh over the last few months. She even won over Mr Grumpy, here.'

She smiled at her Dad, who made a rueful grimace. At least one person in the world was allowed to mock him, then. Her accent was richly Welsh. His accent could have been from anywhere in England.

'We were are at school together, actually,' said Beryl. 'Not friends, though, I was a bit older than her. Probably wasn't even aware of her existence. She remembered, though. Funny.'

'You're both fairly local then?'

'Well, we're pretty local to Caernarfon, Inspector. Dad was a councillor, and everything. Anthea was more Conwy-way. Deganwy, I think. But we were at the same school, yeah. Do you know what happened, Inspector? Any idea at all?'

There was a pleading quality to Beryl Daniels that stood in stark contrast to Sir Anthony's glib show of bereavement. The woman seemed genuinely disturbed by what had happened. He turned to the father.

'You were a councillor, Mr Daniels?'

'Aye,' said Daniels. 'Back in the day.'

'Gave it up?'

'Bottom fell out of it after London. No local powers anymore, everything got centralised. It was just a talking shop.'

'I suppose so. I'd not really thought about it.'

Beryl cut in.

'Local politics blah blah blah. What about Anthea?'

'We're still talking to people, Beryl,' Ted said.

'Did Brother Thomas kill her, then? Then kill himself, like?'

The stark questions threw Ted off for a moment.

'I can't comment on a live case.'

'Ah, no, of course, of course. Sorry. Silly of me. I'm just so cut up about it, see. It's so bloody unfair.'

'Did Anthea seem strange to you, that night? Anything off?'

'Well, there was the argument over the room. You know about that?'

'Sir Anthony's room?'

'Yes, that's it. He kicked off straightaway, saying he wasn't sleeping in the room he was given.'

'Really? He said it was Anthea who raised it.'

'Well. Sir Anthony says things. I'll say no more about that. But it was definitely him as was annoyed. He got Anthea to talk to Brother Thomas about it, and Thomas was a right prick about it. Pardon my English and speaking ill of the dead and all that, but he was. Charming the room one minute, and then being like that the next.'

'You saw this?'

'No. He'd never have acted like that with any witnesses. Anthea told me about it after. She was pretty annoyed about it. Then I didn't see her again before we all went to bed. Didn't even get to say good night to her.'

Beryl Daniels seemed thoughtful for a moment.

'I haven't really thought about that. I'd had a bit too much to drink, Inspector. I should have gone to find her, really.'

Ted caught Frank Daniels looking at his daughter with

the same thoughtful expression. The fruit had not fallen far from the tree.

'Does 19 RPT mean anything to you?' said Ted.

Frank looked away from his daughter.

'To me? No. Why should it?'

'No particular reason. What about *Llanfaes*?'

Frank frowned.

'Do you mean *Llanfaes*?'

To be fair to him, Ted thought, the word did sound completely different when pronounced correctly.

'That's it,' he said.

'Llanfaes was formerly the seat of the old kings of Gwynedd.'

'Gwynedd?'

'You're in Gwynedd, Detective,' said Beryl, obviously the more amenable to ignorance of the two. 'This part of Wales has always been called Gwynedd.'

'Llanfaes is on Anglesey,' said Frank. 'Not much there now. Edward emptied the town after Madog ap Llywelyn's revolt against English rule. There was a friary there dating back to the early 13th century.'

'Did Brother Thomas have something to do with it?'

Frank frowned again.

'With Llanfaes? No. I don't believe so.'

The frown stayed on the face, but the eyes flicked away.

22

The drone was waiting for him when he exited the castle, solicitously hanging in the air some fifty feet away, along with perhaps another two dozen of the things hanging around the castle entrance. But Ted felt he knew which one was his. It seemed almost to cock itself to one side, like a dog waiting for a treat. It wasn't the only watcher waiting. Lancaster stood in the street wearing his well-appointed winter coat.

'Sir.'

'Lieutenant. Keeping tabs on me, are we?'

Lancaster didn't bother replying to that one.

'How was it in the Castle?'

'Not a lot to go on. It's been that sort of day, really.' Ted paused, pondering. 'Sir Anthony says hello.'

'Ah. Yes. I possibly should have told you. He's a friend of the family.'

'Is he? Well.'

Lancaster didn't say anything else. What *was* he? Enthusiastic MI5 appointee who'd 'done the Training' to be part of His Majesty's New Model Police? Or something else again? Maybe only a babysitter. Maybe something quite a bit more.

'And what about you, Lieutenant? What have you unearthed today?'

'Priestley's still at the house. She says she'll be finished tomorrow. Reckons it would make sense for you to pay a visit in the morning. And I've also requested a meet with the Abbot. He's going to make himself available tomorrow morning, as well.'

'OK. And what goodies did Witness have?'

'A lot of noise, not much signal. Data is patchy before London, but there's quite a lot of inference on Thomas Jenkins.'

'Inference? Meaning no evidence?'

'No sir - just the software making connections based on what's in the database. Nothing explicit in terms of the old PND, but it seems there was quite a lot of chatter about Thomas Jenkins. Fair bit of stuff in the local paper. Rumours of backhanders and corruption - bribing of Council officers, stuff like that. I've sent the gist of it to your inbox.'

'Any connection to Robert Hughes or Eurwyn Collins?'

'That's where the software started looking, actually. Yes. Quite a lot of stuff in there. They all knew each other pretty well. Most recent stuff relates to the Y Neuadd development.'

'Where Lucy Jenkins lives now?'

'Yes, sir.'

Had it only been this morning he'd been in that young woman's house?

'And what about Lucy Jenkins? Her name seems to have come up a good deal.'

'Yes, sir. She's definitely part of the same network. And Witness identifies her as a node for Plas Newydd.'

'Meaning she's deeply connected over a period of time.'

'Yes, sir. Put the focus on her and you get an entire network of folks who've been at Plas Newydd over the past five years.'

'How big a network?'

'Up to two degrees of separation - something like seven hundred.'

Ted whistled.

'Bloody hell. Any names pop up?'

'Probably easier to say which names *don't* pop up, sir. Just about anyone connected with government, or either of the arms of the intelligence service, are on there.'

'Including Allan Davies.'

'Yes sir.' A pause. 'And Angela Leybourne.'

Ted supposed this shouldn't have come as a surprise - the mere fact that a senior functionary in the justice administration should have visited Plas Newydd. From what he'd learned in the last 24 hours it would have been a surprise if Angela had not been a visitor. What was notable, of course, was that she hadn't mentioned it. She knew Witness would flag it. So why not bring it up? As a demonstration of the abilities of Witness, it was, of course, flawless - the software cared not for position or rank. All it saw were data points, and it ate through them as emotionlessly as a combine harvester chewing up a wheat field.

'OK. So which of our little crowd of folks had not been to Plas Newydd before, then?'

'The Defence Minister had only been once before.'

'But she's relatively new in post, right?'

'Yes, sir. As are her two aides. Neither of them appear on the Plas Newydd record before this week either.'

'And everyone else?'

'Multiple visits, sir. All of them had been at least six times.'

'Even the two women from the supermarket?'

'Yes, sir. Quite a lucrative sideline, I'd say.'

Ted didn't take kindly to that. He wanted to tell Lancaster to fuck off, to stick his supercilious judgement of the two frightened women in the ordinary little house up his well-tailored arse.

'Right then. That will be all, Lieutenant.'

Lancaster looked momentarily blindsided.

'And what about you, sir?'

'What about me, Sergeant?'

'Well - did you uncover anything interesting today?'

They looked at each other for a moment, standing there in the street beneath the old Castle, the night coming on and the dark rising from the medieval streets.

'Right, sir. I'll be off then.'

'See you tomorrow, Lieutenant.'

23

He stomped away from the Castle and down the hill towards the car park, oddly furious and with no specific direction in mind. The drone, with its invisible geospatial tether, sprang into life and followed him.

It had been what Laura would have called 'a pig of day,' but it looked like it was going to be a clear evening. The drizzle that had dampened every part of him all day had finally gone, and the clouds were giving way to another spectacular sky, as the sun dropped down towards Ireland.

Ted walked in the other direction to the previous evening, along the waterfront in front of the castle, to the point where the river that ran alongside Caernarfon's town walls met the sea. An empty pub stood on this side of the castle, some of its abandoned windows smashed. He remembered the place: The Anglesey Arms. Peg had been hungry, and had demanded to know why they couldn't go in there, and Laura had become tense because she knew the reason why they didn't go in there. Daddy couldn't be trusted inside a pub. 'Let's see what we can find in the town,' he'd said. A bland phrase from long ago, containing so much.

He walked up the street on the far side of the castle, passing into the narrow streets of the old town. Here, immediately behind the Castle, were the council offices, where the likes of his two bankers presumably exploited whatever new and interesting loopholes had opened up in Britain's tattered political fabric. Or maybe that's what they'd always been doing. Thomas Jenkins had been a player, in there, just like he had been in Allan Davies's little modern castle of judicial shenanigans out on the ring road. He'd made money - a good deal of money, judging by Lucy Jenkins's house. And then he had walked away from it all, just as the man or men who had blown up London unleashed their dirty miracle. Why had he done that, Ted wondered?

A left turn, then a right. Finally, a sign of life - a modern-looking pub, still open and apparently thriving. An old Wetherspoons place, now owned by the government, where the state sold booze at a discount to men who had grown accustomed to drinking cheap rat's piss. No-one could afford to drink proper beer anymore, so no one made it. Ted remembered craft beer. Countless pale ales, brewed in business parks, selected by earnest punters with beards who asked if they could try it first. People used to have the time to think of things like that.

And thoughts of drink led, inevitably, back to Laura. She was pouring them another glass of wine - this was in the early days, the days when Peg was still small, back in Streatham, when they used to drink together and Laura never passed a comment on how many glasses he'd had. 'Want to talk about it?' she had said, and Ted always did. Usually, as Ted told his wife the details of a case, it would rearrange itself in his mind, the chains of connection breaking apart and remaking themselves, the hidden narrative beneath the surface twinkling into occasional visibility, until he saw it, maybe a phrase two people had used, separately, days apart, the same sequence of words. Had they practised that phrase? And that possibility led to the possibility that the two were working in concert, and it patched itself together, and Ted would say, 'I think I've figured it out,' and Laura would smile, and sip her wine, and say: 'You're welcome.'

But that night, they'd been talking about Peckham. And Peckham never clicked together in that way. Peckham just fell apart, and he had fallen apart with it.

They were familiar to him now, these sharp-edged fragments of memory. They came all the time - images of Laura and Peg, vivid enough to be present and *now*, invoked by something someone said, or something he saw, or a smell or a noise or a sensation on his skin. These things had become like a mental scrapbook, held open by an unseen hand and accompanied by an unspoken instruction.

It had never felt like madness, or even eccentricity. Ted assumed that everyone experienced their memories of lost loved ones like this. He'd never spoken to anyone of it. There had never been a tap on the shoulder from a superior officer, someone to ask if he was OK, and did he need to speak to someone, perhaps someone professional, about his personal situation? Those kinds of conversations didn't happen anymore. There were not enough analysts to go around, and there was not enough money to pay for them.

'Just fucking deal with it,' Laura said. 'If you think you're losing it, just go to the doctor and get a pill or start meditating or do something, for pity's sake. But I don't think there's anything wrong with you. You just drink too much. Why do you drink so much?'

That was that night. That night they discussed Peckham. They used to talk about his *mental health* after Peckham, as if he had incipient deafness, or a gammy knee.

A shadow unfolded itself from a wall, accompanied by an irregular shuffle on the cobbled stone of the street. Ted kept walking, not breaking stride.

Who was it? Local Police? Security Service? Someone else, maybe someone political, even? Were they watching his hotel? Who wanted to know the movements of Detective Inspector Ted Wood? He'd always suspected this investigation had a political dimension. Was this the proof of it? He pondered confronting the shadow, but to what end? Everyone watched everyone else in the New Britain. Everyone important, anyway. His friendly drone buzzed its way above the street. More watching. Could it see the shadow that saw him?

But why did they need to follow him? They could see him on Witness screens clearly enough. See, he even had his own drone. He wished he still smoked. He could stand out here for a while longer, without suspicion. He even looked around for a shop for a moment, to pop in for 20 Silk Cut, feel the smoke going down into his lungs, his head opening up, his heart racing. Maybe it was just a drug dealer. There were still a few of those.

He stood still anyway. The massive edge of the Castle loomed over one end of the street, lit by spotlights and glowing - and he imagined London glowing like that, its bricks buzzing with electrons - the ash floating in the air, tumbled metal skeletons, buildings exposed to the poisoned air - and everywhere desiccated human shapes, mouths open in screams - Whitehall, sheared of itself, flattened, and somewhere in the rubble Peg, with Laura beside her....

Easy, Ted. Easy, now.

He was alone, with footsteps approaching.

He walked up towards the Castle. There were piles of iron railings laid flat everywhere, ready to be put into place for yet another crowd. An ugly Portakabin had also appeared, ready to sell tourist tat to the same crowd. He went down a side street. The footsteps stayed with him.

'Got any coke?' he said, to no one in particular, and no one replied. The footsteps fell silent. He stopped, and turned, as much to create a marker for himself on the footage as anything. There was no-one in the alley with him.

But no. That wasn't quite true. The drone hung in the air, watching, listening, recording. Maybe it could tell him where the unknown man had disappeared to.

<h1 style="text-align:center">24</h1>

As he walked back to the hotel, he wrestled with a sudden and sharp anxiety, verging on real terror. Perhaps it had been building for a while, only revealing itself as that shadow peeled itself from the wall. He'd hidden himself in Manchester, one of the vanishing breed of old-school detectives, men and women with their own ways and means, increasingly out of step with a new world that didn't want them. It was a grey existence, but a safe one. None of the fears of his old world, the London world.

But now, this. This case. This situation. The Investiture. He hadn't felt this exposed to powerful unseen powers since Peckham, when he'd been unable to sleep and every colleague had been brandishing a knife. He could feel it happening again. Why had Angela sent him? What was her relationship with Allan Davies? Had news of all this reached the ears of the King?

Drink. He found that he needed a drink very badly. But that would have to wait. One of the officers from Manchester, a decent Liverpudlian DC named Hoskyns, was waiting for him in the hotel reception with a suitcase of clothes and overnight supplies.

'Compliments of Crown Prosecutor Leybourne,' Hoskyns said.

'I assume she didn't pack the bag?'

Hoskyns shrugged.

'No. Sent me to do it. 'Cos I'm your bleeding butler now, guv.' He looked around the hotel lobby. 'Fancy. Didn't know they still had places like this. And certainly didn't know they put coppers in them.' He looked back at Ted. 'How are you doing?'

'How do you mean?'

'Just lads were asking back at the station.'

'I'm fine.'

'Right-o. I'll be off then. Want to be home before it gets too late. The wife's already annoyed I missed dinner.'

It struck Ted how comfortable some men were with references to 'the wife.'

'Good. Thanks for driving this stuff over. I owe you one.'

'Yeah, yeah, yeah. No problem.'

He sauntered out. Ted watched him go, remembering a time when he was capable of such a level of sauntering. He watched the outer door swing closed, and then he watched the closed door, and then he headed to the lifts. He couldn't see anyone outside, through the doors. The same receptionist who had arranged for his shirt to be cleaned - no, he was still avoiding the truth, the receptionist *who'd cleaned his shirt* - watched him as he walked across the lobby. He nodded at her and she activated her receptionist's smile and then turned it off again soon enough for Ted to see her doing it. It was fair to say that they had established the boundaries of their relationship.

Upstairs, he unpacked the clothes, pausing a moment

to notice that Hoskyns had put his gun and shoulder holster in one of the internal pockets. He'd left it at home, without really thinking about it. All police officers were supposed to carry their guns when on duty - and most did so even when they weren't. Britain, if nobody had noticed, had changed.

He checked Witness via the laptop which Hoskyns had also packed. Full access was disabled for remote terminals. He could do basic facial recognition but not any detailed database queries until he was on a Witness property, within a secure Witness network. But he wanted to see if the system had captured anything. He plugged in the lat-long of Caernarfon, spooled back to the approximate time, and zoomed into the right street. There he was, walking along by himself. The shadow must have unpeeled itself somewhere, but he couldn't see it. He saw himself stop, and turn. He wound it back, trying to find where the man in the shadows first went into the shadows. He went back a half-hour, but it was pointless. He couldn't follow all the stranger's tracks without full access to Witness. And if the man was working for one of the arms of government - the Security Service or even the Secret Service - he would have known how to cover his tracks, how to obfuscate. He'd even heard rumours that there were some spooks who had become literally that - ghosts in the machine that the software had been trained to ignore.

But it was probably more simple than that - a classic Witness nighttime issue. When darkness fell there were more chances of hiding oneself - of creeping out from one public space (a pub, say) with a hoodie masking your face and sticking to the shadows of buildings. If you knew what you were doing, you could go some distance without being spotted. But it was risky. Internal cameras at the place you'd come from might realise you were missing. There might be a police patrol - there were many of these, in every town, charged with following up instantly on Witness alerts. Or you might cause a punter like Ted to stop, and look, and suspiciously, and suddenly, the cameras were locked in.

And they'd find you eventually, if they cared to. Witness operatives were adept at this - tracking back from someone disappearing in a pub, checking all the people who came and left, cross-referencing their profiles, and because everyone was watched at least some of the time, and some people - dodgy people, frankly, or at least people that the powers-that-be deemed to be dodgy - were watched a lot of the time, they'd get back to a point where they could hazard enough of a guess that the guy in the hoodie creeping out the back was the guy who walked in the front an hour before. And from that point on they'd have a mark on you - a virtual mark, but a mark none-theless. It said *keep an eye on this one, he tries it on*. Ted had heard it referred to as The Eye Of The King, The Black Mark, or The Cunt Stench, depending on the level of education and attitude to profanity of the person concerned.

And then, another thought - connected? The myste-rious phone call to Mair Collier and Diana James. He'd told them not to worry about it, but some process in his mind hadn't stopped thinking about it. So he wondered.

What if the call wasn't meant for them?

What if it had been meant for him? A signal, from someone out there, to say he was being watched, and not in quite the usual way.

What could that mean?

He took a shower, his mind suddenly empty. On the other side of the wall from which the shower extended was the minibar. Is that what was bringing this inner silence?

So many bits of information had come at him today, so many insights and conversations, but his mind remained still and quiet. Occasionally it meandered away into meaningless questions, but the only thought that recurred with any frequency was the bemusement he'd felt at those four words Hoskyns had put to me:

How are you doing?

Like he was a patient. Why had Hoskyns asked him how he was doing? Was he not doing fine? Did people talk about how he was doing, now? Was he a sample for their experiments, an object for their interest, even their pity? Everyone lost people in London and after London. Everyone was wrestling with their demons.

Weren't they?

How are you doing?

Another sharp-edged memory - Laura watching him when he looked up from his dinner plate. They were eating late because he had been at work late, the Peckham case, and there was oh such a mess. It was a month after his father's funeral. He hadn't been sleeping, but other than that he'd been holding it together pretty well, the odd quivering dip into darkness, the occasional teardrop when his car was stopped at the lights and no-one was looking, but he was OK. The Peckham thing was a nightmare - two young men dead, killed separately by persons unknown, their mothers on the nightly news, and he was eating dinner and thinking about that when Laura had said, quietly: 'How are you doing?'

And he had replied: 'How long have you been sitting there watching me?'

He found himself out of the shower, sitting on the bed, naked, looking at a pair of socks. How long had he been sitting there?

How long have you been sitting there watching me?

'Where are you, honey?' he said, and the sound of his own voice startled him. 'Where are you now?'

He stood up from the bed, walked over to the minibar, knelt down and opened it. The white rhombus of light emptied itself onto his lap. They'd refilled it since last night. Somewhere, someone had clocked that Detective Inspector Edward Wood had drunk the entire contents of a minibar in one night. But the hotel had refilled it. Business was business.

No wonder they were asking how he was.

He shut the minibar door, and decided to keep things public. He finished getting dressed, and went down to the bar.

25

The three of them were sitting around a large table covered in papers in the corner of the bar. Two women and a man. The man with a laptop open in front of him, one of the women jotting notes down, and the other woman emphasising some unheard point with sudden chops of her hand, in a way that Ted had seen in countless media reports. Rachel Whitehouse, Defence Minister and politician on the up, was holding court in the corner of the bar of the Lloyd George Hotel.

Well, he supposed he'd spoken to every other attendee of the Plas Newydd party today. It was time to go for a full house. Ignoring the bar, with some effort, he walked over to the group.

'Excuse me, Minister,' he said. 'Detective Inspector Ted Wood, Manchester Police Service. I'm investigating the suspected homicides at Plas Newydd yesterday. May I speak with you, please?'

Whitehouse sighed, rather theatrically. She had a pinched, angular face and long dark hair worn down on either side of her face. She held Ted's gaze for a moment, made a face, and then without saying anything gestured to one of the empty chairs beside the table. He was permitted to enter her presence.

Her two companions watched him pull up a chair and sit down. The woman was a kind-looking soul with an anxious look to her, and she carefully closed her notebook as he sat down, as if she was worried he might see something he wasn't supposed to. Angharad Rees, he assumed.

The man had cultivated artful stubble and wore his hair short on the sides and floppy on top. He put on what appeared to be a deliberate pout as he watched Ted sit down, as if he expected a photographer to appear from nowhere. The pout half-hid an obvious smile, as if he felt sorry for the poor copper. Ted went to him first.

'Sir? DI Wood.' He held out a hand.

'This is Peter Holmes, DI Wood,' said Whitehouse, before the man could say anything. 'My political adviser.'

'Who was on the Island with you, I think,' said Ted, not taking his eyes off Holmes.

'Indeed, Inspector,' Holmes said. 'Me and Angharad went to Anglesey with the Minister. As I'm sure you don't need me to confirm.'

'No, sir. No, I don't.'

Holmes spoke with an unidentifiable accent, the kind of middle-class vaguely Cockneyfied voice that used to be a staple of daytime television. The fellow had a self-importance Ted found himself not caring for at all.

'Ms Rees,' he said, turning to the woman and nodding at her. She smiled, nervously, not saying anything. She didn't ask him how he knew her name.

He took them through the same rigmarole he'd taken all the other party guests through - how the thing had been arranged, who spoke to who, had anything out of the ordinary happened. Holmes and Rees kept quiet while the

Minister answered the questions, with clipped dismissiveness, as if he were a hostile television interviewer.

'And Brother Thomas?' he said. 'Did you know much about his reputation?'

At the word *reputation*, the energy round the table changed. Whitehouse glanced at her adviser, momentarily nonplussed. It was Holmes who answered.

'None of us knew Brother Thomas before we came to Caernarfon,' he asserted. 'As to *reputation*, perhaps you could be a little clearer.'

Holmes seemed to enjoy aping the cadences of Sir Anthony Mayfield, but it was mannered, a performance. A state school boy putting on airs, Ted's mother would have said, and Ted knew what she meant. This man had learned how to speak *proper*, and he wasn't going to have the time he'd spent learning going to waste.

Angharad Rees, however, did not look up from her papers at the mention of Brother Thomas. It occurred to Ted that she was the only one present who hailed from Caernarfon. He suspected she did know what he was talking about, and he also suspected she'd shared some of this with her powerful employers. He wondered how to word the next question without making her a scapegoat.

'Brother Thomas was formerly Thomas Jenkins,' Ted said. 'He had been a property developer in Caernarfon. After London, he became a member of the Community of St Lidwina, and an architect of its location on Anglesey. Did you not do your research, Mr Holmes?'

Holmes's nostrils flared for a moment and vivid red patches appeared on his cheek. His hands, which were sitting on the table in front of him, curled into fists. The real man was quickly exposed. Ted wondered how much skin from those fists had been left on other faces, back in the school playground. A bully, plain and simple. The skull beneath the skin.

'I researched every attendee of that party,' Holmes said.

'Really? But not the man hosting it?'

'Angharad told us something of Brother Thomas,' said the Minister. Angharad Rees seemed to sag slightly, as if anticipating the blow. 'She mentioned nothing in the matter of *reputation*.'

Ted thought that was probably a lie. They'd known about Brother Thomas, but they'd overlooked it, and it suited their purposes now to suppress that fact. What had he been offering them in return, Ted wondered?

'First time on the Island, Minister?'

'You know damn well it was my first time. Now stop playing fucking games and let me get on with my job. Do you have any more questions or us?'

'Probably lots. They'll come to me. But it's been a long day. I'll leave it for now.'

He stood up.

'Tread carefully, Inspector,' said the Minister. 'You may not be answerable to me, or my department. But you don't want to fuck with me. It would not end well for you.'

'I don't understand the implication, Minister.'

'You're baiting me, and you're baiting my adviser. I don't know what you expect to achieve by doing that, but it needs to stop. Don't mistake lack of direct accountability for lack of power, Inspector.'

Ted nodded.

'I'll take that under advisement. Minister. Mr Holmes. Ms Rees.'

He tried to soften his voice before saying the PA's name. He thought he'd probably made the evening difficult enough for her.

26

The American woman he'd encountered in reception the evening before was sitting with her laptop open on the table in front of her, on the far side of the bar to the Whitehouse cabal. There were a few other people in for a drink, all of them in suits, but she stood out, her clothes that little bit sharper, her posture that little bit more self-possessed. The essence of America. Britain had lost its old self-confidence in the face of such assurance. A dirty bomb attack will do that to you.

She had looked up as Ted came in and the thought came that she might have been waiting for him to show up. So it was relatively pleasing to surprise her as he walked back around the bar after his encounter with the Minister.

'Elaine Sullivan?' he said. She raised her eyebrows and looked mildly shocked.

'Well, I'd say who's asking, but I already know that, Detective Inspector Wood.'

She smiled, exposing perfect teeth. Of course.

'You are mysteriously well-informed,' he said, covering his own surprise.

'We appear to have been researching each other,' she replied. 'Sorry. The girl on reception. You kind of pissed her off last night, I think. She was amenable to persuasion.'

'And why did you persuade her?'

'Because you arrived late last night, in a hurry, without any luggage, and because a senior figure on the Community of St Lidwina died yesterday afternoon, and because I'm very good at putting two and two together.'

She smiled again. It was a very good smile. It was direct and unflinching and full of unafraid curiosity. He found himself smiling back.

'My apologies,' she said. 'Professional curiosity, was all. And same remark back at you, Inspector.'

'What remark?'

'*You are mysteriously well-informed.* I get that you're police. What I don't get is why you know my name.'

'I'm investigating the incident on Anglesey that you already seem to know all about. And you've been on the Island recently. You work for the *New Yorker.*'

'Ah. Right. And your nasty little Witness thing has plucked my name from some electronic memory somewhere.'

He shrugged.

'Bingo. Can I get you a drink, Miss Sullivan?'

'Call me Ellie.' She smiled. 'And are you drinking on the job?'

'No,' he replied. 'Are you?'

Despite himself, something must have passed across his face, because he caught himself watching her glance at her nearly-empty glass from which he'd caught the unmistakable odour of rum. She held his eyes for a moment, then said.

'No booze for me, Detective Inspector. I've got work to do later.'

Strangely disappointed, he ordered two Diet Cokes.

'My wife used to read the *New Yorker*,' he said, sitting down. 'Not sure I ever picked it up.'

She reached into her bag, and handed him a magazine. The cover showed a cartoon of the current American president standing in a row of identically-dressed men, singing and dancing.

'Is that a reference to that musical? The Book of Mormon?' he said.

'Sure is,' she replied. 'Remember it?'

'I was thinking about that show just yesterday. Saw it in London, years ago.'

'They've revived the old thing in New York, in honour of our ex-president.'

'Not sure how that would go down over here,' he said. 'He's a hero. Without the money he got through Congress, some say Britain would no longer exist.'

'Some people say it doesn't,' she said. 'At least, not in the form it used to.'

Ted tried to cover a sigh in a smile. He wasn't in the mood for defending his country, or at least the tattered remnants of it.

'So you're here to work?' he said.

'Yeah. I'm actually writing a longish piece on the Investiture. The Royal Family 10 years on, that sort of thing. It's my first long piece for the magazine. There's a special edition coming up: 10 Years After London, they're calling it. It's a big moment for a writer, a long piece in that magazine. And - you will forgive me for saying so - this Jenkins thing is a gift.'

'A gift?'

'Oh yeah. Thomas Jenkins, the co-founder of the

Community of St Lidwina, takes a dive off the roof of his palace four days before the Investiture? Catnip, baby.'

She waited for a response, her eyes wide behind her thick-rimmed glasses and a half-smile on her open face, exposing those immaculate teeth again. It was an elegant face, Ted thought, but a hard one too. She was clearly baiting him, and she was perfectly fine with him knowing that.

'Ms Sullivan, I....'

'Ellie, please.'

The half-smile remained. It was in actual fact an amazing smile, but her teeth were actually a little more crooked than he'd first thought. For some strange reason this was comforting.

'OK. Ellie. Where were you in the early hours of yesterday morning, say between 1 and 6?'

'Why? Is that when it happened?'

He breathed heavily in and out through his nose and rolled his eyes, somewhat theatrically, and she grinned.

'Ah, I'm ribbing you,' she said.

'I know. So where were you?'

'Well. I'd been on the Island the day before. But you knew that.'

'Yes.'

'And you *also* know that I left the Island at midday, and drove to St Asaph's.'

'Well, I didn't know that, but I'm sure somebody does. Why St Asaph's?'

'Because that's where Nicholas Briggs - or Brother Abbot, as his stage name goes - had his original Community. The one where Thomas Jenkins and he cooked up their little Island scheme. I was in St Asaph's until around 5, and then I drove back here. Had some dinner. Drink in this place. Went to bed. As your lovely little cameras will no doubt attest. I seem to have been allocated my own little pet from your roster of flying rats. So, please, officer, please believe me, I did not push that nice man off his roof.'

He wondered, then, whether she knew about Anthea Mortimer. The information had been kept pretty close, but even so the people who'd attended the party must have let other people know, so the facts were beginning to appear. And the thing they would have emphasised was the death of Brother Thomas. Strange. It seemed to him that Thomas's death was an after-effect, a consequence of the death of Anthea Mortimer. He needed to watch himself on that one. It might not have been the case.

'Did you meet Thomas Jenkins?'

'Oh yes. I interviewed him the morning I was on the Island. As you probably already know.'

'I know you were on the Island, that's all.'

'Oh, right! Because your creepy camera shit doesn't work over there.'

She frowned.

'Sorry. I know it's not *your* creepy camera shit. But you are the fuzz, right? As I believe you lot over here say?'

'Yes. I am the fuzz.'

'Right. Well, apologies. Us Yanks find this whole Witness thing creepy in the extreme.'

'If I fly into New York, my face is captured and stored and compared against all national and international databases. Instantaneously.'

'Right. But our fuzz can't lock people up on the computer's say-so. We still have a thing called due process. With a judge.'

'OK. You got me. Now. You met Brother Thomas.'

'Yeah.' She pulled out a notebook, and opened it.

'You didn't record your interview?'

'Yeah, I did. But I took notes too. My shorthand is immaculate. I'm a traditional kind of girl.'

She sipped from her Diet Coke.

'So, first thing to say is, he tried it on,' she said.

'Tried what on?'

'He tried to chat me up, to use a British phrase. Not in a serious way. But he's got an eye for the girls. Or, I should say, he did have. I'm fifty, for Christ's sake. It didn't stop Brother Thomas.'

'Were you concerned for your safety?'

She looked at him.

'Officer, I am a New Yorker who works for the *New Yorker*. No I was not concerned for my safety.'

'And did he give you much material?'

'Not really. He was a polished interviewee. He's done a lot of these things. The Abbot was harder work.'

'You interviewed him too?'

'Did him first. He was very uncomfortable. Said he found talking to the press a real burden. Wasn't about him, it was about God, etc. etc. etc. Brother Thomas was a lot more forthcoming. Not a man backwards in coming forward.'

'Did he seem distracted?'

'Jenkins? No. Not a bit. Apart from by my hotshot looks, of course.'

'And this was two days ago?'

'Yes.'

'And you didn't speak to him again afterwards.'

'Nope.'

She sipped another sip from her insipid drink.

'You don't strike me as a fan of Witness, Detective Inspector.'

'Don't I?'

'Ooh, you're a close one, fella. You and the Abbot will

get on like a house on fire. What did you do before London?'

'I was a Metropolitan Police detective sergeant.'

'I don't know what means.'

'I was a detective in London.'

'You were a Londoner,' she said.

He frowned a little.

'I *am* a Londoner.'

She put her hand across the table and placed it on his, momentarily.

'God. Sorry. Thoughtless.'

She removed her hand immediately and the air moved slightly as she did so, passing over the back of his hand like a current. She smiled. Neither said anything for a bit.

'This pause is definitely Pinteresque,' she said.

'Pinter's still a thing in America?' Ted said.

'God, yes. Not here?'

'Well, probably. I don't know. When London went, so did a lot of other stuff. Cultural memory, I suppose. A sense of…. artistic community. Pinter was a part of that.'

'You like Pinter?'

'Well, I've seen a few things. Good while ago now.'

'Unusual, I should say. Theatre-loving fuzz.'

'Takes all sorts.'

'Huh. Interesting. Mind if I steal that?'

'Steal what?'

'That thought that Britain lost more than museums and theatres. That it lost a cultural sense of itself.'

'Well, I don't know how true it is. But it's interesting to be here in Caernarfon. Here's a place that still has a sense of itself - a sense of history, deep history. And it's a long way from London - geographically, culturally, historically, even linguistically. But there's something else. It feels more solid, somehow. Like London used to feel.'

'Wow,' she said. 'The Singing Detective.'

'Well,' he said. 'Potter, not Pinter. You're quite the Anglophile, Ms Sullivan.'

'And you're quite the reader, Inspector.'

'Back to Thomas Jenkins.'

'OK.'

'Where did you meet?'

'In that house,' she said. 'That house, man. That house is weird. Ugly-beautiful. Know what I mean?'

'I do. What did you talk about?'

'The history of the Island. Its unique status under the Witness statutes. The Abbot said that had all been the work of Brother Thomas.'

'Did you have a look around the Island?'

'Yeah. They lent me one of their funny little golf carts. Went to Beaumaris, didn't get into the castle. Had a look at that Church they're building. Spoke to some Brothers and some Sisters and even had a word with the inmates. What do they call them? The Suffering. And then I came back. I didn't see anything suspicious. I just kept my eyes open and wrote some stuff down.'

He drained the last of his Diet Coke, and stood up.

'OK,' he said. 'I think I'm done.'

'I've seen the old British cop shows,' she said. 'Don't I have to come in and make a statement, or something?'

'No - we don't do that anymore.'

She frowned, looking up at him.

'Witness really fucked you detectives up, I guess.'

He raised an eyebrow.

'Fucked us up?'

'I mean, it's unusual now, right? A detective looking into a murder like this. I'm guessing the only reason you're here is that this happened on the Island. Away from Witness's prying eyes.'

'You might say that. I couldn't possibly comment.'

She laughed.

'Nicely said. Very British. Look. Can I buy *you* a drink now, Detective? Are you off the clock?'

She smiled, a practised, professional but still extraordinarily pleasant smile. He closed his own notebook, and slid it into his jacket pocket.

'Have you eaten?' he said.

They were in Skegness, he and Laura, and though it was only 9pm every restaurant in the town was closed. Laura had laughed and laughed. They found a fish-and-chip shop that was about to close and persuaded the old Chinese man who owned it to fry them up a couple of pieces of fish and some chips. They ate on a bench by the sea in the deepening gloom. Seagulls squawked and below them on the beach they could hear young people talking and giggling, as if nothing had changed at all.

'Penny for them, Detective.'

An American voice, firm and assertive, pulled him back into himself.

'Sorry. Miles away.'

Ellie shook her head slowly.

'I've seen that face before,' she said. 'It's like you're all playing a movie in your head.'

This disturbed him, because that was exactly what it was like.

There were still Chinese signs on the walls of this little restaurant, but the owner was Welsh and the menu was… well, what was it? Seventies British? Sausages and pies and beans and oven chips. They had ordered something, and the owner had gone away to cook it. Or microwave it. Probably the latter.

'You sure know how to treat a lady,' said Ellie, looking around.

'Options are somewhat limited these days,' Ted said, remembering the House of Constantine, the stench of corruption, the deliciousness of the food.

'For real,' she said. 'I'm dreaming of New York.'

And I'm dreaming of London. He didn't say anything

'Can I ask you something professionally?' she said. 'Off the record.'

He pointed to the notebook, which she had put, pointedly, on the table. She'd been scribbling shorthand notes in it since they arrived.

'What's the phrase?' he said. 'Deep background?'

'Yep!' she said. 'Deep, deep, Marianas Trench background. Who are you, as a detective, accountable to anymore?'

He sipped his drink. Another Diet Coke. Ellie had ordered the same but he'd sensed that, if the company had been different, she'd have ordered something else.

'Ultimately?' he said. 'The King. But that's always been the case. Well, it was the Queen, but now....'

'And what about Parliament?'

'What about it?'

'So I get that the King has executive power, now - like our President. Except he's not elected.'

'No. He's a King.'

'And he's advised by his Privy Council.'

'That's right.'

'Who he appoints.'

'Yep.'

'So what's the role of Parliament?'

'Same as it's always been. The legislature.'

'Like our House and Senate?'

'That's it. It meets in Birmingham.'

'Yeah, I've seen the new building. It went up fast.'

'Within the year. Thanks to your President and his funding programme.'

'It's kind of an achievement, that building,' she said. 'How they managed to copy something beautiful and make it so ugly.'

'Well, context matters, I suppose.'

'Yeah. No rivers in Birmingham.'

'Only canals.'

'And you kept the royals,' she said. 'A fact which we Americans find bizarre.'

'Well, that's what you don't understand. Continuity was the thing. Change as little as you can. It's what people wanted.'

'But, come on - you can't have something like a king in a democracy.'

'Well, what is a democracy? You have two Senators in each State, right? Regardless of the population of said state. California has the same number of Senators as North Dakota. And the Senate decides who does or doesn't sit on the Supreme Court, which ultimately decides on the legality of any legislation. So - is that democracy?'

'Jesus. Did you swallow a history book?'

'*Longman History of America.* I read it last year.'

'Thinking of emigrating?'

'No.'

'And the King. Is he, well, *respected?*'

'He's *loved.* Is that the same thing? See, it's like this. People didn't want big changes after London. They didn't want politics. They wanted leadership. All the leaders were gone. So they turned to the bloodline.'

'And what do you make of that?' she said.

'What do I make of what?'

'This... government of yours. This King. It sounds pretty medieval.'

'It does, but you're not seeing the full picture.'

'I'm not?'

'Well, what I mean is - people see the King as their Protector. That's been the biggest change, since London. They're happy to cede their privacy to him - and to his agents, and to the State - because it keeps them protected. The old state - the old combination of police and courts and security services - well, it failed, didn't it? It failed *big time*.'

'Is that how *you* see it, Detective?'

'Yes, that is how I see it, Ellie,' he said. 'The truth is, somebody walked into London with a dirty bomb. They set if off on the one day of the year when the whole Royal Family and the whole of Parliament were assembled in one place. They blew the whole thing to pieces.'

'Guy Fawkes.'

'Well, we gave him a name. Jesus, we don't even know if it was a *him* or a *her* or a *them*. No-one ever claimed responsibility. ISIS, Al-Qaeda, Hamas, Iran, Syria, Russia, some alt-right crackerjack fucker with a MAGA hat on. Who fucking knows?'

'You know what it was like?' she said. 'It's like they scared themselves. It's like they didn't expect it to work, and when it did they were shocked and scared. They blew up Westminster, for Christ's sake. It was almost.... too *big* to claim.'

'That's right. Everyone's got their own theory.'

'And yours is?'

'One of the kleptocracies. Russia, maybe. Remember the months before London? We were closing down offshore banks, changing the law, cracking down on money laundering. London was leading the way, having led the way for so long in the opposite direction. Nobody knew quite why. Nobody *voted* for that change. But it was happening. And then somebody blew London to kingdom come, and nobody talks about money laundering anymore. It doesn't seem…. *important.*'

'And now you're all watched, all the time.'

'So are you, in America. *All the time.*'

'Yeah, but we still have due process. We still have judges issuing warrants. Not software.'

'Yeah. I see that.'

They were the only two people in the restaurant, and, for the time being, it felt like they were the only two people in the whole world. The food arrived, and they ate it, and there was something astonishingly comforting about it. The conversation rambled around: they talked about New York ('I fucking love it, Ted, but I hate the men there'); football ('Yeah, we still have football, but crowds are down. People are suspicious of crowds); family ("she was called Laura, and my daughter was called Peg.').

Until finally, Ellie asked: 'And privacy, Ted? What about privacy?'

'Drones don't go into bedrooms, Ellie.'

'And toilets, I hope. Because I need one.'

She stood up and wandered off to find the toilet. He reached over for her notebook. He couldn't read any of it. She did write in shorthand, after all.

DAY THREE

27

The weather was not getting any better. The Island was obscured by mist and rain. Ted was trying to avoid the metaphorical. Driving over the Menai Strait bridge, he could only see outlines, a suggestion of settlement. The Brothers on the far end clustered under old golfing umbrellas. One had the name 'Donald Trump' on it.

Halfway over, he drove into the grey. He knew where the line was, because once again his faithful drone - or the latest in the chain of faithful drones that had been assigned to him - pulled up short, suddenly, fifty metres from the end of the bridge, just before the first tower. He watched it go in the rear view mirror, without stopping the car this time.

He hadn't stopped last night, either, when walking back to the hotel from the restaurant with Ellie. But someone had been there. He was sure of that. The irony was that, after years of being watched by the State, his sense of being watched by a living breathing human was still in operation. Ellie hadn't noticed - or if she did, she must have put it down to the same air of distraction he seemed to emanate all the time. There had been an awkward moment outside her bedroom door, and as is the way of such British moments it wobbled Schrödinger-like between two outcomes, and in her direct American way she had ended the awkwardness by holding out a hand and wishing him good night. He'd gone back to his room and opened the minibar. Kneeled down before it. Closed it again.

'We meet again, Brother Enoch,' he said as he pulled up at the Brothers' gate and wound the window down. But it was not Enoch who greeted him - the mist had obscured even that.

'We meet again, Detective Inspector Wood.'

Michael, the Scottish brother who'd accompanied Enoch to the mortuary, stood in Enoch's place. He had the look of an ex-con about him - a man who'd done time for something violent. He wouldn't be the first ex-con to turn to God. Broken nose, tough chin. Slightly hangdog, worn out expression. He could have been an armed robber. Or a copper.

Michael took Ted through the same procedures as the day before, only this time they did it in the car, to prevent the paperwork becoming drenched.

'Is it far?' Ted asked, when the niceties had been completed.

'To where?' said Brother Michael. He was stone-faced and abrupt, just the other side of rude, as he had been in the mortuary.

'To the Abbey. Or whatever the Abbot's place of resi-dence is called. Maybe he's in a beach bungalow.'

Michael did not respond well to attempted levity.

'We're not going to Penmon. The Abbot is waiting for you at the inn on the other side.'

'Bit early for a drink, isn't it?'

'That's up to you, Detective Inspector Wood.'
What do you mean by that, Brother Michael?

They drove onto the Island. Ted thought of the man in the leather jacket who'd been standing, silently, on the roadside, two days before. He wondered what had happened to him. The encounter with his first member of the Suffering seemed to have happened weeks ago, separated from the present as it was by the enormous minibar bender he'd experienced that first night. Yesterday had been hard, but today was very different. His memories of yesterday were as sharp as the air had seemed to be yesterday, as clear as yesterday's memories of the day before had been muddled. His freshly-laundered shirt, courtesy of DC Hopkyns, crackled pleasantly against his skin, under which no bugs were crawling. A day without a hangover awaited.

He drove Brother Michael onto the roundabout on the Island side of the crossing. Michael steered him to the old supermarket ahead.

'You can leave the car over there,' he said. 'Your colleague is already here.'

Ted parked the Dyson on the weed-strewn tarmac, next to the black and gleaming saloon of nondescript origin that despite being devoid of identifying features had *Security Service* written all over it. Lancaster climbed out of the car as Michael and Ted got out of the Dyson.

'Guv,' Lancaster said, in that forced way he had, as if he was playing the part of a copper.

'Lieutenant,' Ted replied, in that guarded way he had.

The three of them walked back round the roundabout to an inn. 'The Bridge Inn' said one sign, on its left-hand side. On the right, the same sign, but in Welsh, 'Tafarn y Bont'. At least, Ted assumed it said the same thing in both languages. It might have read *English pigs go home* for all he knew. The entrance looked like the French doors onto a Cotswold country garden, set between two bay windows. The place was less like a pub than a retired banker's residence, though Ted doubted there were many retired bankers left on Anglesey anymore. An odd vehicle was parked outside, a kind of freight-sized electric buggy. They went inside.

28

The Abbot, Nicholas Briggs, was sitting at a table in one of the bay windows. He stood as Ted, Lancaster and Michael came in, and bowed his head slightly to Michael, who did the same.

'This is Detective Inspector Wood, Brother Abbot,' said Michael. 'And Lieutenant Thomas Lancaster.' He pronounced it *lootenant*, like they did in the movies. Maybe Brother Michael had never encountered a lieutenant before.

Michael's words were as to an equal, but his attitude was not. The older man - bald-headed, as if he were tonsured, broken teeth, tall and imposing - was clearly the one with authority, and deference towards him oozed out of Brother Michael, despite the thug face and the way he looked at Ted like he knew where he lived and wanted you to know that.

'Thank you, Brother Michael,' said the Abbot. 'Would you please wait for us outside? The Inspector may require your services after our conversation?'

This last to Ted, as if enfolding him into his personal

authority. He said *Inspector* with a studied reverence, the way he might have said *Archbishop*. Ted pondered sending the rock-faced Scot off to fetch him a sandwich.

'That depends on how happy you are for me to drive around the Island,' he said. 'I shall want to visit the crime scene again after this.'

'Even in this weather?' said the Abbot, smiling. He seemed oddly jovial, under the circumstances.

'If we let the weather stop us, where would we be?' Ted said.

'Indeed!' said the Abbot. 'As fine a summary of the Celtic Christian Church as I've heard, if you will permit me.'

'So. I'm OK to make my own way to Plas Newydd after we speak?'

The Abbot smiled, as if he'd thought of something particularly pleasing.

'My dear Inspector. This is not a prison island. You must go wherever you see fit.'

Ted wondered how true that was.

'Well, in that case, Brother Michael need not wait on my account.'

'Splendid. Then thank you Brother Michael. I will meet you when I am done with the Inspector and Lieutenant Lancaster.'

Ted watched Michael's face as the Abbot adopted the traditional English style *lefftenant*. He made no sign of having noticed - just bowed his head to the Abbot (and only the Abbot) and left.

'Do take a seat, Inspector, and Lieutenant,' said the Abbot.

Ted looked around as they sat down. He noticed Lancaster did not do the same. He sat, almost reverentially, looking at the Abbot and then looking away, as if blinded by his holiness.

'This place is remarkably well-kept,' Ted said.

'Yes, we like to keep the pubs in good working order,' said the Abbot. 'There are few places in which the Suffering can forget themselves, but a good pub is as fine a balm to the soul as anything.'

'You let them drink?'

'By *them*, I take it you mean the Suffering, Inspector? It is not a question of *letting* them do anything. This is not a prison, or a concentration camp. It is a community. We have shops, we have pubs, there is even a cinema, though I do not think it has more than one screen operating, these days. And I imagine we are not on the main distribution circuit for such things anymore. Do people still go to the cinema, on the Mainland?'

'No. They're not thought to be safe.'

'Ah! Well, there you are then. Perhaps the Suffering are a little *more* free here than they were on the Mainland, eh? Would you like a coffee?'

'You have coffee?'

'Oh yes. There's a machine, behind the bar. Allow me.'

Ted watched as the Abbot stood up and walked behind the bar, and began fiddling with a shining metal coffee machine. Ted also stood, and sat down at the bar. The beer pumps gleamed at him. *What do you say, fella? Fancy a quick half?*

'Why can't you have just one pint?' Laura used to say. 'Put you in a pub and you lose all track of yourself. When was the last time you came out of a pub sober?'

Today. Today might be that time.

'Brother Thomas. Thomas Jenkins,' he said. 'You knew him as well as anybody, I think.'

'Ah, yes,' the Abbot said, still moving cups around

beneath the coffee machine. 'Brother Thomas and I founded the Community together, a few months after London. He suggested it, in fact. I was a member of a small contemplative community near St Asaph's, barely a dozen of us, living within the Celtic Christian tradition. Thomas was staying with us at the time.'

'He'd been visiting for a while before that, though.'

The Abbot looked at Ted, as if surprised at what he already knew.

'Yes. He'd been coming for about a year, as I recall it. Thomas was a deeply spiritual man, Inspector, but he had fallen out of the habit of religious observation. It is not uncommon.'

'But why did he come to you? Why go all the way to St Asaph's?'

'He felt we offered something the established Church at that time did not. And then London shook him deeply. As it shook all of us. But Thomas felt a spiritual response was needed. And then there was the matter of the Suffering. There you are.'

The Abbot placed a cup of coffee in front of him, and a second in front of Lancaster.

'I believe we used to call that an *americano*,' the Abbot said. 'Is that right?'

'It smells magnificent,' Ted said, because it did. It smelled like no coffee he had had in years.

'Would you like some milk?'

'No, thank you.'

He lifted the cup and sipped. The temperature was perfect, the taste exquisite.

'My… word,' he said, stepping clumsily around a blasphemy. If the hotel coffee had been an improvement on the usual, this was like another category of drink altogether. He'd have taken it for granted, before London, when coffee like this was available in tedious quantities. Now it tasted like sipping nirvana.

'Is it satisfactory?' said the Abbot, anxiously.

'It's perfect,' Ted said.

'Well, good. Yes. We were talking of Thomas. Well, I don't know if you remember much about the months immediately following London, but they were a bad time.'

He remembered waking up to an empty house, and then the world falling apart. *Yes, Brother Abbot, the months that followed were a bad time.*

'We were somewhat protected from it, in our little St Asaph's community,' said the Abbot. 'But after a few days, people began appearing at our door. Sick people. Sad people. Desperate people. They were drawn to us, like bees to a flower bed. I believe some churches experienced…. bad things. There were many who saw the hand of God in what happened, and believed he was punishing us. But those who came to us didn't think that. They sought comfort in God, and in Jesus.'

Ted found himself staring into the coffee. Its black surface was like a slick mirror within a cold white circle.

'The coffee machine's broken again,' Laura had said. 'This is the worst thing that has ever happened to me.'

The worst thing.

He pulled himself out, looked up to see the Abbot and Lancaster watching him. The Abbot's face was warm but not sympathetic, and Ted marvelled at the man's empathy, because if there had been anything resembling pity in that face, then… well. He didn't know. Something. Lancaster just looked puzzled.

'And Thomas thought he could, what, cure them? The Suffering?' Ted said, after a moment.

'Well, for a while we thought it was just… shock, I suppose. Some anger, as well. A lot of despair. But then, there was something else. *Explosion sickness*, people began to call it. I remember the first time I heard that phrase. It was a woman from Denbigh who came to St Asaph's with her husband. The man was virtually silent, and he was terribly thin. *He's got the explosion sickness*, she said to me. I asked her what on earth she meant, and she looked at me as if I was stupid. *The explosion sickness! He's got it! From London.'*

The Abbot sighed.

'But you probably remember how people came to think of it like that,' he said.

'There were a lot of theories flying around,' Ted said. 'People talking about Hiroshima.'

'So I understand,' said the Abbot. 'There was that Japanese word.'

'Hibakusha.'

'That's the one,' the Abbot said. 'I believe you can buy fashionable T-shirts saying that in Paris, these days. The world moves on. But the truth of it was, there were more and more people saying they had it, this *explosion sickness*. And after a while people started appearing who had made their way from.... well, from the south-east, shall we say. And some of those people really *were* ill. It was, as I say, a bad time. And so Thomas suggested moving our Community from St Asaph's to here. To the Island. And then a Miracle happened.'

'A Miracle?' Ted said.

'Ah, I am being facetious, I fear. But it felt like a miracle. Thomas put his idea to the King.'

'How did he do that?'

'Well, Thomas knew people. A great many people. It was his great skill, you know - the power of connection. He told somebody about our idea, who told somebody, and before we knew how any of this was happening, the King was standing before the new Parliament announcing our new Community, where those suffering from the sickness would be cured or allowed to die in peace, away from the eyes of the world.'

Ted remembered the speech. *The eyes of the world* had featured heavily, because at the same time an early version of Witness was being rolled out.

'It was *all* Thomas's idea?' he said. 'This place?'

'Well, yes, in the first instance. As the planning went on, others became involved, of course. But Thomas was the inspiration. He even suggested our patron saint.'

'Saint Lidwina.'

'Yes. Do you know of her?'

'No. I admit to never having heard of her.'

'And you, Lieutenant Lancaster?' said the Abbot, turning to the younger man, drawing him into the circle. 'Do you know of her?'

'I know… a little,' said Lancaster, in the small voice of the boy at the back of the class called on by the teacher he adores. 'She lived in Holland at the end of the 14th century. She fell when ice skating, as a teenager. She never recovered. Accounts tell of her shedding parts of her body, and of eating nothing but river water flavoured with sea salt. She was canonised by Leo XIII. She is the patron saint of the chronically ill.'

'And of ice skaters,' the Abbot said. 'The Catholic Church always did have a curious sense of humour. Well done, Lancaster. A man of God, I think.'

Lancaster bowed his head, slightly, and Ted thought of the way the Abbot and Brother Michael had bowed to each other.

'Abbot, it is my job to find out what happened to Brother Thomas,' he said, abruptly. 'And what happened to Anthea Mortimer.'

'Indeed, I know this,' said the Abbot. 'But it is also *my*

job. You understand, I trust, the unique *legal* status of our Community?'

'I know something of it. But I hope I can still rely on your cooperation.'

'Up to a point, Inspector. Up to a point. It will come down to this, I think. First, we must ascertain what actually happened.

'You mean if Brother Thomas was murdered, or killed himself.'

The Abbot bowed his head.

'My days,' he said, quietly. 'The words are so simple, but the things they describe are beyond despair. Yes. Murder or suicide. Either is unthinkable to me. But are there any real reasons why one should consider this a *murder*, Detective? As I understand it, the initial indications point to…. point the other way.'

Ah yes, Abbot. They do indeed point the other way. But he was here, wasn't he? He had been summoned here by the Powers That Be. And the Abbot, an intelligent man, must wonder why that should be, as Ted himself was wondering. For once, Why Am I Here was not a religious question.

And anyway - suicide was only half the story.

'Anthea Mortimer was killed,' said Ted. 'Of that there is no doubt.'

'Oh I do understand,' said the Abbot.

The Abbot's face had gone cold and still.

'And Brother Thomas was a man of such importance, you see,' said Ted.

The Abbot smiled now, but his eyes were still cold.

'If it transpires that Brother Thomas was killed, as well as the poor woman,' said the Abbot, and his voice was now as cold as his eyes, 'and he was killed by someone *outside* the Community, then justice will be served by the forces you represent. But if the killer is from *inside* the Community, then the authority I represent will be the presiding judge and jury.'

'The authority you represent?'

'I think you understand my meaning, Detective.'

Ted sipped the last of my coffee.

'Benefit of clergy, is it?' Ted said.

'If you like. The phrase is no longer meaningful. But we are allowed to look after our own.'

'And what, Abbot, will transpire if Brother Thomas killed Anthea Mortimer and then killed himself?'

The Abbot did not reply. Did not even blink.

'I mean, killed himself because of remorse. I assume he believed in the hereafter.'

'Is that a question, Inspector?'

'Did Thomas worry about his enemies?'

'His enemies?' said the Abbot.

'He must have ruffled some feathers. You both did.'

'What do you mean?'

'Taking over the Island. People must have lost their homes, their farms.'

'A misconception,' said the Abbot. 'But a common one. No-one on the Island was forced to leave. But if they wanted to, they were offered very generous terms. Those terms are still available, if any of the former property owners wish to move on.'

'At a time when money is short.'

'Yes, of course. But you must remember, Inspector - the NHS collapsed. We picked up a lot of the pieces. The compensation bill was large, of course, but we reached an accommodation. There are still a good many people living on the Island who are not of the Community.'

'And all this was negotiated by Brother Thomas?'

'Thomas was a.... worldly man, Inspector. He knew how these things worked.'

'And what about his wife?'

The Abbot looked away.

'Are you married, Inspector?'

'I was.'

'You lost her?'

'Yes.'

Why was he telling the Abbot this? How did the man get people to speak so loosely? Ted felt unaccountably angry - with himself, and with the Abbot.

'Then you understand the pain that must have been involved when Thomas left one home to build another.'

'He left her behind.'

'He had his Calling.'

'He swapped his wife for his God.'

The Abbot turned his face back to face Ted.

'That is not how I would describe the transaction, Inspector.'

'It's how she describes it.'

The Abbot actually looked terribly sad at that.

'You have spoken to Lucy, then?'

'I have.'

'I wish…. well, I wish she could have felt the same way as Thomas. That she could have joined us here in the Community.'

'She doesn't strike me as a celibate.'

The Abbot ignored that.

'And Plas Newydd?' Ted said.

'What of it?'

'Brother Thomas lived there alone.'

'He did.'

'The house is enormous. How big is your house, Abbot?'

'Somewhat smaller.'

This with a smile.

'You don't think it looks odd, a monk in a palace?'

The Abbot laughed.

'It is by no means a *palace*, detective. I don't see what you are driving at. *Someone* has to live there. Almost half the houses on the Island are empty. Our population declines by the year. Why should Plas Newydd not be held by someone who appreciated it? And cared for it?'

'It caused no jealousy?'

'Are you suggesting that someone killed Brother Thomas because of his *house*?'

'Why not?'

'Well, why not, I suppose. But why now? He has been in that house for years.'

'So, you can imagine no reason for Brother Thomas being killed?'

'If you mean, do I know of anyone who might have killed him then, no, Inspector. I do not.'

It was not, Ted noted, quite what he had asked.

'And are you worried for your safety?'

The Abbot looked confused.

'You mean - am I worried that someone might kill me too?'

'Yes. That is what I mean.'

'But I simply cannot imagine why anyone would want to do that.'

'Precisely. Just as you cannot imagine why anyone would kill Brother Thomas.'

The Abbot made a rueful face.

'I take your point,' he said. 'In any case, men like me are somewhat insured against such anxieties. A better place awaits, etc.'

'And what about his parties?'

'Parties?'

'Brother Thomas held parties. People came to his

house from the Mainland. By boat. There was a party there the night he and Anthea died.'

The Abbot laughed, the sound as rich as his coffee.

'Hardly *parties*, Inspector. Thomas offered a safe space for discussion and debate. The Church has played a similar role down the centuries. People came to him as a conciliator, a counsellor. It has always been the way of clerics to facilitate discussions.'

'Discussions held outside Witness.'

'Well, yes. But that might have helped people to be open. What was the old phrase? The Chatham House Rule?'

'So, you did not participate in these *discussions*?'

'Oh, I did, of course. When I was asked to.'

'You knew when he was holding them?'

'I did not police them,' said the Abbot. 'If you will forgive the term.'

The Abbot came out from behind the bar.

'And now, I'm afraid I must be about my day, Inspector. It is a busy time. The new Prince is expected to visit us after the Investiture. My days are full with making ready.'

'I will need to see the all your records of all those coming onto the Island, and all those leaving, for the 48 hours before the murder. To check they align with ours.'

'That will be fine, Inspector,' said the Abbot. 'But no more than 48 hours. That would be unreasonable.'

He smiled, as if they were haggling over the price of a rug.

'Witness will give me the records going back three years,' said Ted.

'Well, then, *our* records will no doubt disappoint. But I would ask something in return.'

'What is that?'

'The Brother Thomas's body be returned to us for

burial on the Island in line with our customs and observances.'

'That is not my decision, Abbot.'

'You mean - it is the decision of his wife.'

'They never divorced. She is legally his next of kin.

'Ah, well, *legally*, you are of course correct. Then I must ask a favour. Will you speak to her?'

Is this how it happened? Is this how the Church got its fingers into you? By asking for a favour, or by returning a favour, or by promising sanctuary from evil in return for a favour? They were like the Mafia.

But he needed to speak to Lucy Jenkins anyway. What harm could it do?

29

At morning prayers, Brother Patrick seemed close to tears again. Several of the novice Sisters, and even one or two of the Brothers, were crying again. Moira, drawn along by the emotional waves and, in any case, wanting to be part of the drama, sniffed mournfully alongside Jenny. But all Jenny could think about was the bike.

'When a great man is taken from us, we are of course left somewhat empty,' said Patrick. 'And when that great man is also a friend, the space within us is even deeper and darker. But God brings light into every darkness, and God lights this one as well. For Brother Thomas was a man of God, and he has been taken up into the Godhead. He was a friend of the soul - and, as Pelagius teaches us, we each need one special friend of the soul. We must open our souls completely to these friends, hiding nothing and revealing everything. And we must allow this friend to judge what he sees. And Brother Thomas still sees us, brothers and sisters. He still sees our souls.'

At breakfast after the service, she tried pondering

Patrick's words. Did Brother Thomas see her? And what did that mean? Did he see her shyness, her affections, her questioning uncertainty - and most of all, did he see her rage? It was always there, the snake in the garden. And however hard she stamped on it, the rage was still there.

Perhaps that was why her mind kept going back to bike - unlocked, down the street behind the old Beaumaris gaol which held the dormitory for the novice Brothers and Sisters.

She knew a little about what had happened at Plas Newydd - the stuff they'd told the novices, of course, but also the gossip in the gaol. She had told no one what had happened on the roof of Plas Newydd, because to tell people would be to invite conversation about cigarettes and she wanted no part of that. She knew she was already on shaky ground with the senior Brothers of the Community (and they were all Brothers, the senior ones, not a woman among them - why should that be?). And she did not want to be thrown off the Island, perhaps to be dragged back to the orphanage in Salford. Sweat and misery and tears, rows of children and teenagers on camp beds inside an enormous space which someone had told her had once been a television studio. That had been Salford. And Mary, of course. Mary Dudley Edwards. The girl she had hurt.

It had been Mary who had opened the way to her to come here. The Abbot had told her that, soon after she arrived. 'There were those who considered you…. well, they thought you might be a divisive influence,' he had said. She had felt like a hole had opened inside her, and she stood at the edge of it, waiting to fall. 'But Mary Dudley Edwards convinced us.'

'Mary?' she had said.

'Yes, Sister. Mary explained to us the circumstances of

the…. incident. And what she told us did you great credit. And thus we accepted you.'

'And Mary? What happened to her?

The Abbot smiled, a sad smile, full of bitter experience.

'Mary was in a difficult place, Sister. She ended her own Suffering there soon after you left the orphanage.'

A great wave of sadness had passed through Jenny then, and it accompanied a sudden awareness. Of the connections between herself and others. Of the world outside, passing through tragedy and dilemma and resolution. Of an adult world, where adults spoke to each other of children like Jenny and Mary and the rest, of the sharing of information, news, gossip. She saw, then, that the Island was cut off from the Mainland only by water, but it was joined by everything else. She had gripped her hands, tightly, and had taken control of herself once again.

The encounter with the woman on the roof had been of a piece with that - a filament tying her back to the Mainland. Talking to the young woman on the roof had given Jenny her first glimpse, in months, of what living over there might be like. So when she heard that Brother Thomas had died, that was one thing. But when the rumours started of another death - the death of a young woman - well, that was something else.

'They say,' Moira had whispered, the night before today, 'that she was naked on the bed. And *tied up*.'

One of the other Sisters had gasped. Jenny had felt her face grow hot and red, as if the old anger was bubbling up again. She did not wish to hurt Moira, but she did not like the way the girl was talking.

'Brother Thomas was a great man,' the Abbot had said to them, the morning before. 'A very great man. You know the man he was and so does everyone on this Island. His death is a mystery, and an abomination, but somewhere within this disgusting episode, God's will is to be found. We just have to wait for it to express itself. And while we wait, we will cooperate with the Mainland authorities in their own investigation. And in the meantime - please, stay away from Plas Newydd.'

She had been thinking about that injunction to stay away, and about the bike down the side street, for over 24 hours now.

She found herself near the back entrance of the Gaol. On the other side of the wall was the bike. So she leaned on the wall, closed her eyes, and whispered to herself a prayer, her favourite prayer, the one that always brought comfort.

God to enfold me,
God to surround me,
God in my speaking,
God in my thinking.

God in my sleeping,
God in my waking,
God in my watching,
God in my hoping.

God in my life,
God in my lips,
God in my soul,
God in my heart.

God in my sufficing,
God in my slumber,
God in mine ever-living soul,
God in mine eternity.

She opened her eyes again. But still all she could see was the bike, and her riding it, out through the streets of Beaumaris and down to Plas Newydd.

And so she opened the little gate, and left.

30

Ted stood beside Plas Newydd, the Strait behind him, looking up at the roof. He wondered how often Thomas Jenkins had stood up there looking across the Strait, looking at the house he had left behind, and the woman inside it to whom he'd done the same.

He'd ordered that the tent and the tape be taken down on the island side of the house, where Brother Thomas's body was found. There was nothing more to be found. The uniforms did as he asked, but the silence with which he was greeted told its own story about what they thought of him, and of this entire situation. It wasn't easy, being plod these days. You were a glorified water-carrier, sent by algorithms to clean up messes made by others.

He turned around and faced the Strait, his back to the house. He looked across and saw the boat-house from which the guests at Plas Newydd had departed for their little parties. It was barely visible, such was the drizzle and mist, but it was there.

He walked down to the water's edge. A stone balustrade ran the entire width of the house, punctuated by those strange cannons Peg had loved, which he assumed were put there for decorative reasons. This wasn't Caernarfon Castle, the military base of a warrior king. It was a posh house with aspirations. The tide was low, and he could see an old abandoned jetty which had been submerged by the tide when he'd come here before, with Laura and Peg. But over to his right, there was a proper dock, with a breakwater and a quayside. He walked down to it. He noted the two gleaming mooring bollards, and wondered whether the shine on them meant they'd been recently and regularly used. He turned and walked back up to the house.

In the daylight, the rooms and halls were magnificent, and magnificently clean. He found himself wondering who cleaned the place - surely not Brother Thomas Jenkins, God-on-earth, Chief Poobah Of the King's Laying-on-of-Hands. The place made him suddenly angry, its splendour unjustified and vaguely obscene.

A woman's shout came from somewhere, and Ted walked through a few corridors and rooms to find its source: one of the uniforms standing at an open door that led onto a little servants' hallway between the main living rooms, one of those secret places you didn't get to see on house tours, in the days when they still did house tours.

'We've found something, guv,' the uniform said. Ted found himself appreciating the *guv*. She was young, with a Liverpool accent. A recent recruit, post-London. Ted wondered what she thought about her job, her role, her place in society, and then he told himself to stop his bloody mind wandering.

She led him down a tiny staircase, into the basement. A big door hung open, its lock mechanism crushed, presumably by a uniform wielding the Enforcer, the device they used to smash in doors. A light was on inside, a very bright one.

The first thing he saw when he went in were the black windows of computer screens, lining a workbench that ran along one side of the vaulted room. Around these screens was a confused spaghetti of cabling, yanked out of whatever sockets might have been accommodating them. Then there were the remnants of several keyboards, random boxes of letters thrown up into the air and brought down again in new combinations.

'Bloody hell,' he said. Priestley, who was sitting at the workbench and trying to make sense of the cabling, snorted derisively.

'It's a bloody hell for me, all right,' she said. 'I'm not very good with tech.'

'Can you make sense of it?' Ted said.

'No,' she said. 'Or at least, not right away. You'd need an IT or audiovisual guy to sort this little lot out. But it's behind a locked door in the basement. I'd say that pretty much guarantees that what was here was plugged into the rest of the house in some way.'

'Any sign of stuff being removed?'

'Lots of signs. None of them definitive. If you're wanting a tell-tale square patch on the floor, I'm afraid I can't help you.'

'Just screens and keyboards,' he said. 'No computers or hard drives.'

'Yeah,' said Priestley. 'I thought that too. Looks like whoever did this took at least that stuff away.'

'So, what are we thinking? One computer with a hard drive, or several?'

She shrugged.

'Any resource in your part of the forest to have this looked at?' he said.

'Not anymore,' she says. 'I'd have been calling in the forensic technology bods in the old days. They've all been sucked up into Witness. I'll test for fingerprints and all that good stuff, but a full shakedown of a place this size is just impossible.'

'OK.'

He thought for a moment.

'What led you down here?'

Priestley grinned.

'Bloody good question. Come with me.'

He followed her out of the basement, telling the uniform to secure the room as far as was possible. Some forensic evidence might be found. Priestley went out into the main rooms of the house, and then up onto the first floor. She went into one of the bedrooms.

'So, I've been under a lot of beds this morning,' she said.

'Any particular reason why?'

'I've been inspecting the dust.'

Ted raised his eyebrows.

'I don't know if you're joking or not.'

'Not. This is the biggest bedroom. Nice isn't it?'

He looked around. It was nice. A huge four-poster. A red leather armchair. Thick curtains. A view of the Strait.

'This was the bedroom Anthea Mortimer was found in.'

'Correct. Through there's an ensuite bathroom,' said Priestley. 'Very modern. Very unmonkish. I'd say it was installed in the last few years.'

'You mean, since the Community was formed?'

'Yes, I mean since the Community was formed. And the room is immaculate. No dust under the bed. Now, look up.'

Ted did so. The ceiling - smooth, white, decorated with

an ornate cornice, its surface interrupted only by a light fitting and a smoke alarm - looked back down at him.

'It's a ceiling,' he said.

'Yes, it's a ceiling. Well done, Inspector Morse. Now, come with me.'

Priestley walked out of the bedroom and onto the landing. She passed two open doors and entered a third. Ted followed her.

It was another bedroom. In some ways, it was even nicer than the first one. An old fireplace dominated one wall, above which stood a picture of a fat man in Turkish costume holding a rifle. The bed was another four-poster, seemingly identical to the one in the first room.

'No ensuite in here,' said Priestley. 'And there's dust under the bed.'

'Who was in here?'

'Sir Anthony.'

'Ah. He swapped with Anthea.'

'Really? How interesting.'

'Why interesting?'

'Look at the ceiling.'

Ted looked. This ceiling was old and cracked - still perfectly impressive, but very different. The cornice looked older, too - modelled on the same design, but put here in another era.

'There's eight bedrooms on this floor, by my count,' said Priestley. 'Four of them are modernised. Four of them aren't. Two of them have the same beds - this one, and the first one I took you into. Now. Look at the top of the bed in here.'

Ted looked.

'Now, come with me into the first bedroom.'

Ted followed her.

'Look again - at the bed, and the ceiling.'

Ted look, and he saw straightaway.

'The bed post is closer to the ceiling.'

'Bingo. Which means either the bed has been raised up, or.....'

'Or that's a false ceiling.'

Priestley nodded ceremoniously.

'So why would there be a false ceiling?' he said.

'Well, it's not entirely decorative, is it?' she says. 'They could have laid a piece of plasterboard over that whole surface, and it wouldn't have caused as big a drop as that. I reckon there's wiring up there.'

'Wiring? What kind of wiring?'

'These are excellent questions, Inspector, to which I don't yet have answers.'

Priestley's eyes twinkled. The morning's discoveries had excited her, it was clear. How old was she? Mid-fifties? Maybe even 60. Before London, she'd have been contemplating retirement by now. She looked up at the ceiling again. She pondered.

'There are smoke alarms in all the rooms,' she said. 'What's the betting they're not really smoke alarms?'

She looked at him.

'OK, me and these coppers are going to start making a bit of a mess up there, I think. But I don't think it'll tell us too much. This house is, I'll put a bet on it, networked. There'll be cabling running up there, and that cabling will run down to the basement. Cabling connected to what, I wonder? Cameras, perhaps? And if there were cameras, they will have been able to see what was happening in those four bedrooms, and they will have been able to store it down there. Otherwise, why is all this stuff here at all?'

Why indeed?

'And if we get hold of the recording...' she said.

'We'll find out what happened that night,' he replied.

'Well, some of what happened, I suppose,' Priestley said. 'I didn't find any cameras or anything on the roof.'

'OK. OK. Good work, Priestley.'

She made a pretend bow with her head and held her hands together, as if they had just completed a yoga class. Ted left her, wondering to himself who *they* were.

31

He went out onto the roof, up the little stairs and through the door they'd been shown two days before. He needed to think.

The weather was coming in - but then, the weather always seemed to be coming in. A curtain of rain hung over Snowdon and seemed to grow thicker and darker while he watched, though beams of sunshine still kissed the water of the Strait below him. There were no views like this in London, or anywhere in the south of England. This was a Wagner view, demanding knights and bards and the thrumming of approaching hooves. He could do it scant justice.

The problem was: who to trust?

He badly needed to get full Witness access. He needed to track down the man (or men) who had been following him in Caernarfon. He needed to see who was phoning Diane James and Mair Collier.

But if he went onto Witness - or even into the main building at Parc Menai - he would be tracked. His interest in such matters would be instantly logged. He realised how much the stranger in the dark in Caernarfon had affected him. Who did he work for? Were they tracking his activity on Witness? He realised, for the first time, what freedom from Witness might mean, standing here on this roof, unaccompanied by a drone, unwatched and unheeded.

A boat pulled away from Lucy Jenkins's boathouse - and with it, a drone, hanging in the air behind it. But as the boat reached the middle of the Strait, the drone froze, hovering in the air above the waters. But unlike Ted's drone - he thought of it as a possession, now, even though it wasn't a single drone, just a series of identical ones - this one didn't turn around and head back to the Mainland. It stayed where it was, as if waiting for something, hovering over the water like a gull eyeing a fish.

He watched the boat pull into the little harbour he had been standing at barely an hour before, saw a man jump off and tie a rope to the bollard he had been looking at. And then a woman stepped off the boat and onto the quayside.

'Bloody hell,' Ted muttered, and began to make his way down to meet her.

Angela Leybourne was standing on the top terrace of Plas Newydd, looking up at the house as Ted emerged to greet her. The wind, which had been picking up, whipped her hair and her thick dark coat, and she stood with one hand against her head, keeping her hair out of her eyes.

'You should have seen the place in party mode,' she said as Ted approached.

'Party mode?' he said.

'At night time, with all the lights on, people wandering around with drinks in their hands, sharing secrets they probably shouldn't have been shari. It was like something Gatsby would have laid on.'

'Shall we go inside?'

'No, I don't think so. Let's walk, Ted.'

She began to walk around the house, Ted following.

'You have your car here?'

'Yes, it's up in the car park.'

'Right. Never been to the car park. Show me the car park.'

Her Oxbridge voice was almost regal. *The Duchess*, she was known as in the corridors of the Manchester Police Service, although Ted had never found anything noble or conceited about her, apart from the cut-glass vowels and the immaculate couture, the source of which was a perennial mystery to the rank and file. Her private life was obscure. He'd looked her up on Witness, like any interested employee might, but it had not been forthcoming. She didn't live with anyone, she never seemed to meet with anyone, she must have lived only for her work.

'I wanted us to talk unobserved,' she said, as they walked.

Ted looked out to the Strait. The drone still hung there. It was big, presumably powerful enough to be able to see the two of them. So how *unobserved* did she mean? She caught him looking.

'Impossible to avoid it being noticed that we're meeting, of course.'

'Of course,' he said.

'But then there's always the chance that one is being listened to, as well as being watched. At least this place puts paid to that. Well, to a greater extent.'

Ted wondered what she meant by that.

'You've probably been wondering how to check on the men who were following you. But you can't look on Witness without alerting whoever it was that you were interested.'

She did this a lot, he found. Blindsided you with what

she knew, and what she inferred. It was bloody annoying, frankly.

'I had a look for you, though,' she said.

'You were watching me?'

'Of course I bloody was, Ted. I get a report on the hour as to your movements and interactions. What did you think, that I'd just leave you to get on with it, and then have you report back? You've got your own drone chain, and a small team of clever young people watching your every move.'

She grinned as she looked at him.

'I'd be careful around that American woman, by the way. She's very good at her job, by all accounts. So keep it in your trousers, there's a good boy.'

'I wouldn't know what to do with it even if I could find it.'

'Hmmm. Well.'

She breathed in through her nose. The salt of the sea air did merge rather delightfully with the wet green air of the trees.

'The man who followed you in Caernarfon works for the competition. So does the woman who called your two shopgirls just prior to your visit.'

'Don't they have better things to do?'

'Hmm. Interesting reaction, Ted. I thought you'd be more bothered.'

He was bothered, of course, but didn't want Leybourne to know that.

'Is Lancaster with the other lot as well?'

'What?' She glared at him now. 'Of course not. I'm not an idiot, Ted. I wouldn't have put a double agent in your team.'

'Double agent? Aren't we all on the same side?'

She laughed, though it sounded more like a growl.

'Good one. But I came to say: you're right to be cautious about using Witness. The other lot are watching you. And those two little incidents are meant to let you know they're watching. I even rather resent having to come here to tell you, as it's all part of their silly little game, but there we are.'

'But why?'

'Because they can. Because it's not their investigation. Because they're miffed about the whole bloody affair.'

'Miffed?'

'Annoyed. Pissed off. Irritated. Look, their own bloody minister was here on the night in question - and you barging in on them in the hotel bar wasn't appreciated, by the way - and they can't get a handle on it. They don't know who you are or why we sent you. They can't see what happened on Witness. They're just flexing their muscles, is all. Letting us know they're watching.'

'It seems pretty childish.'

'Does it? I don't know. I'd probably be doing the same, if the boot was on the other foot.'

'And is it, often?'

'The boot on the other foot? Often enough.'

They reached the car park. She smirked when she saw his car.

'Still driving that ridiculous thing, Ted? How marvellous. You know you could always put in for a smart new one? Something black and German and powerful.'

'Like Lancaster's, you mean?'

'If you like. He really is on our side you know, Ted.'

'I'll take your word for it.'

'Hello. Who's this?'

Ted's heart stopped for a moment. It looked like Peg waiting there by his car.

'Made a friend, did we, Ted? Looks like she has something she wants to say to you, anyway.'

Angela turned back to face the house.

'Ugly bloody thing from this side, isn't it? Yet so beautiful from the waterside. Probably a metaphor in there, somewhere. Harvey Dent. Right?'

Ted had no idea what she was talking about, and was barely listening to her. The young Sister standing by his car was alone, and looked anxious. Had something happened to her? Was she in danger? He barely heard Angela Leybourne say goodbye.

32

Peg had come home furious. They had struggled not to laugh, when they looked at each other, so theatrical was her rage. She had brought news from school of her whole class being put into detention. A supply teacher, a loss of control, a feisty bunch of kids with a hypersensitivity to injustice. Her eyes were blazing with the wrongness of it all. This must have been soon after they moved from Streatham to St Albans, because back then *everything* was blamed on that move.

'This would *not* have happened in London!' Peg had yelled, slamming her satchel down onto the breakfast bar, before spinning around to exit. Her new trainers - the trainers they'd bought for her to go to school in, the trainers she'd not have been allowed in Streatham, where the uniform policy was draconian and often decried - her trainers squeaked on the solid wooden floor they'd had put in, and as she marched away he and Laura looked at each other and nearly, so very very nearly, laughed out loud.

The Sister waiting by his car was wearing trainers. There was something defiant about those trainers. They peeked out from beneath the hem of her thick brown robe. They looked almost brand new, like they would squeak on a wooden floor. Her hair was long and dark brown and ill-behaved, parted in the middle, and she managed to look both quarrelsome and self-conscious all at the same time. There was anxiety there, yes, but there was also anger and suspicion. This was a girl who'd seen things she shouldn't have seen.

'Hello,' Ted said. 'Are you OK?'

'Are you a policeman?' she said. She had a broad Birmingham accent, which was astonishingly endearing.

'Yes. I'm Detective Inspector Wood. And who are you?'

'Sister Jennifer. Jenny.' She paused. 'Jenny Spencer.'

'Nice to meet you, Sister Jenny.'

'Are you in charge?'

'Of the investigation? Yes, I am.'

'Oh. Good. I was… hoping to run into you.'

There was something funny about the form of words, and he found himself smiling. Thankfully, she smiled back.

'Is there something you want to tell me, Sister Jenny?'

'Who was that woman?'

'She was my boss.'

'Why was she here?'

'To check I'm doing a good job.' He shrugged. 'It's what bosses do.'

She frowned, but in an interested way. Then she walked to the edge of the car park, and looked down towards the dark shape of Plas Newydd. He followed her over.

'I was working here. The other night. The night of the party.'

'OK.'

'And I was on the roof. When the party was nearly over.'

'Why were you on the roof?'

She closed up for a moment. He backed off.

'That's OK. It doesn't matter why you were on the roof.'

'She came up as well. The woman. The one who….'

'Anthea Mortimer?'

'Yeah. She said her name was Anthea.'

'You spoke to her?'

'Yeah. She was nice, actually. Seemed a bit sad.'

'What did she say to make you think that?'

'A few things. She talked about the drones. The ones you have on the Mainland. She said it was weird, the way we didn't have them here.'

She stopped, as if replaying the conversation in her head.

'She said you could get away with anything if no one was watching.'

'She said that? Exactly that?'

'Well, maybe not exactly. But near enough.'

'What time was this, Sister Jennifer?'

'I'd finished tidying up. So around half past eleven, I'd say.'

She stopped again. She had come all the way from wherever she'd been to find him here. It hadn't been to tell him that. But he kept his mouth shut, and waited.

'She was talking to herself. Before she saw me. She was talking to herself.'

'Could you hear what she said?'

'Yeah. I could. It was a bad word. The same bad word, over and over.'

'OK. Can you tell me the word? It's OK, I won't be angry.'

She glanced at him, suddenly amused.

'I'm not worried about swearing. We all swear.'

'OK. Sorry.'

Another long pause. Then she began talking again.

'Her hands were shaking. When she lit her cigarette. They were shaking and it wasn't *that* cold, and she had a coat on. And all the time she was doing it - lighting her cigarette, then smoking it - she was saying the same word, over and over.'

He waited.

'Bastard.'

33

The boatyard was halfway between Parc Menai and Caernarfon, between the main road and the sea. There was a stretch of what Laura would have called 'sailing stuff' strung out along the shore of the Strait, most of it either abandoned or at best neglected. One marina which must have once housed prosperous-looking pleasure yachts was now emptily desperate.

The Britannia boatyard was different though - it seemed almost spruce. Ted pulled his car up before the gates. The day was getting on, and the drizzle was finally letting up. The wind had dropped. It was almost calm, and the boats that were moored here were still. Ted could begin to believe that people actually climbed into the floating death traps for fun.

He remembered Laura and Peg reclining on the webbing of a catamaran, while the instructor held the thing in place. He had been removing his lifejacket and shaking his head, and then he was watching the two of them pull away, the sail stiffening in the wind, the bored instructor already moving onto the next boat, and there went all he cared for in the world, protected from the depths by flimsy looking fibreglass and the arcane workings of the wind.

He remembered Sister Jenny clambering on to the ancient looking bike which she refused to say was 'hers' and which made her blush furiously when he asked about it. She had seemed in a hurry to get it back. He had watched her wobble away and, *oh my days*, he'd remembered his daughter sailing out across the ocean deep.

He pressed a button on a post beside the marina's locked gate. Nothing happened. So he pressed again.

A man came out of a portakabin at the back of the yard. He stood on the steps for a moment, then shouted at Ted.

'What do you want?'

'Emyr Phillips?' said Ted.

'Who wants to know?'

'Police, Mr Phillips,' said Ted. 'I'd like a word about the *Dulcibella*. And Lucy Jenkins. And her husband.'

The man stood still for a moment, deliberately defiant, then walked over, fishing a set of keys out of his pocket. He looked at Ted through the wire fence while he unlocked the gate's padlock. He was a tall, fierce-looking fellow, about Ted's age, but with thick black hair that hung down below his collar. He was wearing faded jeans and an ancient hoodie bearing the legend *Weyland-Yutani: Building Better Worlds*. He opened the gate.

'You'd better come into the office.'

The portakabin was neat and well-maintained, just like the yard outside. An ancient-looking computer sat on the deck, next to a more recent state-issued screen. Phillips sat down behind the desk. He did not offer Ted a seat.

'What's this about?' he said. His accent was richly

Welsh, and he spoke slowly and deliberately. He appeared to be a careful man.

'As I said, the *Dulcibella*,' said Ted.

'Aye. What about her?'

'I understand that you keep her.'

'I do.'

'And pilot her as well, when asked.'

'Uh-huh.'

'And the boat was originally acquired by Thomas Jenkins.'

'Ah, now. Well, you wouldn't know that through official channels, would you?'

'Wouldn't I?'

Neither of them said anything for a moment.

'Are you a big reader, Mr Phillips?' he said. The big man's eyes didn't register a response.

'Are you preparing an insult, then?' Phillips said.

'No,' Ted said. 'I just wondered about the name of the boat. Where it came from.'

Phillips frowned.

'I've no idea.'

'No, I don't suppose you have. I imagine Thomas Jenkins had an idea, though.'

The frown lingered.

'*Had* an idea?'

'He's dead. Died two days ago. Falling from a roof. Over there.' Ted pointed out of the Portakabin window towards the Island. Phillips followed the line of his finger, and looked out of the same window.

'Well, now,' he said. 'That's the worst thing I've heard in quite a while. Who killed him?'

'Who says anyone killed him?' Ted said.

'Well, he didn't kill himself.'

'Do you have any reason to think he wouldn't do that?' Ted said.

'Tommy?' said Phillips. 'No, not Tommy. He was one of life's optimists, he was.'

The man was lying seemingly for pleasure. Of course he had known about Jenkins's death. Pretending not to might lead to information, was all.

'So, Mr Phillips,' said Ted. 'The *Dulcibella*?'

Phillips breathed out through his nose, a decisive sound.

'Aye, she's Tommy's. I look after her, and I piloted her across the Strait when he asked me to.'

'Taking people from the dock at his house?'

'Well, it's Lucy's house, these days,' said Phillips. 'But yes.'

'How often did you take these trips?' said Ted.

'Every few weeks. Usually six or eight people.'

'What sort of people?'

'People like you. Police people. Politics people. Men and women in suits.'

'You left them at Plas Newydd.'

'I did.'

'You waited for them there?'

'Usually. Easier than going home.'

'That seems very diligent of you.'

'Tommy was paying me by the hour. Least I could do. And I'm not married.'

'Paying you how much?'

'Paying me enough to keep this place open.'

'So his death will make things difficult for you.'

'What do you think?'

Phillips spat the words out.

'The town council,' I say. 'You are a councillor.'

'Yes. Not that it means much, these days.'

'Been a councillor long?'

'Twenty years.'

'Ah. Then you must have known Mr Jenkins before.'

'I did.'

'Work with him on any planning developments, did you?'

'A few.'

'Any problems? Did he make any enemies?'

'Developers always make enemies.'

'They don't tend to get killed.'

'No. Nothing like that.'

'Did he build that for you, then?'

Ted pointed at a picture on the wall. It showed a modern-looking house looking out onto a blue sea. Again, Phillips looked at where Ted was pointing, but turned away from it, his eyes hooded.

'Yes,' he said. 'Well, he developed the land.'

'And where is it? This land?'

'On Anglesey.'

'Whereabouts on Anglesey?'

'What, you in the market?'

'No.'

'Near Beaumaris.'

'Anything dodgy about the transaction?'

'No,' said Phillips. 'There wasn't.'

'But you no longer own the house?'

'Yes, I still own the house. But it's bloody worthless now, isn't it?'

'Because of the Community?'

'Of course, because of the Community.'

'You didn't take up the King's offer of compensation?'

Phillips grinned and sneered, all at once.

'What, swap bricks and mortar for some virtual

currency when there's nothing to spend it on? No thanks. I'll take my chances.'

'What does that mean?'

'It doesn't mean anything.'

'You're going to, what, wait it out? See what comes next? Think the good old days are coming back, do we?'

'Is that illegal?'

'It's a bit treasonous.'

'And you're going to bring me in for being a bit treasonous?'

'No. But I'm going to be looking into how that house got built, Mr Phillips. And will I find anything fishy when I do look?'

'No.'

'OK. Well, I won't take your word for that, Mr Phillips. Now, we're going to need forensics to take a look at that boat tomorrow.'

'Why?' said Phillips.

'Because it's there,' Ted said. He was beginning to enjoy himself. It was sometimes like this. You felt like an Old God. He had felt the same thing when talking to James Moncrieff - the power of the badge. 'And because this yard is a bit too neat for my liking. As the young'uns used to say: do you feel me?'

Phillips didn't answer.

'Tell me about Robert Mountjoy,' said Ted.

It happened, then. The moment when Phillips became uncertain how much Ted knew. It had been a punt, but then every case had a punt somewhere along its spine, and here was this one's. The moment someone started covering his own back.

Emyr Phillips told Ted all about Robert Mountjoy.

34

Sir Anthony wasn't available at the Castle, so Ted had to make do with his sidekick. Lawrence Greenwood was as crisp and well-polished as before, greeting Ted as if he was about to show him into a ballroom. They stood together in the courtyard of the castle, watching the final preparations for the ceremony.

'Can you imagine?' said Greenwood. 'In less than 48 hours, this place will be filled with the great and good of Britain. It is so exciting.'

Ted, successfully containing his excitement, changed the subject.

'I'd like to know a little more about this disagreement at Plas Newydd, on the night of the party.'

'Disagreement?'

Greenwood didn't look at him, but his sudden wariness was carved into the set of his shoulders, the way he folded his arms. He wasn't the type to fold his arms.

'About Sir Anthony's room?' said Ted.

'Ah, yes. Yes. The small mix-up. Dear Anthea sorted it out.'

'So I understand. Sir Anthony told me that she was the one who raised it initially.'

'Did he? Well, I expect that is right.'

'So you're not sure?'

'Sure about who raised it first? Well, yes, yes, it was Anthea.'

'I think perhaps it wasn't, Mr Jenkins. I think perhaps Sir Anthony asked Anthea to sort it out. She didn't do it off her own bat.'

'Oh, dear, well really, I cannot be sure one way or the other. But really, does it matter?'

'Everything matters, Mr Jenkins. First law of policing.'

'I do believe Robert Peel said the first law of policing was to prevent crime and disorder, as an alternative to military oppression.'

Ted was surprised. Greenwood smiled complacently.

'Apologies. I studied social history. Was always rather taken with Mr Peel. I wonder what he would have made of *you*, Detective Inspector.'

'I'm sure I'd have been a great disappointment, Mr Greenwood. But I'm sure he would also have had views on motive. Tell me, what was the motive for Sir Anthony wanting to swap rooms?'

'I'm afraid I don't know.'

'Really? He didn't discuss it with you at all?'

'No. He just....'

Greenwood stopped.

'He just insisted?'

'I didn't say that.'

'You were going to, I think.'

'You are mistaken.'

'Tell me, Mr Greenwood. To your knowledge, has Sir Anthony ever been blackmailed?'

Greenwood turned to face him. His expression of

surprise was theatrical.

'Blackmailed? Why on earth would Sir Anthony be blackmailed?'

'Well, that is the question I've been asking myself, Mr Greenwood. Why *would* Sir Anthony be blackmailed?'

'I cannot imagine.'

'Well, perhaps it's *you* who has been blackmailed, Mr Greenwood.'

'What? But this is preosterous. Nobody has been blackmailed!'

'Does Sir Anthony send money to the Community?'

'What does that have to do with anything?'

'Does he?'

'Well, yes, he does, as it happens. A rather generous monthly allowance. I'm sure you can check the amount so I will spare myself the difficulty of explaining to my employer why I revealed it to you.'

'When did he start paying this monthly allowance?'

'I don't know.'

'I can check, Mr Greenwood. I would advise you to assist me on this one.' He paused, as theatrically as Greenwood might have done. 'It might help with whatever happens next.'

Greenwood said nothing for a while. Ted watched the man gently bite his lower lip. It gave him a strangely idiotic look.

'Last year,' he said eventually. 'He started paying it last year.'

'And did this decision follow soon after a visit to Plas Newydd?'

Greenwood didn't answer that one. His arms remained crossed. His eyes were fixed on the perspex-covered stage where, two days from now, a Prince of Wales would rise to speak to his father's subjects. Ted left him to it.

35

He phoned Lancaster from the car park at Parc Menai. He could have gone inside to find him but felt an odd reluctance to do so - something about not wanting to go through the security rigmarole a second time.

He'd decided it was time to trust the lad. He couldn't be everywhere he needed to be for the next bit. He would need help, and Angela Leybourne had at least been reassuring about her faith in the square-jawed Lieutenant. He sat and waited in the car while Lancaster made his way out, and then folded his tall frame into the uncomfortable little seats of the Dyson.

'Anything new?' Ted said.

'No, sir. We've rather been waiting for you.'

'Fair enough. Some things I want you to check, please.'

He went over them, methodically, while Lancaster wrote them down. The PR man James Moncrieff, and his links to the bankers, Collins and Hughes. Sir Anthony Mayfield's previous visits to the Island, and who he came with each time. Any links between Thomas Jenkins and

Frank Daniels, of the Welsh Historical Society, especially links involving property pre-London. Evidence of financial support for the Community from either of the bankers, Sir Anthony, or Frank Daniels.

'The Community doesn't have to declare its supporters, sir,' said Lancaster.

'I know, lad. So you're going to have to go a-sleuthing, aren't you?'

Lancaster smiled, a genuine smile for once, and Ted wondered if they might end up getting on OK after all.

'Any reason why I'm looking into all this, sir? Anything I should know about?'

Ted breathed out through his nose, an airy sigh.

'I'm fishing, Lieutenant. A desperate man in need of a nibble.'

'Is this related to what Priestley found up at the house, sir?'

'Sharp lad. Could be.'

'Right. And where will you be, if you don't mind me asking?'

'I'm off to see a grieving widow.'

He watched Lancaster walk back across the wet carpark, then pulled out and got back up to the main road.

Unlike the last time he visited, he went through the front gates to reach Lucy Jenkins's house. His drone followed him out of the business park gates, turning right and then right again, driving up to the gates of the huge estate of Y Neuadd, flashing his police pass at the guard on the gate. There were various other properties that had sprouted up in the grounds, all of them part of the enormous redevelopment project that was completed the year before the Emergency. Developed by Thomas Jenkins. Funded by Robert Hughes and Eurwyn Collins. Approved by Robert Mountjoy, Leader of the Council.

A camera doorbell flickered at him as he rang it. There was a long pause before the bell responded.

'Detective Inspector Wood.'

He just about recognised Lucy Jenkins's Southern accent.

'Can I come in please?'

'What can I do for you?'

'I need your help.'

'With what?'

'I want to talk to you about the best means of securing planning permissions.'

There was a pause. Quite a long pause.

'I don't know what you mean, Detective.'

'Really? I understand you had the inside track.'

The little doorbell went silent. After a few moments, noises came from the door. It opened, and when her face finally appeared, Lucy Jenkins had on her brightest sparkling Estuary face. He looked for something scared under the surface. He couldn't find it. He prepared himself to be played.

'Day's getting on, DI Wood,' she said. 'Though it is always delightful to see the plod.'

'Mrs Jenkins,' he said. 'Can I come in?'

'Well, it's not the *best* time. I was going to have a bath. Get spruced up for the morrow, and all that.'

She smiled, and looked him up and down.

'You look tired. And a little bedraggled.'

'I am. And hungry.'

'Well, I don't know why you're here. But OK. Come in, we can have a chat, and I'll knock you up a sandwich.'

She stood aside to let him in, leaving only a little room, such that he had to brush against her as he passed. He smelled her expensive perfume. It smelled strong enough to have only just been put on - in the gap between the bedroom and the front door, perhaps. He pictured her reaching for the atomiser as she walked up to open the door to him. He told himself not to lose his temper with her. She was doing her best.

'You've come alone?' she said, looking outside. Ted's drone hung in the air, like an obedient dog waiting outside a shop.

'I have.'

'No back up for little old me?'

'Little old you? Come off it. They're not far away,' he said, nodding to where Parc Menai was, just behind the trees.

'Ah yes - watching watching watching.'

He turned towards the living room, but she put a hand on his arm and steered him away. She left the hand there for a little while. For a moment he imagined shouting at her, telling her to leave it off, that this was repulsive and demeaning. But she did what she did. It was all any of them could do.

'I think in here would be best.'

She walked him towards the kitchen. He sat on an expensive-feeling stool at the breakfast bar, and she moved her hand from his arm to his shoulder before walking away.

'Something to drink, Inspector?' she said.

'A glass of water would be great.'

'Nothing stronger?'

'Not just yet, I think.'

'No worries.'

She opened a cupboard beneath the other side of the breakfast bar, leaning down towards it. Her loose top hung down. She stood up again, and smiled at him.

A slow walk to the sink, a careful splash of water into the glass. And then back to him. She put the water down on the breakfast bar, and went to the fridge, to take out what looked like expensive imported Cheddar. She was wearing skintight jeans and strapless heels. Her artificially-tanned skin glowed in the light from overhead. She pulled out sandwich paraphernalia - chopping board, knife, bread, butter. It was all effortless, and effortlessly available. Like a top-of-the-range middle-class kitchen in the old days. Her fridge and cupboards were full. None of this was normal anymore.

'So, Inspector,' she said, as she made the sandwich. 'What is all this about?'

'You know, for a good long while I thought you'd had your husband killed.'

'I'm sorry?'

'I mean, I couldn't quite square it. Why wait until now? Why not have him killed as soon as he left you? Or at least, soon afterwards. You had motive - he left you for God. But I can't square method, and I can't square opportunity. But it's odd.'

'What's odd?' She stroked the knife as it worked the bread and cheese. Her fingernails were painted bright purple and were immaculate. Her fingers were long. Her hands smooth.

'It's odd that a woman like you has no contact with the Island. Has never been there. And yet there's a boat that leaves, from your property, at regular intervals. And, as far as I can tell, you've never got on it. Why?'

He stood up, and walked away from the breakfast bar.

'I'm having trouble, you see,' he said. 'Trouble squaring two different pictures of Thomas Jenkins. One picture is of a holy man, a kindly man, loved by the Sisters and Brothers of the Island. A man who got God, and established a religious community. A man of the cloth.'

Lucy slid over the sandwich. She watched him carefully.

'But then there's the other Thomas Jenkins,' he said, walking back to the breakfast bar and picking up one half of the sandwich. 'The one who built this house. Who acquired himself a trophy wife.'

'Fuck off.'

'The one who developed property, made millions, had important friends. And who suddenly, *before* the Emergency, found God and scarpered off to be with him?'

Ted pointed at the window, chewing on bread and cheese.

'You can see Plas Newydd from here, Mrs Jenkins,' he said. 'You can watch the house of your ex-husband. I find that pretty odd as well. But not as odd as what we've found in that house today. That, I think, is very fucking odd indeed. And, however this plays out, your life is pretty much snarled up in my investigation, now.'

'I didn't have anything to do with it,' she said.

'With what?'

'With Tommy's death.'

'But what about the rest of it?'

'The rest of what?'

'The scam, Mrs Jenkins. The grift. The blackmail.'

She didn't say anything to that. He munched for a few moments, letting her stew on what he had just said.

'If I thought you were an entirely innocent party, Mrs Jenkins, I might feel bad for you. But I don't, particularly.'

He waved a hand around, the one with the half-eaten sandwich in it. A few crumbs fell to the floor.

'This place is the most well-appointed house I've been in since the Emergency. Now, I don't move in particularly rarified circles, but that's pretty noteworthy, I think. You don't work. I find myself wondering how it's all paid for.'

Her beautiful face was still, her eyes open and direct, as they had always been since he first met her. She did not reply.

'This started before the Emergency, I'm guessing,' Ted said. 'I think your husband was a wheeler dealer at the local level who had some pretty serious access to cash and influence. A man who could rustle up a few hundred grand or even the odd million without much effort. He knew the local bankers. Men like Eurwyn Collins. Robert Hughes. But sometimes money isn't enough, is it? Sometimes you need a bit of leverage. Some pictures, maybe. A dirty video. The chair of the planning committee with his or her trousers down. All grist to the mill, right?'

'I'm getting a drink,' she said, getting up and walking to a cupboard. 'You sure you don't want one?'

'Well, Mrs Jenkins, I think we both know that I'm not that good with drink. I don't know how you know, but you've been dealing in information you shouldn't have for years now. Which is why you keep offering me a drink. So, can I say, with great emphasis, just fucking stop it, OK?'

She began moving bottles about in the cupboard.

'The whole redevelopment. It had to be approved at the top level. And it was. Robert Mountjoy. Remember that name, Mrs Jenkins?'

He wondered who was listening, if anyone, if the house was even empty, if that was why she'd steered him away from the living room, but found that he didn't particularly care.

'Because it wasn't all palm greasing, was it? Oh no. Tommy had another string to his bow. Blackmail. He blackmailed the leader of the council, didn't he? Robert Mountjoy. The one who killed himself. And somehow someone started sniffing around. They discovered something, I don't know what. And then, your husband found

God and ran into the arms of Nicholas Briggs and his little Community of God botherers. And then, God really did intervene.'

'Yeah,' Lucy says. 'He blew up London.'

'Yeah. He blew up London.'

And my wife. And my daughter.

'And so your husband and his new friend established their new Community. And he got away with it. All of it. And you stayed here. And then, the great and good started making their way over the Strait. What did they do over there, other than hold these so-called seminars? Maybe some minor narcotics, brought in from Ireland? Or maybe other things brought in from Ireland. Girls. Boys. Kids.'

He was trying to rile her. She just said 'fuck off', mildly.

'Ah, then, you have some limits, do you?'

She looked at him, appraisingly. She raised the glass she had filled, and sipped at it.

'I think you're the procurer, Mrs Jenkins. Or, as we used to call them, the pimp. I don't know how you communicated with him without Witness knowing - a good old-fashioned walkie talkie, maybe? You're close enough. But you sent people over there, and he recorded them, doing whatever they were doing. And then you helped him distribute the good stuff. I imagine it was you who went to see the targets, told them what you had, told them what you wanted. I imagine we'll be able to join that up on Witness pretty easily, now I know the pattern. But you know what? I can make all that go away if you tell me why you think Anthea Mortimer had to die.'

She put her glass down on the breakfast bar, and looked at it.

'The truth is, DI Wood - I have no idea.'

He picked up the other sandwich, and left the kitchen.

He heard her heels clattering on the floor behind him as he walked across the hallway into the living room, where the chiselled and groomed face of the banker Eurwyn Collins was rising from the sofa. Lucy stumbled into the living room behind Ted, and all three of them looked at each other for a while. Ted took a mouthful of sandwich, chewed on it a moment, and then turned, and walked out.

Sometimes, you didn't need to ask any questions. It was all there in front of you.

36

He walked back up the hill past the Castle towards the hotel. Night was coming down. The Investiture was the day after tomorrow, and now the signs of it were everywhere, the metal railings increasingly finding shape and structure, and after today something else watched over them - towers of scaffolding dotted throughout the town square, with cameras beginning to sprout from them. Come the day, those towers would be manned by men and women in dark uniforms sporting rifles and AR goggles which could show them, at any time, the face of anyone in the crowd below. Identities would be mapped and recorded, digitised faces turned into miniature narratives, tracking who each of them was with, who they'd been with, who they'd met and talked to and corresponded with, nothing secret and nothing hidden away.

Ted carried on walking. Bunting had been established, he saw. Pictures of the King and his son had appeared in windows, somewhat disguising the fact that the shops contained very little else. At least the two faces were something to look at. They were fresh-faced, well fed, smiling.

They were missing something that pretty much everyone else had now - cheekbones. The pictures had appeared suddenly, during the day - they had not been here when he'd left this morning. It was as if a last-minute panic had gripped the town, and nobody wanted to be seen to be less than totally enthusiastic.

He thought of the T-shirt he had bought at the hotel reception, two evenings ago. He reminded himself that the day of the Investiture was also the anniversary of the Coronation. Caernarfon was preparing to celebrate the most famous sons of England. It was another in a long line of political statements, stretching back to old King Edward dangling his infant son from the half-built ramparts of the Castle and saying to the Welsh below *look, I can give all of you to this baby, that is how little power you have.*

He found himself drawn towards the station, as if by filaments of memory.

The railway line ran along the river Selont, squeezed between a small riverside road and the main road which ran above it. A great stone terrace separated the railway and the small road from Caernarfon proper. The line was narrow gauge. He vaguely remembered it being opened, back in the time before London. The signs around the place had half-recalled names: Ffestiniog Railway. Rheilffordd Eryri.

The station was deserted. All stations were deserted. Many of them had become half-tolerated spaces for the homeless to cluster, as the authorities cleared them off the outside streets. The huge Victorian sheds in the towns and cities provided a kind of shelter. At least the authorities knew where they were. And there were no trains running, so nobody took them. After London, the railway system which had, as its ultimate purpose, the ferrying of humanity into the capital, encountered its own day of reckoning. They couldn't afford it. Or so they were told. If you needed to get somewhere, you got yourself there.

There were no homeless here. The only building on the little station was locked up and inaccessible. The narrow platform faced only the stone wall of the terrace that ran down the side of the place. A single bench was festooned with seagull shit. There was nowhere to sit.

He stood for a while, feeling like a fool, remembering an episode of some half-remembered television show set in a haunted railway station. Caernarfon station wasn't haunted, but he felt he might be. Haunted, appropriately enough, by the memory of a train his wife and his daughter must have taken.

But no, he'd been wrong. This station was haunted, as well, by a ghoul from before London. A poster on the glass of the waiting room, stuck up there illegally by persons unknown. The ugly-handsome face of a blonde former actor, smiling his crooked smile over a single word: *Freedom*.

It took him right back there, to the months leading up to London. The demos and riots in the street. The escalating social media babble. The 5G conspiracies. The lunatic president, the marches, the attacks on public buildings. The sense that countries were going mad. He'd been part of it, this crooked-faced man. And the Peckham killer had been part of it too.

He'd been called Churchill. The newspapers made a good deal of that. No relation, he'd said. Thin, quiet. 'He looks like Slender Man,' Peg said, and he hadn't known who Slender Man was, and when he found out Peg wasn't allowed near the computer for a fortnight.

He'd issued statements, this man. He'd said he was fighting against something called White Armageddon. His victims were black and brown, all young men, violently raped and eviscerated. And all of them had criminal records. Churchill said he was doing the job the police wouldn't do. Many of Ted's fellow officers thought he had a point. And as the killings continued and progress continued to be slow, one by one the senior officers dropped away, until it was only Ted making statements, only Ted hurrying into Peckham station, pale and grim-faced, failing failing failing, until finally his own head had given way and he'd suffered a complete nervous break-down. Four days later, Churchill attacked a drug dealer just off Rye Lane, but the dealer was an undercover cop, and after a struggle the young officer had shoved Churchill's own knife through the man's poisoned heart.

He'd been a cop. Of course he had. The stench was immense. Somewhere within it, they'd moved to St Albans and he'd gone back to work. The man who failed to find the Peckham killer. The man who'd failed to save them all from one of their own.

If Laura had seen him standing there in that Welsh station - a raggedy man on a deserted platform - she might have wondered how he had come to this. If they had separated or divorced, back when they might have done, she might have been living in Caernarfon by now, her daughter grown up and maybe even living elsewhere. She might have been hurrying to find a restaurant before they all closed - as most of them would soon - so she could eat before the curfew, now firmly in place so close to a celebration such as the Investiture. Or perhaps she would now be working in the Royal party, and she would be out for an evening constitutional, security service agents following her, protecting her. Or perhaps she would be a magazine journalist, an intelligent woman paid to observe people and write about them, like Ellie Sullivan, standing by the side of the road, watching a man she had often put to bed coming to pieces at the seams.

But she would only see the outside. Just like Witness. She would have no conception of the inside. She would assume - and it would be reasonable to assume - that the inside was a maelstrom. But it was not. The inside was quiet. It was a man sitting in an interrogation room, with a tape machine running, recording everything. There was no window in this room, just a single light hanging from the ceiling. It was a scene from a film, from television, from the shared collective consciousness. But the scene was wrong. Because there was no-one else in the room.

Could he wish her into being?

No. He could not.

She would not come to join him in this room.

There was no 'Laura'. No voice would come from the tape machine, even though the wrecked device of his subconscious had put the machine there, as if to draw her out, so he could ask the question. The only question.

Could she ever forgive him?

The receipt had flooded out from under the washing machine when the blasted thing finally gave up the ghost.

Gave up the ghost. Now there was a phrase. He could do with giving up the ghost.

He had fished it out and looked at it. Laura was at work, Peg was at school. He was on nights, bumped down after Peckham, and therefore terribly tired all the bloody time. He'd been doing the washing, as he often did during the day, and then the damn machine had broken down, and the receipt had washed out with the excess water, and he had fished the receipt out.

It was for Pizza Express in Peterborough.

Pizza Express in Peterborough.

It sounded like the start of a poem.

He had never been to Peterborough.

He had gone to his smartphone, opened the calendar app, and had checked the date of the receipt.

Laura in Cardiff at conference.

Two pizzas in Peterborough. A bottle of Montepulciano. Two coffees. Lunchtime.

A stupid little coincidence really. A dumb way to unlock an investigation, but dumb is what these sudden breakthroughs often were. A receipt, and this disjunction of dates and appointments. For the next two months, he had surveilled the suspect, and she never even suspected that a campaign of surveillance was underway. He held her letters up to the light. He hit redial on every phone he came across, apologising to countless strangers for dialling the wrong number. He checked browser histories, hacked into email accounts, and on three occasions even inspected the police database for CCTV footage. He became his own trial version of Witness, a pair of haunted eyes connected to a half-blind surveillance network, because it was only half-blind back then, barely even a prototype for what what to come, for how could they imagine what was possible back then? If only they'd been watching China as carefully as Ted was trying to watch his wife. Trying to catch her on a hook, and not knowing if when he caught her he would throw her back or bash her head in with a rock.

Once, he watched a stuttering recording of Laura stepping off the train in Peterborough when she was supposed to be in Cardiff.

Once, he saw her walk across a square in Peterborough.

Once, he saw her coming out of Pizza Express in Peterborough with a man, and watched them walk off screen together, and he had wondered to myself - he distinctly remembered it even now - he had wondered to myself *why don't these fucking cameras move so I can see where they're going?*

Careful what you wish for, eh?

He had assembled a body of evidence. He had everything he needed to confront her. But before he did that, he thought he wanted to speak to the man she had met. He knew where he worked. He knew where he lived. All he needed to do was get on a train.

He had been sitting on this station platform for a while, and he thought those watching him were beginning to become impatient. He saw the flare of a cigarette lighter and then the dancing red circle of a cigarette taken from a mouth, placed by the side of the shadow smoking it, raised again to the mouth, like a red lamp being swung in the distance. Angela Leybourne said it was the intelligence service bods, and he supposed he had to trust that she was right. They weren't being very careful about revealing themselves. That much at least seemed true - they wanted it known that he was being watched. He looked up to his faithful drone, and while looking at it pointed along the platform to where the cigarette smoker was. He saw several of the miniature cameras hanging beneath the drone follow the line of his finger. He doubted that was the software. Someone was operating the drone, as Angela had said. He pulled back his hand, stood up, and walked towards the red dot of the cigarette. It fell to the ground, there was a suspicion of shadow, and then there was nothing. He helpfully stubbed out the cigarette with his heel as he walked past.

They were all in the same game, after all.

37

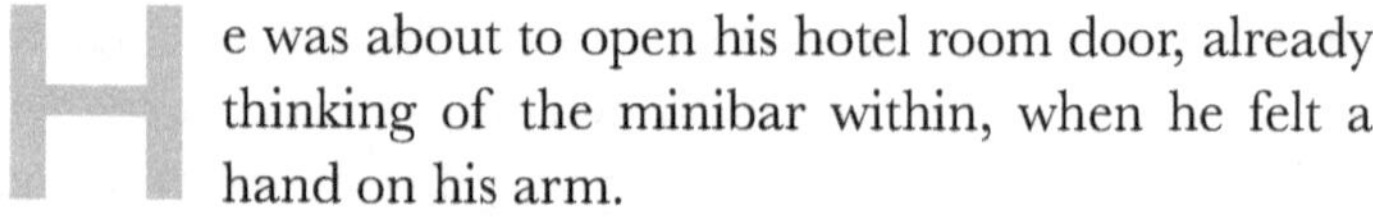

He was about to open his hotel room door, already thinking of the minibar within, when he felt a hand on his arm.

'Detective Inspector Wood. If I may.'

He turned to look. A man in his thirties, wearing a smart suit, with sleepy eyes and a suggestion of a pout. Good looking, and knew it. Spent time on his hair, and artfully created the impression of rebellion with a carefully-groomed stubble. He looked like a right little bastard. Peter Holmes, the majordomo to Rachel Whitehouse, last seen glaring at him across the table in the bar, yesterday evening.

'Mr Holmes. Keeping an eye out, were we?'

Holmes didn't smile. Ted rather got the impression he didn't smile very often. He reminded himself what Angela had said - that the opposition, aka the intelligence service, aka MI6, had been watching him, had wanted it to be known he was being watched. *Standard fuckery*, she had called it. But whoever was watching had alerted Holmes of his arrival at the hotel. So perhaps not as standard as all that.

'The Minister would like a word, Detective Inspector.'

'All she needs to do is ask nicely, Mr Holmes.'

'The Minister would like a word. Please.'

They stared at each other for a few moments, two relatively powerless men dropping into old ways to try and feel better about it. Ted sighed theatrically.

'Lead on, Macduff.'

The top floor of the Lloyd George Hotel was reserved for serious VIPs. Only a half-dozen doors went off the only corridor, suggesting sizeable suites behind. Maybe the PM would stay up here when she arrived for the ceremony. Ted doubted she'd be invited to stay with the Family.

Rachel Whitehouse stood at a large window looking out at the town square, sipping on something brown in a heavy-looking glass. Just outside the window hung a large drone. It looked to Ted as if the Minister had been talking to it. She turned as he entered the room.

'Detective Inspector. Thank you for taking the time.'

'It felt rather like a summons, Minister. But you're welcome.'

'Please. Sit.'

Her hand swept regally across the room. Ted glanced at Holmes, waiting for him to sit down, and then sat down himself somewhere he could see the other man.

'Drink?' said Whitehouse.

'A glass of water,' said Ted.

'Angharad?' said Whitehouse, mangling the name, and Ted heard someone in the kitchen, or whatever it was this room boasted. He looked behind him to see Angharad Rees filling a glass from a tap. He smiled at her, but she did not smile back.

'I was hoping, DI Wood, that you might give me an update on the progress of your case,' said Whitehouse.

'An update, Minister? I'm not entirely sure I can.'

'I think, for the sake of argument, that if I say you can, you can.'

'Respectfully, Minister, I don't agree.'

Angharad Rees placed a glass of water on a table beside him, and receded back into wherever she'd come from. Ted picked it up and sipped it. His mouth was terribly dry, all of a sudden. Peter Holmes stared at him like a bull terrier pondering a lunge.

'I am the Defence Minister, DI Wood.'

'Indeed, Ms Whitehouse. Indeed. But as you know, the police force is accountable to the Home Office, not the MoD or even the FCO. Although I believe I've had colleagues of yours on my tail these last few days. Seems like something of a waste of resources, if you ask me. After all, there are bigger fish to fry.'

'Fish?'

'The small matter of the Investiture.'

'Ah, yes. The Investiture.'

She came and sat down in her own chair, still holding the glass of liquid. Ted wondered if she might throw it at him.

'I did not care for your approach or tone the other evening, Detective Inspector.'

'I'm sorry. That you didn't care for it.'

'It seems strange, to me, that you are not making use of my resources on this case.'

'Your resources, Minister?'

'We have people here in Caernarfon who could help you.'

'I know. As I say, some of them have been keeping me company. Perhaps you could explain to me why that is?'

'Perhaps you could explain to me why it is that you are here at all?'

'To investigate the deaths of Anthea Mortimer and Thomas Jenkins.'

'But why *you*, Detective Inspector.' She flicked a hand towards Peter Holmes. He had his little speech prepared.

'Detective Inspector Edward Wood. Formerly with the Metropolitan Police Force, now attached to Manchester Police Service. Widower. Lives at 55 Prince's Drive, Stretford. Given health leave from the Metropolitan Police for three months after leading the botched investigation into the killer of nine people in Peckham, South London. Spent some of that time at the Maudsley hospital for mental health conditions. Drank the entire contents of his minibar on his first night in Caernarfon.'

Holmes stopped. He looked pretty pleased with himself.

'Is that supposed to impress me, Mr Holmes?' said Ted. 'Cutting and pasting from Witness is an entry-level activity.'

'Our point, DI Wood, is this,' said the Minister. 'You are a middling detective with a background of unreliable behaviour. You're carrying untold mental scars from the loss of your wife and daughter and this business in Peckham, which some of us still remember, not least our Prime Minister. And yet Angela Leybourne has seen fit to send you, of all people, to investigate the high profile death of a senior member of this country's religious community. In the days running up to the most significant political event in this country in years.'

'And a young woman of promise,' said Ted.

'I'm sorry?'

'Thomas Jenkins wasn't the only one killed. Anthea Mortimer. A young woman of promise.'

'All right, yes, a young woman of promise. The question still stands, DI Wood. Why you?'

'Well, perhaps that's a question for my superiors, Minister.'

'Hmmm.'

The Minister looked at him, and he felt himself wilting a little under her gaze. She had that presence about her he'd experienced with other politicians and leaders - to some extent, he'd seen it in Angela. A raw kind of magnetism. Unteachable, and dangerous - particularly if those wielding it had their own sense of it. Here was a politician on the up. She had found herself in a situation - a murder investigation, of all things - that endangered her position. Ted didn't think this woman would ever do anything that endangered her position.

'Am I still a suspect, DI Wood?'

'Minister, I'm afraid everyone who was in that house is still a suspect, and will remain so until we find the person or persons responsible.'

'Of course. Of course.'

'If I may?'

She nodded, gently, and he stood up. She watched him as he turned to make for the door.

'Day after tomorrow,' she said, in barely a whisper. 'You've got until the day after tomorrow.'

Why did it sound like she was sorry?

<h1 style="text-align:center">38</h1>

He found he wanted, very badly, to get out of the Hotel. Something about that drone bobbing up and down in the window behind the Minister's eyes, as if an infinite chamber of faces were gazing at him, whispering as one *you have one more day. You have one more day*.

A drink. One drink. Somewhere else. What harm could it do?

There was a big pub in the middle of town, the one he'd walked past the previous evening when he'd first encountered his mysterious companions. They were with him again tonight, or at least he assumed so. His own drone was waiting for him at the hotel entrance, and though it was presumably scanning the streets, could it see those silent companions? *The competition*, Angela had said. MI6 or similar. Spooks, to use the commonly accepted term of abuse within the security service (so what was Lancaster, then? A trainee spook? An ex-spook? A home office spook?).

He made his way to the old Wetherspoons place he'd seen the night before. His drone waited outside. There would be plenty of cameras inside. These megapubs were always well-surveilled. Many people were happy to swap personal privacy for cheap booze.

There was a manufactured brightness to the interior, a function of loud music, over-powered lighting and a vivid and sticky carpet. Men lined the bar, some standing, others sitting. They were, almost without exception, holding glasses of state-subsidised lager. There was no food being served. There was no food to serve, probably. Unlike the old days, the men in here were thin, despite the beer consumption. They would not be rounding the day off with a curry or something disgusting from a kebab shop. The kebab shops and the curry houses were almost all gone, and no one asked what had happened to the people who had run them.

Some of the pub's punters glared at him as he entered. He had the stench of authority about him. He didn't let it bother him.

An empty-faced barman made his way over and Ted, without a moment's thought, ordered a double of whatever gutrot whisky they were selling to accompany his pint of cheap state lager. He was holding his phone up to pay when he felt a hand on his arm.

'You sure about this?' an American voice breathed in his air.

He turned to see the journalist, Ellie Sullivan, standing beside him.

'Sure about what?' he said. She raised an eyebrow, shrugged, and walked away, leaving Ted to look at his held out phone and the two untouched drinks on the bar.

'And a pint of Diet Coke,' he said. 'Here,' he added, pushing the two untouched drinks over to some unseen neighbour at the bar, paying for them, and walking away with his awful bloody consolation prize.

There was a snug off the main saloon with a power point and an Ethernet socket. Ellie was sat there with a laptop computer, which would have been a pretty ballsy move for a woman on her own back before London, but as the place was festooned with cameras these days she was unlikely to meet any trouble.

'I was looking forward to that,' he said. She smiled up at him.

'You're welcome,' she said. 'Do join me, Detective Inspector.'

'Ted, please.'

He sat down. She closed her laptop.

'Interesting surroundings for a *New Yorker* journalist,' he said, sipping at the Diet Coke. It tasted of nothing. Nothing at all.

'The reason I write for the *New Yorker*, Ted, is that they let me come into places like this and draw conclusions.'

'Conclusions?'

'You don't think there are conclusions to be drawn from the fact that His Majesty's Government subsidises places where people - mainly men, actually - can drown their sorrows while being watched by machines? You don't think that's almost *too* on the nose?'

He sighed through his own nose. She sipped her own drink - an orange juice. He was going to assume there was nothing stronger in it. She grimaced at the taste.

'Man, this stuff is fucking disgusting. I doubt it's been anywhere near a goddamn orange.' She put it down again, leaned back and looked at him. 'So, how goes the case, Ted?'

'It goes.'

'Ah, no morsels for the journalist lady from New York, then.'

'None at all.'

There was a not entirely uncomfortable moment of silence.

'You know, Ted, I've been thinking a lot about a book I read once. Written by a guy from the *New Yorker*, actually. It was visiting the Community that got me thinking about it. The word they use for the people who go there.'

'The Suffering.'

'Yes. The Suffering. I've been thinking about that word a lot. *Suffering*. The Suffering. Collective noun? Suffering. Adjective? Could you be a singular Suffering? Or did the Suffering suffer together? And do they hold hands when they jumped into the sea?'

'Jump into the sea?'

'Turn of phrase. I'd heard that was something they do.'

Ted thought about the man he had seen on his first trip to the Island, standing, blank-faced, looking down into the waters.

'So, this book I read,' Ellie continued, 'it was called *Hiroshima,* one of the survivors of the bomb was a German Jesuit priest. He survived the initial blast partly because his mission house had been reinforced by the priests - all the buildings around it were flattened. He saved many people from the aftermath of the blast, and managed to get out of the city to safety. The depiction of what he saw and experienced was horrific. There weren't many eyewitness reports of atomic aftermath. Not in those days.'

'No,' said Ted. 'Not in those days.'

'So, anyway, this German priest was taken to Tokyo after the blast, and treated there by doctors who had no idea what was happening to his body, because no one knew about radiation poisoning then. But he recovered, to his own amazement as well as theirs. He became something of a newspaper celebrity. His health improved and declined, improved and declined over the years. Years after the bomb, he became a naturalised Japanese citizen, taking a Japanese name. He developed back pains, was treated for cataracts, caught mysterious fevers and frequent attacks of the flu. Then, more than twenty years after the bomb, purple spots appeared on his palms. The doctors at that time didn't know what caused these spots, and were just as confused by the battery of other conditions suffered by the priest.'

She sipped again at her orange juice, made the same disgusted face, before continuing.

'The point is, Ted, he *suffered*. He died in the 70s, three decades after the American bomb dropped. Just before he died, he showed a visitor a copy of his medical chart, on which one of the doctors had written, in Japanese: *living corpse*.'

'And that's how you see us? Living corpses?'

'Us, Ted? Who is us?'

He smiled.

'Explosion-affected persons.'

She raised an eyebrow.

'You've read it,' she said.

'Yeah,' he said. 'I've read it.'

'Well then, a toast.' He raised his half-finished glass of Diet Coke. She raised her orange juice. They clinked them together. 'To the *hibakusha*.'

'The *hibakusha*.'

DAY FOUR

39

Occasionally you arrived somewhere and it felt astonishingly normal - and by normal, people tended to mean *like it was before London*. The places that felt like that tended to be those which were either very poor or very well-off before London - the poor places continued in their misery, the well-off places seemed to have enough people with time on their hands and commitment to the social fabric to find a way through, opening coffee and nick-nack shops, campaigning for supermarkets and leisure centres. The only thing British people cared about when it came to politics was the NHS and their bins being emptied. Well, the NHS was no more, but in some places close attention was still being paid to the emptying of bins.

Chester was one of those places - spruce, bustling, presenting its best face to the world, the kind of place where people tutted if you dropped litter. The shops were mostly only half-full, but they were making the best of it, while the faces were gaunt but well-moisturised. Anthea Mortimer's flat was in keeping with the general character -

tidy and unassuming. She had obviously given the place a thorough cleaning before heading off to Anglesey for her last trip. Even the dishwasher had been run.

Priestley and Lancaster did most of the looking - he just stood in the living room, looking out of the third-floor window into the street below. He felt he could almost smell the young woman - a fresh scent, tragic in its clarity, a mixture of household cleaner, supermarket air freshener and overtones of something more expensive and refined. He'd always had a good nose. He'd been one of those husbands who'd bought perfume for his wife, but not the same perfume every time - he had liked to experiment, knowing what Laura liked. He'd enjoyed it until the stench of alcohol snuffed out every other scent.

He felt a slightly panicked clarity this morning, had felt it ever since he'd woken up. No drink yesterday, was the probable reason. He'd opened the minibar again when he'd got back to his room, but had closed it again. He'd even considered phoning Ellie's room and seeing where that might lead to. But in the end he'd showered and gone to bed, his skin as clean as the sheets, his mind relatively quiet, and had slept the sleep of the righteous.

This morning he'd woken up with that jittery panic. The Investiture was tomorrow. They still hadn't cracked this case. They'd learned things, lots of things, about the stench of corruption around Plas Newydd and the Community, around Thomas and Lucy Jenkins and the great and good of Caernarfon, but it was all background, mood music, accompanying literature. Had Thomas Jenkins killed Anthea Mortimer? And then himself? Or had a third party killed them both? Method: strangulation and a shove from a roof or a brick to the head. Opportunity: pretty much anyone in the house could have done it, and with the hard drive absent from the cellar they didn't even have video to go on, if there had indeed been cameras and videos, as he now believed. Motive? Why now? Why them?

Priestley came out of the kitchen. Lancaster was rifling through photo albums on the small dining table to one side of the living room. All three of them were wearing white evidence suits. It felt oddly pointless to Ted, though. Any forensic evidence they gathered would not be processed for days, and his deadline was end of tomorrow. If the Investiture passed without a resolution to the case, he doubted anyone outside would notice. But he'd be off the case, or maybe even worse. He wasn't sure why he thought that, but he was convinced of it.

'Have you done her bedroom?' he said.

'Yep. Done and dusted. Literally.'

'OK. Come back in with me.'

He went through to Anthea's bedroom. A bedspread and cushions, some generic art on the walls, a book by the bed. A historical novel from the old days, queens and cousins.

'Where was her underwear?' he said.

Priestley indicated a chest of drawers. He opened the top one. He felt a momentary dislocated queasiness, rifling through a dead woman's knickers. But it passed. He was a professional. He pulled out various undergarments, knickers and bras and a few vests. He went to the bottom of the drawer.

'Pretty standard stuff, wouldn't you say, Priestley?'

'What, I'm an expert in knickers because I'm female?'

'I should ask Lieutenant Lancaster?'

She snorted, amused, and picked up a couple of pairs of knickers.

'Bog standard, I'd say, DI Wood.'

'Nothing fancy for this young woman.'

'Any reason why we're looking?'

'Do these knickers look like the kind of thing a woman who's into being tied up would wear?'

'Do you think sexual preferences dictate underwear choices?'

'You don't think she'd have some raunchier stuff if that was her thing?'

Priestly just looked at him.

I have no idea what women do.

It was the kind of thing he might have said, once. But he had as much idea about women as he did about men. They left the bedroom.

Lancaster had one photo album open. There were several of them. Ted had seen this before. The arrival of Witness had sparked a vogue for old-school printed photographs which, people believed, could not be tracked and stored in the same way as digital pictures. Mostly, they were deluding themselves - there were other ways of iden- tifying people, and most people had made digital copies of old photographs anyway. But they also had a point. If you took a photo with your digital camera, it was stored in some Witness-accessible way from the moment you took it, regardless of how quickly and diligently you then deleted it. The picture maps formed from individual photos knitted together by the AI was a fundamental part of the tapestry of Witness.

'Old school photo,' said Lancaster. 'She would have been in year 8, Beryl Daniels in Year 10. That's them, I think.' He pointed to the two of them. The whole school was in the picture, a few hundred kids, and Ted needed his glasses. Beryl Daniels was unmistakable, Anthea Mortimer less so.

'The brother? The one who died in London? What was his name?'

Lancaster checked the notes on his phone.

'Roger Mortimer. Father was called Philip.'

'Did he go to the same school? Presumably so. Any sign of him in the picture?'

Lancaster carefully peeled the photo away from the album. He flipped it over. Attached to the back were the names of every child in the photograph. He read across, flipped the picture back, and ran his fingers along one of the rows. It stopped.

'That's him. Roger Mortimer. Year 11.'

The tiny face peered back at them. Unsmiling, wide-eyed, ready to leap at the camera and the viewer. The hair was shaved down to the skull. There was a clear smudge on the forehead. The faces on either side told their own story - leaning away, unsmiling too, but judging by the sideways glance of one of the faces, these weren't angry, these were just anxious about their proximity to a dangerous animal.

Ted got out his phone. He snapped a picture of the photograph, opened it up, and zoomed in on the face. It blurred as he want further in, but it allowed his old eyes to see what that smudge on the boy's forehead might be. Lancaster, leaning over and looking at Ted's screen, breathed out.

'My God,' he said.

'Christ almighty,' said Priestley, leaning in from the other side. 'Is that a swastika?'

40

The offices of Moncrieff Delaney were a simple affair above an unusually bustling shop on Northgate Street. It was an open plan place, with one notable exception - a glass-fronted executive office in the far corner through which James Moncrieff was clearly visible.

Lancaster spoke to the receptionist, leaving Ted to look around the place. Perhaps a dozen people were seated at desks. They all seemed to be on the phone. An unfeasible proportion of them seemed to be young and female and dressed to emphasise the fact. Passing his eyes across the room he happened to see Moncrieff looking through the glass partition of his office directly at him. Their eyes locked. Moncrieff was talking, presumably through a hands-free phone or ear pod. His hands were in his pockets, but as he and Ted glanced at each other he lifted his hands and folded his arms across his chest. The kind of move a bouncer would make when faced with a situation outside a nightclub. It was time to throw slick Mr Moncrieff off guard.

'You go in and speak to Moncrieff,' said Ted.

'What are you going to do?' said Lancaster.

'I'm going to speak to her,' said Ted, pointing to one of the young women in the office, the one who had been placed nearest to Moncrieff's office. 'You keep him talking in there while I talk to her.'

'Who is she?' said Lancaster.

'I've no idea.'

The two of them made their way into the office. Lancaster walked briskly up to Moncrieff's office and stepped in without knocking. *Good lad.*

The young woman watched him as he walked up to her. He kept his eyes on her, not looking at Moncrieff. He put on his best incorruptible smile.

'Morning,' he said to her. 'My name's Detective Inspector Wood.' He flashed her his badge. 'And what's your name?'

She looked anxious. People tended to, when the police came calling.

'Janet Marlow,' she said.

'Well, Ms Marlow,' he said, 'we're investigating the death of Anthea Mortimer two days ago. On Anglesey.'

The anxiety flooded away and for a moment she almost smiled. But then she remembered to look sad.

'Oh, yes. Poor Anthea.'

'Did you know her?'

'Oh, yes, we all knew her. She was very popular. Everybody loved Anthea.'

'Did she have any particular problem with anyone? Was there someone who might wish her ill?'

'No. Nothing like that. I really think everyone liked her very much.'

'Good. And how long you have you worked here, Ms Marlow?'

'Only six months.'

'OK. What's your job?'

'I'm Mr Moncrieff's executive assistant.'

'That's your title is it? Executive assistant.'

'Yes.' She frowned, as if she put out by the suggestion there was anything wrong with her job title.

'So you must know how things work round here. Who comes and who goes. That sort of thing?'

She looked anxious again now. She didn't like where this was leading. There was a suggestion of movement behind her and Ted glanced that way. Moncrieff was staring at him furiously and clearly trying to get out of his office, but Lancaster was standing in his way, dutifully noting something down in his notebook. He was playing the role of the plodding sidekick to perfection.

'Well, Ms Marlow, there's a few names I'd like to put to you. See if you can remember them, if any of them have ever been in here. Allan Davies?'

She frowned, and shook her head. She seemed to be about to look behind her to see if her boss might rescue her, but Ted had other ideas. He leaned in as conspiratorially as he was able.

'I need to let you into a little secret, Ms Marlow. Your boss? Mr Moncrieff?'

Her eyes widened. He had her full attention now.

'Yes?'

'Well, we've been tracking him on Witness for some time. Someone so involved in the Investiture, we have to keep tabs on them. Where the safety of the Royal Family is in question. You do understand?'

'Yes. Of course.'

She was agog, all ears.

'I can't say much in here, but there have been some

questions raised about Mr Moncrieff's movements. He has been seen with a particular woman.'

He held out his phone, a picture of Lucy Jenkins ready for her viewing. She looked down at it, and her face clouded. It had been a guess, but it seemed to have paid off.

'Have you ever seen this woman?'

'Yes.'

Her voice was now cold and flat. The voice of a woman betrayed. She wasn't trying to look at Moncrieff anymore.

'Where did you see her?'

'At a party.'

'Where was this party?'

'In Caernarfon. Two months ago.'

When she would have been four months into her new job. Ted wondered how long it had taken Moncrieff to do his work on her.

'She spoke to your boss?'

'She spent half the sodding night speaking to him.'

She was on the edge of tears now. He needed her not to cry.

'It's OK. It's OK. It's not what you're thinking.'

She looked directly at him, pleading with her eyes.

'They're business associates. Nothing more.'

'Business associates?'

'Yes. I can't say anything more. Now, have you ever seen this man?'

He flicked through his phone, finding a picture of Sir Anthony Mayfield and showing it to her.

'Yes. He was at the party too. He's been here, as well.'

'To the office?'

'Yes. A few times.'

'With this man?'

He flicked to Sir Anthony's factotum, Lawrence Greenwood.

'Yes. Him too.'

'OK. OK. You're doing very well, Ms Marlow, your help is invaluable. Couple more faces, if I may. This one.'

Rachel Whitehouse. A shake of the head.

'No? What about this one.'

Whitehouse's assistant, Peter Holmes. Again, a shake of the head.

'Right. One last question. Have you ever heard anyone speaking about Robert Mountjoy?'

Another puzzled frown.

'*Robert* Mountjoy? No. But someone called Mountjoy works here.'

He was for a moment stunned.

'Here?'

'Yes. Jean. Jean Mountjoy.'

'Is she here?'

He looked around the place.

'No, she only works a couple of days a week.'

'What does she do?'

'Something to do with the accounts, I think.'

A big movement from behind them signalled the arrival of her boss.

'If you've quite fucking finished, Detective, Janet has important work to do.'

He didn't look at Moncrieff. Just smiled slowly at Janet Marlow, and gave her a soft conspiratorial wink.

'All done, I think. Let's be off, Lancaster.'

41

The now-familiar rigmarole at the bridge completed, Lancaster drove them onto the Island. This time, instead of bearing left towards Plas Newydd, they turned right, heading anti-clockwise round the Island, taking the road towards Beaumaris. They drove along a winding road alongside the coast, behind the backs of seaward-facing houses, some of which looked notable and impressive. How many were still occupied by private owners? How many had been co-opted into the work of the Community? What must it be like to be a freeholder in the midst of this religious takeover? Ted could think of nothing like it.

Beaumaris was an unlikely place, springing up from a flat plain beside the sea, a high street of impressive Georgian properties followed, as the road headed north, by a castle of heart-stopping beauty. Next to it, its half-built brick tower already almost as high as the towers of the castle, was the new church. St Lidwina's would soon be competing with Beaumaris Castle for the eyes of visitors.

'Both unfinished, by the looks of it,' Ted said.

'Yes, but one of them *will* be finished,' said Lancaster, firmly.

'Ever been here before?' he asked Lancaster as they continued north from Beaumaris.

'Beaumaris?'

'No. Penmon.'

'No,' Lancaster said. He looked like he might be heading for a job interview. Or to meet his Creator. Probably, this encounter was a dizzying combination of both.

'I'd have thought you would have been,' Ted said. 'You seem to be quite signed up to what this place is doing.'

'If you mean, sir, that I agree with their religious mission, then yes, I do. And I am not ashamed to say so.'

'All right, son, no need to get exercised.'

Lancaster breathed out through his nose.

'Sorry, sir.'

Ted didn't feel like letting him off with that, though.

'You're not reporting to two bosses, are you, Lieutenant?'

'Two bosses, sir?'

'Me and the Big Man,' Ted said, gesturing skywards.

'My religion is one thing. My work is another.'

That just means you're not taking one of them seriously. But he didn't say that. There was nothing to be gained by antagonising the lieutenant. But this was the kind of nonsense that came up when you injected religion into public life.

They turned off the Beaumaris road, and found themselves on a narrow but well-kept lane that twisted and turned through fields and copses. They passed more wealthy-looking properties looking out to the sea. He wondered if one of them belonged to Emyr Phillips, as developed by Thomas Jenkins. Then the road dropped down to sea level and they were driving alongside a beach. Amazing, how thrilling it still was to find oneself alongside a sandy beach in Britain, with the sun out. The day now had a crystal, warm clarity and the view over to the Mainland was tremendous, dominated to the east by the unlikely mound of the Great Orme above Llandudno.

The lane bent away from the beach and they passed fields surrounded by a half-ruined stone wall enclosing… well, what exactly? Ted could see no house. They climbed another hill, and then he saw the edge of a medieval ruin. They had arrived at Penmon, residence of the Abbot of the Community of St Lidwina.

The place had a very different feel to Plas Newydd. It was ramblingly ancient. The ruin of some big old monastic building sat up next to a small church, and connecting the two of them was what appeared to be a small house. On the other side of the lane Ted could see another ruin, massive and shaped oddly, a rectangular block topped on one end with a kind of cupola, with a small covered opening at its peak, whose use he could not fathom. There didn't seem to be anyone about.

'Let's go and say hello, shall we?' he said. Lancaster was looking at the place with a kind of anxious reverence, as if their presence was somehow profaning the air. But he followed Ted up the steps. A sign told them, in English and in Welsh, that this was Saint Seiriol's Priory Church.

'Saint Seiriol?' he said to Lancaster.

The lad shrugged.

'Not a name I know, sir.'

They went through a small metal gate into a sort of front garden. It was really just an open space between the ruin to their left and the church to their right. The little house that sat between the two was just ahead of them. The door of the house was closed, but two of the three windows above it were open. From inside, Ted could hear music.

'Is that Barbra Streisand?' he said to Lancaster.

'I've no idea,' Lancaster said.

Ted knocked on the door, and they waited for a moment. No-one came. So Ted turned to his right, to the church entrance - a great white door beneath a blue wooden portico, at the top of four stone steps. He was halfway up the steps when the door of the house on which he'd knocked opened, and the Abbot stepped out.

'Ah! Inspector. I thought I heard something. Apologies. I am glad you finally made it to Penmon.'

'You were expecting us?'

'Well, I heard you were on the Island, but I did not presume. Would you like to see inside the church?'

Ted looked at Lancaster. It was as if all his Christmases had come at once.

'Why not?' he said.

Inside, the church was much bigger than it appeared from outside. It seemed to consist of two distinct parts. To the right of the door was the altar, and this end of the church had a reassuring churchiness, with its wooden pews, wooden pulpit on a stone base, and altar behind a sturdy wooden altar-rail. It was like the inside of a morally upright Victorian prelate's brain - tidy, symmetrical, beautifully maintained.

It was a different story to the left. There, the light was heavier and older, the stone rougher and thicker.

'It is, in fact, two churches,' said the Abbot, speaking softly beside him. Lancaster was creeping in behind, a look of awe on his face. 'To your right is the Victorian church. They built on top of the old medieval chancel, and raised the altar a few feet. The body of St Seiriol is buried beneath it. But to your left is the original medieval building, beneath the Norman Tower. It has some interesting elements in it, if you care to look.'

Ted walked into the vaulted space beneath and beyond the Tower above. Turning back to face the Victorian pews, he saw a great medieval arch, or perhaps something even older, untidy and unsymmetrical, almost pagan in its lack of classical finish. He found what appeared to be a carving of a man carrying an axe.

'That is said to be Gofannon,' said the Abbot. 'The god of blacksmiths.'

'In a church?' Ted said.

'Well, if that surprises you, look at this.'

He pointed to something on the wall. It was hard to make out what it was.

'It's a sheela-na-gig,' said the Abbot.

'A what?

'An early Christian female deity. Some say even pagan. She is opening her legs. See the slit between them?'

He did see it, suddenly, and felt a deep sense of the strangeness of it. Churches were churches, a particular kind of safe space, constructed from formal designs, all fundamentally looking the same. He rarely went into them, but when he did, the sense of familiarity was part of the point. But *this* church inverted that, even more powerfully because of the homely Victorian nature at one end.

'I have a nice speech, though I say so myself, about the way this place embodies British Christianity,' said the Abbot, as if turning Ted's thoughts into a student essay. 'The Church here thrived for hundreds of years before the Normans came, building on older spiritual traditions. When the Romans left Britain, the lands to the south and east were overrun by pagans. But not here. Here, the Christians had accommodated pagan viewpoints many centuries before.'

'And that's what you mean by Celtic Christianity?' Ted said.

'In a sense, yes. There is a good deal more to it than that, of course. But fundamentally, we absorb the Victorian into the ancient.'

'Is this accepted canon? Does the Archbishop go in for paganism?'

'Well,' said the Abbot, smiling. 'I imagine York has more than its fair share of the stuff. Vikings, you see. Apparently the King finds the Scandinavian stuff *deeply* fascinating. Come, look at this.'

He took Ted deeper into the vault in the old part of the Church. He stopped before a great stone pillar. But no, it wasn't a pillar. On closer inspection, Ted realised it was a Celtic cross. It stood on a stone plinth, with the round shape of the cross perched on top of a pillar. The arms of the cross had been worn down almost to nothing.

'A stone cross, found four hundred metres from here,' said the Abbot. 'It is more than a thousand years old. Older than any cathedral. Older than St Peter's. Some say it has Viking influence. It's said you can see St Anthony facing off his demons in its surface.'

'I know as much about St Anthony as I do about St Seiriol.'

'Ah, really? Seiriol was a hermit. His cell is behind the church, by a well. It is said that there was another hermit, called Cybi, who lived at Holyhead - the Welsh word for Holyhead is Caergybi. The two of them used to walk and meet in the centre of the Island. Because he walked with his back to the sun in the morning, and the setting sun behind him in the evening, our particular saint became known as Seiriol Wyn - that is, Seiriol the Pale. Cybi walked in the other direction, with his face to the sun in the morning, so he is known as Cybi Felyn, or Cybi the Golden.'

'It's all very Middle Earth.'

The Abbot laughed out loud, a big booming disrespectful sound inside this ancient space, and it made Ted jump to hear it. Lancaster turned around, wide-eyed.

'Middle Earth! Very good, Inspector. Although I always worry I'm coming over a little Lord Summerisle.'

He put out a hand, and touched the stone of the ancient cross with great reverence. Crazy with blasphemy, all Ted could now think of was Christopher Lee.

42

Five minutes later, and the Abbot was making him coffee again. Lancaster, starstruck, sat on the other side of a rough-hewn kitchen table. Ted watched Nicholas Briggs., as was, pottering around the little country kitchen, as he had watched him the previous day pottering around behind the bar of the pub at the Bridge. It was a good act, to be fair, and Lancaster was sucking it up.

'I remember the day Tommy first came to us at St Asaph's,' the Abbot was saying. He said 'Tommy' the same way Lucy Jenkins did. 'He was terribly depressed, anxious, quite beside himself really. He said he'd done some bad things, and he needed help to come back to God.'

'To come *back* to God?' Ted said.

'Yes, I do believe that is what he said.'

'And this was… what…. a year before London?'

'Yes. I suppose it would be.'

The Abbot looked rueful.

'Odd, how London has become our dating benchmark, isn't it?' he says. 'The fixed point from where the world started again. *Anno Londinium.*'

He looked suddenly pained at that. Ted couldn't blame him.

'Given how sharp your memory is, Brother Abbot, can you perhaps answer me this: did he give any *specific* reason for coming to join your Community?'

'Well, he didn't *join* the Community, not at first. That came later.'

'Not long later, according to his wife.'

The Abbot looked confused, then his face cleared.

'Ah. Lucy.'

'Yes. You don't think of her as Tommy's wife?'

'I confess I do not. I had rather forgotten he *had* a wife. It is a common mistake, in my line of work. She doesn't like me, I fear.'

'She believes you stole her husband.'

'Yes. Tommy said it was something like that.'

'She has some harsh words to say about the Almighty, too.'

The Abbot shrugged.

'I'm sure she does. These things are never easy. Perhaps they're not supposed to be.'

'I asked you about Jenkins's reasons for coming to the Community.'

'What kind of *reason* do you think he might have given, Inspector?'

'Well. Did he tell you anything about his line of business?'

'He said something about it. Property development, wasn't it?'

'And did he say whether he had any qualms about the way he'd been developing property?'

'I can't think what you might mean. Is that the kind of thing people have qualms about?'

'In your experience, Abbot, what normally brings people back to God?'

'Any number of things.'

'Guilt, I would have thought, would be one of those things.'

'Oh, certainly. We all have something to be guilty about.'

He said this, rather theatrically, while looking into Ted's face. Ted found he wanted to shout at the Abbot, to tear down his self-possession, because he fundamentally did not trust him. Not one little bit. Certainly not enough to have him hear his confession.

'So, initially, Jenkins was just visiting your Community occasionally.'

'Yes. For almost a year, he only came occasionally. We kept an open door for anyone who wanted to pray, or think.'

'What kind of Community was it?'

'Well, first of all, it was not a Community as such. More a Community House, attached to the Northumbria Community. We kept a residence, a small place gifted to us by a wealthy supporter. And in that place, we kept to the Rule of Life of the Community.'

'And what is this Rule?'

'To be available, and to be vulnerable.'

'You will have to explain that to me, Brother Abbot.'

'Well, we must be available to God, first of all, to allow him into our heart. And we must be available to others, both in terms of offering hospitality and by taking care for their concerns and worries.'

'People like Thomas Jenkins, you mean.'

'Yes, indeed. And, secondly, we must be vulnerable, both in the sense of being open to God's teaching, and by being out in the world. We are a monastic order, but we are also out in the world, part of it, being affected by its concerns. That is what we mean by vulnerability.'

'So, you were required, by your beliefs, to offer Jenkins shelter, and to be involved in his concerns?'

'That is it, yes. Not all of it, but that is as good a summary as I could manage. It is not an entirely simple set of beliefs. We also believe in the shifting sands of the real world - in the need for our beliefs and practice to accommodate external realities.'

'Like London, and the aftermath.'

'In God's name, yes. Exactly.'

'So tell me - what changed with Jenkins?'

'In what sense?'

'Why did he stop visiting regularly, and come to stay? Just before the Emergency?'

'I do not know.'

'He never told you?'

'No. And I did not ask.'

'Was such behaviour common?'

'Yes, very normal. A proportion of all our associates took on a deeper role, some of them within the Community itself, some of them out in the world.'

'Do you think he was running, Brother Abbot?'

'Running? Running from what?'

'I don't know. The Devil, perhaps.'

The Abbot frowned. He was not happy with that line of enquiry.

'And Brother Thomas was at St Asaph's on the day the bomb went off in London?'

'He was.'

'And he stayed afterwards.'

'Yes.'

'And it was during this time you both decided to found a Community? This Community?'

'Yes.'

'And it was Jenkins's idea?'

'In some ways, yes. But it was also inevitable. People began flooding to us soon after London. This Community grew out of that moment - the need to do things on a bigger scale.'

'And Jenkins handled the politics?'

'Well, I'm not sure what that *means*, Inspector. He did tend to cover more worldly matters. I tried to adapt our previous practice to the new reality.'

'So, tell me, Brother Abbot - how much did you know about Brother Thomas's little *soirées* over at Plas Newydd? Were these what you mean by his *worldly* activities.'

'Are you attempting with your use of the word *soirée* to suggest there was something illicit about them?'

'Wasn't there?'

'Not to my knowledge. He invited certain VIPs from the Mainland to discuss important issues under conditions of confidentiality. The Chatham House rule. Wasn't that what they called it?'

'Well, sadly, Chatham House is now a pile of rubble. And Brother Thomas is dead.'

'Is that a question?'

'So you had no involvement with these VIP events?'

'Thomas kept me appraised of them, of course. But no, I did not help to organise them. I attended a few, when Tommy felt my contribution would be useful.'

'But they were beneficial to the Community. Kept you close to the seats of power.'

'I suppose so. I've never really thought of it like that before.'

'And Jenkins also handled the money side of things.'

'The money side of things?'

'That church in Beaumaris did not build itself, Brother Abbot. Where did the money come from?'

The Abbot made what Ted could only describe as a simpering expression.

'We have been most fortunate in our patrons.'

'Jenkins dealt with them?'

'Not exclusively. I have received many of them here. This place has a profound impact on the soul. Don't you find?'

Ted ignored that.

'Did you know about the works to Plas Newydd?'

'Works?'

'There has been work done to some of the bedrooms. The ceilings have been lowered. We suspect it's to accommodate wiring for some kind of computer network.'

The Abbot's self-possession seemed to wobble a bit.

'Well, I know nothing about that.'

'But he must have spent money on it.'

'Possibly. But, you see, Brother Thomas looked after that side of things. Temporal matters, you see.'

'And you're more about the spiritual side of things.'

'That's right.'

'This is the first you've heard of any of this?'

The Abbot frowned. He sipped the last of his coffee, put the cup down, and stared at it for some time.

'I cannot help but think, Inspector, that you believe I am keeping some essential truth from you. That there is some bigger picture of which I am aware. You seem to be suggesting, with some force, that Brother Thomas had some reason to kill himself. Which lends itself to suicide, as you have consistently said. But then this talk of illicit computer networks. And the terrible matter of the young woman. Her death. How on earth are you intending to draw all these threads together?'

The Abbot, it seemed, had rather hit the nail upon its head, as he would probably have said.

43

'Walk with me, Lancaster.'

The lieutenant did as he was told, following Ted up a road beyond Penmon that climbed a hill into some trees. There was, it surprised and vaguely disturbed Ted to learn, something mystical about the Abbot's coffee. Or perhaps it was something to do with the water here. Whatever it was, as they left the little house and the church, a terrible sense of clarity walked with him, and with it, a biting despondency. He knew that every hangover came walking a black dog, but there was no hangover today, and all it seemed to mean was that the black dog was more visible, more present, its sick smell in his nostrils rather than his own.

He didn't think of Laura, or of Peg. For some reason, he thought of Ellie. Did he feel something for her, after only two encounters? He hadn't been in bed with a woman for two years, and that had been a disaster, a random encounter at a conference in Amsterdam, an Austrian detective of his own age, married with children, drunk and unhappy and emptied by remorse after they'd finished. She wept for an hour while he drank. He'd fallen asleep to the sound of her weeping. In the morning she was gone, from his room, the hotel, the conference. He never heard from her again.

'Penny for them, Inspector.'

Lancaster walked alongside him, less black dog, more faithful Labrador. If Ted started accepting all these pennies people kept offering, he'd have enough for a state-subsidised lager.

'Not sure they're worth a penny, son.'

'If you don't mind my saying so, sir, I'm not feeling I'm exactly in the loop.'

'The loop?'

'Yes. The train of your thoughts.'

Ah. The train again.

'Right. No. Fair enough, Lieutenant.'

They came through a gap in the trees.

'Oh,' said Ted. 'Wow.'

The road came to an end in a small car park, to the right of which was the abandoned shell of an old pair of terraced houses which must, once, have been quite grand. Before them was the sea. The sun had come out, and the surface of the water was flat and still, broken only by a small island about a hundred yards off the coast, and a perfect black and white lighthouse which stood, impossibly, in the water itself. The sky was bigger than the world. With one spin of the finger, you could pull the horizon round to Ireland itself.

'Quite the view,' said Lancaster, matter of factly.

Yes. It was quite the view.

'OK, Lieutenant,' Ted said. Speak, think, work - and then maybe he would be able to ignore the other, older stuff that kept coming back. Maybe he'd be able to ignore his dead wife and child. 'Let's have a little chat.'

'Here?' said Lancaster, sweeping his arms across the prospect.

'I can think of no place better. Why not? No one can see us.'

'Is there a reason you're worried about being seen?' said Lancaster.

'Do I have reason to be, Lieutenant?'

'I don't know what you mean.'

Was there a pause there? The merest breath of one perhaps. Paranoia, probably.

'OK, then,' Ted said. 'Did the pathologist file his report yet?'

'No, sir.'

It occurred to him, for the first time, that he hadn't discussed any real part of this case with Lieutenant Lancaster. And by real, he meant hypotheses, theories, hunches, superstitious stuff. In the old days, Lancaster would have been a sounding board, an amanuensis. The faithful sidekick of detective dramas, there for purposes of exposition. So was he going to let him in now?

He had to let *someone* in, didn't he?

'I keep thinking about her on that bed,' said Ted.

'I'm sorry?' said Lancaster.

'Anthea Mortimer. Tied up on that bed. It doesn't sit right with me, and hasn't all along.'

Lancaster looked deeply uncomfortable with the line of argument. God, he was at times an irritating little choirboy.

'Anthea Mortimer wasn't the type. Nothing we know about her - nothing at all - suggests the kind of person who went in for that kind of horseplay.'

'So, let me get this straight. You're thinking the killer forced her into being tied up?'

'Yeah.'

'Why would he do that?'

'Two options: for a sexual kick. Or to blackmail her.'

'Blackmail her?'

Detective work was mostly a solitary activity, the working out of thoughts which seemed to blink into existence, thoughts which even Witness couldn't see. Sharing those thoughts with another was an act of trust, and it was not the kind of thing one did easily. He used to share them with Laura. Lancaster was not Laura. He was MI5, not Police. He was Witness, not CID. He was God, and not.... what? Mind? Self? Ego? He was not Ted's partner. He was not even Ted's friend. Which made all this acutely difficult.

It occurred to him - was the Lieutenant wired for sound?

Well. Something needed to happen. The King was due here tomorrow.

'Thomas Jenkins was operating a semi-clandestine route onto the Island, for the purpose of holding semi-secret discussions on.... well, on this and that. We don't know the content of those discussions, but we do know who attended them. And the attendees included Allan Davies, your Prosecutor.'

'Not my Prosecutor, sir.'

He sounded almost put out. As Ted would have been.

'No, he's not. He knows about you, though.'

'He knows about me?'

'Described you as the *coming man*, son.'

'That doesn't exactly fill me with warmth.'

Was that almost insubordination, Lieutenant?

'The boat for these little outings operated from a dock on the property of Lucy Jenkins, Brother Thomas's estranged wife,' he said. 'She looks to have had a key hand in organising these little *soirées*. And the boat was operated by Emyr Phillips, a former associate of Thomas Jenkins.'

'And Lucy Jenkins also procured female company for some of the attendees.'

'Exactly. But I don't think it ended there. We suspect that four of the bedrooms in Plas Newydd were bugged. They may have offered full video and audio feeds from within the room. The works seem to have been done since the foundation of the Community.'

'Since Brother Thomas took possession of the house.'

'Exactly. I think Brother Thomas had the house bugged. I think the intention was always to record what was going on in those bedrooms. And to use the material.'

'For what purpose?'

'Well. I can't prove it - but I'll say to you what I said to the Abbot.'

Lancaster finished the thought for him.

'That church didn't pay for itself.'

'No, Lieutenant. Indeed it did not. Which is where we come to Robert Mountjoy.'

This is the stuff the lad maybe didn't know. The stuff from the boatyard.

'Robert Mountjoy was council leader in Caernarfon before London. Successful one, too. There's a plaque to him in the town square. Though, if London hadn't happened, I think they'd have taken it down by now. Because Robert Mountjoy was as bent as a three pound note. As we used to say.'

'Where are you getting this?'

'From Emyr Phillips. The one who operates the boat that Lucy Jenkins uses to send people to Plas Newydd. I had quite the chat with him. You probably saw me having it.'

'I'm not keeping tabs on you, sir.'

The lad's voice was tight.

'Aren't you? Well then. So. Mountjoy has property on

the Island, as does Phillips, as does Allan Davies, as do both the bankers who were at the house three nights ago. As does Frank Daniels.'

'The historian?'

'The historian. And former adviser to Caernarfon council on matters regarding planning. OK. So we can assume something was going on between these people. Backhanders, I'd wager, dodgy planning permissions, the classic local corruption stuff.'

'I'm not sure I follow.'

For a moment, Ted was nonplussed. Wasn't this pretty obvious? But no. Perhaps not to a man of Lancaster's age. Because the type of corruption Ted was describing didn't really exist anymore, did it?'

'Put it this way, son. There was a time when owning land, and planning permission to build on that land, was worth a lot of money. Lots of things could devalue that land, including, say, an expert analysis saying it was of historical importance, so you couldn't build on it. Thomas Jenkins got rich off developing land - his own house, the one Lucy Jenkins now lives in, was developed with input from Frank Daniels, with money from Robert Hughes and Eurwyn Collins, and with planning permission organised by Robert Mountjoy.'

'And all of them - apart from Mountjoy - were in that house three nights ago.'

'Yes, but that could just have been coincidence. There's no evidence that I can find that Sir Anthony or Rachel Whitehouse or any of the government lot were involved in all this. But they needed money to put on their show tomorrow, and they knew who to speak to to secure it.'

'How does that work?'

'It works because I think this grift has continued after London. I think Jenkins and his little posse have been working the angles for years. I think there's been all sorts of blackmail and coercion going on, to the benefit of the Community, of the Abbot, and his church. And then there's the fact that Robert Mountjoy's wife has been employed by Moncrieff. Which links him to the affair as well. Guilt, or keeping her close?'

Lancaster didn't say anything. Ted turned and walked to the left, down towards a little sandy beach. He stepped out onto the sand. The ground softened beneath him. He heard Lancaster following. The lieutenant asked the obvious question.

'So, where does Anthea Mortimer fit into this?'

Well, that was indeed the question, wasn't it?

'She moved rooms, remember,' he said. 'When Sir Anthony made a fuss.'

'Did she know about the cameras?'

'She might have done. If she did, it meant she didn't expect anything worth recording to happen to her that night. She took one for the team - letting Jenkins and his cronies spy on a lone woman in return for keeping Sir Anthony happy and the Investiture plates spinning.'

'Or - she didn't know about the cameras.'

'Yeah. I lean towards that, I think.'

'But the killer can't have known?'

'No. He must have not known any of the rooms were bugged.'

'He?'

They paused. Ted was thinking about Rachel White-house. He assumed Lancaster was too.

The lad was standing beside him now. They were both looking out to the sea. The water and the air both seemed to be stirring the thinking juices.

'What possible motive could Rachel Whitehouse have for killing Anthea Mortimer and Thomas Jenkins?' said

Lancaster. 'We've found no link between them. They hadn't previously even met.'

'Unless Whitehouse killed Jenkins first,' said Ted. 'Pushed him off the roof, but Anthea witnessed it, so she had to see to her as well. The pathologist found brick in Jenkins's skull. There was no brick on the ground.'

'Anthea would have raised the alarm immediately, surely?'

'Possibly. Unless Whitehouse was armed. Was she?'

'She has clearance to carry a sidearm. All ministers do.'

'She could have got her man to do it. Peter Holmes. Presumably he has clearance to.'

'I can check. But even if he did it, she must have known.'

Lancaster sighed.

'I can't believe I'm having this conversation,' he said. 'The day before the Investiture.'

Ted thought about the shadows in Caernarfon, the man or men following him. Did they work for Whitehouse, or Defence, or MI6? Were they protecting their Minister? What might they do in the line of defence? He imagined a sniper in the impossible lighthouse, a landmine on the beach, a helicopter appearing over the horizon, strafing the sand, Lancaster, him.

And always the same recurring question: *why did Angela send me?*

44

The small brown shape wandered by the side of the road from Beaumaris, and Ted asked Lancaster to stop the car. The lieutenant did so, rather suddenly, with no little noise, and the small brown shape, startled, stopped by the side of the road and looked back at them.

'Wait for me here,' Ted said to Lancaster, and got out of the car.

Sister Jenny watched him as he walked up to her.

'Where are you off to, Sister?' he said.

'I missed the minibus. I'll be late for the Mitchells.'

The panic, the gestures, the inability to know how longs things took - it was all heart-breakingly familiar.

'Who are the Mitchells?' he said.

'A couple. From London. I visit them every day. It's my duty. But the minibus drops me off and I've missed it.'

'How far is it?'

'Too far!'

Her voice was rising, and it wouldn't be long until 'it's too far' morphed into 'it's not fair', if Ted was any judge.

'Why don't we drive you?'

She looked at Lancaster's night-black car, eyes wide.

'In that?'

Ah, the rudeness now. It was like talking to his own past.

'Take it or leave it.'

He smiled at her, his old broken heart at least capable of that, and he was rewarded with something that might, given time and attention and patience, have turned into a smile.

'OK,' she said, and stepped towards the car. He opened the back door. She got in, and he walked round to the passenger door, and got in.

'Sister Jennifer, this is Lieutenant Lancaster.'

Lancaster put on his best pro smile and looked into the rear view mirror.

'Hello, Sister Jennifer!'

The false bonhomie made Ted wince. Jenny didn't answer.

'Where to, Sister?' Ted said.

She looked at him helplessly.

'Oh, I don't know the way.'

That emerging panic again.

'Got an address?' said Lancaster.

She gave it to him, from memory, and he punched it into the satnav. That, at least, still worked on Anglesey.

They drove into the heart of the Island. It was cold and clear now, the greens and greys of the Island established in perfect detail. Lancaster followed the directions on the satnav. Ted didn't say anything for a while, but stole a glance into the back seat every now again. Jenny looked out of the windows at the scenery as it passed by.

'So tell me - how did you end up here, Sister?' he said, after a moment.

'I was brought here.' The tone was sullen and resentful now, wary of questions. Another in the set of Peg Behaviours he was collecting from his encounters with this angry girl. She didn't take her eyes from the window.

'From where?'

'Salford.'

'Salford! Wow. That's a coincidence. I live in Manchester.'

She didn't respond to that. Lancaster chipped in.

'Interesting,' he said, glancing at the satnav. 'This used to be the main road to the Mainland before the Expressway was built.'

Neither Ted nor Jenny said anything, and Lancaster fell silent.

They turned off the road in a little place called Gaerwen. It was a half-abandoned village, not quite a town. Many of the houses had smashed-in windows, and none of the businesses looked open. A lot of the former residents must have taken the King's money and moved to the mainland. There was a caravan park opposite an old structure which might have been the remnants of a windmill, then another one of the small industrial units which seemed to infest North Wales, this one devoid of clients, before the road narrowed into a lane. They turned off into a driveway, and parked up in front of a modern, fairly well-to-do bungalow surrounded by an overgrown lawn and some rampantly overflowing flower beds. Rhododendrons were the main thing. At least, Ted thought they were rhododendrons.

Ted got out of the car, shakily. From beyond the field on the other side of the road, he heard a once-familiar sound - the rumble of lorries on the Expressway, going to and from Ireland. The house, he noted, was called Manderley. The rhododendrons were explained. Jenny was already knocking on the door when it was opened by a smartly-dressed, attractive woman wearing old jeans and a sweatshirt. She had the look of Joanna Lumley - fit, elegant, up for anything.

'Can I help you?' she said.

'Mrs Mitchell?' Jenny said, and Ted was taken aback by her voice. It sounded grown up and in control, almost like she was talking a child. 'It's Sister Jenny, Mrs Mitchell. I've come to see you.'

The woman frowned.

'Oh, I see.' Her voice was polite. 'Yes, I see. Well, I suppose you had better come in. Do come in. Would you all like a cup of tea?'

She didn't ask who Ted and Lancaster were - just turned and went back into the house. Jenny followed her, and Ted and Lancaster followed Jenny.

Jenny told her they would very much like a cup of tea, and then a man appeared at the door beside her, suddenly, as if he'd walked quickly from another part of the house, or perhaps from outside. He was dressed for gardening. He had none of the practised politesse of the woman. He stared at them as if he had never seen people before, and Ted thought back, suddenly, to the man who had stared at him on the bridge to the Island on that first day. This man was Suffering.

'Mr Mitchell, this is Mr Wood,' said Jenny, cheerily, as they clustered in the hall. 'And this is his friend, Mr Lancaster. They're here to help me today. Shall we do some gardening?'

She had, bless her, remembered both their names, but had no conception of their titles. She took the silent man by the arm and led him through into the lounge, from where French windows gave onto a chaos of a garden. She led him outside, turning back to Ted.

'Go and help her!' she whispered, and Ted obeyed, leaving Lancaster staring out of the window at the ruined garden.

He went into the kitchen. Mrs Mitchell was standing by the sink, a kettle in her hand, staring at it as if she couldn't remember what it did. Ted caught a whiff of expensive-smelling perfume.

'Don't mind him,' she whispered. 'He's grumpy today. He had a…. a…. bad night…..'

But Ted could see that it was perhaps Mrs Mitchell, not her husband, who had had the bad night. She teetered slightly, and he took her hand and walked her into the living room as she began to cry. Ted sat her in an armchair, and she looked out of the lounge window. Ted, startled, saw her husband on the other side of the glass, looking back at them. His expression had changed. He looked suddenly purposeful and angry. The man stepped through into the living room. Ted saw Jenny and Lancaster behind him, following him into the room, but Mr Mitchell only had eyes for Ted.

'Get away from her!' Mitchell said. 'Get the bloody hell away from her!'

Jenny appeared at his side, taking his hand and stroking it.

'It's all OK, Mr Mitchell,' she said, soothingly. 'It's all OK. These men are friends. They're actually policemen. Like you were! Remember?'

Something settled in Mitchell's face. He hadn't taken his eyes off Ted, but now they swung into focus.

'Police? You're police?'

Ted pulled out his badge.

'Detective Inspector Wood, sir. At your service.'

'Sergeant Peter Mitchell. How can I help you, sir?'

The words snapped out automatically. He looked almost surprised by them.

'He's not here for work, Mr Mitchell,' said Jenny. 'He's my friend.'

Ted, feeling a bit wobbly at those words, suggested to Sergeant Mitchell that they might head to the kitchen to make tea. Lancaster stayed in the lounge with Mrs Mitchell, who was gazing at all of them peacefully. Jenny came and stood in the kitchen while Ted spoke to the old police sergeant. Mitchell stared out of the window onto the rear garden.

'We used to have a tree in the garden,' he said, in a south-east accent. Kent, maybe. 'A lovely thing. I hung a tire in it for the children to swing on. Took it down when they stopped coming, put it up again when the grandchildren came. Then they didn't come anymore. So I cut the tree down.'

Ted filled the kettle from the tap and set it to boil. He suppressed the obvious questions - where are your children and grandchildren? Are they well? There were reasons for this man's despair.

'Maidstone,' said Mitchell, after a while. 'I was a copper in Maidstone. Where were you, sir?'

The painful deference was hard to hear, but Ted ignored it.

'The Met, sergeant. Out of Peckham.'

Mitchell breathed in a jagged air.

'The Met. Ah yes, the Met.'

Ted decided to change the subject.

'Do you like it when Sister Jenny comes to visit?'

The old copper turned back to look at Jenny in the kitchen doorway. She flashed on a smile which hit Ted hard, harder than anything yet, because it was everything that was magnificent rolled into one, that smile, the sun over a mountain, the fresh cold of a hill spring, the first notes of a song you love on an old juke box in the best pub in the world.

The old copper didn't smile. He didn't say a thing. He just turned to look back out of the window. Jenny's smile faded away, and she just looked at Ted, an old look, a too-adult look. *Well. What are you going to do?*

Just then, there was not enough hate in all the world left for Ted to throw at whoever had bombed London.

'She woke up in the night,' Sergeant Mitchell said at last.

'Your wife did?'

'She woke up in the night, and she screamed and she screamed. And I put a pillow over her head.'

Ted felt suddenly and acutely sick. He looked out at the derelict garden to avoid looking at Mitchell.

'I put a pillow over her head, and I pushed down a little bit, just a little bit, and held it there. And she stopped screaming. She went very, very still. And I lifted the pillow up, and she was looking up at me. And she looked disappointed.'

Ted could smell him - an old man smell, underneath, but on top a clean smell, with a hint of cologne. A smell from another time.

'Christ Almighty,' was all he could manage.

'I'd do myself,' Mitchell said. 'I bloody would. If it wasn't for her. I think about it. Every. Fucking. Day. But if I do for myself, who's going to do for her?'

'Would anyone like some tea?'

Mrs Mitchell's voice from the living room was brittle-bright. Her husband turned to the sound of her voice, and straightened his back a little.

45

ancaster dropped him in Caernarfon before heading back to Parc Menai. It was late afternoon, and there were now crowds - actual crowds - gathering in the square. Many of them had pop-up tents and sleeping bags, preparing to spend the night to secure their slice of history. Drones hung in the air, dozens of them, cataloguing and cross-checking. Ted watched as three men in suits, not uniforms, approached one couple. They spoke to the man for 20 seconds or so, then both the man and the woman bowed their heads, quietly and utterly. The men in suits led the man away. The woman watched them go, turned away, and began packing their sleeping bags away.

Penny for them, Detective Inspector.

It had been hard, leaving Jenny in that sad house, but she had insisted. The minibus would be along later, and she had various chores to do around the place. They had left the Mitchells in the living room, the wife staring into space, the husband staring at her. Suffering.

Ted checked the map on his phone, and made his way past the castle down into the old part of town, where old

King Edward's grid system divided the quadrants between the walls. He passed the House of Constantine, and stopped to peer in the window. It was a whirlwind of activity in there, presumably preparing for the coming influx of VIPs that would accompany the arrival of the King and what remained of his family. They would be staying in the Castle itself, impregnable and secure, one way in and one way out. Some things didn't change, and a massive wall and gatehouse were still the best defence against maniacs with dirty bombs. And drones, of course. The drones helped. He imagined the Witness machines churning, the AC current pulsing into transformers like the beating of a gigantic metal heart.

The Daniels lived in an upstairs apartment above a dusty jewellers that still seemed to be open. A grey bearded face glared at him from within as he walked up to the door for the flat. It watched him while he waited, and his drone, hovering behind and above him, watched the face watching him.

Beryl Daniels answered the door. For a moment she didn't recognise him. Why should she?

'DI Wood, Ms Daniels. I've got a couple of questions I'd like to ask you and your Dad, if that's OK?'

'Umm, it's not the best time, Detective Inspector,' she said. He realised she was upset and worried by something that had preceded his arrival.

'I'm afraid it's important and it can't wait, Ms Daniels. If you don't want to answer questions here, I'll have to ask both of you to accompany me down to the station.'

The station. The words still held some power. Certainly more power than *the business park out on the ring road.*

Beryl Daniels thought for a moment, sighed, and then let him in.

The reason for her reluctance at the door was immediately apparent. Frank Daniels was drunk. He glared at Ted as he sat down and accepted Beryl's offer of a cup of tea. She sent a pleading look Ted's way as she went to the kitchen.

'Mr Daniels,' Ted said. 'Remember me?'

'The policeman.' Daniels's voice was flat and truculent, but the words weren't being slurred. He wasn't completely out of it. But his eyes were hooded and his head wobbled slightly as if he were sitting on an unseen train carriage for just one man.

'Mr Daniels, I'd like to ask you some questions about your time as a councillor.'

Daniels frowned, and looked to one side.

'Why?'

'Because I believe your relationship with Thomas Jenkins goes back further than I'd thought. To before London.'

'Never denied it.'

'No, sir, you did not. But you didn't bring it up either.'

Daniels pushed his lower lip out and above his upper lip, like a petulant child.

'What of it?'

'Why did Robert Mountjoy kill himself, Mr Daniels?'

The name startled Daniels. His head went back and his eyes widened, like Ted had just thrown a glass of ice cold water in his face.

'How the bloody hell should I know?'

'Well, what would your hypothesis be?'

'Can't read a man's mind, can I?'

'Auditors closing in, were they?'

The word *auditors* had an extraordinary effect on Daniels. He seemed to collapse in on himself, folding even further into his chair, his head dropping forward as if someone had just whipped the batteries out. He folded his hands in his lap, and took great interest in them.

'That was the truth of it, wasn't it? Auditors from the Senedd in Cardiff. Showing up and asking questions. Questions about property developments in and around Caernarfon. Developments you passed as a member of the planning committee. You, and Emyr Phillips, and Robert Mountjoy. Was that it, Daniels?'

'Can't prove anything. Long time ago.'

'That isn't a denial, Daniels.'

He didn't say anything to that.

'What did Thomas Jenkins have on you, Daniels?'

The head lifted then, the eyes looking straight across, full of an exhausted anxiety.

'Did you kill him for it?'

A fragment of a pause, and then a shake of the head.

'What did he have on you?'

Beryl came in then, with cups of tea. She fussed around with them, arranging biscuits.

'Sugar, Inspector?' she said. Ted, needing her out of the room, said yes. She went back into the kitchen. He leaned forward.

'Tell me, Daniels. Tell me now or I take you down the station and put all this on record.'

'Her mother,' Daniels whispered. 'Affair. Beryl's.... not mine.' The exhausted eyes, pleading now. 'She's all I have, Inspector. *She's all I bloody have.*'

Daniels fell back into his chair. Beryl returned with the sugar. Ted put a spoonful in, grimaced his way through half a cupful, then bid his farewells.

Beryl let him out.

'I'm sorry for his state,' she said. 'He's been under a lot of pressure, with the Investiture. Did he tell you what you needed to know?'

'He was very helpful, thank you. One more thing. Anthea's brother. She had a school photograph in her flat. He was in it. It looked to me like he'd drawn something on his face just before the photo was taken.

Beryl made a disgusted face.

'You mean the swastika,' she said. 'Yes. There was a big fuss about that. School only realised when the prints showed up, and there was nothing they could do about it. Most of the pictures were sent back. Anthea must have kept hers because, well, Roger was her brother, wasn't he?'

'He was, what, a fascist?'

Beryl made a sad laugh.

'Who knows? He was a sad, lonely little boy. Right weirdo. Don't take this the wrong way, Inspector, but not everyone who died in London was missed.'

46

He walked back towards the hotel, weaving his way between the people in the square settling in for the night. It was getting towards evening, and if there had been a sun it would have been setting, but instead the grey sky was just deepening towards charcoal. There was rain in the air. The crowds were quiet, subdued by the damp weight of the atmosphere above them. The feeling was the opposite of festive.

As he approached the entrance to the hotel, Ellie emerged from the door.

'Turn around, and keep walking,' she said.

'What?'

'Walk with me. Somewhere. Anywhere. Just don't go in there.'

'Why on earth would I not go in there?'

'Because there are men in suits with little wires going into their ears waiting for you. Two outside your room. Two in the lobby.'

'Waiting for me? How do you know?'

'Because I'm a good journalist and I know how to listen. Now, keep walking.'

She had his arm and they walked away from the hotel. He saw two suited men emerge from the entrance and watch them leave. After a moment, they began to follow.

Before he had a chance to speak to Ellie, his phone began ringing. Angela Leybourne's name appeared on screen. He accepted the call.

'Don't go back to the hotel,' Angela said, without introduction.

'So I've just been told.'

'Who the hell by?'

'Elaine Sullivan.'

'The reporter. Jesus, Ted….'

'What the hell is going on?'

'SIS.'

'You mean….'

'Yes, Ted, I mean the spooks are waiting for you. Apparently trying to scare you off isn't enough for them. They've been given the order to get you out of the way before tomorrow.'

'Given the order by who?'

'I don't know. But I suspect the Foreign Secretary.'

'Oh, come on.'

'I guess you must be getting close.'

'Close to what?'

'Close to her.'

Neither of them said anything for a moment. There was no such thing as a secure line, not on a public mobile network. Witness was listening. And who was listening to Witness?

'They won't approach you when you're with her,' Angela said after a moment.

'With Ellie, you mean?'

'She's American. She's a name. It's too high profile. Stay with her.'

'I'm not putting her in any danger, Angela.'

'All right, John Wayne. Cool your jets. She's not in any danger. Nor are you. I reckon this is just about shunting you to the side for the next day or two. You're not going to have weights tied to your legs or anything. You near your car?'

'It's in the Castle car park.'

'Too far from the crowds. Are they following you?'

'Two of them. On foot.'

'OK. Hang on.' He heard the tapping of a keyboard down the phone line. 'Yeah, I see them. OK. Lancaster's on his way. He'll meet you in the car park behind the pub.'

'The pub?'

'The one you went to with her. Last night.'

He was so old, and his mind so entrenched in the past reality, that he nearly asked her how she knew about that. Angela rang off.

'Who was that?' said Ellie as they strode across the square.

'My boss.'

'And what was that about putting me in danger?'

'You're not in danger. Neither am I.'

'So what is all this?'

'To be honest, I barely know. Politics of some kind. I've got the barest view of it. But we need to back to the pub we were in. Pronto. Lancaster's going to meet us there.'

'But they'll follow us.'

'Yes. But they're on foot. I think Angela's trusting on them not being to get to a car as quickly as we can.'

Somehow, there had been a transfer. Rather than her holding his arm, he was now holding hers. But softly. Her muscles were taut beneath the fabric. Americans still went to the gym, then. Or maybe some complicated yoga routine.

They walked for four or five minutes. The two men following kept their distance. Maybe Angela was right - maybe Ellie did project some kind of protective forcefield around him.

The pub was packed, in the last hour before protective curfew. Some optimistic soul had put up bunting, but the effect was hardly cheery. There were pictures of the future Prince of Wales dotted around the place. One had been placed next to a cardboard display of peanuts, half the packets sold to reveal a topless woman kneeling in sand, holding her breasts out to the unseeing men, who gazed only into their beers. A comeback from an older time.

They forced their way through to the back of the place. Lancaster's timing needed to be first class, and it was. He saw the lieutenant's big black tank pulling into the little car park just as they made it to the rear exit. Then they were down the steps and into the back seats, and as Lancaster pulled away Ted looked back to see the rear exit open and the two men in suits appear at the top of the steps. The lieutenant drove hard and fast, speeding out of Caernarfon with his blue light flashing, not worrying about secrecy because none of this was secret; even now a drone was speeding along beside them, his drone, perhaps, his faithful and persistent friend.

'Where did she tell you to take us?' said Ted.

'Plas Newydd,' said Lancaster.

Of course.

47

Ted stood in front of Plas Newydd, the Strait behind him, looking up at the roof. He pictured Jenkins standing up there, looking out towards the mountains. But then he saw Lancaster, up on the roof, patrolling. He raised the cup of hot tea he held in his hand. Lancaster raised something in reply - the dark brutal silhouette of a gun. The lad wasn't messing around.

'Not very *monkish*,' said Ellie, beside him.

He smiled.

'Yes. I remember you saying. And no. Not very monkish.'

'So have you worked it out?'

'Not quite. Not at all, really.'

She chuckled. It was extraordinary, given everything that had happened, that she could chuckle like that.

'Detectives. Always keeping their little secrets. You're a cliche, DI Wood.'

He found that he still liked her enormously.

Lancaster had driven like the wind, and Ted had left him

to it, asking no questions, keeping an eye in the rear window for pursuing vehicles. If there were any he didn't see them - only the light of the drone followed them close behind. And even that stopped and moved back as they moved across the Bridge to the Brothers waiting on the far side.

There had been many more of them, and police too, some of the uniforms from his arrival recognisable to him. Brother Enoch had been there, giving him a narrow-faced smile, and Brother Michael too, apparently controlling things in his stern Scottish accent. He had waved them through with none of the previous rigmarole. Ted thought about that as they drove onto the Island. Had Angela and the Abbot had a word? Had they been having words all along?

The house had been dark, locked up, but Lancaster had keys. The first thing they did was turn on all the lights, and patrol the perimeter. No one else arrived. This was to be a low-key hideout, apparently according to Angela Leybourne's wishes.

'I'm assuming this is off the record,' he said to Ellie. She laughed.

'Who knows anymore? Maybe I'll say I was kidnapped.' She sipped her tea. 'We can work that stuff out after this is over.'

'Whatever *this* is.'

'Well, indeed.'

He turned and went into the house. Ellie followed him. He went into the old study at the corner of the house, drawn by a realisation that this was something he should have done before now. There was the desk and the chairs, two old leather sofas, and a gigantic screen that took up one entire corner of the room. He stood in front of the screen, and flicked it on. A feed from the satellite dish on the roof filled the picture - a news broadcast, previewing the Investiture tomorrow.

Feeling a little queasy, Ted flicked the input button. Lucy Jenkins's boathouse, on the other side of the strait, filled the screen, the picture coming from a camera outside. He clicked the control again. Another view, from the side of the house. Click, again. The back of the house. And again, the other side. And again, back to a view looking over the Strait, but from down nearer the water - the dock, presumably. He pictured Brother Thomas sitting on his sofa, watching his own house on the other side of the Strait. Had he seen Lucy Jenkins sitting at his old desk, looking at her own screen? Did they, perhaps, watch each other watching each other? It would be an appropriate kind of marriage for the times.

'Eyes on the prize, Brother Thomas had,' said Ellie.

'Yep.'

Ted kept on clicking. This time the screen went black, as on his previous visit. Another click. Another black screen. And another. He clicked perhaps a dozen times, before the screen reloaded with the image of the dock and the Straits.

'Why does it cycle round again' said Ellie.

'Because those other feeds are dead. Cameras unplugged or removed.'

'So where were the cameras.'

'In the bedrooms, I think.'

'The bedrooms?'

'Yes.'

He looked at her. She looked back. There was a world of understanding in that glance.

'Were there recordings?'

'I think so.'

'Where are they now?'

'We don't know. The box which stored them was probably removed. From the basement.'

'By who?'

'These are really excellent questions. You should be a reporter.'

He walked round to the desk, tried all the drawers. All of them slid open easily, but they were all empty. Which was rather strange, wasn't it? And wasn't it rather strange that there didn't seem to be any paper files anywhere in this place? No filing cabinet, no storage of any kind. Hadn't Lancaster said they preferred to write things down? So where had that writing been stored? He remembered the print out in Brother Thomas's robe - the seating plan, the annotations. He obviously did write stuff down. But then what?

'You have a thinking face on, detective,' said Ellie. 'I like it.'

He smiled, distractedly. He forced himself not to think too hard, to look at the room and allow it to talk to him - it was a trick he'd used countless times, and sometimes it worked, and sometimes it didn't. It hadn't worked with Churchill, the Peckham killer.

The hiding place would need to be convenient - easy to get to in case he was disturbed. So no clambering up to ceilings. Somewhere accessible - hidden, but not *too* hidden. Somewhere to hide a flat shape, about the size of a large book. Somewhere Priestley would have missed, though that didn't say much - she'd been hard pressed to find anything in this gigantic place, with no assistance.

He imagined Brother Thomas coming in here, closing the door behind him if there were others in the house, leaving it open if there weren't. Walking towards the desk, stopping somewhere on the way to retrieve the thing he'd hidden.

A drinks cabinet. An odd thing for a monk to have. But Ted now barely thought of Brother Thomas as a monk at all. He had been wearing a disguise, a costume. And Thomas Jenkins, the old blackmailing rogue, would definitely have had a drinks cabinet. Ted opened the cabinet's doors. Bottles sparkled attractively at him, sparking the old thirst back into life, but he ignored it. Priestley would have opened it, looked inside, closed it again. She wouldn't have noticed that there was a small void beneath the shelf on which the bottles nestled. She wouldn't have put her hand in, flat, and felt the metal surface sitting there.

He pulled it out. It was an old Macbook Air - more than 10 years old, by Ted's reckoning. More than London old. More than Witness old. The same kind Ted himself had had once. He took it over to the desk, Ellie following. It was charged already - the charger would be another thing they'd have to find. It flicked on at the press of a button.

But then it asked him for a password.

'Bollocks,' said Ted.

'Bollocks doesn't sound good.'

'This is a pre-Witness machine. New computers sold in Britain have to have backdoor access for the police and security services. I can access any of those with a password override. But not this one.'

'So we have to guess the password?'

'Yeah. I don't imagine it's super-secure. He wouldn't want to write it down, or change it so regularly it would be hard to remember. Just enough to keep randomers away.'

'Randomers like you, you mean?'

'Yeah. I wonder.'

He pulled out his phone, opened the Witness app, scrolled through some contact details and phone numbers, clicked on one of them. He pondered putting the thing on speaker, and then reminded himself Ellie was a civilian, not police. It was nice having her around and everything, but she wasn't his partner.

Lucy Jenkins answered her phone.

'Lucy, hello,' she said. Informal but guarded.

'Mrs Jenkins, this is Detective Inspector Wood.'

'DI Wood. What an unpleasant surprise.'

'I'm going to make some generalised threats now, Mrs Jenkins. Locking you up for procuring sex work. Blackmailing VIPs. Conspiracy to obstruct justice. If your friend the banker is with you, he'll be facing some of the same stuff. You could go away for a long time. Or worse.'

A bitter laugh crackled down the line.

'Make me disappear is it, detective?' Lucy said. 'Didn't take you long to show your true colours. But I presume this charade has a point. You want something.'

'I do. I want a password.'

'A password?'

'Your husband had an old laptop. A pre-Witness laptop.'

She breathed out.

'And you've found it. Well. Fuck me sideways.'

And then she laughed again.

'And you can't get into it, can you, detective? Your sneaky little backdoors won't work. Heh. Clever bastard. Clever dirty bastard.'

He waited. She waited. She blinked first.

'So, what? You're offering me immunity?'

'You know I can't do that. I'm offering to tell the prosecutor that you helped. That stuff matters. Now more than it ever did.'

'Allan Davies? That prosecutor? Wouldn't trust him with my used toilet paper.'

'Not Davies. Angela Leybourne.'

She breathed again, this time with a slight shudder.

'Oh, Jesus. Leybourne.'

'Yeah. She's tough, but she's straight. She'll listen to me if I ask for leniency.'

Lucy Jenkins was well informed, he'd give her that. The name of the north west prosecutor wasn't well known. But he imagined Mrs Jenkins had learned to keep files as effectively as her husband.

'OK. OK. I think I remember what the password to that laptop was. But there were three he used regularly. He might have changed to one of the other three.'

'Give me all of them.'

'y-n-3-u-8-d-d'

'The name of your estate with numbers?'

'That's it.'

'Lower case?'

'Yes.'

'And the second?'

'3-r-1-c-c-8-n-t-0-n-8'

'Eric Cantona? With some numbers?'

'Yeah.'

'OK. And the third?'

She breathed out again. Paused. Then finished it.

'lucyj8n3'

And then she hung up.

He looked at the passwords he'd written down, thought for a moment, and then tried the last one she'd given him - her birth names.

The screen opened up. On the desktop was a picture of Lucy Jenkins. Ted smiled.

'You gave up a lot, didn't you, you slippery bastard?' he said.

'Who is that?' said Ellie. He had almost forgotten she was there.

'Lucy Jenkins. His wife.'

'She was the one you were speaking to?'

'Yeah.'

He opened the browser - an old Google Chrome thing. An extension was running providing a VPN - the kind of thing that was no longer permitted, but had once been common. Witness wouldn't have been able to track the activity from this machine because, by the looks of it, Witness thought the machine was in Norway, one of the few countries that had stuck to the older privacy laws.

He opened the browser history screen.

The last entries were from just after midnight on the night of the two deaths. There were perhaps a dozen website addresses related to Rachel Whitehouse. It was all standard public internet stuff - news sites, biographies, the Minister's departmental profile page.

'He had a serious jones for Ms Whitehouse,' said Ellie.

Ted wondered about asking Ellie to leave. But she'd been spirited away from Caernarfon in a police car, having been pursued by agents of Britain's Secret Intelligence Service. She was hardly a bystander any longer.

There was one page with Peter Holmes in the title. Ted clicked on it. A departmental page listing Peter Holmes. His petulant, sulky photo gazed back at him. A face which sparked immediate dislike.

'Who's that?'

'Rachel Whitehouse's personal secretary.'

'He looks like a right little shit.'

Ted sat back in Brother Thomas's leather chair.

'Is that all there is on him?' said Ellie. 'One page?'

'Yep.'

'Shame.'

He turned to look at her.

'No, it's not a shame. It's interesting.'

She thought for a moment.

'You mean it's interesting because there isn't *more* about him.'

'Uh-huh.'

'And because Brother Thomas was checking him out. But hang on, surely he checked out *all* the guests.'

'Maybe. But look at the time in the history window.'

She looked.

'Just after midnight.'

'Yeah. When Whitehouse and Holmes had already been here for hours. I mean, I'm sure he looked into them *before* the party. But afterwards? Why would he do that?'

She thought about it.

'Because something happened at the party.'

'Because something happened at the party.'

'He saw something?'

Ted looked back at the screen. Two search result pages caught his eye. Philip Mortimer. Roger Mortimer. He clicked on the result pages. They weren't particularly helpful - a search on one name on the Internet wouldn't be helpful, unless it was a very unusual name. But there was another related search - for Roger Mortimer's name, with one added word. 'Fascist'.

'What the hell?' said Ellie.

'Roger Mortimer was Anthea Mortimer's brother. Died in London. We found a picture of him with a swastika on his forehead.'

But the search results page was clear. No results.

'Seems unlikely,' said Ellie. 'How often do you see a search page with no results?'

'Not often. Not often at all.'

He was picturing it now. Anthea Mortimer had been in here, with Brother Thomas. She'd seen or heard something, and she'd brought some scraps to Brother Thomas.

Something connecting Rachel Whitehouse and Peter Holmes with her brother and her father.

There was one other search query in the history. This one was for the map search, which had only grown more sophisticated under Witness. It was a search for Trearddur Bay. Ted's memory ground through gears while his eyes scoured the map. A road ran all way behind the beach. Ravenspoint Road.

Ravenspoint.

RPT?

19 RPT. That had been scribbled on the seating plan in Mitchell's robe. 19 Ravenspoint Road. Was that what Anthea had told Brother Thomas? But why on earth had Anthea suggested looking at that?

48

Somehow, Ellie managed to rustle up some fresh steaks and potatoes and even butter - 'Brother Thomas kept a decent larder,' she said, emerging from the kitchen in the basement (she didn't go near the other room down there, the one from which they'd taken all the technical paraphernalia) with a tray on which were three plates. Lancaster, meanwhile, surprised both of them by appearing with an opened bottle of something red and French.

'There's a *cellar?*' said Ted, disbelievingly.

'Well, it's a cupboard,' said Lancaster ruefully. 'But it's filled to the brim with decent wine.'

'And how would Lieutenant Lancaster know about decent wine?' Ted said.

'Leave the lad alone,' said Ellie, taking the bottle off Lancaster and sniffing it. 'Wow. He's not wrong. This is the real stuff.'

They ate in a room looking over the Strait, with the lights off - a decision they arrived at silently, without discussion, but it meant they could both see the lights across the Strait and the dark imaginings of Snowdon behind, but it also meant they could see down to the water's edge and the terraces outside, meaning they'd see anyone moving around out there.

They ate silently but companionably, Lancaster in particular making occasional noises of delight, both at the steak and the wine, while Ted just celebrated the potatoes and the butter, simple pleasures on a complicated evening. The wine was, indeed, delicious, but he sipped at barely half a glass, controlling himself, and though Ellie said nothing he caught her noticing a few times.

At the end of the meal, they all sat back and looked at the view for a while, saying nothing. It was the kind of moment one experienced rarely - heightened by the extraordinary circumstances in which they found them-selves, sweetened by the rarity, enriched by spending it with two part-strangers who had each become, each in their own way, a kind of companion.

After a few minutes, Lancaster stood.

'Time to take a look around, and lock up, I think. The beds aren't made up, but there are blankets in a cupboard at the end of the hallway upstairs. I've left it open for you both.'

A moment of acute embarrassment, then, as if the lad didn't know what he might be suggesting, and didn't want to be thought badly of, but it passed when he walked out of the room.

'A sweet man, I think,' Ellie said.

'Yes. I think you might be right.'

She didn't say anything for a while, and neither did he. He didn't want this suspended moment in time to end. But then she ended it, or at least moved into another phase, with what she said next.

'What are we going to do about tomorrow?'

Oh, God. The coincidence. The terrible bloody coincidence. He actually groaned with it. Groaned out loud, loud enough to look at him.

'What is it?'

'I need to tell you something, I think.'

'You don't need to tell me anything, Ted.'

'Well. Tell someone, then. Anyone.'

He sipped at the wine, the tiniest of sips, a microbe of Dutch courage.

'The night before London, I went for a drink with some locals. We were living in St Albans. It's a place just north of London. The other men were dads at my daughter's school. I don't know why they invited me, to be honest. I never had very much to do with the school. My wife used to complain about it, though Peg never did. When I asked her if I should get involved more, she'd roll her eyes and say something like 'oh God, no, that would be the worst."

She'd leaned to one side in her chair, kicking off her shoes and pulling her feet under her so she was curled up in the seat. She rested her chin on one hand, and gazed at him while he spoke. The word seemed right: *gazed*. He couldn't remember ever receiving anyone's attention like that - well, not since Laura, anyway.

'I certainly didn't endear myself to this group of men that night. I got astonishingly, sickeningly drunk. When I drank beer in quantities like that - and I usually don't, I prefer my oblivion delivered in short measures - it worked as a kind of sedative on me. I found myself unable to make decisions, including the one decision that mattered: the one that says 'you've had enough."

'I hear you,' she said. It was a big phrase for something so small. It meant *I understand what you mean, and I share your concern, because I've felt that too.*

'They left me in there, the bastards. Or perhaps I refused to leave. I never saw any of them again. I don't know how much more I drank, sitting there on my own. All I do know is that, at some point, my wife came to pick me up. I was sitting there, in this pub - it was called the Jolly Sailor, the Jolly Fucking Sailor - and in she walked. She looked at me, and I was drunk, and I didn't care. And I said it, then. I said it.'

His voice broke. She lifted her chin from her hand, and the hand reached out to his, and she held his hand, and squeezed.

''I know what you've been up to,' I said. 'You've been enjoying yourself in Peterborough.' Enjoying yourself. Oh Jesus Christ.'

He heaved a massive breath in through his nose. Her hand held on, which meant he was able to.

'She didn't reply, at first. She just looked down at the table. It seemed *ages* before she said anything. I knew, you see, that she'd been seeing someone else. A man in Peterborough. I knew *everything* about him. I'd been keeping tabs on the bastard for *months*. But I'd not gone up there, and I'd not said anything to her. And there it was. Finally, she looked up at me. She *stared* at me, and she didn't say anything. But I think I know what she meant. She was begging me with her eyes, you see. Begging me not to do this. And then she said: 'I'm driving you home.''

He wiped snot away from his nose with the back of his hand.

'It's bloody odd,' he said. 'Bloody odd. Normally when I'm drunk I can't remember a thing from the night before. But I can remember every detail. Every single bloody detail. I was in the car, and she was driving. I looked out of the window, didn't say anything. She was a really good driver, really scrupulous and quiet and systematic, and I remember thinking, I bloody well *remember thinking*, that I could have just reached over if I'd wanted to, reached over and touched her shoulder or her hand as she drove, and everything might have been OK, somehow that would all have been fine. But I didn't reach across the car. And then we were home, and I was walking up the stairs to bed, and she was in the hallway downstairs, and then she said it, the last words she ever said to me, and the thing is, Ellie, the bloody thing is, you just said them too.'

She turned round and now held his hand in both of hers.

'Oh God, Ted. I'm so sorry.'

'*What are we going to do about tomorrow?* That's what she said. And I didn't know what she meant. I didn't understand. I just carried on up the stairs and fell onto the bed and slept for hours and hours and hours.'

Another shuddering heave of breath in, a last shot of oxygen before the finishing line.

'When I woke up, I understood. I knew exactly what she'd meant. Peg had been due to go on a school outing. I'd taken the day off to go with her. We'd never done anything like that before. Peg thought it was amazing that I was going with her. And you see the thing was the outing was a school history trip. To Westminster. To see the Queen opening Parliament.'

'Oh God, Ted.'

'I woke up at just past two o'clock. Just past it. And the thing is, Ellie, the thing I always wonder is: did that bomb going off wake me up?'

DAY FIVE

49

He decided, given how lovely the morning was, to take his coffee up onto the roof. He barely remembered the way, getting pretty lost in the stairwells and hallways. The doorway into the bedroom where Anthea Mortimer died was open, but he did not go in there. He found himself back on the similarly municipal-looking hallway, and then found the final little staircase, with the door at the top of it, and then he was out on the roof.

The air was clear, and so was his head. There'd been a moment, that morning, when he'd woken up as old Ted, his brain foggy with hangover, half expecting his outstretched hand to brush against Ellie's side as she slept, already processing the mistakes that had been made and the apologies that would need to be offered. But there was no Ellie. He was asleep alone on an unmade bed, still wearing yesterday's clothes, and Ellie was in another bedroom, because they'd gone to bed sober and self-aware, and nothing untoward or unnatural had occurred.

Unnatural? Yes, unnatural. Some things were not

meant to be. Some things were the stuff of unlikely thrillers.

He made his way carefully towards the front of the house, the side which faced out onto the Strait, away from the side from which Thomas Jenkins had fallen, for whatever reason. The mountains were drawn clearly against the azure sky, a child's sketch of mountains, all sharp downslopes and symmetries. But the eye was drawn more to the buzz over Caernarfon, over to his right. A column of objects stood in the sky - circling helicopters the most visible components, but smudged against the sky a squadron of drones, each one barely a dot at this distance, but in aggregate a cloud, a fog of Witness to record every aspect of this astonishing day. Somewhere beneath that cloud a boy was preparing for his big day, a speech in English and in Welsh, under the watchful eyes of his Father. A celebration of renewal and, for the Welsh, a reminder of the political realities.

Though not just for the Welsh - a reminder for all of them. Power always collected itself round a pole of attraction in this ancient kingdom, and that power was itself attracting a cloud of devices, sky high, electronic courtiers to an electronically-sustained throne.

Ellie would be back there now, underneath that crowd and, he trusted, safe enough from the men who had been waiting for him at the Lloyd George Hotel. She'd insisted on returning - 'I've a job to do, Ted, don't take that away from me' - and, after a quick phone consultation with Alison Leybourne, it had been agreed. Lancaster had driven her back to Caernarfon, before making his own way to Deganwy. Ted's own drone-chain, no longer employed while he was on Anglesey, was allocated to Ellie. 'They'll see we've done that,' Alison said. 'It's like a big flashing red light on Witness.'

She didn't elaborate on who *they* were. She'd called them 'the competition' back when they'd last spoke.

So he stood on the roof, sipped his coffee, and he waited.

At just after 10am, his phone pinged with a new message from Lancaster. *I'm here*, it said. Ted replied. *OK. Call me as soon as it's done.* A moment later, another ping - a thumbs-up emoji.

Trusting this to Lancaster still seemed like a risk. He still wasn't entirely sure what game the lieutenant was playing. Was he working for Ted, for Angela, or for somebody else entirely? Was he tied up with those men who'd been waiting for him at the hotel, the Foreign Secretary's mob, the Secret Service, the 'competition'? Traditionally, men like Lancaster - expensively-educated, well-connected men - had headed in their direction rather than Ted and Angela's way - spies and spooks, not police and surveillance. Witness might sit across both camps - Security Service and Secret Service, MI5 and MI6, Home Secretary and Foreign Secretary - but men and women didn't. They backed their horse and they stayed with it. The new thing, of course, was Security Service men and women doing the police training and joining the likes of Ted in the reorganised police divisions, now conjoined with the Security Service into one domestic instrument - or *secret police*, as those with long European memories might call it. Lancaster was part of that new breed. But did he feel the old tug in the other direction - the glamour of old spy movies, the secret poisoned glitter of the secret agents?

Well. Ted didn't have anyone else. Angela had seen to that, apparently. Lancaster it was going to have to be.

His phone buzzed, pulling him out of his reverie. It was Lancaster, calling via video, as the young folk seemed to like to do. Harder to fake, he supposed.

Lancaster was sitting in his black German tank. He looked elated.

'Sir?'

'I'm here, lad. How did it go?'

'Exactly as you predicted. She ID-ed him right away. His real name is, or was, Simon Evans. She had a really strong response to the picture. Burst into tears, said he was a devil and a monster, and he was the one who had put her lad on the wrong path.'

'And the father?'

'Ah, she clammed up a bit on the father, sir. Just kept saying he was a 'proud man, a proud man'. That's how she put it. Wouldn't be drawn any more than that. But she said Evans knew him too, said the two of them together used to go out with Roger Mortimer. And you were right about that too.'

'Anglesey?'

'Yeah. They spent weeks and weeks on Anglesey. Trearddur Bay, like you thought. They were there for a fortnight just before London. She wasn't allowed to go with them, she told me. Not for that last few months before London, and certainly not for that last visit the fortnight before.'

'Right. Right.'

'So do I bring him in, sir?'

Ted didn't answer at first. There was something else here, something curled up and hissing beneath all this. He almost had his finger on it, but didn't dare touch it in case it bit him.

'Sir?'

'Not just yet, lad. I want to go to that house first. If I'm right, it'll be just how they left it. Pick me up at Plas Newydd. We're going fishing.'

50

They drove in Lancaster's German tank, cutting across the countryside north of Plas Newydd and hitting the A55 Expressway to Holyhead after about five or six miles. The old road signs had been painted over and replaced with IRELAND FERRY TRAFFIC ONLY notices aimed at deterring random motorists, most of whom would be Community tourists. There were some cars pottering along the Expressway, most of them driven by elderly folk who, Ted assumed, still owned property on Anglesey and were clinging on to it with their fingernails.

They followed the Expressway almost into Holyhead itself before turning off to the left and taking a road which fell down onto another beach - Trearddur. This had once been a destination of some repute, it seemed - there were abandoned pubs and restaurants and dozens, if not hundreds, of bungalows and holiday homes.

Ravenspoint Road ran the full length of the beach and more, but then: a problem. Number 19 did not exist. There was a row of fairly modern properties, but a vacancy between numbers 23 and 15. Had this been a target for property development, then? For a moment, the case was gone, slipping away into the waves on the beach below.

But then they came upon something else. Lancaster spotted it. A grandiose pair of gates, with the gatepost topped by metal ravens, their wings outstretched. Three wings rather than four - one of the ravens was missing its left one. The gates were locked shut with a forbidding chain. RAVENS POINT read a sign.

'Got a crowbar?' Ted said. Lancaster looked at him. Ted sighed, somewhat theatrically. 'There was a time, son, when no self-respecting copper went out without a crowbar in his boot.'

He got out of the car without waiting for a reply. The wall on either side of the gate was pretty low, but he still made a meal out of getting over it. He didn't look behind him to see Lancaster sail languidly over it, probably - he just began traipsing up the hill.

Ravens Point was an estate of some forty homes built on a headland above the sea. The houses nearest the sea backed onto cliffs and the sound of waves crashing below was loud. But apart from that there was silence. No cars were parked, no children played, no dogs were being walked. Many of the windows were smashed, and weeds grew out of the pavements, the tarmac and the running-riot front lawns.

Number 19 - *Cigfrain's Rest*, Mrs Mortimer had called it - was no exception to these rules. It was in keeping with all the other houses - painted white, some exposed brick, a driveway and a separate single garage off to the side. The name was etched into a faux-wooden sign. Built in the 1970s, Ted reckoned, with perhaps three bedrooms inside. None of the windows were smashed, but that seemed more by accident than design - it was a fair way into the estate, and whichever kids had enjoyed themselves to the sound of breaking glass probably couldn't have been bothered with the longer walk. Or maybe there were other reasons locals avoided this place.

He sent Lancaster to the front door while he went to inspect the garage. There was a single window at the side of the little square block, but it had some kind of light-blocking blind or curtain on the inside so he couldn't see within. The main garage door was locked, and so was the side door, down a passageway between it and the house. A hefty padlock secured this door, which was opposite a back door to the house, also secured by a padlock. Both were rusted and ancient-looking. He found himself asking what police procedure said, these days, about forcing entry. Before Witness, he'd have needed a warrant to start forcing doors when no-one was in. Since Witness, such niceties had essentially been automated. Witness itself supplied the warrant, based on its own database results, which were themselves based on probabilities. He didn't fully under-stand how this worked. In fact, he wondered if anyone did, really. But the upshot was this: if the system said nefarious activity was probable, you got your warrant. They could send it to your phone, instantly.

But what happened on the Island? Did Witness policing procedures apply? Then he noticed that there was an illegal satellite dish on the roof of the garage, and told himself to stop dancing around the issue and get inside. All bets were off. In many ways, all bets had been off for years.

The driveway up to the garage door was lined with white decorative rocks. He picked one of these up, and chucked it through the glass window at the side of the garage. Then he wheeled an ancient wheelie bin round to the side, and used it to climb into the window, his knees creaking and, at one point, his back wrenching itself awkwardly, such that he knew it was going to hurt for at least a week, that he'd wake up tomorrow wincing and grumbling. But tomorrow was another day.

He pushed broken glass out of the way, then shoved the blackout curtain aside, and then stepped down into the garage. The curtain fell back into place, so it was almost pitch black inside again, but he used the light on his phone to find his way to the door, felt around for the light switch, and then flicked it on. Nothing happened. Of course it didn't. Whatever bulb there had been had died years ago. He was left to sweep the phone light around the space.

The place was a mess. Dozens of bottles and cans littered the floor, covered in dust. There was an old and rancid smell of spilled beer - years old, he had never smelled anything quite like it. There had been a party in here. It did not look like the kind of party to which Ted would have cared to be invited.

For one thing, there were the swastikas. Not even just swastikas - actual Nazi flags, six of them lining the walls, hanging down in some naff, desperate echo of Nuremberg, picked out one-by-one by Ted's phone light, like a spotlight picking across a triumphant rally. *Riefenstahl's garage*, he thought to himself as his light picked out the flags, one by one.

Then there were the framed photographs. Hitler, Mussolini, Franco. Trump. A face which was not immediately familiar, but soon rolled into focus: Timothy McVeigh. A roll-call of hate on the walls. He recalled that poster in Caernarfon station - there were any number of faces for this kind of hate.

And finally, in pride of place at the end of the garage, a familiar face from the past now locked in shadow in an Anglesey garage. A smiling brown face, grey hair, the familiar look of vague discomfort at having a photograph taken, Ted's phone light passing across the features like a searchlight in an air raid. The deceased Mayor of London looked down at him, unaware of the liberties that had been taken with his face, scrawled as it was with obscenities and hidden behind eight letters and an exclamation mark, exerting all who looked at it to hail victory.

Amazing, the power this stuff still had to spark fear and rage. The old magic still worked. He could almost smell the hate in here. It bubbled beneath the old beer bottles and cans, the damp concrete floor, the heavy Welsh air that promised rain as it always promised rain. He imagined them, these men, shouting and singing and hugging each other in celebration.

But in celebration of what?

He heard a knock at the main garage door, and he walked over to it. A locking mechanism on the inside handle took some fiddling with, given the rust, but he eventually popped it open, shoving the garage door out and upwards, and letting daylight and fresh air into the place. Lancaster was standing outside. It must have been quite a sight for the lad, looking down into this tunnel of hate, the flags lining the walls, the face at the end. The colour drained from his face. He looked like he might be sick. Ted let him take it in for a moment. Some things didn't need commentary.

'Did you get into the house?' Ted said after a moment.

Lancaster looked at him, almost in relief.

'I…. smashed a window, sir. Haven't been in yet. Wasn't sure of the regs, to be honest.'

Ted smiled at him. The lad really was something. He wasn't going to give him a hard time. After all, the regs were the last line of defence against the hate within that awful space.

51

The window Lancaster had smashed in was on the far side of the house to the garage. It was small enough and high up enough for Ted to refuse entry.

'In you go, son,' he said to Lancaster. 'See if you can find some keys. Or a bigger window, lower down.'

Lancaster clambered inside, leaving Ted with his thoughts. He wandered around outside the house, looking but not really looking, walking and thinking. He looked at his watch. Approaching midday. The great and good would be gathered inside the Castle. The crowds outside would be looking at the screens. In the old days, the breathless BBC coverage would have claimed *the world was watching* at moments like this, and perhaps there had been a time when it was. Not any longer. He thought of Ellie, hoped she was safe, thought about texting her, but then there was a shout from the back of the house. He walked round between the garage and the kitchen, and found Lancaster standing at an open patio door.

'Good work, son,' he said. He followed Lancaster into the house, relieved at not having to climb into anything.

The living room was in a similar state to the garage, though without the far right paraphernalia. Here there were bottles and stale, rancid ashtrays. A widescreen TV of the old type stood in the corner. Sleeping bags lay along the two sofas. Perhaps this was where they slept it off. Whatever *it* had been.

He exited the living room, went into the hall. It was filthy - men coming in and out with all kinds of shit on their boots, and no women to shout at them. The kitchen was similar - a horror of unwashed dishes, years old, presumably nursing new forms of life by now. Which left upstairs.

The stairs led straight up into a second living room, open plan, with a large window looking in the direction of the sea. You couldn't *see* the sea, but it was almost enough to know it was there, a cleaning, destabilising force in this place of filth. And the filthiest thing of all was the body.

It was more skeleton than cadaver by now, and must have stunk to high heaven for a good time after it had been left. It lay, face down, in the middle of the carpet. There was little enough need to establish cause of death - a rusting kitchen knife stood, straight up, from its back, locked in place by its rib cage.

Ted looked at Lancaster. The lad's face was grim and set but had lost none of its colour. This house of horror had lost some of its ability to shock.

'Got any gloves, son?' he said.

Lancaster felt in his jacket pocket, pulled out some blue latex.

'Good lad. See if you can get some DNA off that. Don't disturb the knife.'

Lancaster got to work, and Ted began moving around

the room. He didn't know what he'd been expecting to find, quite. The body was a surprise. He might have hoped for incriminating maps on walls, or scale models, or something, but there was nothing like that.

He spent a fruitless half-hour looking round the room (pondering, in the meanwhile, that the new Prince of Wales must have been delivering his speech by now). Lancaster finished his swabbing, going out to his car a couple of times to collect bits of apparatus to take and store swabs. The body remained face down. A semi-decomposed skeleton inside what looked like a Supadry jacket, the only damage to which seemed to have been the knife going into the rear. Supadry. Another echo from the time before.

He looked at the jacket for a while.

'So, whoever did this left the body here,' he said to Lancaster. 'They didn't come back to dispose of it.'

'No, sir.'

'Perhaps they weren't able to?'

'Because something happened to them?'

'Yes. Because something happened to them. They just left it here. Which means they didn't have time to dispose of it before they left, either.'

'They were on a schedule.'

'Precisely. They were on a schedule.' Ted thought for a moment. 'Is there an airport or anything near here?'

Lancaster pulled out his phone, tapped onto the screen. He looked at Ted.

'There was, yes. Anglesey airport. Leased from the RAF. About five k from here.'

'OK, then. OK. They're rushing to catch a plane - either scheduled or private, we can check that. They can't miss it, because it's part of a grander plan. Something happens as they're leaving, an altercation or something, there's a fight, again unplanned, because that poor sod has been got with a kitchen knife, not a hunting knife or anything like that. Someone went downstairs to get it, someone, maybe the same someone, shoved it in his back, and then whoever was left scarpered for the airport. Make sense so far?'

'Makes sense to me.'

'OK. OK. Which has got me thinking, Lieutenant Lancaster - what's in his pockets?'

'His pockets?'

'Yeah. What's in his pockets?'

There was a time when Lancaster might have stopped him. Chain of evidence, and all that. But this time, when Ted squatted down next to the body, the staunch military man said nothing at all. Ted carefully felt around both sides of the body, pushing his hands up into the jacket. Of course, the bloody thing was zipped up.

'I'm going to have to turn it over,' he said, not looking at the lieutenant, who said nothing in reply. Ted took hold of the kitchen knife, gave it a couple of tugs, and when nothing happened gave it a sharper one, and it came away with a sickening screech. He held it up to Lancaster, who took it off him and placed it in an evidence bag. Ted turned back to the body.

He put a hand on each shoulder, breathed in hard, and turned it over.

The first thing that happened was that the head separated from the torso, its connective tissue long corroded away. It rolled gently the other way, ending up facing the far wall, and not facing Ted. Thank Heaven for small mercies.

The legs didn't twist with the torso, so Ted thought they were probably separated as well. No time to worry about such things. He unzipped the Supadry jacket, and felt around inside. There was a wallet, which he took out and handed to Lancaster. While the lad looked through it, he continued to feel inside. There was a narrow sharp edge. Something on paper. Presumably terribly fragile after all this time.

'Philip Mortimer,' said Lancaster from behind him. 'Anthea's father.'

'Right,' said Ted, in barely a whisper. 'Right.'

His finger and thumb grasped the edge of the paper. Slowly, ever so gentle, he began to pull it out. For a moment it seemed to stick on something inside, and he was terribly afraid it was about to rip, and then it came, sliding out silently and swiftly.

A piece of folded paper. He placed it on the floor and gingerly opened it. The print was fading, almost gone, but was still perfectly legible. It was a boarding pass, for an early morning flight from Anglesey Airport.

'Look at the date,' he whispered. 'Look at the bloody date.'

London.

52

The cloud of drones hung over the church, looking down through the unfinished roof, the skeletal walls, the half-completed construction funded by who-knew-what kinds of back channels bifurcating out from Plas Newydd and its secret cameras and microphones. Did blackmail pay for the whole thing? Or just the final bit of financing? How far did the King unlock his purse, and did he know that his beneficence was in a co-funding arrangement with something far older and darker?

Rumour was, the King had insisted that the church remain unfinished for this day. Someone somewhere (Frank Daniels, perhaps?) had told him that the first Investiture, of Edward the Second, had taken place in a half-built Caernarfon Castle, and he'd liked the idea of blessing a new structure with the sanctity of the Family. Ted wondered if he'd anticipated the light drizzle. At least the King presumably had someone to hold his umbrella.

Most of the hangers-on were outside the church, to the extent that they could be outside a structure that was still only notional. They clustered under large black umbrellas -

all the same colour. Sir Anthony's attention to detail, presumably. The women wore bright dresses which looked weirdly inappropriate in the dreary rain. The men wore suits of varying hues, overwhelmingly dark, because North Wales didn't lend itself to something in beige and linen. The whole effect was as if a massive August hen party from Lisbon had stumbled on a massive February stag party from Belfast.

'They're right in the middle of the crowd,' said Lancaster to Ted, holding his phone to his ear. 'Witness has a lock on him.'

There had, of course, been no question of drones not being present on the Island at this final part of the Investiture. For one day, and one day only, the cloud of electronics that accompanied the Family wherever they went would fly over Anglesey. Every single member of that crowd had been scanned and catalogued hundreds of times since they first arrived in Caernarfon, and would continue to be so long after they left the Island. Which made it all the more remarkable that Peter Holmes had gone unremarked for so long.

'We'll wait until the crowd begins to break up,' said Ted. 'I'm not plunging in to that lot.'

They stood fifty metres away from the unfinished church. Ted couldn't see a thing, so fired up the news feed on his phone and watched, the rain spitting onto the screen, as the Abbot of St Lidwina blessed the head of the new Prince of Wales, who knelt on newly-fashioned stone steps before an altar on which stood a Celtic Cross. His Father stood to one side, unconventionally, it was said, putting himself at the centre of the ceremony alongside his Son. The Archbishop of York stood off to one side, playing second ceremonial fiddle for the only time in his ecclesiastical career. He didn't look particularly happy about it. And then a choir of young Brothers and Sisters began singing a song Ted did not recognise, a hymn of the Celtic Church, presumably, something that skipped and danced in a way no Protestant Hymn ever did, speaking of salt seas and rocky islands as much as it spoke of God and the Trinity. It was, Ted found, rather lovely.

The Prince stood, bowed his head, and turned. He embraced his Father, the kind of folksy, non-traditional gesture the King liked to be known for, then turned and walked down the aisle, or rather the gap between the crowd inside, for there were as yet no pews, giving the whole thing a medieval air. Ted would only have been half-surprised if a dozen knights on horses had rode in, swinging their swords in acclamation.

The crowd outside now also parted, turning slowly to follow the progress of the Prince and his father out to the waiting bulletproof limousines. Ted put his phone in his pocket, and looked up to see the drones following the procession in just the same way as the attendants, arranging themselves in patterns of artificial intelligence to map the progress of the Family.

'He's seen us,' said Lancaster. 'He's moved behind the Minister.'

'Are we off the news feeds yet?' said Ted.

Lancaster paused.

'Yes, we are now. BBC has switched to the studio, as planned.'

'OK. Then we're going in.'

They walked towards the crowd as it now began to disperse towards the same line of limos. Lancaster guided him, and they walked unerringly towards where the Minister and her factotum were momentarily paused, chattering frantically to each other beneath their umbrella. Ted saw Holmes look at them and then look to the right and the left, and for one mad minute he thought the man was going to run, the flight reflex strong enough to overwhelm logic. Run where? But Holmes stayed put. It was Rachel Whitehouse who moved first.

'I wish it to be known, on the record, Detective, that I am the victim of extortion.'

'No doubt, Minister. You can explain the whole thing to our officers. They're waiting for you at Parc Menai, if you could make your way there immediately.' He nodded upwards towards a drone which had hung back, watching. 'You're obviously going to be accompanied.'

Her face was pale and tight with fury. He hoped the case against her was as watertight as he thought it was. She was obviously going to throw Holmes over the side. If she saved herself as well, things could get uncomfortable for him. But this was how Angela had wanted it - the Minister given the chance to make her own way off the Island. A visit to Parc Menai after the ceremony could easily be painted as normal business for a woman in her position. Only Witness, and those who watched it, would know about this little encounter.

Appearances needed to be maintained.

He saw her make the same calculation, swiftly and efficiently. Saw defeat enter her features. And then she was gone, over to a limo, the faithful drone drawn along with her by an invisible thread.

The half-built castle of Beaumaris was a hundred metres away. Ted turned to Peter Holmes.

'Shall we?'

53

'Wow,' Laura had said. 'That's actually pretty impressive.'

'It's *amazing*,' Peg had added, pulling at his hand, desperate to be over there. She'd taken to holding their hands again on that trip, even though she was a teenager, and could be expected to find such things disgustingly embarrassing.

It was their return visit to Anglesey. In the Mini Countryman, this time, not the Mercedes. Leaving from St Albans, not Streatham. After, not before, Peckham. And after, not before, the cloud of suspicion that had come down on him, suspicion of his wife and what she might be up to. His belly was bigger, his chins more numerous, his heart broken.

They'd parked the Countryman by the sea wall, facing the mountains over the water in Snowdonia. The Castle of Beaumaris seemed to be nuzzling its way into the town itself, as if afraid it was going to miss out on something. Underneath its walls there was a children's playground, adding to the air of unreality about the place. He'd imagined knights looking out over the ramparts watching kids use the slide.

Laura's phone had rung as they walked round to the entrance. She'd taken it out and looked at it, and then had put it back in her handbag.

'Who is it?' he'd said.

'Nobody.'

The playground was on one side, but the other three sides of the structure were surrounded by the castle moat. A real moat, with real water in it. The entrance was beside the road, and they'd walked into the little building just like they'd walked into the little National Trust gift shop to get into Plas Newydd, on that first visit, years before. Similar-looking young women greeted them cheerily, and had taken his money (£6.90 for the three of them - what a strange thing to remember).

They'd walked along the outside of the moat, then turned left onto the little footbridge that led to the original outer gatehouse of the castle. Peg wasn't holding either of their hands anymore, just walking ahead excitedly. He remembered thinking how odd it was that a fifteen-year-old girl should be so enthused by a castle.

Laura's phone had buzzed. She'd switched it to silent when she put it back in her handbag, but there was so much stuff in her handbag it sounded like a sack of bees when the phone vibrated. She'd let it ring.

'Aren't you going to answer that?' he'd said.

'No. It's nothing important.'

They'd walked under the grey stone towers, and into the grassy courtyard within. The place was a mystifying mass of walls, ramparts, staircases, and Peg had wanted to climb them all. Laura had never had a head for heights, and had said so.

'I'll go with her,' he'd said.

'Thanks,' she'd said. 'I'll go and sit on the bench over there.'

He had watched her walk across the courtyard. He'd turned away and followed Peg up a twisting stone staircase, and out onto the rampart above. Metal barriers lined the walkways, put there to protect tourists. He'd felt the shape of the rocks and pebbles embedded into the rampart by its builders. The view was spectacular.

Peg had scurried excitedly along the rampart, following the outer edge of the castle wall, and he'd walked carefully behind her. They'd come to another winding staircase down into another tower, and they'd followed it down to another low wall, passing along the inner walls of the castle. Then they'd come out onto the courtyard, and he'd looked down and seen his wife sitting on her bench, talking into her phone.

'Why the fuck are we going in here?' Peter Holmes said, sourly, as they walked up the road and into the entrance to the castle, abandoned and empty.

'Because we need somewhere quiet to talk,' Ted said, looking into the sky. The drones had gone. They were unwatched. Unwitnessed.

Two ghosts walked with him along the outside of the moat, as he, Holmes and Lancaster turned left onto the little footbridge, and then headed under the grey stone towers. Ted looked across the courtyard and saw that the bench where Laura had made her phone call was still there.

'Why don't we go and sit over there?' he said.

At the bench, Holmes slumped himself down. Ted sat beside him. Lancaster stood and watched, like the faithful guard he had presumably always been. The day was getting on, now, growing gloomier, but at least the drizzle was leaving. Beaumaris had that empty sense of a room in which a party had just finished.

'They have a prayer, here, in the Community,' Ted said. 'Something about the eye of God. Do you know it, Lancaster?'

'Yes, sir, I do.'

'By heart?'

Lancaster was looking at Holmes, guardedly. But he followed Ted's cue.

'The eye of the great God,
The eye of the God of Glory,
The eye of the King of hosts,
The eye of the King of the living,
Pouring upon us
At each time and season,
Pouring upon us
Gently and generously.
Glory to thee,
Thou glorious sun,
Glory to thee, thou sun,
Face of the God of Life.'

Lancaster stopped.

'Rather beautiful,' Ted said, meaning it. Holmes didn't say a word. 'Where's it from, Lieutenant?'

'It's a song from the Outer Hebrides,' Lancaster said. 'It tells of the rising of the sun, and of their sense that God is watching us, kindly.'

'Watching us, kindly. Rather appropriate, Mr Holmes. Or should I say, Mr Evans. Mr Simon Evans.'

Evans's petulant face grew even sulkier. He looked like a kid who'd been caught lying and was going to brazen it out, but a defiant kid, one with a sneer, the kind who would gaslight you so hard you'd start doubting your own mind. He'd seen the type before.

'She recognised you, of course,' said Ted. 'Anthea Mortimer. She recognised you straightaway, right? Friend of her brother's. Companion in his little fascist games. Not in the school photo, but maybe you'd been chucked out of school by then? I don't think so. I think you were the little shit who was always in the background, goading them all on, and then disappearing when things got real. A right little worm of a man.'

That stung him. Evans turned his eyes on Ted, looking furious. He decided to push further.

'Touched a nerve, did I, you little Pound Shop Hitler? People like you sicken me. All mouth and no fucking trousers.'

Evans narrowed his eyes.

'Trying to wind me up, are we, Detective?'

Ted smiled.

'Accent coming back, I see, Mr Evans. Must be a constant effort to hide it, right? I can hear it in your voice now, though. The authentic voice of the Welsh Mussolini. But you didn't have the balls, did you? To see it through?'

Again, no response. The man had settled himself down again.

'But Anthea recognised you, at the party. And she went and told the only person she could think of telling - Thomas Jenkins. Peter Holmes isn't who he says he is, she said. He's Simon Evans, he knew my brother, and he was a right little nasty bastard, too. But Jenkins didn't do anything. Not right away. The two of them were in the study, discussing you. And because you recognised her just like she'd recognised you, you were listening in, I'm thinking. Outside the door, outside the window, maybe even with some super-secret military microphone, I don't know. We'll find out. But you listened in to them talking, and you had a problem, right? Couldn't let that stuff get out. A little Welsh fascist at the side of the Defence Minister, with an assumed name? Be the end of you, that would. So you waited a bit, saw Brother Thomas head out onto the roof. Maybe you called him up there for a chat? 'Let's do a deal,' you'd have said, and he liked a deal. He had something on you, he thought he could get something more. So you went up there, and you shoved him off the roof.'

Ted frowned as he thought.

'No, you didn't. You killed him up there - lamped him with a brick, I'd say, we have the pathology on that one - but you didn't shove him off. Not yet. Didn't want anyone finding him before the second act. Killing Anthea Mortimer. So you go to Anthea Mortimer's room, and you strangle her. And then you tie her to the bed. Make it look like kinky sex gone bad, right? And the dead guy on the roof, he's going to be the main candidate for killing her. Then he kills himself, out of remorse. Except you killed him. And then, when you're sure everyone's safely in bed, you pop back up to the roof, and flip him over the side.'

'You've no proof for any of this,' Evans said. His Welsh accent was now fully apparent. The effort to suppress it for a decade must have been enormous.

'Haven't I? Maybe I won't need it. There's the Minister, for one. She'll throw you under the bus to save herself - she's already talking about extortion. And then there's Trearddur Bay.'

There was a change now. A very definite change. He hadn't been expecting that. His whole body stiffened, and his tongue crept out to lick his lips.

'We found the body of Philip Mortimer, Evans. Found him lying face down with a kitchen knife in his back. He had a train ticket to London in his pocket. For the day of

Queen's Speech. Remember that, you little fascist cunt? Do you fucking well *remember that*?'

Lancaster made a movement, as if to hold Ted back, anticipating, what? A lunge? A thrown punch? How much did he know about the tragic family history of Detective Inspector Edward Wood? Or was he just imagining that?

'Your little fascist mate, Roger Mortimer, and his little fascist Dad. What were they up to? And did you have the same ticket, arsehole? Did you just lose your nerve?'

He had gone quite white now, the pound shop Hitler. This was new. This was unexpected. Ted heard Lancaster's phone buzz. The lieutenant turned away to take the call.

'I wasn't there,' Evans said, quietly, as if he didn't want Lancaster to hear. 'You have to believe me, I wasn't there.'

'What were they planning?' Ted said. 'What was going on?'

'Roger's Dad, he found out about it, and he went there to stop them,' Evans said, still in a whisper. 'He came to me, said if I knew where they were, and I told him they'd gone to the holiday cottage, that they'd been there for a couple of days, so he went there.'

'How do you know?'

'Because... afterwards. Afterwards, I went there. I wanted to see. I saw his body and the other stuff. But I *wasn't there.*'

'So who killed him?'

'Roger. I think probably Roger. He was crazy with it, towards the end. Saying all sorts of scary shit. That's when I started... moving away from him. He'd made contact with some other groups. Some real psychos. I didn't want any part of it.'

'Any part of what?'

Evans frowned. And then there was a huge sound, and

Evans's head snapped back, a round red dot on his forehead already expanding and distorting into something ugly and terrible. As he slid off the bench, Ted stood and turned, and saw Lancaster holding a pistol.

AFTER

54

Six weeks later, the house in Stretford was on the market, and Ted was settling into a house on the fringes of Beaumaris, one of those nice houses he'd seen on the road from the Menai Strait, between the road and the shore, looking out over the water to the mountains of the mainland. He'd flirted with the idea of somewhere more remote, maybe one of the abandoned houses at Penmon, facing west towards the setting sun, towards Ireland and then America. But he'd not wanted that kind of oblivion. Besides, there were other, better reasons to stay in Beaumaris.

Jenny would be here soon. She came most mornings, presumably at the orders of the Abbot, who would have been charged by the Powers That Were with keeping an eye on the ex-detective, his comings and goings, who came to visit. He guessed, in her way, Jenny was a kind of spy. But the leap in his heart whenever her knock came at the door was real enough, a sufficient connection to humanity for now. Maybe even for ever.

He poured himself a cup of tea, and looked out of the

kitchen window. Bangor Pier pushed out into the waves from the shore on the far side. He saw a boat pull away from the pier, or perhaps from a jetty or marina behind or beside it. It was heading his way. He watched it for several minutes, and when it had nearly reached him he sighed, put his cup down, and went out into the garden.

The wind screamed in his ears, as the wind often did here, but there was sun in the air, a warm golden fire. He remembered that morning driving from Manchester to Anglesey, all alone in his now-relinquished Dyson, thinking about the mind of God.

The motor launch pulled up beside the little jetty which, he supposed, belonged to him now, or at least was his responsibility. Angela Leybourne was helped out by the pilot of the launch, a man Ted recognised. He nodded at Lieutenant Lancaster, who nodded back, but stayed in the boat.

'Interesting, you came with him,' Ted said, as Angela walked up the slope towards the flat terrace in front of the house, a small echo of the terraces of Plas Newydd.

'What, you think it's some kind of gesture?' she said.

'Isn't it?'

'Not everything's a signal, Ted.' She looked up at the house. 'Nice place. Hell of a view.'

'You can certainly see anyone approaching from the water.'

She smirked.

'Got any decent tea?'

'Yorkshire.'

'How's the water here?'

'Soft.'

She made a face.

'Just like bloody Manchester. I miss London water. The kind that messed up your kettles. Ah well, beggars can't be 'choosers.' She walked up towards the house, and Ted followed.

Minutes later, they were standing at the kitchen window drinking their tea, with a line of sight to Lancaster on the boat, a fact Ted wondered at.

'Any more signs of the competition?' she said.

'The competition?'

'Don't be a smart arse. Intelligence. The public school-boys with their secret codes and leaky files. The Minister's lot.'

'No. No sign of them.'

'Good. Well you gave them a bloody nose, all right, Ted.'

'Was that what this was all about?'

'Partly. They don't like it when we have information they can't get hold of.'

'Well, Simon Evans certainly isn't talking.'

She chuckled.

'You're too clever by half, Ted,' she said. 'I thought you'd be another couple of days figuring it all out. But you had to go and jump in on the big day itself.' Her glassy vowels made him think of old BBC sitcoms.

'Was it always the plan?' he said. 'To shoot the poor sod at the end?'

'What do you think?'

'He knew stuff. About the house on Trearddur Bay. About Mortimer and his son.'

She chuckled, wearily.

'Cheeky bastard.'

'Are you bent, Angela?'

'Like Allan Davies you mean?'

'No, not like Allan Davies. In a different direction.'

'Sod off, Ted. I'm not bent.'

'So he did have stuff on you, then? Evans?'

'Just don't, Ted. You don't know what you're dealing with.'

'So tell me,' Ted said. 'Tell me what I'm dealing with.'

'How does the phrase go? I could tell you, but then I'd have to shoot you.'

'Or get Lancaster to do it.'

'He would, too.'

'I don't doubt it. I suppose the lad's been feeding you stuff all along.'

'Christ, Ted, you *work* for me. So does he. I'm not the bloody enemy. I'm your boss. Yes, he's been keeping me informed. I knew you wouldn't. Not how it's done, is it? Old school, Ted Wood is. Likes to keep his cards close to his chest.'

'You set me up.'

'Oh, diddums.'

'Christ Almighty, Angela, this is like some Russian whack-job. Is this how we do things now? Silent assassinations?'

'There's a bigger picture,' she said.

'I'm sure. There always is. Something to justify you lot doing what you bloody well like.'

'Us lot?'

'The Security Service, for want of a better word. The secret police, as they used to be called in other countries.'

'Been doing a lot of thinking, Ted, have we?'

'It was Intelligence that warned me off. MI6. SIS. The spooks. Whatever they're calling it now. You're still at it, aren't you? The old game. Spies versus counter-spies, playing your silly bloody games over the carcass of the country. Secret agents and secret police.'

'Very poetic.'

'Lancaster was broadcasting that conversation between me and Evans, wasn't he? Getting the whole confession on the record. Streaming it back to you. You called him when the subject turned to Trearddur Bay. To London. You told him to shoot Evans before he said something the competition could hear. The competition being, of course, the spooks. You're probably recording me now, beaming it back to some Witness facility for all and sundry to hear. So *they* can hear what you know about them.'

'No, Ted. I'm not recording this one. This one needs to be off the record.'

'The thing I've thought about most, the thing that's got me most puzzled, was why you brought me here at all.'

Her silence felt like encouragement. *Go on, then. Run with that thought.*

'Why send a washed-up has-been all the way from Manchester to Anglesey? Why not let the local plod deal with it?'

'Because the local plod's bent.'

'Part of the reason, maybe. But not the whole reason. You needed a witness.'

She smiled at that.

'Do you know, that's very good?' she said. '*You needed a witness*. I like it.'

'That house, you see, it's a trap. Quite a clever trap, as it happens. It catches two types of prey. The first type are naive and ambitious. Jenkins lured them onto the Island with promises of the usual stuff - food, drink, sex - but also proximity to power, gossip, *influence*. And he put them in one of those wired-up bedrooms, and he recorded them, and then he used those recordings to peddle his own influence, just like he'd done in the good old days, before London.'

She was listening, and listening carefully.

'And you all let him do it. I've wondered about that. And the reason's obvious, I think. You let him do it because everything he recorded was being shared with you. You had all the same juicy stuff. And you had a man on the inside, as well. Someone cleared out the hardware after Jenkins was killed. I can't prove it, but I'd guess Brother Michael. He was there that evening. He called the police when the body was discovered. He had plenty of time to clear things out.'

She sipped her tea, looking out of the window, listening with every fibre.

'Lucy Jenkins? Was she on it too?'

'Oh, hello, now it's time for Ted to do his Gallant Policeman act. What about her?'

'You going to arrest her?'

'For what? Arranging parties?'

'Collusion in blackmail.'

'No-one will know about the blackmail, Ted. Lucy did a deal with us, a long time ago. She keeps her nice house by the water, and she keeps - or rather, kept - the party's organised.'

'And you'll get it going again,' Ted said. 'As night follows day. It's too bloody useful to you, isn't it? Because there's nothing more valuable, in a country where everyone is watched all the time, than a place where they can go where they think they're *not* watched. Where they can let down their hair and loosen their tongues. I bet if I track back from all the partygoers over the years I'll find some interesting related investigations.'

'Maybe. Except that's not going to happen.'

'No. That's not going to happen.'

He took their cups, rinsed them off under the tap, put them on the side.

'But there's even more to it than that,' he said. 'And this is where it gets really fiendish. Why not wire *all* the rooms? Why make it so obvious that some rooms were wired and some were not. Why could an idiot like Sir Anthony work that out? Because it's not true. The rooms *were* all wired. Only some of them made it obvious. So the people in the less obvious rooms thought they were even more safe, and, more to the point, they felt in on the game, too. Same principle, on a smaller scale. All the rooms were wired, for sound and video, with different levels of sophistication. We didn't have the time, or expertise, to figure that out for ourselves. But if I'm right, there's an obvious conclusion. You knew who killed Anthea Mortimer. You knew *all along*. And that's why you sent me.'

'Bravo, Inspector Hound.'

'You needed an old copper, someone who did things the old way. But you also needed someone you knew, someone you could influence. You put Lancaster on me to make sure I didn't linger too far off the beaten track. Because the really important thing here, the thing you absolutely didn't want to happen, is for the competition, the spooks, to learn about your little goldmine at Plas Newydd. Because they don't know, do they, Angela? The Minister didn't know. Simon Evans didn't know. Even Allan Davies didn't know, and he's supposedly on your side.'

'Allan Davies is a galactic moron. It helps us, to have a massive idiot thinking he is running things in North Wales.'

'Who's 'us'?'

She didn't answer.

'And will he still be running things?' he said. 'Davies?'

'Yes. For the same reason as before.'

'Keeping control. Keeping it away from the spooks.'

'Yeah.'

'Which is why they were buzzing me. Sending signals. Letting you know they were keeping an eye out.'

'That was clumsy of them. But they were worried.

Really worried. They're not stupid, Ted. They could see how strange it was, sending you in. They wanted to know why. And if they couldn't figure that out, their best bet was to throw you off. Maybe get you running back to Manchester. Run the clock down to the Investiture. As I say, clumsy. They look like proper Charlies now.'

She sighed in satisfaction.

'Can't tell you how nice it is, giving those bastards a bloody nose for a change.'

She turned away from the window, and leaned back on the work surface, folding her arms.

'Problem with Witness, Ted, is it's *too good at its job*. We can see so much. We can see *virtually* everything. We can see patterns - in the people you know, in your interactions with them. Tie that up with all the other things you do - the stuff you buy, the messages you send, the telly you watch - and we have a vivid, three-dimensional picture of you. But it's not complete.'

'Sounds pretty complete to me.'

'No. It's not. Because we don't know what you're thinking. We can *infer* it. That's the best we can do. But we can't see the thoughts inside your head. At least, not in an actionable way. So we have to give people the chance to expose those thoughts to us. It's not about seeing bad things happening. It's about preventing them before they happen, by identifying bad people.'

'Plas Newydd is a blackmail machine.'

'A what?'

'Something Lucy Jenkins said.'

'Well, in a way, she's right. If you leave pockets where people can behave naturally - behave as if they were unobserved - then you can learn even more about them. Did you really think, Ted, that the King and his advisors would just give a whole fucking Island to some cheesy God-botherers because they asked him to? Especially when one of those God-botherers was a colossal creep?'

But he had. He had thought that. And, to be fair, *everyone* had thought that. But that wasn't what had happened at all. Somewhere down the line, some clever little tosspot had whispered into the King's ear: *Listen, your Majesty. If we want to get the real skinny on how bad people are doing bad things, we've got to give them a chance to* do *those bad things. And look, here's a whole Island we can say is off our grid. Oh, they'll come from miles around, claiming to be sick and damaged, and we'll give them a house, and then we'll let them be who they really want to be.*

'You're watching Anglesey,' he whispered. 'You've been watching it all the time. The whole Island is a blackmail machine.'

She sniffed.

'Not really, no. We can only watch from high-level stuff - satellites, some high-level drones. Too far away for reliable facial recognition, although that will come, and we can't hear anything. But we saw what happened on the roof. We see who's coming and going. Lorries from Ireland, visitors from the Mainland, all sorts of little details.'

'Why are you telling me this?' He nodded out the window. 'Is our lad out there going to walk up from the boat and put a bullet in my head.'

'No, Ted, he's not going to do that. For one thing, Witness would see it.'

'Which means the spooks would see it.'

'Indeed. And for another, I think you're going to keep your mouth shut. About all this. And about the other thing.'

The other thing. So there it was.

'No one knows who put the bomb in London, Ted. No one. Even the spooks. It's a mystery. No one claimed responsibility. You remember. It was as if whoever did it was astonished by what they'd done.'

'I remember. I also remember how the narrative unfurled. That Guy Fawkes had a brown face.'

'Not me. Not any of us. That was people seeing what they wanted to see. No, Guy Fawkes is the great unknown. The great mystery. And then along comes Ted Wood, Detective Extraordinaire, making wild discoveries in a rundown holiday house on the edge of nowhere.'

'Discoveries that connect a senior aide to the Defence Minister to a cell of far-right extremists, with evidence connecting them to the day of the London bomb.'

'Or, to put it another way, evidence about a group of pound shop Hitlers, to use your memorable phrase, playing at being Nazis before heading off to London to see their good old Queen, but getting into a pissed-up row about who was paying for the chips, with one of them ending up dead.'

'That's the narrative, is it?'

'We can't connect Roger Mortimer to this, Ted. He was a bloody kid ten years ago when he went to London. Do you really believe a bunch of Welsh fascists blew up London? Why? How did they get hold of the device?'

'That isn't the story, Angela. And you know it.'

'What's the story, then?'

'The story is that the secret police - our lot, Angela, the police, MI5, the works - didn't have our eye on the ball when it came to the far right. We weren't looking at them because we were too busy looking at brown folk who prayed five times a day. And all the time we were looking in that direction, the poison was growing. Do I think Roger Mortimer and his mates blew up London? Of course I bloody don't. Do I think there's a possibility that they were aligned with a group who might have arranged it? Yes. I think that's a distinct possibility. And do I think there are people around, right now, who know what happened? Some of them quite senior. Secret police and secret agents both. One of them ended up as an aide to the Minister of Defence, for Christ's sake. I think it's at least worth asking the question.'

'Do you, Ted? To what end, exactly?'

He didn't have an answer for that. *Burning the whole rotten edifice down* was one reason. But wasn't that just an act of terrorism?

'Maybe Witness isn't all it's cracked up to be,' was all he had.

She raised an eyebrow, archly.

'Oh. So you're some kind of freedom fighter now? Let me tell you something, Ted. France is installing a version of Witness as we speak. There's a procurement bill going through Congress. Germany's holding out, but there's a majority for it. New Zealand has a ring of surveillance which someone down there charmingly called Fortress. The tech is there. Do you think governments are just going to put it to one side? Britain's leading the way, sunshine. That and Yorkshire tea. Almost makes you proud, right?'

She reached into her coat, pulled out a package, though he half-expected to see a gun. She handed it to him.

'What's that?' he said.

'Retirement gift. You're going out on a high, remember. Experienced detective unlocks impossible case, murderer shot while trying to escape. To be fair, it's a good story. And you deserve to retire.'

Her voice had softened. She was playing with him, of course. But then, she'd always been playing with him.

'And what if I don't retire?'

'Then the story changes, Ted.'

'Let me guess. Brave Lieutenant Lancaster made the running.'

'Yes. Because you were drunk. And you're drunk a *lot*, Ted.'

'And you just fire me.'

'Or worse.'

'I just disappear.'

'And that would be a shame, Inspector.'

She made her way to the back door.

'Oh. One more thing. If I read something in the *New Yorker* I don't care for, I'll know where it came from.'

And then she did leave.

hat would Laura have done?

That was the question in his mind as he watched the boat pull away from the jetty (*his* jetty, now). The world he lived in would be unrecognisable to his dead wife. In ten years, all the givens had gone. Like everyone in Britain, he spoke while assuming he could be heard, he acted while assuming he could be watched, he lived under a panoply of eyes and he knew that his identity was a public thing, that only his thoughts were his own, though those thoughts became public property the moment they were uttered. He could seek privacy in his bedroom and in his bathroom, but it was a brittle privacy, because he knew that they knew he was in his bedroom, because they saw him go into it, and they saw anyone in there with him go into it too, and they could, with barely any bureaucratic fiction, slip in a camera or a microphone to turn his bedroom into a public space, too.

He could see Laura's face, listening in to that conversation with Angela Leybourne. She looked appalled, sickened, angry. So was he, truth be told. Because now Witness was not the whole story. Even in the brightest light, there were shadows. Men and women he did not know had a different category of access to the truth. They could pretend that some areas were beyond their vision - but it was a lie. They could use religion as a cover for surveillance. They could encircle and entrap. *For what wouldn't we do if we thought they weren't watching? What wouldn't we reveal about ourselves?*

Thomas Jenkins had understood that. He just didn't have the imagination to realise that others would figure it out, and that those others would have the whole panoply of Witness at their fingertips - the low-level and high-level drones, the fixed street cameras and listening stations, the satellites, the digital records of the mobile communications networks, what people bought, what they watched, where they walked, how they talked - and all of it tied into machines of growing intelligence, so-called *artificial* intelligence but actually it was more like an *aggregate* intelligence, the aggregate of all their actions, building into profiles of each of them, the profiles aggregating themselves into a national profile, such that one powerful Superman - the King, perhaps - might switch on his machine and say *show me an Englishman* and it would be able to show him *the* Englishman, or perhaps Englishperson, a collaborative hermaphrodite, an avatar for them all.

He knew how Laura would respond to that, because he was thinking the words she would have used. Better words than he was capable of, angrier words, passionate words. She would burn it all down.

But here's the thing, my love. It would have stopped it. *It would have stopped it.* If Witness had been available on that May day years before, it would have seen it all. Guy Fawkes would not have been able to hide his - or their - intentions beneath the comfort blanket of individual privacy. He would not have burrowed away between the gaps, importing his machinery of death in the shadows between the patches of light available to MI5 or GCHQ or the dear old Metropolitan Police. He'd have been stopped even for *thinking* of doing what he did.

There is a trade-off, you see. Individual liberty and privacy - even general democracy and freedom - against the life of their daughter.

Our precious, delightful, beautiful Peg.

Ted knew which he'd choose. And he knew Laura would have disagreed.

The day was deepening to evening. Sister Jenny would be here soon. They'd go for a walk, perhaps, and talk about her day - the prayers, the dutiful service. Maybe she would share a bit more about herself, her own terrible history.

He opened the package that Angela had left. He smiled at it. An old, leather bound King James Bible. A gift, but also a message.

His eyes adjusted, and he found he could sill see the deep-grey carpet of the sea, and the ridged complexities of the old pier on the far side of the water. There was a generous and opulent blend of salt and oxygen, a rich mix of earth and water. The wind blew consistently and strongly, as the wind almost always did in this part of the world. He looked towards the distance, and felt something stretch within him as he gazed at the dark shapes of the mountains climbing towards God, away from him, into the ancient heart of Gwynedd, and for the first time he found himself wondering what it would be like to join this Community.

www.ingramcontent.com/pod-product-compliance
Lightning Source LLC
Chambersburg PA
CBHW051433190726
48289CB00001B/163